Runner
Jags Arthurson

N⁰|0

Jags Arthurson

Runner
By Jags Arthurson
Copyright (c) 2023 Jags Arthurson
All rights reserved

This book is subject to copyright under the Berne Convention. No part of this publication may be reproduced or distributed in any form or by any means or stored in a database or retrieval system without the author's consent.

The right of Jags Arthurson to be identified as author of this work has been asserted in accordance with sections 77 and 78 of the Copyright, Designs and Patents Act, 1988

This is a work of fiction. All names, characters, places and incidents are the product of the author's imagination or are used fictitiously and any resemblance to actual persons, living or dead, events, businesses or locales is entirely coincidental.

Number90

ISBN 978-0-9928226-7-5

First published in UK by Number90

Runner

Chapter One

It's not easy to drop into conversation. "Nice weather for the time of year and by the way I'm a psychopath." Doesn't work, does it?

Anyway, why would I?

Professor Robert Hare, a world expert in psychopathy describes us as "social predators who charm, manipulate and ruthlessly plow (sic) their way through life, leaving a trail of broken hearts, shattered expectations and empty wallets."

There's an unbiased scientist for you.

Everybody makes assumptions about me – even you. You've known me for just a few seconds and already assume you know me. Well don't. I warn you … I KNOW WHERE YOU LIVE!

Joke!

See? You're assuming I'm some sort of latter-day Norman Bates; cold-blooded and mirthless, with no sense of humour – wrong again.

The truth about 'primary psychopathy' is that it's not an illness, it's a trait, like hair colour, and is caused by a variation in the behaviour of the amygdale.

There are tests, based on Hare's 'Psychopath Checklist' with 20 items. For instance, Item 1 is *Glibness/Superficial charm*. Notice how negative and pejorative that is? Not 'a good communicator' but 'glib'. So I live in a world where I'm forced to lie about who I am because if I don't everybody wants me treated, locked away or worse. And then Hare puts down as item 4 that we're pathological liars!

Who knew!

Each item is scored 0, 1 or 2 to give a total up to forty. But note that item 15: *'Irresponsibility'* – or, as I would put, 'carefree' is awarded exactly as much weight as item 20: *'Criminal versatility'*. So somebody who's a bit relaxed about things will get as many points as a bank robbing, axe-murderer.

On Hare's scale 'normal' people score less than six. Scoring over 30 labels one as a psychopath. I score twenty-eight. So I could argue that I'm not *actually* a psychopath or, at least, thirty percent of me isn't.

Also, for every psychopath locked away there are dozens wandering the streets. More than one percent of the population are psychos but as many as twenty percent of the directors of big multinationals score higher than average on the 'psycho scale'.

You see, we psychos are the risk-takers, the no-nonsense, cut-the-crap-and-get-on-with-it types with scant regard for consequences. We think fast when the chips are down. If you're ever in a tight spot then hope the fellow next to you has a large dollop of psychopath because he's the one most likely to get you out of it.

The problem is simple: we ... I ... just don't 'get' people; I don't see why they're *special*. In your world you have the environment – the stuff that just *is*. Me too. Then you have other stuff that may be useful to you, like furniture and, again, so do I. Then you have people that you care for and empathise with ... well that's where I fall down because, to me, people and furniture are the same. People are useful to me or not. But get this: you don't go around smashing up furniture, even other people's furniture, on a whim. Neither do I. And I don't do it to people either ... usually.

What else about me would interest you?

My degree is in psychology. That's when I found out

about my 'condition'. When I was young my parents thought there was something odd about me. For a while 'the experts' thought I had autism and I suppose all this psychology stuff made me interested in what made people tick, which led to the degree. The next step was a doctorate and practice but I soon realised I couldn't give a toss about other people's little problems so I switched to a Masters degree in Business Analysis.

It was while I was doing the Masters I got married but it didn't last. We wanted children – well, *he* wanted children and I was happy to go along with it.

Oh? More assumptions? Like a psycho wouldn't want to be a mother? Why not? I would have made a great mother ... unlike my own. I got pregnant but miscarried. Then they told me I couldn't have any more so that rather put the mockers on the relationship.

Mind you, I walked away with a tidy sum. He was on some sort of guilt trip because while I was in hospital bleeding and screaming, he was off screwing one of his juniors. And if you want more proof that I'm not a homicidal maniac there it is because if I were going to go all 'Hannibal Lecter' on anybody it would certainly have been on my ex or his 'bit on the side' but I didn't. Why should I worry if he shagged some slut providing he was there when I needed him? That was where he fell down. I didn't really need the money because after the separation I moved back with my parents – Hare would have given me full marks for number 9; '*Parasitic Lifestyle*', although that covers every teenager, doesn't it?

I blew a chunk of my settlement on some super transport. The Yamaha YZF R1, cost nearly thirteen grand. I call it 'Potex-1' ... 'Pissing Off The Ex', get it? It's only the third fastest production bike on the road but as I rarely find anywhere to wind it up to its full one hundred and ninety miles an hour I guess it's fast enough. Another wad went on an Audi R8.

Why am I telling you this? I'm not normally this open but I suppose it explains some of the stuff that happened. I don't know how relevant my condition is to how I reacted but when you make a decision do you say to yourself, 'I did this because I'm heterosexual/gay, male/female, black/white or whatever?' Or do you just go ahead and act without worrying about what drove you? So I guess we'll never know. I *do* know that we female psychos don't conform to the popular image, which I suspect is based on the male of the type who tends to be more sociopathic and violent. We're just as 'psychopathic' but we're more devious. *Okay, Hare, I'll take the points for that one.*

Something else; I hardly drink. I hate not being in control so I rarely have more than one glass of wine and then only if it's very, very good. In fact, I've only been drunk five times in my life. The first time was when I was fifteen at a party. Davy Reilly slipped some vodka in my orange juice and, when he thought I was beyond fighting back, took me to the bedroom, dumped me down on some coats, whipped off my pants and stuck it in me. I screamed at him to stop and, when he didn't, sank my teeth in his ear whereon he suddenly lost interest. He had ten stitches but they couldn't sew back the bit I'd bitten off. I'd swallowed it.

I got drunk a couple of times at university. You know, just fitting in.

I got smashed when I came out of hospital after losing the baby while Graeme was out screwing his nineteen-year-old, big-tit bimbo.

And I got absolutely hammered the day my family was massacred.

Chapter Two

The door slammed, cutting off Kylie being *Lucky, lucky, lucky* while, unknown to me, the horror was already unfolding just a few miles away.

I was slipping off my dress as the others trooped in. All but two were men, bow ties swinging loose and pretending not to notice I was wearing nothing but my pants. We so often end up changing in the toilets that a mixed dressing room was almost a luxury.

We're a small band: about fifteen of us. For me, it's just a bit of weekend fun. The bandleader is Stefan Reingard – you've probably heard of him. I'm one of the regulars: vocals and tenor sax. I have just two *real* loves; music and exercise or, bringing them together; dance.

On a gig, we play three sets. We start with 'wallpaper music': cool jazz, that sort of thing, while the punters scoff the rubber chicken and get lubricated before our first break when the organisers do their speeches ... there are *always* speeches.

We'd just finished the second set.

I have a problem with clothes. I love 'elegant' so the long, midnight blue satin I wear for the first set is great. The second set dress: yellow, knee length with flared skirt and a pattern of green sequins is 'OK.' I'm happy in dress-down-casual; even jeans, t-shirt and boots ... providing they're well-fitting. 'Girly-girly' is a total 'no-no' – there's not a millimetre of lace in my entire wardrobe.

But worst of all is 'slapper-tarty'.

Which brings us to my 'third set frock'. A screaming, eye-damaging pink – I abhor the colour – the skirt is low on the hip and as short as possible. The top is little more than a pair of wide straps. The whole is covered in tassels so when I spin I look like a carwash brush. *Better legs, though.* Poo-Brain, my little brother, calls it my 'belt-and-braces'. I would never, ever, be seen dead in it ... except on the dance floor because you can't do a samba in an evening dress.

As I wriggled into it, Maxie appeared: tight black dress and big, blonde hair. Maxine plays guitar and sings backing. We harmonise like angels.

"Wow! I thought you said you weren't going to wear that again ..."

"Stefan insisted." I gave the hem a pointless tug. "Does the job."

"Depends on the job." She grinned: a dazzling tribute to the orthodontist's art, and turned her back. "Unzip me." I obliged. She stepped out off her dress and tugged on a well worn, silk robe before joining the scrum around the drinks table, emerging with what looked like a glass bucket containing half a bottle of Cabernet. After a long swig and a long sigh she subsided into a chair with her bare feet on another. The robe fell open revealing a yard of leg. Most of the others had snatched their drinks and headed for the fire escape to light up so they missed a treat.

By now the table was bare.

"Anybody got my water?" I asked nobody in particular and got no answer. The management was supposed to supply the drinks and it looked as if they had forgotten mine.

"Bugger." We only had twenty-five minutes before we were due on again. I could really do with putting my feet up rather than fetching my own drinks. *Note to self re: new shoes on a gig.*

At the bar, I waved to a barman and demanded my water then, turning away, bumped into a short, corpulent man. This evening, we were playing for a local electronics company and I had nearly poured half a litre of Perrier over the boss. Like all the men, he wore a dinner jacket with black tie: somewhat askew, and a purple cumberbund possibly intended to pull in his gut but actually emphasising it.

He smiled and ran his eyes over me as a hungry tiger might regard a gazelle.

"Hello, beautiful lady. Don't be in such a rush ... tonight's for enjoyment."

I beamed at him. *The customer is always right*. "You won't be getting any enjoyment if I'm not up there singing in a while." I nodded at the stage.

"We can all wait a few minutes." He told me his name was Gupta-something-or-other then introduced his tall, overweight wife clad in an elegant purple and gold thread sari I would give my right arm for and enough gold to encourage the guys at Fort Knox to likewise donate a limb. A heavy gold chain swung between her nose-ring and earring like the rope barrier on a museum exhibit.

I started to 'work him' – as you do – all wiggles and giggles and flicks of the hair. It's what the arrogant dicks expect from any young woman and my favourite hobby is 'running' people so it's an excellent match. *Manipulative*.

Wifey stood there gurning as if it's the most natural thing in the world for some young girl to be making up to her hubby in front of her and it was all going well when a younger couple joined us.

"This is our daughter Priti ... that's P-R-I-T-I." As if anybody could have mistaken it for 'Pretty'. *Never going to happen, Girl*. She was as scrawny as a cocktail stick with most of the wood scraped off, had zero muscle tone and wore a short, black sleeveless number that showed too much of her pipe-cleaner limbs. She gave off a solid thump of the sort of citrusy perfume that immediately made her the mortal enemy of anybody with normal olfactory function.

"And this is her fiancé, Jordan," Gupta said. Jordan

was tall and blonde with broad shoulders; not bad looking. Things were looking up. I started working him as well, standing too close, smiling, batting my lashes, brushing imaginary fluff off his lapel. Scrawny looked at me like I was meat on a market stall and mouthed, "Slut!"

Stefan's rules fairly are strict about band members scratching the eyes out of the paying public. So she got away with it – but it was a close shave. *Unlike your top lip, Love.*

Something a bit unusual about our show is that Stefan and I do some exhibition dances, which have become really popular since programmes like *Strictly Come Dancing*. Before the first break we do a foxtrot then start the second with something to get them going. We have a fairly decent repertoire. I like the Argentine tango ... 'vertical expression of horizontal intent' ... with lots of intertwining body parts but we can also do quickstep, foxtrot, samba and others.

Tonight we opened part three with a pornographic salsa and then pulled out a couple of the guests so as revenge I made straight for Jordan and really gave him the business. Scrawny, sitting on the sidelines, almost had apoplexy. Afterwards, as we were singing, Maxie and I kept catching his eye and making up to him just to wind her up. You can imagine my delight when I saw the body language of a full-on row, culminating in her storming off with folks in tow.

At the end of the evening there's not much for me to do because packing up a sax and three frocks only takes a minute. When I went out to my car – Potex-2 – Jordan was there, waving his phone in the air, his face illuminated by the light of the display.

"Problems?"

He shrugged. "No signal. I came with Priti and her parents but they've gone so I'm stuck. I need to get a taxi but ..." He shrugged again and waved his phone some more.

"Where do you need to get to?"

"Just Burgess Hill."

So I offered him a lift and at his flat he invited me in 'for coffee'. *Really?*

I excused myself to use the bathroom and took a sneaky look around. Makeup filled the bathroom cabinet, dresses hung in one of the wardrobes, lots of underwear. *Drawers of drawers.*

When I got back to the lounge he had poured two huge white wines. One sip and I almost spat it out.

"Does your fiancée live here?" I asked. No way I'm going to say her name, it would stick in my craw.

He had the good grace to look guilty. "Well, er, sort of." *Worried you'd just wrecked your chances of a leg-over?*

"Aren't you concerned about what she'd say if she walked in?"

"No, no … " *Too quick with the denial.* "She's staying over with her parents. We're splitting up."

Personally, I thought it would be a hoot if she *had* caught us.

There you go, Professor, one more tick for your checklist. No 11: 'Promiscuous sexual behaviour'. *Every* man I know scores maximum points on that one.

* * *

Next morning I packed up and left. I always keep a few things in the car so I was able to change my underwear. I amused myself by leaving my twenty quid lippy in the bathroom cabinet with her *Number 7* stuff and would have called it quits there but, at the last minute, stuck my pants – black and sparkly – in the basket of dirty washing with Jordan's dress shirt. I'd bet anything she does the washing because that's the way of the world and she ought to recognise them because I'd been waving them at the audience half the evening.

Maybe you won't be so keen to bandy around the epithets in future, Scrawny.

Chapter Three

I swiped my card to enter – no old fashioned keys in our house – and the alarm box on the wall started bleeping at me. Eleven on a Sunday morning and the alarm was still set! And the silence. No music. There was *always* music: Mozart, Tchaikovsky, Bach, Chopin.

There's a special quality to an empty house.

A strange, metallic aroma hovered on the cusp of smell and taste – an olfactory hint of the butcher's shop.

Next it's 'Off with the Christian Louboutins.' Not because I'm trying to creep in unobserved – the noise of the Audi's 4.2 litre engine would make that pointless – but my father is outraged by the carnage the killer heels inflict on the wooden floors. This original part of the house is all right: all dark wood walls with a granite-slab floor worn smooth and curvy by eight hundred years of foot traffic.

Facing the front door is a balcony with a staircase either end and, under it, the door to the dining room which stood half open. But it shouldn't have been because there's another house rule: "All doors closed." On the floor, stretched across the doorway, was a leg. It looked like my mother's.

Shoes forgotten, I dashed over, heels loud in the unnatural silence and peered into the sunlight bright room. For a second my brain stopped, refusing to compute the data: a red, gelatinous mess everywhere.

When rationality returned, I saw she had been shot in the back of the head. I say 'shot' even though I've never actually seen anybody shot but there was a small, dark hole in her skull and the contents of her braincase sprayed across the top of the sixteen-seater, teak table and up the patio doors opposite. There was hole in the double-glazing. I bet my father has a rule about bullets through the windows. Whatever. He'd be regally pissed off about it.

As she'd gone down, she'd pulled over a chair, which now lay half over her. Another chair, a carver, was missing.

I touched her arm; icy cold, and when I rolled her over I saw her face or, rather, *didn't* see her face because it looked as if somebody had scooped it out with a spoon. There was circular hole between her eyebrows and mouth. *Sometimes a lack of empathy can be an advantage.*

Granny? My father? Poo-brain?

I sprinted to the sitting room; in the room before I remembered the shoes.

On the floor was a young man, flat on his back, staring at the ceiling. Jet black hair and slightly epicanthic eyes: he could easily have been mistaken for Poo-brain but wasn't. He had the handle of Granny's bamboo knife in the centre of a gummy red circle on his chest. He was cold too.

Granny sat in her chair with her knitting bag in her lap. She had a hole in the middle of her forehead and her brains were, just as my mother's had been, sprayed across the room behind her.

All sorts of strange feeling flooded me. I'm not used to emotions. I can't cope with them. My brain can't sort them out. All I knew was that I was churning up inside. This is Granny. Nobody can do that.

My father was in the chair from the dining room, gaffer tape binding his wrists to the arms and his ankles to the legs. He was naked and his clothes lay scattered in bits on the carpet. Several of his toes had been smashed to pulp – presumably by the hammer lying beside them. He was also dead but there was no sign he'd been shot. His face was red and his lips were blue. There was no sign of Poo-brain.

Here was a quandary. My duty was to call the police

but did I have time to change my dress? *Okay, Josie, call them then charge upstairs and change while you wait for them.*

Back in the hall I dialled triple-nine, asked for the police and told the woman I wanted to report a murder. "Four, actually," I corrected myself. When she asked me for my name I had to make a quick decision but I've always lived by the adage: *If you've got it, flaunt it*, so I said, "Jocelyn Bergomay-Trelawney."

"Is that Bergomay-Trelawney as in—"

"Yes," I interrupted. "As in *Assistant Chief Constable* Bergomay-Trelawny." I doubt I would have noticed the pause if I hadn't been listening for it. *Very professionally done.*

She took the address and promised somebody would be there "as quickly as possible."

"I'll bet." That will have lobbed a hand grenade into the cess pit.

I never did get time to change my dress because at the top of the stairs, where I would have turned right toward my rooms, was little brother. He'd also been shot in the back of head but when I reached him he groaned and tried to speak.

"Stay there, Poo-brain."

I was weighing up what to do when I heard a car pulling up outside so I hammered back down and grabbed the phone. The doorbell rang as I was demanding an ambulance so I opened the door with the receiver pressed to my ear.

Then the party started.

* * *

I had barely let in a female sergeant and a male constable when the detectives arrived so I was saved the trouble of going through my tale twice. The Detective Sergeant, a good-looking guy of about forty who introduced himself as Mullin, sent the uniforms to search the house to ensure the offender was not still lurking, then he and his younger colleague toured the sights. The medics arrived and got Harrison – that's Poobrain – packaged up and slung in the back of the ambulance. I offered to go with him but Mullin wouldn't let me. I knew the drill. I was a suspect and he was not letting me out of his sight.

"Tea?" I asked and went off to the kitchen without waiting for an answer. I know coppers – I was married to one – they drink tea like camels in a drought. More important, there's a hatch between the kitchen and the dining room so I could eavesdrop.

"Jeez, boss, did you catch the legs on that?" the DC said and gave a low whistle.

"Try to be just the tiniest bit professional, Hooper." The DS's voice was a low snarl. *Ease up, Mullin, it's fine by me.*

"Sorry, Sarge." He hesitated before adding, "But what's she wearing? I've got more material in the label of my coat."

"Hooper!" Mullin snapped. There was silence for a while before Mullin added "But there *is* something rather odd about her, though. She seems a bit, y'know, *distant* ... as if we were discussing broken ornaments rather than her family. Know what I mean?"

Shit! 'The Act'!

Because I struggle with empathy I've had to learn how to act 'normal'. In public I have to constantly monitor everybody so I can project the proper emotions and plaster on the correct expression. At home I don't have to do that, I can just be ... *me*. Now I'd blown it. Could I pull it back?

I snatched up the china teapot and dropped it on the stone floor where it shattered, scattering potsherds and scolding tea. Then, with my back to a cupboard, and careful to avoid the hot liquid, I slid down and let out a loud wail. Within seconds I heard running feet and a confusion of people burst in. The female officer tried to support me but, not one to miss an opportunity, I flung myself into Mullin's arms and sobbed onto his shoulder. He tried not to react but I felt it in the way he held me.

I allowed myself to be led into the library where they surrounded me and spoke soothingly. Somebody sent the woman to make a replacement pot. *Bloody typical ... girlies make the tea!*

A SOCO van arrived and technicians, dressed as if there had been a nuclear war, started their investigations. Mullin and some DC took my statement. She said her name was Elaine something. Mullin let her take the lead. *All girls together?*

"Regina," she began and I bridled. "Do you mind if I call you Regina?" True, it was my first name but I loathed it – especially when, like this moron, it was rhymed with 'vagina'. I had been about eleven or twelve when my classmates had caught onto this. Their problem was that they couldn't make me cry so as part of their campaign they weaponised my name against me

I'd stormed into the principal's office and announced that, henceforward, I would use my second name, Jocelyn, and that all school records were to be amended accordingly. She had not said a word but the records were duly edited. It took more direct action, usually with the point of a technical drawing instrument, to edit my classmates. Our friend Hare would probably have used that to give me full marks for Item 18: '*Juvenile delinquency*' or 12: '*Early behaviour problems*'.

"I don't like the name. You can't even pronounce it." *Twat.* "You may call me *Ms Trelawney* or, if you really must, *Jocelyn*."

She coughed and Mullin looked down, hiding his

mouth behind curved fingers.

"You say you had just arrived home?" she continued. "What time was that?"

"About eleven or just after. I called you immediately. It will have been logged." I managed a quite convincing sob.

"And where were you until then, Jocelyn?"

"I play in a band. We had a gig last night until one this morning—"

"So you have witnesses for where you were last night until one? What about afterwards?" *Afterwards? Have the techies got a time of death already?*

"I stayed with a ... friend ... in Burgess Hill. I left there at about ten-thirty this morning and came straight here."

"I'll need his ... his?" He raised an eyebrow and I nodded. "His name and address." I suppressed a smirk. *That's going to shake up Jordan's domestic idyll.*

Insisting that 'I must keep busy,' I took tea outside to the first two officers who'd been relegated to the role of bouncers. I found them examining the Yamaha; the PC crouching beside it while the sergeant stood back, hands hooked in the armholes of her stab vest. I handed them the cups.

"This your dad's?" the man asked. I laughed, picturing my father astride Potex-1.

"No. I couldn't see him involved in anything more sporty than watching rugby on TV. He'd scream like a girl on this." I imagined how I would rag him until it hit me that I would never speak to him again.

"Crikey. Your brother's only ... what? ... eighteen. This must cost him an arm and both legs in insurance."

Another assumption. *Here we go again.*

"Oh, don't worry. He doesn't have any insurance on this." Both heads jerked around at me and the sergeant slopped tea over her hand but I ignored them and went back in.

Graeme, the ex, turned up in his official, chauffeur-driven, jaguar and there was an immediate change in the others. I don't suppose they often had an ACC turn up at a crime scene. He was togged up in full brass and braid, looking like a recruitment poster. Only his tailor and I knew he spent thousands on made-to-measure uniforms; customised to accommodate his asymmetric shoulders. He still looked the part with his chipped-from-granite features and his black, steel-wool hair, shading to grey at the temples. At over six feet he had an inch on me, even in my four inch heels. But his most outstanding features were his beaklike nose and dark eyes, giving him the appearance of a hunting raptor. As soon as we were alone he reached out to me but I slipped under his arm.

"Josie, how are you?" *Like you care!*

"My family …" It genuinely hurt. *I never expected that.*

His face dropped. "Harry …?"

"Yeah, Poo-brain's not dead but he could be a vegetable. No change there." Despite the situation he made a half-grin. It had always amused him, the constant sledging and the nicknames we had for each other. From the day he was born, on my fourteenth birthday, I always associated Harrison with the least pleasant human emissions. I originally called him 'Shit for brains' or 'Esseffbee'' until my mother forbade it when I changed it to Poo-brain. I told her it was for 'Pooh – a bear of very little brain' … but he and I knew the truth. In return he called me … *well, a derogatory Chinese phrase about being flat-chested.*

We sat and Graeme made me go over my movements for the previous evening. As I'd spent the night with another man, it amused me to rub his nose in it. I was tempted to ask how his sex life was now his current wife was up the duff.

Now here's something to ponder: when Graeme Thomas Bergomay married Regina Jocelyn Trelawney-Penhaligon he'd insisted on rebuilding the names to Bergomay-Trelawney and when we got divorced he kept the name. Isn't that rather odd? More importantly, I wonder how my replacement, Leonora, feels having to use *my* name: Mrs Bergomay-Trelawney ... *the second!*

At least she *is* having a baby. *Score one point for her.*

"Is there anything I can do?" He placed a hand on my wrist but I jerked it away. My head was like a merry-go-round and I couldn't say what I really wanted so I just sat, head down. "Is there anybody we should inform?"

"Thanks. Somebody ought to tell my father's secretary because otherwise she'll be coming here tomorrow morning and walk into this circus. And the cleaner." I scribbled their contact details into his pocket book.

"Can you find somebody to stay with? You shouldn't be on your own and, anyway, you won't be able to stay in the house until SOCO's finished. Personally, I don't think I would want to stay here after all this." I suddenly realised that I had never felt so alone. "How about Uncle Leo?" he asked.

"I could do that, I suppose. I'll drive up now. I can break the news and stay there tonight, perhaps tomorrow. I'll have to be back by Tuesday as I've a client to see."

He gave me a long, steady look and shook his head. "You know, Josie, sometimes you're the coolest customer I've ever met. If these were my folks I'd be in bits but you just grit your teeth and carry on. You always do. Even when we lost the b..." His voice trailed away and he put a gentle hand on my arm but I shrugged. I didn't know what he wanted me to say. It was all too painful: him, the baby. What I wanted most was for him to put his arms around me and tell me that everything would be all right but that was never going to happen. I wouldn't let it. *You're not going to hurt me again, you bastard.*

"Whatever. I'll need to get into my office so I'd appreciate it if you'd get your guys to clear out asap." Both my father and I worked from home and had offices in the house, just along the corridor from the library. He was an accountant and I have a business analysis consultancy.

"I'll see what I can do but these things grind slowly. And you'll need to go into the station to give a full statement—"

"Under caution?" We both knew the answer but wanted to put him on the spot. He pulled a face but he wouldn't go out on limb to let me off that particular hook. *Don't want to get involved in anything do you, my love? Unless she's got big tits.*

He left and I finally got away.

In my room I paused in front of the mirror and have to say, despite the slutty frock, I looked good. People have described me as anything from 'very pretty' to 'drop dead gorgeous' but I suspect much of *that* was coloured by how much he – or she – wanted to get into my knickers. I'm not keen on my hair, which was long but too straight and not any particular colour. Justin, my hairdresser, who earns a fortune for doing nothing but trimming the ends every couple of weeks, calls it 'honey blonde'. Poo-brain calls it 'mousey'. I'm probably with him.

What to do?

Given all my options I would have gone for a long run. It's what I do when life closes in. I don't need 'The Act' when I'm hammering along, settled inside my own head, music in my ears. When my body is screaming in protest and my heart is trying to dig an escape tunnel out through my ribs, I'm just *me*.

Or the gym. Straining with heavy weights. Nobody approaches. Nobody hits on me. Nobody wants a conversation.

But I couldn't even do any yoga. The police filled every crevice of the house and would soon be kicking me out so I had no options.

I took my time: stripped, showered, applied my makeup before chucking on my leathers, stuffing some clothes in a backpack and setting out. The two plods looked stunned as a mounted Potex-1 giving them a nice view of my leather-clad butt.

"This yours?" the PC said and I just smirked at him. "I thought—"

"No you didn't." I pebble-dashed them with gravel as I went.

Uncle Leo and family live in Laleham overlooking the Thames so I headed north. I got up to one hundred and fifty on the M23, slowed to eighty on the cloverleaf and didn't get over one-twenty on the M25. The adrenaline surge is extraterrestrial! I covered the seventy two miles in forty six minutes so it was not yet seven when I rang the doorbell. Aunt Tazzy opened the door and ushered me in. The house was, as ever, overheated and over-perfumed. Uncle Leo, my father's brother, sat reading in his high-backed, tan leather chair.

"Hello, Josie," he said, smiling. "We didn't expect you. Everything all right?" I suddenly realised I hadn't planned this out. *How does one tell somebody his brother and family have been murdered? What facial expression is appropriate? What tone of voice?*

"No," I said and, as he rose in alarm, all I could say was, "They're dead."

Then I took a look inside me ... at the thirty percent ... to see how a normal person would react but it seemed to take over unbidden. I suddenly realised I was sobbing and could hardly stand. I never expected that.

Chapter Four

I regained consciousness at about six, my head feeling as if it was stuck in a revolving door somebody was whirling. Fast.

Much of the previous evening was all bits and pieces. I remember that, as I slumped onto the sofa, Leo poured me an enormous single malt. Then I told them.

I'd swallowed the drink: searing my throat, making me cough and my eyes water. Despite that, I grabbed the bottle but he seized my wrist and eased it from my grasp.

"Don't want me getting sloshed on your posh booze?"

"Not at all, but if I let you get plastered on this stuff you will end up with the hangover from hell." He passed me a bottle of vodka. "Believe me, you'll thank me tomorrow." I didn't thank him but hate to think how it could be have been much worse. Everything went hazy soon after that but when I looked under the covers I was in my bra and pants. I guess Tazzy put me to bed. *I* hope *it was Tazzy*.

From the bed I looked across a river that slid past like oil, pockmarked by raindrops. A sky like old pewter promised worse to come.

I scrubbed the compost from my teeth, put my hair in a ponytail and donned my running gear: minute top and shorts that show of the fab-abs, all in dried-blood red with orange piping and bright orange Nikes. I thrash my body with some hard exercise every day and had missed yesterday so I wasn't going to let a headache stop me.

I set out along the towpath with Suzerain's *Apocalypse Disco* beating time. Every step hammered straight into my damaged cortex and, of course, the rain stepped it up a gear.

By the time I had done my ten miles I was soaked but more human. I drove myself hard over the last mile along the Laleham Road from Staines and attracted a few hoots from drivers in misted up cars but didn't look around. The driver of a battered white van opened his window and shouted something obscene so I flicked him the finger and turned back down towards the river. Tazzy was preparing breakfast as I entered the kitchen door, dripping everywhere.

Showered and changed, I tucked into an enormous breakfast; only then realising that nothing had passed my lips the previous day except tea and booze … if you don't count my Jordanian activities. *Let's not go there.*

"Are you all right? Is there anything I can do? What do you want to do today, Josie?" Tazzy wittered as she juggled a couple of hot slices from toaster to rack. She was trying to sound solicitous but was actually just annoying. I smeared lime marmalade on toast.

"Nothing definite planned. Overton is out of bounds so I've nowhere to live." *Damn, why did I say that?*

"Leo is going to see the boys at school this afternoon and break the news to them then he'll bring them home for a few days. I don't know how he'll tell them. It's just so bloody, bloody awful. Then she cried and was even more annoying. Once she'd calmed down she said, "You can stay here if you like. The boys will be delighted to see you. Just delighted." *Oh deep joy.* I could think of nothing worse than having to entertain that particular amalgam of testosterone and teenage attitude. I had to think quickly.

"Thank you but I have to report to the police station and give a statement. I might as well get it out the way. I need some clothes and with any luck they'll let me in to grab some, then I'll find a hotel."

"There's absolutely no need for you—"

"No, Tazzy." I retrofitted a look of brave forbearance.

"I've got to keep busy, otherwise I'll go mad. I have to see a client tomorrow and it will do me good to bury myself in some Domain Class Models." She looked puzzled. *That's the idea.* "It's something I use to analyse data." It was all the explanation I was going to give and I saw it whistle over her head without even ruffling her brain. *Not the hottest coal on the barbecue, my aunt Tazzy.*

Back in 'my' room I put on some slap, just lippy and eyes, pulled on my leathers and headed out. I passed Leo who said he'd 'been into the office to put a few things on hold.' He seemed remarkably calm ... just as I imagine my father would have been. *Peas in a pod. Frozen peas.*

I kissed him dutifully on the cheek, leaving a red smear and promised to stay in touch. Tazzy was still in the kitchen so I called goodbye and hit the road. I made decent time but nowhere near what I had done the previous evening.

* * *

At the cop shop I waited for twenty minutes and was on the point of having a strop and walking out when Mullin appeared. Rather officiously, I thought, he led me to an interview room where I was introduced to a DI Frank Leyland: massively overweight in a badly fitting suit who must have been on the edge of hanging up his handcuffs. *Him, the suit was well past retirement age.* He said he was now in charge of the investigation. He added that I was not under caution and could leave whenever I liked but made it sound like a threat. I get really hacked off when some little Napoleon thinks a badge gives him dictatorial powers over the rest of humanity. Mullin searched my bag and then took me to another room where I was fingerprinted – for elimination purposes, he said – then he escorted me back to the interview room.

I wanted to 'calibrate' Leyland, something I do when I meet somebody new.

"How did my father die? He wasn't shot." He looked up and to the left; the merest flick. Got him. Now I could tell if he was *recalling* or *creating*.

"The pathologist hasn't had time to do a full PM but we suspect your father – Bruce isn't it? – died of a heart attack." Yup, up to the left.

He started by going over the details of the crime scene. We talked about my mother and how I'd found her, then about the dead youth.

"Did you recognise him?"

"No. Never seen him before."

He pulled out a Ziploc bag that held Granny's knives. "And these?"

"Yes, of course. They're Granny's bamboo knives. I last saw one of them sticking out of his chest." I pointed at the picture on the table between us.

"Granny? The little Chinese lady?" I nodded. "You call her 'Granny' …?"

"Maybe it's because she's my, er, grandmother."

"You don't look very Chinese …"

"You don't look like a knob." I scowled at him. It's one of my best looks. "She's my mother's mother. So I'm one quarter Chinese." I screwed my eyes to slits and tucked in my lower lip to simulate buck teeth. "So solly me no lookee likee Chinkee lady." He looked embarrassed and I slumped back in the chair, arms folded. I was getting fed up with this.

"Bamboo knives?" He tried a different tack to save his blushes. *Got you!*

"Yes." I picked up the bag. "As you see, there are two knives with bamboo handles and very slim blades. Each blade is slightly offset from the centre and alongside each is a slot in the hilt so the two knives slip together side by side, each hilt being the sheath of the other blade. When they're pushed together they look like a single piece of bamboo. She always kept it in her knitting bag and ... I'm only guessing here ... when the lad got close enough she stabbed him so they shot her."

"Why would she keep a knife in her knitting bag?" His eyebrows climbed towards where his hairline had once been.

"You would need to understand her background." I could barely conceive of how she has survived: the barbarism of the Japanese occupation of China, walking halfway across that vast country on her own when she was only fifteen years old, slipping out of communist China and living from hand to mouth in Hong Kong. But that story had been our secret and I had no intention of sharing it with him. "How is any of this relevant to finding the killers?"

"Just information. You never know what's relevant." He leaned forward, elbows on the table. "Something else you might be able to help me with. Can you think of any reason there was only one fingerprint on the knife?"

"One ...?"

"Yes and, based on a quick look at the prints you gave, it could well be yours."

"But—"

"You see, the handle had been wiped but whoever did it missed one near the blade."

"It's highly likely I've handled the knife—"

"But you see, Josie, here's my problem: If your grandmother stabbed the man then I would expect to find *her* prints on it so why, then, would anybody wipe the handle?"

"How would I know?"

"Okay. Can you help me with something else? You know how to operate the security system at your home?"

"Of course."

"Good. And it's a very sophisticated system that protects different parts of the house. So, for instance, at night you can have all external doors and windows and the whole downstairs fully alarmed but the corridors upstairs not. Yes?"

"Yes."

"And it's all monitored by a specialist security company, SecScan?"

"True."

"Well, their records show that when, presumably, everybody is indoors, the system is normally set so you can move about in the house but with all external doors and windows monitored."

"Yes. So anyone entering needs to scan an electronic key or the alarms will go off—"

"And did you scan your key when you arrived home yesterday morning?"

"Yes, of course."

"And the security company confirmed that. So the alarm was still set?"

"Well ... Yes ... I ... I guess so."

"So my question is: how did the raiders get in and out without setting off any alarms? How would they be able to do that?"

"Well ... I ..." A thrill ran down my spine and I felt goose bumps.

"Unless they had a key card."

"I suppose they must have. But I don't see how—"

"Indeed they did. And SecScan came up trumps on that, too. The alarm was deactivated, from the outside pad, at 11.05 on Saturday evening and reset from inside at 11.07 – just long enough for a person or persons to enter. It was deactivated again at 2.08 until 2.11 and finally from 3.14 to 3.15 – time enough for people to leave. They even told me whose key was used."

I had a sudden sinking feeling but I had to ask. "Whose?"

"Yours." It felt like a punch.

"But I don't see how …" I rummaged in my bag and produced my key.

"Do you have a spare?"

"Probably. Maybe in my desk." *Whoa, where is this going?*

"There are cameras as well."

"Of course, they will show anybody in the grounds."

He extracted a black and white picture from the cardboard folder on the table in front of him. Two slim figures stood at the front door. They wore 'hoodies' and ski masks. "We've estimated their heights." He tapped on the image of one of the images. "About five feet nine or ten." He studied me. "How tall are you?"

"You know or you wouldn't be asking. Equally, either of them could be the young lad that was killed with Granny's knife." Too late I heard the trap slam shut.

"Exactly!" He tried not to appear triumphant but failed. "One could be you and the other could be the lad."

"Wait. Watch the film later on and you will see me arrive." *Got you.*

"Unfortunately not, because immediately after this picture was taken, this one here …" He tapped the photograph, "… sprayed paint on the lens." *Damn.*

Then he launched in on me, going over my, as he called it, 'story' – but in a tone which suggested no reasonable human could ever believe a word of it.

"We went to the address you gave us in Burgess Hill to confirm your alibi." I didn't like the way he emphasised the last word. "We spoke to a woman there called Priti—"

"A misnomer if ever there was one."

He ignored the remark. "It seems this Jordan has

moved out." I had to grin. "She did, however, confirm that you had been there." He took out another evidence bag and I saw, through the clear plastic, my pants and lipstick. That was a result: to get those back. But when I examined them I saw that she's taken scissors to the one and stamped on the other.

"Do you often go to bed with men you've just met?"

"What's it got to do with you?"

"If it's not something you usually do then it seems very convenient that you should step out of character to create an alibi on that particular night ... and go to a lot of trouble to leave evidence to prove it." He shook the bag at me. "So you'll forgive me if I need to assess your credibility."

"Assess your chances, you mean?" I looked him up and down and sneered. "Well I would rather stick pins in my eyes." Leyland made a sort of muffled cough and shuffled some papers. Mullin, sitting beside him, slapped a hand over his mouth so I winked at him. Is that one of the subjects at Hendon ... smirking when a fellow officer is embarrassed? *Works for me.*

"Do you know if your father had any enemies?"

I laughed. "He was an accountant, for God's sake. The nearest he came to conflict was discussing the finer points of Value Added Tax with the taxman."

"He must have had something they were prepared to torture him for." He leaned forward over his hands, studying his interlinked fingers, appearing to be pondering a difficult conundrum, then looked up. "You see, Josie, I have a bit of a problem. If, as you say, your father was 'just an accountant' where did he get his money from?"

"Duh? Working as an accountant?" I ladled as much sarcasm in as I could. "Doubtless you're looking at his financial records."

"Indeed we are. He was quite successful. A decent

turnover on the business. But you live in a house worth about four million—"

"Bought about twenty years ago—"

"For cash. And he has quite a lot in various bank accounts and investments."

"I don't know anything about that—"

"About six million, we reckon, but we're still looking." That knocked me back. I knew we were what my father described as 'comfortable' but this was way beyond that. "For instance," he continued, "why would he have sixty thousand pounds cash in a hidden safe in his office?" I could do no more than shrug. "Do you know who your father's clients were?"

"Of course not. Apart from anything else, I suspect there's some arcane rule of client confidentiality which means he couldn't tell anybody. Like I'd even be interested."

"You shared an office with him."

"No. I had an office *next* to his. I had a bedroom along the hall from him but I've no idea how often he and my mother had sex."

He glared. "This is not very helpful." He leaned back in his chair and glared some more. "You don't seem particularly interested in helping us solve the horrific murders of your family."

I leaned forward across the table to emphasise my earnestness and snarled, "You don't have to tell me anything about the murders … I saw them. After I leave here I'm going to have to go to the morgue and identify my father, my mother and Granny. After that I will go to the hospital where they are trying to decant the brains back into my brother. Don't you *dare* tell me I'm 'not particularly interested in helping you solve the horrific murders of my family,' you prat." I even managed a few real tears. It was a bravura performance. Then he hit me with a curve ball.

"What was your relationship with your father like?"

"What?" Building his case against me?

"Did you get on with him? Any arguments for example?" *Yes. First: motive – money. Then a trigger – a family row.* "I notice, for instance, that you always refer to your parents as, 'my father' and 'my mother' – not, for instance, 'Dad' or 'Mum'. That strikes me as somewhat – shall we say – impersonal. To my mind it implies a certain ... *remoteness* ... in your relationship. Am I right?" *Cheeky bastard.* He was trying to get me needled, perhaps hoping I'd flare up and make a slip – reveal something to incriminate myself. *Good luck on that one, Buster – I'm not one of the mugs you usually deal with.*

"No. Of course not. What are you suggesting?" Perfectly calm. Expression number 2: How-may-I-help-you-sir?

"With your father's death you have become an extremely wealthy young woman." *Yup, I'm right. Pin this on me you'll have the case solved and your 'attaboy badge' all before teatime.* That did it. *No more 'Miss Nice-guy'.* I stood, snapping my legs straight so they flicked the chair and sent it crashing to the floor behind me. *Nice touch, that.*

"I'm *already* 'an extremely wealthy young woman.' I've got more money in loose change than you'll earn in your whole sad career." Then I hoisted my bag on my shoulder and snatched the door open. At the last instant I stopped and turned. "Actually I lied." That got their interest. "You *do* look like a knob."

* * *

I went to the morgue and did the official identifications. They didn't look like my family – just Madame Tussauds waxworks. And not very good ones at that. My mother was difficult, with most of her face gone, and they gave me the option of not doing it but I felt I had to keep up the act: tissue, face in hands, loads of tears ... mostly genuine.

At the hospital I found Poo-brain all hooked up to machines and with tubes in every orifice. I sat with him for about twenty minutes but there's only so much inactivity I can stand so I rode to Overton – with Leyland's permission, of course – where I found a swarm of vans and people: the press. *Of course.* As I stopped and hoisted the bike onto its stand they rushed forward and thrust cameras and microphones at me but I kept my dark visor down so they had no idea who I was. At the gate I started to punch in the code that would open the gate – taking care that the vultures couldn't see it – but was interrupted by an idiot in blue.

"Hold on, mate, who're you then?"

"Not your 'mate' that's for sure."

He ignored my snipe. "I'm going to have to ask you to remove your helmet, *Sir*." He squeezed every ounce of insolence he could into the honorific.

"Not until you get these ghouls out of my face."

"In which case, I'm going to have to ask you to move away."

"Please," I begged. *Try a different approach, Josie. You never know, it might work.* "I only want to go into my own home to collect some clothes and things. Inspector Leyland has cleared it." I kept my visor, my voice and my temper down.

"Not with me he hasn't." He got up close and personal. "Move away or I'll nick you." He put a hand on my arm and I wondered if I would get away with sloshing him 'in self defence'. *Probably not.* I moved down the road and called Graeme. It was a last resort – I don't like antagonising people with any degree of power because you never know when they may be useful ... or spiteful ... but I could see no option. A few seconds later the PC's mobile rang and, when he clapped it to his ear, I saw him stiffen. After a few more seconds during which, I guess, the ear was barbecued, he waved me over but I refused to move, making him come to me. "You could have told me who you were." It was almost a whine.

"I probably would have ... if you had been a little more civil, *Mate*." I punched the code and fishtailed Potex up the drive, leaving him to fend off the press and prevent them following through the closing gate.

I packed what I needed and loaded it into the back of my mother's Volvo XC90. The police had removed all our computers and filing cabinets so I rang Leyland and fired a barrage of epithets at him.

"But they're evidence," he protested.

"How is *my* computer evidence in my family's murder? Listen, I've got a business to run and all my records are on it. What am I supposed to do? Email all my clients and tell them to sit on their hands until you lot get around to letting me have everything back? Oh no, I can't even do that, can I? Because my email address book is ON MY SODDING COMPUTER!"

He mouthed a few more anodyne apologies but I just slammed the phone down. I wasn't as hacked off as I made out but it's always good practice to let people think they've upset you because it puts them in your debt ... never a bad thing.

I found a seafront hotel in Brighton with an 'Okay' room, had a late lunch and got on the phone to find a serviced office. At a computer retailer I bought a laptop with *Microsoft Office* and a few other applications preinstalled and told them to deliver it to my new office for the next morning. I would have to download all my records from my offsite data storage. Typical plods, they'd taken my computer but anything I wouldn't want them to see wasn't on it anyway!

It all took until five o'clock so I had a sandwich then

went to kickboxing to spend a couple of hours kicking the snot out of anybody stupid enough to volunteer for the job.

Chapter Five

Next morning I decided to walk to my new office so after my run and a quick visit to Poo-brain, I grabbed an overcoat and descended the stairs. As I emerged into the foyer I saw the unmistakably slobby outline of Leyland, Mullin in tow, entering the lift so I ducked back and waited until they'd gone before putting as much distance behind me as I could. I had a client to see later that day so didn't feel inclined to faff about with that cretin. I hadn't given anybody the address of my temporary office so felt safe. I was halfway there when my mobile rang and displayed a number I didn't recognise. The voicemail message was a very brusque Leyland *ordering* me to call him back 'immediately'. *Cheeky git.* He continued to call every twenty minutes or so until I set it to go straight to voicemail – making it appear as if my phone was off.

I was bidding for a contract with a company called TMO so the morning was taken up with preparing my pitch then I had lunch with the Managing Director: Luke, the letch, Battersby. I had dressed for the part: elegant, charcoal grey business suit with off-the-knee skirt and plain white blouse – top two buttons undone. I wore my hair in a bun; businesslike and it shows off my neck. As I slipped into the booth beside him I showed a lot of thigh and he spent the entire two hours with his line of sight half a metre below my brains while I never once looked down to where he keeps his.

I got the contract.

Later I had a fitting with Diana, my dressmaker. Diana was gorgeous, loud, bouncy and up for anything. She's my ... er ... Well, to call her my 'girlfriend' would be stretching the facts. I guess she thinks we're closer than we are.

But most importantly, she was a great seamstress and I just *have* to have my clothes made. You know what it's like; trying to get something that fits waist, hips and legs. Even two out of the three is a miracle.

I'd met her through her husband, Garret, a member of my kickboxing club, after admiring a shirt she'd made him. Within seconds I realised she was a puppy dog: into everything and I'd be able to run her as easily as I can run a bath. She and Garret presented themselves as so 'into' each other she seemed a challenge I had to accept.

She agreed to make me a trouser suit and we arranged for her to visit me at home. I'd worn a short skirt and, as she slid the tape up the inside of my naked leg, I gasped – as if involuntarily – and clamped down on her hand. Her eyes flicked up so I held her gaze and gave her a tiny smile as I eased the hand upwards. Her face was pure confusion. She didn't know where to look and a red hue suffused every inch of visible skin. After that, I started playing up to her at every opportunity: the little touches to her hand, a finger trailed down her back, brushing a strand of auburn hair – like polished copper – from her face, that sort of thing. She never once objected or shrank away from the contact.

Asking me whether I prefer boys or girls is a bit like asking me if I prefer sofas or tables, so I was quite happy to take it further. For a partner I have three requirements: good looking, great at sex and married. No commitments. And that knocked Hare's item 17 into touch. '*Many short-term marital relationships*'. I'd only had one that wasn't … and see how well that turned out.

In Diana's case I decided it would be better if I kept her dangling.

The trouser suit was perfection.

She was the manager of a small supermarket but once I

realised her talent I set her up in a small workshop, which we called *The Studio*, located above a coffee shop in North Laine. It wasn't purely altruism as I got all my clothes tailor-made for the cost of the material, plus a slice of the profits.

Today, I wanted company, somebody to talk to, to take my mind off everything for an hour or so. Normally I would go to Maxie but she was on a trip with her heavily engaged sister ... pre-wedding shopping.

As soon as I walked through the door Diana enveloped me in arms, perfume and deep, open mouthed kisses. She really is beautiful, everything I would like to be: superb figure, a gorgeous wide face and eyes I would die for. I love her hair: long tresses the colour of fire that cascade over her shoulders and down her back. I could really fancy a fling but an earlier incident had led me to suspect she would read too much into it and make it awkward to get out of. *Sex and business ... not a great combo.*

I spotted the local newspaper lying nearby. The headline screamed LOCAL FAMILY SLAIN.

"Sorry, Di," I put on a disappointed face, "I can't ..." I picked up the paper and showed it to her. "That's my family so I ... I ... excuse me ..."

She reacted immediately, hands flying to face, look of horror. You know the sort of thing. "Oh my God, Josie, how awful." She started to cry and *I* ended up comforting *her*. Not exactly what I had in mind so I bailed out.

Downstairs in the coffee shop I perused the article. It said the police were trying to trace 'the daughter, Regina' under a picture of me. The only copy of that photo was on my father's desk and the only people with access to it were the police so it had come from one of Leyland's men. *You know, Frank, you and your little team are really,* really *beginning to hack me off.*

* * *

I didn't arrive back at the hotel until after six but as soon as I walked through the entrance I was accosted by a man, so obviously police that his plain clothes may as well have had numbers on the shoulders, flashed a badge and hauled me off to the station.

For somebody who had been so desperately trying to get hold of me, Leyland didn't seem very happy now I'd arrived. "Where the hell have you been?" he snarled at me through bared teeth. Good at snarling, our Frank.

"Working. I'd try to explain the concept to you but I suspect it would be beyond your comprehension." I flicked my hair back over my shoulder.

"You've been ignoring my calls."

"No. I've been busy. Not the same thing." I then abused him for the 'theft' of the photograph and said I wanted to make an official complaint. That calmed him.

He led me to the interview room where Mullin already waited. A uniformed woman officer stood at ease by the door behind my back.

I started to become alarmed when he slipped a tape into the machine and pressed a red button. I became *very* alarmed when first Leyland, then Mullin introduced themselves to the tape, instructed me to state my name and then cautioned me: "You are not obliged to say anything but failure to mention, when questioned ..." *You know the sort of thing.* He told me I was entitled to legal representation and I pondered whether to take him up on it but it would only mean hanging around even longer. I decided against it. *I can outthink you two in my sleep.*

"How much money do you have, Jocelyn?" he began.

"What? On me?"

His face said he'd smelled a bad odour. "In total. Bank

accounts, investments, that sort of thing."

"How would I know? Two and a half ... three million. Something like that ..." I shrugged.

His eyes opened wide. "You really expect us to believe you don't actually know how much money you—?"

"I don't care what you believe. I'm guessing you've been through my records so why don't you enlighten me."

He did. It was marginally over three million. "Where did you get that sort of money?"

"When I was twenty-one, Granny gave me four million to avoid death duties providing she lived another seven years. She gave the same to Harry but he's fourteen years younger than I and was only seven at the time, so it went into a trust fund until he's twenty-one ... in three years."

"So where did *she* get it from?"

"Oh, come on!" I was getting really fed up with this. "She had it before I was even born and – to the best of my knowledge – it is all perfectly legal and the authorities knew everything they were entitled to know about it."

He switched tack. "There's a file on your computer—"

"I guess there are several, most of which are private and confidential to my clients and they will be decidedly displeased if—"

He ignored me and continued. "... this file's encrypted."

"What's it called?"

He referred to a sheet of paper. "FBA07OSP." I shrugged. It meant nothing to me. He took a printout from a cardboard file. "Obviously, we cracked it." *Obviously*. He slid the paper across the table but, when I examined it, there seemed to be nothing but a random collection of the weird symbols seen in the ASCII computer character set. *How did it get on my computer and what was it about?*

I shrugged again. "No idea. I've never seen it before."

Then he started on again about money, my father's money, where he got it from, where he kept it. He pulled out some thick documents and pushed one at me. "Your father's will."

"And ...?"

"He left all his worldly goods to your mother and, failing that, to you and your brother." He slapped down a second and read, "Jeanne Trelawney-Penhaligon," from the front. "Your mother. Ditto." A third. "Mae-lu Harris. Your grandmother even cut out the middle man – or woman – and left it all to you two direct."

"Quelle surprise! Call the media. Tomorrow's headline: 'PARENTS LEAVE INHERITANCE TO THEIR CHILDREN!'"

I caught the flick of his eyes: up to the right. He was 'creating'.

"They each have a clause which says something to the effect that 'If any bequest fails then the residue is to go to the surviving heirs.' So if your brother dies you get the lot." I could see where this was going and I didn't like it one bit. He gave another eye flick. "So if somebody broke into your parents' home and killed them all ... you suddenly become very rich—"

"Enough!" I shouted and leapt to my feet. My heart was racing and my face felt tropical. But he just smiled and slid back in his chair, arms crossed.

"Sit down." It was an order. The officer behind me put a heavy hand on my shoulder and I subsided back onto the hard plastic chair. He grinned. "A little bit of a temper there, Josie?"

"It's Ms Trelawney to you." Even that flash of petulance seemed to amuse him.

"So let's summarise what we know." This time his gaze hovered on some point above and behind my left ear until he switched to look me in the eye and held up his forefinger. "If your family dies you get a lot of money – and I mean *millions*." He raised an eyebrow but I ignored him so he raised the second finger. "Intruders access the family home using *your* key." Third finger. "Not only are you, seemingly, not there but you've gone out of your way – to a suspicious degree – to leave evidence you were elsewhere."

"So ...?"

"So how's this? You pick a night when you're going to be in front of an audience until gone one, slip your spare key and a few quid to some 'mates' so they can go in and polish off your family for a nice lottery win on your part. Any good?" He held my gaze with a fierceness that seemed to be boring into my inner thoughts. I could see how it would work with your run-of-the-mill villains. *There's nothing run-of-the-mill about me, Leyland.*

"And the knife you're so interested in? How does that fit into your fairy story?"

"I'm not convinced about a seven stone octogenarian suddenly whipping out a blade and offing some young thug whereas a falling out amongst thieves sounds far more plausible. You stab him and try to erase your prints."

"When did I get to perform that magic trick?"

"You had plenty of time to get home after your concert. Nobody in the band saw you more than a few minutes after you packed up and we only have your word you went off with this 'Jordan' fellow."

"But my lipstick and—"

"Exactly!" He was triumphant. "You give him the evidence to drop at the flat to act as an alibi while you nip home to ensure your co-conspirators have done the job. You get there just after two ... and we have the evidence because the alarm was switched off when you went in. Then you fall out with the lad – or decide to reduce your overheads – stab him and then slip away again just after three, so you can return and call us at eleven that morning."

By now I'd had enough. I wondered what the reaction of a 'normal', innocent person would be to this onslaught. Probably tears and hysterics I should think. I was tempted but in all honesty he was boring me, I was hungry and I was missing my gym class: 'Body Pump' tonight.

"Am I under arrest?"

"No, just under caution …"

"In which case I'm out of here."

" … but I *can* arrest you if that's what you want."

"Okay. Either arrest me and lock me in a cell until my solicitor arrives when we'll do a 'no comment' interview or you can have your boy here escort me to the front door." He sighed. I watched his eyes and saw him 'creating' again. This was going to be another bluff.

"What's the name and phone number of your solicitor then?" He picked up a pen and glared at me, unblinking. Yes … a bluff. *Don't play poker with me – you'll lose your shirt.*

"Don't bother with my solicitor. Just call Graeme – sorry, ACC Bergomay-Trelawney – and let him know the situation." *Cover your bet and raise you. Your bid.* He turned to Mullin, who had not spoken a single word the whole time, and just jerked his head at the door. At the desk I was bailed 'under my own cognisance' to reappear in a week and told not to leave the area 'without clearing it with Leyland … personally.' Five minutes later I was on the street.

I made my exercise class with seconds to spare – but hungry.

Chapter Six

A month ground by. Poo-brain was still in hospital drifting in and out of coherence so I visited him every spare second I had. I even took a laptop so I could work by his bed. I really wanted to be there if he came round.

Eventually the bureaucracy ground to a conclusion and the coroner opened and adjourned the inquest so the bodies could be released and the funerals held. The three coffins went into the ground side by side on miserable Thursday morning.

The previous evening I'd rehearsed in front of the mirror. I'd tried 'grief-stricken and tearful' and even 'hysterical and self-flagellating' but realised I wouldn't be able to sustain either for any length of time so in the end settled for 'rigid self-control and stoical'. That worked. In truth, I felt a strange swirl of emotions I couldn't sort out. I felt like I wanted to cry but didn't know why. It was all so outside my frame of reference. I'm a psychopath, I'm supposed not to care. So why did it feel like this?

Several dozen people, many whom I knew only slightly, stood around in fine drizzle and then we returned 'home' ... all except the police who, dressed in plain clothes, insinuated themselves throughout the mourners but had the good grace to stay away from the wake.

The house had been released for my return the previous week but I chose to remain at the hotel until a team of specialist crime scene cleaners put it into some semblance of habitability and the glaziers had replaced the patio door. So the first time I went back was the day before the funeral when went to organise the caterers. Personally, I wouldn't have done anything – *what's the point of supplying free booze and food to strangers?* – but Leo and Tazzy had insisted it was 'the right thing to do' and would have organised something in a local restaurant if I hadn't, so I was more or less coerced.

"I'm sorry for your loss, Regina," a voice behind me said quietly in my ear. At least he had pronounced it correctly.

"Don't call me that." I whirled to face him then, realising I had been too sharp added, "It's 'Jocelyn' if you don't mind." I added a tiny smile. Granny had taught me: *Politeness is an impenetrable mask.*

He was about fifty, I guessed, smartly dressed with a full head of salt and pepper hair, slicked back hard. I took an instant dislike to him.

"Have we met?" I was still annoyed but gritted my teeth and offered him my hand. We shook. He seemed sardonically amused. He glanced around at another man as if to share the joke. This other was a shaven-headed brute with broken nose and massive beer belly who stood at his shoulder like a servant attending a master.

"My name is Neil Shepherd. I am – was – one of Bruce's clients." He had an unnatural accent, almost digitally precise, as if it had been created by computer. He slipped a silver business card case from an inside pocket, clicked it open and passed me a rectangle of embossed cardboard. It felt as if he was about to try and sell me something.

"Why would I want your card?" He looked quickly around, gauging how close any eavesdroppers might be.

"Bruce was holding a sum of money for me."

I looked him up and down, keeping my face impassive. "I'm sorry, Mr Shepherd, but what does that have do with me?"

"It is rather a large amount and I want it back." I sighed. *Who does he think he is?* He was coming on like some James Bond villain *sans* white cat.

"I'm sorry, there's nothing I can do. As his estate is probated the executors will go through his accounts and any monies held for clients will be returned in due—"

He got into my personal space and went into full 'intimidation mode'. "It is unlikely to be in any account." His voice had gone towards the subsonic and I could feel his breath on my cheek.

"Get out of my face, Shepherd," I snapped and shoved past him, half spinning him with my shoulder. A few other people looked around as I stalked into the kitchen to get a glass of water. When I returned he was gone. *Sorry Granny. Fell at the first hurdle.*

That evening we: Leo, Tazzy, the boys and I, went into Brighton. We ate in a huge, noisy Italian restaurant in the Lanes. Afterwards we parted – tears and hugs on their part, a decent simulation on mine – and I drove Potex-2 back to Overton. Across the gate was parked a large luxury SUV, all in darkness. I stopped, slipped my bamboo knives up my sleeve – I hadn't told Leyland that Granny had given me a pair – and stepped out. I could see a dark figure in the driver's seat and rapped on the window but he remained rigid, staring ahead so I rapped again. With a whir the rear window descended and the internal light went on.

"Regina?" *Shepherd.*

"What do you want?"

"Get in, I want to talk." There was no way I was getting in a strange car with two creepy guys in the middle of the night.

"Get this heap out my way in ten seconds or I'll call the police." I started to walk back to my car, counting loudly enough for him to hear. The driver's door flew open and a huge figure uncoiled itself from inside so I started to run but he grabbed my arm. It felt as if I was held in a vice. He spun me around and slammed me against the side of the SUV, partially winding me, and clamped a hand on my throat. I thought he was going to crush my tonsils although, in some ways, this was a blessing as I was almost suffocated by the reek of cigarette smoke emanating from his shabby clothes. I hung on to his wrist and tried to break his hold but it was like gripping a log. When I had seen him earlier I had assessed him as just fat and slobbish – and he was – but he was also very quick and very, very strong.

"Mr Shepherd says 'e wants to talk to you." His flattened nose whistled.

I think I was supposed to feel scared but I was actually becoming angry. And when I get angry I tend to lash out. Wrong, I know, and Granny always schooled me to govern it, to use that anger, but sometimes I forget her lessons. I still had both hands free so I could easily get my knife and open up his belly and, to be honest, was quite tempted. I reckoned I could probably plead 'just cause' ... a girl on her own, two men, dark, that sort of thing. I took as deep a breath as the circumstances allowed and tried to calm myself. If somebody was this keen to speak with me then maybe I should listen.

I grinned at my captor ... not a response he had expected.

"OK," I croaked around the constriction. "With him. Not you." And with that I brought my knee up as hard and as fast as I could ... straight into his gonads. I swear he rose onto his toes but only for a second before he made a strange gurgling noise and dropped to the ground. I recommend it; it's so cathartic. I hadn't done it in years and now kickboxing had taught me how to *really* concentrate the force.

I stepped over him where he writhed and leaned in the window. "All right, Shepherd, let's talk."

"Was that necessary?" He nodded to his driver.

I shrugged. "Not sure, but I enjoyed it. Now ... what's

so important?"

"As I said, Bruce had some of my money and I want it."

"And as *I* said—"

"Just shut up and listen. He was doing a, er, *special job* for me ..."

"What sort of job?"

"It does not matter. He received the money on my behalf and he was going to pass it on but, of course, he didn't. Now I want it. The money must be somewhere and it is up to you to find it."

"And if I don't?"

"Believe me that would be a huge mistake." *Oh come on, you sound like a B-movie.*

"And how much am I looking for?"

"About fifty million ..."

"POUNDS?"

"Dollars, but I will take sterling. That would be about thirty-two point six million at today's rate."

"You're mad. Where in hell do you think I am going to get that sort of—?"

"Know what? I do not give a damn. If you have to sell the house, the fancy car ..." he nodded at Potex, "... or even your baby brother ..." he leaned towards me, face a pallid mask in the dashboard light. "Just get it."

"And I just take your word for it that he owes you—" I was becoming angry.

"Just get it."

"So can I assume you had something to do with the demise of my family?" I reached into my sleeve. *Just cause.*

"Of course I did not, you stupid whore. Why would I kill somebody who owes me money? Dead men do not pay their bills." *Stupid whore? And me with a blade.*

"So who did?"

"God knows. I am guessing that somebody found out

he had the money – maybe he talked to the wrong person – and they tried to get it from him." He leaned back into the soft leather with a self satisfied half-smile. "But you might let it be a guide to your future behaviour to know Bruce was tortured until he died of a heart attack rather than reveal the secret and incur my displeasure. You have one month." I could tell the interview was over. *How did he know about the heart attack?*

"Maybe he didn't keep silent. Maybe he talked and the money has already vanished."

"Not my concern." He pressed a button and the window started to ascend.

"Are you going to get this passion wagon out of my way?"

"Is Ray up to driving?" I looked around and the driver was sitting in the mud nursing his injured manhood. I kicked him in the side of the head and he went over sideways. *This was getting better.* I don't suppose it hurt too much because I was only wearing my lightweight, driving flatties.

"No. He's not."

Without waiting I jumped into the driver's seat, started the engine and drove forward. There was a screaming and shrieking as I liberally scraped the nearside panels along the gatepost and adjacent stone wall. When the vehicle was sufficiently clear I leapt out, returned to my own car, punched the button on the dashboard and drove in through the opening electric gate.

I couldn't hear his abuse over the roar of my engine although I saw the gestures.

But I kept thinking …

Thirty two point six million pounds.

Chapter Seven

Eric Malone, our solicitor and the executor of the wills, unravelled the family's affairs and it seemed there was about eight million pounds in assets in total ... plus the house. It made up only a small proportion of the demanded amount but, even if I felt inclined to pay this mysterious Shepherd ... which was far from certain ... the shortfall was so far beyond my means I reckoned I may as well front it out and see how things developed.

What on earth could my father have been doing with somebody else's thirty two point six million pounds? Money laundering? Surely not. But he was well placed to do something like that: a highly qualified and experienced accountant with plenty of overseas contacts.

But THIRTY TWO POINT SIX MILLION POUNDS!

One would associate money laundering with drug dealers, people traffickers or arms dealers. But wouldn't they launder their money bit by bit as they accrued it? Would any criminal really save up his ill-gotten gains until he had accumulated THIRTY TWO POINT SIX MILLION POUNDS?

My staid, boring old father? A money launderer? *NEVER!*

As a side issue, I had to consider where to live. I wondered whether to stay on at Overton but it was way too big for me and, if I'm honest, too far out in the sticks.

Leyland called me in for another interview but we just went over the same old ground. I offered him the information about Shepherd demanding money. I didn't tell him how much but I thought if the police started sniffing around

Shepherd's business he might give me a bit of breathing space. It proved totally counterproductive. Leyland made it obvious he didn't believe a word I said but agreed, begrudgingly, to follow it up. Shepherd called me a few days later saying that if I set the police on him again he would, I quote, "Make sure that you don't cause me any more trouble." *Not one of your better moves, Girl.*

I had a call from the hospital. Poo-brain was out of his coma so I visited him. Leyland had beaten me but I chased him out.

"Give him a chance, he's barely conscious," I yelled.

Harrison was still coupled up to tubes and wires but his eyes were open.

"Hello Poo-brain," I said, standing over him. "Do you know who I am?"

"The woman with a chest like an ironing board, Wú rŭfáng." His voice was slurred and he seemed to struggle for the words but he managed a distorted grin. Granny always conversed in Mandarin with us both but he limited his use to his derogatory nickname for me.

I pumped him on what he remembered of the attacks but his memory was blank.

Afterwards I spoke with his doctor, who told me, "I'm afraid he has quite a bit of brain damage. We've not finished all the tests but it appears he has substantial paralysis and may well have significant cognitive impairments." Harrison was going to need substantial care for the rest of his life. So I was going to have to find somebody to do it. And a place to do it in.

That swung it. Developers were building a new block of flats just along the coast to the east of Brighton and I bought the two on the top floor: the 'penthouse flats'. Each had three en suite bedrooms and had a staircase up to a 'solarium.' I had the staircase removed from the flat I was fitting out for Harrison so I had sole use of the roof. I also specified a number of other improvements.

An agency found me a Romanian couple who would occupy two of his bedrooms and tend him fulltime.

Meanwhile, I was still a murder suspect, on bail and unable to leave the country, which hacked me off because Maxie's sister, Lucy, was having a hen-do in Madrid. The suspicion also prevented me from touching my parents' assets. Malone put Overton up for sale and had a buyer within two days. I arranged to have all the furniture cleared out and put into storage but before the removal men arrived I took a look around for anything I wanted to take; severely restricted as the flats would not be habitable for two weeks.

* * *

I almost missed it ... hiding in plain sight. In my father's office, in the middle of his desk alongside the now disconnected and redundant monitor, sat a beautifully made, highly polished wooden box. When I lifted the lid it revealed a second lid – a glass plate set into a rebate – that covered some cigars. My father never, ever smoked. He detested it and would not even associate with anybody if he could smell it on their clothes. Very odd.

What would you have made of the malodorous Ray, Father?

Peering through the glass I saw one of the cigars was the opposite way round to the others. This was also strange as there was no way he would have allowed that. The sides of the box were about a centimetre thick and in one edge was a vertical hole holding about a dozen red matches. Two of them were the wrong way up – another contravention of 'the rules'. Next to the matches was a strip of carborundum, presumably to strike them on. On the opposite edge was a long slot holding a chrome and jade cigar clipper. The disorder of the cigars and matches conjured up an image of the police, searching the room, hurriedly tipping things out of boxes and drawers then roughly stuffing them back. In my hand the box was about the weight I would have expected – but I'm no expert on hardwood.

I looked around the room but kept being dragged back to the humidor that seemed to squat, glaring at me, in the centre of the near empty desk. So I tipped out the cigars and found another puzzle because they only occupied about two-thirds of depth of the box … and I suddenly knew what I was holding.

On my tenth birthday Granny gave me a present that appeared to be a solid lump of wood except that the surface was smooth and polished so it shone: craftsmanship of the first order. She told me it was a box except when I looked for a lid there wasn't one. All she would tell me – in Mandarin, of course – was I could open it 'with study and diligence' but added that it contained something of untold value. It took me a whole day to find that one slim strip of the glossy wood could be slid a few millimetres. This released others. But it was not simply a case of moving one to allow movement of the next. Each strip had to be moved a precise distance because if, for instance, I moved the first strip too far it subsequently prevented movement of the fourth strip. But neither could I reset the first strip because the third strip now obstructed it.

There was more than one occasion when I was close to smashing it open but Granny warned me this would destroy the value of the contents.

Over the course of a month I learned and relearned all the possible combinations of the pieces and then one day it just … opened. Eagerly I plucked out the contents and found it was a narrow sliver of paper inscribed with Chinese

Runner

characters ... which she refused to interpret for me. My ten-year-old brain expected a treasure map so I slowly and painstakingly deciphered it:

Patience and perseverance lead to great knowledge.
Knowledge is more precious than jewels.
Thanks Granny. Appreciated.

I put the cigar box into the Volvo with everything else I was taking and returned to the hotel. In the room that night I examined it, turning it over and around in my hands: pushing, pulling – the sides, the edges. All to no avail. I inverted it over the bed and the glass plate fell out, cigars and matches tumbled onto the bedspread along with the striker stone and the cutter ... which was when I noticed an anomaly in the otherwise pristine workmanship. The carborundum sat in a slot so precisely cut that, when it was in place, no gap could be seen around it. With the stone removed, the bottom of the slot was also precise – except there was another, smaller, slot in the bottom of it. I probed it with a nail file and then tweezers – nothing. I prodded, I shook. Still nothing.

Then my eyes lit on the cutter and I tried the end of the ornately shaped handle in the slot. It fitted exactly and, when I gave a slight downward push, there was the tiniest 'click' and one narrow sliver of wood suddenly stood proud of the side and I found it slid as smoothly as if oiled.

I didn't get the box open that night, nor for several after. Night after night, just before I slept, I pushed and pulled, slid and twisted. Frustration mounted and at times I threw it down in disgust ... only to pick it up again after a few minutes.

As before, I was tempted to smash it open but I resisted in the fear it would destroy the contents. Whatever was in there I was convinced it would lead to the answer of the riddle.

To thirty two point six million pounds.

* * *

Fifteen days later, my last night in the hotel, it opened. There was no drama, no fanfares or loud clicks, l just slid a single strip from the centre of one end and that allowed me to ease the floor of the cigar compartment out and reveal the contents. When I inverted it, something dropped into my hand ... and I had no idea what it was. I'm quite computer literate so I immediately recognised it as something to do with computers. It was rectangular, slightly larger than a credit card and about six or seven millimetres thick. On one short edge was a standard USB port and from the other hung a lead with a USB plug but when I connected it to my laptop I just got a message that this was an 'unrecognised USB device'. And no matter what I tried, it was the only response I could get.

I'd made a huge leap forward – straight into a brick wall.

The next day was taken up with moving into the flat so, despite my curiosity I could spend no time working on the mystery. The man I needed was Adam. But Adam really didn't want to see me or, at least, he got all awkward when we were together.

It's a whole sorry tale.

Chapter Eight

I first took up kickboxing at my local club but found it unsatisfactory because it was mixed. Whenever we did any sparring they would put me up against another girl but as soon as I thumped her a bit there would be upset and tears. On the rare occasions I got to fight one of the boys he would treat me like porcelain and not put the effort in. Totally useless.

So I joined the SKB Club.

There was a bit of fuss when I asked to join because it was all male. I proposed that, to prove my aptitude, I would face any of their number they nominated and this long, lanky lad stepped – or was pushed – forward. We padded up: blue, gel- and foam-filled protection that would absorb much of the impact of a punch or kick, and faced each other. Ron, who ran the club and obviously didn't want me in, read us the riot act.

"Don't punch her in the tits, Micky," he ordered "And you ... don't kick him in the bollocks." As he was speaking he kept his eyes on me to see how I would react to the language. I didn't.

Compared to Poo-brain you're a rank amateur, Ron.

As soon as we started, Micky smacked me straight in the middle of the chest so I kicked him hard between the legs to the resounding cheers of his mates. What I think really won them over though was his kick: a long, sweeping roundhouse. I didn't see it coming until too late and reacted too slowly. It would have hit my left shoulder but my attempted block deflected it upwards so it actually caught me on the side of the head. I went down like a sack of wet straw but, determined not to lose so easily, hit the floor, rolled over onto all fours before springing up and launching a furious attack with fists, feet, knees and elbows. I actually won on points but Ron called time, announced a draw and I was accepted as the only female member of SKB.

One of the main objections they had against females was that they had only one set of showers. "No problem," I said. "I'll either just slip on a tracksuit and shower at home or wait outside until you've all finished. And that's the way it worked.

But one of the traits of psychos is we tend to be impulsive. Hare made '*Impulsivity*' item 14 on his list. We see what we want and just go for it. And it's got me into so much trouble in my life. Usually I'm clever enough to get out of it, often by passing the buck but sometimes one impetuous act puts me in a situation where I'm forced to take further action on the spur of the moment. That can lead to still deeper 'situations'. And that's what happened.

Every Friday the guys would retire to *The Jetty*, a lovely little pub near the harbour where we would meet the wives and girlfriends ... this was where I'd first met Diana. We'd all get together and have a few drinks, play pool or darts, chat ... that sort of thing. Except that, when I had to wait for all the blokes to clear the changing room, I was always half an hour or so behind them.

Then came the night of the quiz.

It was something the pub did regularly and this week it was to support a local charity and Artan, the Albanian landlord, persuaded us to enter a team. If I had to hang around for the boys to finish I'd miss the start but I certainly wouldn't go without a shower!

On impulse I waited until they'd had long enough for some of them to have got out the shower and walked into the changing room. Somebody gasped. Someone else said,

Runner

"Hey!" I fixed my eyes on the far wall as I strode between the two rows of semi-naked men – *although I have great peripheral vision*. Silence fell like a lead weight and I felt a dozen pairs of eyes on my back and heard a dozen intakes of breath as I stripped off first my top, then my shorts. I wrapped myself in a towel: breasts to thighs and, again with eyes straight ahead, walked back through the tunnel of amazement and into the shower area just in time to meet Adam coming out – stark naked. I must say I was impressed but pretended not to notice. Showering was no problem as there are eight curtained cubicles.

After that it became my usual routine. I couldn't really see the problem. What did amuse me was these strapping blokes all – or, at least, most – of whom would love to be naked with me suddenly going coy when their mates were also there.

When we met on a Friday we tended to drop into traditional behaviour patterns: men propping up the bar or playing the pub games, wives and girlfriends in groups around tables and, despite the fact that I was, by my reckoning, 'one of the boys' – a fully paid-up member of the SKB – it was taken for granted I would join 'the girls'.

About three weeks after that incident, we met as usual but I sensed a difference amongst the women when I slid into the quiet booth beside them, clutching my fizzy water. There was a little bit of chat but one by one they drifted away until I was left, knee to knee, with my friend, Diana. She made one or two attempts to introduce whatever topic was on her mind but I finally had to ask her outright what the problem was.

"Well, it's like this," she hesitated. "Some of the men have been talking and …" Again a pause followed by a deep breath before she twisted in her seat to hold my eye and charged. "Do you share the showers with the men?"

I couldn't hold back a little chuckle. "Is that a

problem?" This seemed to puzzle her. Her face said there must be but it appeared her brain couldn't rationalise exactly what it might be. Eventually she found something.

"But they see you naked!"

"Only my back really. The guys may have got a good look at my bare bum or the occasional glimpse of boob but ... well."

"Do you see them? Their ... you know?"

"Not really. I might get a glimpse but I'm not really interested."

I could see where this was going. If the WAGs were concerned I might be poaching they could make life difficult for me. If they turned against me they might apply pressure on their men to throw me out. I had to act. So I did. Impulse.

"To tell you the truth I'm not really interested in ... men." She looked shocked, disbelieving. I decided to press on. For weeks I had been 'teasing' her and I was sure she was 'temptable'. *You never know, it might be fun.*

I reached out a gentle hand and placed a palm on her cheek, no more than the softest brush, my fingertips trailing against her neck below her ear. I had all my senses turned up to maximum – I needed every single signal. And I got it! Because, as my hand rested against her face she actually tilted her head slightly, increasing the pressure of the contact.

"And if you're worried about me and Garret then don't. No man could fancy me when he has a woman as beautiful as you at home." I saw a gentle flush rising across the top of her breasts up to her throat so I allowed my hand to trail lazily towards the back of her neck. She actually turned her head minutely to maintain the contact of her face against my palm and I leaned inwards, towards her.

Even as I approached, her lips parted but as our lips met, social conditioning took over. She pulled back and her right hand flew up to my chest to push me away. However, with my hand now on the back of her head, she couldn't escape and the resistance lasted just a second or two. That was it. A single kiss. No big deal ... at least, not for me.

I held it for several more seconds and broke 'reluctantly.' The look on her face could have been anything: a mixture of horror, amazement, disbelief.

"I ... I ... " she muttered and stood, struggling out from the confines of the booth. "Josie ..." she began but failed again and stroked her lips with gentle fingertips as if to resurrect the contact. "I need to ..." and scuttled towards the bar where her husband stood in conversation with one of the regulars.

Diana dragged a befuddled looking Garret out the door and I suspected he was in for the night of his life as she reaffirmed her sexuality.

But the episode had got me a bit overheated so I made a beeline for Adam. He was my target for a number of reasons. Firstly, I knew that his girlfriend, Becky, who was in the final year of an art degree in Leeds or Manchester or somewhere, had been away for seven weeks so I assumed he would be missing the sex. Secondly, Becky's brother was also a member of SKB so Adam was unlikely to go around bragging about any liaison. And, of course, I had seen him in the changing room so I'd been able to assess the full package ... *so to speak*.

The next morning he acted as if I had violated him and wanted nothing to do with me.

Now I needed his help.

* * *

It took me a whole day to track him down. I left voicemails and texts but he did not return them. I called his friends, but nobody knew where he was ... or that's what they said.

Finally, sitting at my office desk, I sent him a simple text of just 6 words:

Call me or I call Becky

That did it. Just four minutes later my mobile blared out its pop song ringtone.

"What do you want?" he snapped without any sort of conversational prefix. Leyland, Mullin, Shepherd, assorted coppers ... now Adam.

Ever feel nobody likes you?

"There's something I need to see you about." Adam was an expert in IT security, hacking and all things technological. If anybody could crack this little device he could. I heard his sigh down the line.

"What can be so important?" There was a long pause. I let him stew until finally he sighed again and said, "All right. When? Where?" We agreed to meet for lunch the next day at Zizzi in Brighton Marina. "And Josie ..." he said.

"Yes Adam?"

"This had better be genuine ..."

"It is. I promise." There was click. A great thing about mobiles is you can't slam them down but somehow it felt as if that's what he'd done.

When I arrived, he was already sitting at a table by the window over a half finished *Peroni*. He half rose as I entered, waving a hand at the empty seat opposite him, finished the beer and signalled for another. I declined beer and ordered bottled water.

"What's so important?" He thrust his chin at me like a weapon.

I reached into my handbag, extracted the device and lay it on the table between us. "Do you know anything about this?"

His eyes widened and he looked around as if I had just dumped an Uzi machine gun in front of him. He snatched it up and plunged it under the table onto his lap.

"Jesus Christ, Josie!" he said in a harsh whisper. "Where on earth did you get this?" He looked around again before leaning backwards, arms straight and chin tucked hard against his chest, so he could examine it without bringing it out from its hiding place. I propped myself forward over my elbows, catching his mood.

"Why? What is it?" I asked, also in a low voice.

"This is an H4SD ... a high security, solid state storage device. They were developed by GCHQ as portable storage for highly sensitive material. I've only ever seen two of them and one was just a development model." Once more he examined it under the table – as if somebody in this Brighton restaurant would look over his shoulder, recognise it and run screaming for the secret service.

"Tell me about it ... what does it do?"

"I'm not sure I should tell you anything." He mulled it over for a while before looking up with a hunted look. "Basically it's a very small computer with the sort of flash storage they use in memory sticks and tablet PCs."

"But no keyboard?"

"No. It plugs into the USB port of your computer—"

"I already tried that but it said 'Device not recognised.'"

"It wouldn't. You need a special dongle – a sort of USB pen drive – and plug it into the USB port – here." He pointed at the slot. "Then you'd get some sort of screen that allows you to access the data. But here's the kicker ... because it's also a computer you have to access it through whatever programs are installed and if you can't provide the required access codes it will wipe the drive. No discussions. No warnings. No 'are you sure you want to do this.' Just *bang* ... data gone."

"Can't you just bypass the program and copy the data?"

"No because the only access is via the cable and at the

other end of that is the software. If I tried to do anything like, say, a bitwise copy, it would immediately wipe the data. If you tried to dismantle it—"

"It wipes the data?"

"Exactly. And, unlike your normal hard drive, once the data is deleted from the flash drive it has gone forever ... irrecoverable."

"So there's no way to hack it?"

"That's rather the point ..." Suddenly he whistled and his eyes widened again. He actually looked scared.

"What?"

"It's not one of ours!" He shoved his chair back and started to rise, slipping the device in his pocket.

"Wait," I said and clung onto his arm. "What are you doing?"

"We thought we were the only people in the world to have these things. Not even the Yanks have got them. But this is not one of ours. It's an almost exact copy. Don't you see what this means?"

Was I being particularly dense? Then, in a flash, I got it. "Espionage?"

"Yes. I've got to take this to the authorities."

"I thought you weren't with GCHQ anymore."

"I'm not, but I still understand the repercussions of some foreign power getting hold of—"

"But you don't understand the repercussions of me not getting the information that's on it."

"Sorry, Josie, this is not up for discussion. National Security takes precedence over any problem you may have."

I pulled on his sleeve and put on my most imploring face. "Please, Adam. At least stay and eat. World War Three won't start in the time it takes to eat a pizza." He subsided into his chair and we ordered: Margherita Rustica with a mixed salad for me and something spicy with lots of pepperoni for him, accompanied by a bottle of Chianti. I accepted a glass of the wine but only took a few sips.

"Where did you get it?" he asked around a mouthful of pizza.

"It was hidden in a box of my father's effects."

"So what's *he* doing with it?" He patted his pocket as if to confirm it was still there.

"God knows. But I've got a problem and I think that thing may be the solution."

He took a good swallow of wine and raised an eyebrow. "Go on." I took a while to arrange my thoughts, working out what to tell him and what to keep to myself. "There's this man; calls himself Neil Shepherd. He approached me after the funeral with some cock and bull story about my father owing him money – a lot of money – and he wants it back." I put on my 'helpless female' face – right on the edge of tears. Adam was a sucker for that sort of thing. "I tried to tell him I didn't know anything about it but later, when I arrived back home, in the dark, he and some thug grabbed me and threatened 'consequences' if I didn't find it and hand it over."

He dropped his cutlery on his plate and stared at me, wide eyed. "My God, Josie. What did you do? Did you go to the police?"

"Yes but with no effect. The police suspect I killed my family so when I went to them with stories of thugs and missing money they just thought I was trying to muddy the waters."

"How much are we talking about?"

"Lots." He waited. What the hell. I leaned forward adding an air of confidentiality. "Millions." His mouth dropped open and his eyes became wide circles.

"God in Heaven." It was almost a sigh. He drained his wine. "What are you going to do?"

"Find it ... if I can." I topped up his glass. "And I

think that ...thing ... has got something to do with it. That's why I need it or, at least, the information on it. After I get that, I'll be happy to do my civic duty and hand it over."

After we finished, I persuaded him to come and help me find the 'dongle' ... on the grounds he would recognise it. I'd moved all the furniture I needed into the new flats. We opened every box and found nothing but there was a huge amount in storage. It could be in there.

"I'll have to start going through the stuff in storage tomorrow," I told him, pouring coffee into two cups. "Can you forget this H4SD-thing for another couple of days? After all, if it's no good without this dongle and it will be even more use to the spooks if we can give them *both* parts."

He pulled a face which I interpreted as reluctant compliance then we carried our cups up to the solarium and sat, side by side on the sofa, looking out to sea.

"Why did you do it, Josie?" he asked all of a sudden.

"Do what?" My mind whirled with thoughts of money, murder and dongles.

"Seduce me." I was amazed.

"I seduced you?" What? "Just hold on there. It takes two to tango, buster." Okay, technically he was right but a girl should never admit it, should she?

"But you knew I was with Becky—"

"What? And you didn't?" I half turned towards him. "So suddenly *I'm* the guardian of *your* morals because you're too weak willed, that it?" He had the good grace to look embarrassed.

"Well. No. When you put it like that but ... well, you know." He stared into his cup. "It was almost as if you slipped something in my drink—"

I was outraged and leapt to my feet, towering over him. "Listen to me, Fellow, the only drugs controlling your actions were the alcohol from three pints of lager and an excess of testosterone." There was an immediate change. He too stood, taller than me, but instead of shouting he seemed somehow shy, diffident.

"I'm sorry, Josie. That was uncalled for. I suppose I'm a bit … you know … guilty and that. Guess I'm taking it out on you." Then he kissed me and I was thinking, *What the hell?* I needed this guy on my side.

Carrot always better than stick, right?

For the next two hours he seemed to forget about Becky altogether. *It's not my job to remind him.*

Chapter Nine

I had to visit a client in central London so I ran to my six o'clock yoga class and back before I left and I got back to Brighton just in time for my Body Attack class and that was the day gone. This meant it was Friday morning before I got to search my storage unit. I did as thorough a job as possible but found nothing. I contacted Malone to see if he was holding anything or knew of a safety deposit box or the like but just drew blanks all round.

Nothing.

Zero.

Zilch.

At kickboxing that evening Adam was awkward whenever I caught his eye and, as soon as we met the WAGs at *The Jetty* he claimed a headache, grabbed Becky – back from uni – and cleared off. At least he hadn't mentioned the H4SD.

All weekend, when I wasn't in the gym or taking my flying lesson – I'm now doing helicopters – I spent sorting the flats into some sort of habitable order. That was when I noticed the removal company had brought me the wrong desk. Mine and my father's were identical but mine had a stain on one side where I'd dropped a bottle of nail varnish some months earlier. Conscious of how ironic it would be if the dongle I sought was here all the time, I went through it with a fine tooth comb – even though Adam and I had searched it just a couple of days before. Still nothing.

On Monday I had an idea. I wondered if the mystery file the police had found on my computer it might help – maybe a sort of treasure map for the missing device or something. I discovered I had inadvertently saved a copy in my cloud storage but when I downloaded it I could not open it without the password. As usual, Leyland was totally uncooperative: unwilling to tell me the password or provide a hardcopy printout. He made a snide comment about 'nasty men' intimidating me.

So I called Adam. He was, as ever, decidedly sullen. What was it about the man? He couldn't keep his hands off me ... not that I was unhappy about that ... then behaved as if his moral incontinence was somehow my fault.

"What?" he snapped.

"Calm down, Darling, I just need a bit of help ..."

"I can't see you now. I'm busy." Yeah, right. *What you really mean is you don't trust yourself.*

"There's no need. I've got a computer file but it's password protected."

"So what do expect me to do?"

"I know you've got a load of specialist hacking stuff. Can you open it and then see if you can decrypt it?"

"Where did you get it? Is it legit?"

"Of course it's legit. It was on my computer. I think my father put it there."

"Okay. Email it. I'll see what I can do." He rang off without even saying goodbye. *Ouch.*

About four hours later I got an email with the unlocked file, and it was the same rubbish Leyland had shown me. I read Adam's accompanying email.

Josie
Unlocked file attached. Ran it through some decryption software but it comes up with nothing. It just seems to be 256 random ASCII characters. It might be a code that needs a key, i.e. a set of letters or numbers that are 'added' to the characters to make the message make sense. If it does then,

unless you find this key, you're not going to crack it. The key could be anything, e.g. a paragraph from a book, a person's nickname ... anything. See if it means something to you.
Adam

I emailed back: 'Thanks, J'. Is my entire world surrounded by brick walls erected just to get in my way?

Damn, damn, damn.

Chapter Ten

Poo-brain was coming out of hospital. It was two months to the day since he had been shot. They suggested he could stay longer but all he was doing was lying in a bed being visited by therapists. He could do that at home and the couple I had employed, Florin and Ionela Babluc, were nurses back in their own country and able to give him all that.

And I *really* wanted him with me.

Our parents' estate was frozen pending the completion of the police investigation. With the possibility that I had bumped them off, the law had to ensure I didn't get to spend any of it before I was cleared. Malone was prepared to release some of Harry's share to equip rooms on the grounds that he obviously hadn't done the deed. The Ballucs moved in and over the next week we were occupied buying and installing all manner of hoists, baths and other equipment.

A private ambulance delivered Poo-brain at three in the afternoon. He was practically paralyzed and his speech was so bad we frequently struggled to understand him but we got him installed and he gurgled contentedly at the sea view from his front window. He had one of the bedrooms and the Ballucs had the other two: one fitted out as their private sitting room. They also had the use of the kitchen as it was going to be a goodly while before Poo-brain was making his own peanut butter sandwiches. So they lived quite comfortably and I paid them over the odds.

As I let myself back into my flat the phone rang. Shepherd.

"Month's up," he said without preamble.

"How'd you get this number?" I demanded.

"It's surprising what I have access to." I could hear the self-satisfied smile in his voice. "And as I said, 'The month's up.' So what have you got for me?"

"Nothing."

"How unfortunate." It was a sneer. "You have obviously not been searching assiduously enough. Maybe you need a little, er, persuasion ... something to inspire you, perhaps." He was trying to sound sinister, to scare me, but he actually sounded more like a pantomime villain. I almost laughed but what would be the point in winding him up even more?

"Look, Shepherd, I've searched everywhere I can think of." I tried to sound reasonable. "I've had a friend help me look. The police have had experts going through everything. None of us has found anything. Apart from a huge sum of money – and I only have your word my father owed it to you – I don't even know what I'm looking for. Give me a clue—"

"Okay." He sighed. "Have you found a piece of equipment that looks like a thick credit card with a computer lead on one end and a socket on the other?"

BINGO!

"No. Nothing like that. What is it?"

"It doesn't matter. If you find it just give it to me." *Ah, did he have the dongle?*

"That's all? Just that?"

"No. There will something else with it. It looks like one of the miniature flash drives that you carry computer files on, only smaller. Know what I mean?"

"Yes."

"They might be plugged together."

"Right." *Pity they weren't.* "What colour are all these things?"

"Black. Both black." *So he's seen it.*

"I'll look again."

"Call me. You have my card. Two days. No more reminders. Got it?"

He sounded serious. Maybe I should start feeling scared.

Chapter Eleven

Saturday. Flying lesson in the morning. I'd already qualified on single engines, twins, instrument rating and was now working on my helicopter papers. Wouldn't it be cool if Potex-3 was a Bell Ranger? *Dream on, girl.* I escaped from the marriage with just over six hundred thou. A decent 'copter would cost much more than that and I'd already blown nearly half of it.

We were playing a Masonic Ladies' Night near Croydon. Nothing special. At about twenty past one I was walking back to my car. The streets were dark and deserted: a bit creepy but par for the course. And, of course, I was wearing 'belt and braces' so I was getting chilly.

As I passed a particularly dark alleyway a hand rocketed out and snagged my arm, yanking me into the urine-smelling canyon and slamming me against the wall. I was winded and almost collapsed but a hand slammed into my throat and pinned me to the wall. In the half light of reflected streetlamps I recognised the bull neck, the shaven head and the fat belly. Ray! I didn't need light to recognise the tonsil-crushing hold or the body odour.

"Mr Shepherd 'as a message for you, Girly." I heard a click and felt the cold of a knife blade against my cheek. "The two days expired yesterday and, as 'e 'asn't 'eard from you, 'e told me to leave you a permanent reminder."

"Okay. Wait a second," I croaked, playing for time, my mind in overdrive. Was he really that stupid? He'd tried this stunt before and had come unstuck. Just as before, I brought my knee up with all the force I could muster – and it was like hitting a brick wall. He grinned, a glint of teeth and a reek of bad breath.

"Cricketer's box. Padded and reinforced fibreglass. It'll protect the old family jewels against cricket balls. Your knee don't stand no chance."

And this time I hadn't got my bamboo knife. *Nowhere to hide it.*

So here we break for a little bit of mathematics. The heel of my shoe, a Blahnik this time, is about five millimetres in diameter. Divide that by two for the radius and multiply that by itself and by pi – that's approximately 3.14 – and we end up with less than twenty square millimetres or one fifth of a square centimetre. I weigh marginally less than sixty-five kilograms so when I put my heel on his instep and put my full weight on it I was exerting a force of over three hundred kilograms per square centimetre or, if you still think in old money, nearly two tons per square inch.

He screamed and tried to slash me with the knife but I was hanging onto to his arm with all my might.

"Drop the knife," I yelled in his ear and twisted my heel to drive home my point – *see what I did there?* There was a rattle as the knife hit the ground and I felt it fetch up against my left foot but I still had a problem: the guy was huge and much stronger as I. As soon as I let him go, was he going to grab me? Thump me? And I was in no position to run – in these heels? I couldn't even step out of them and sprint for it in bare feet because these were ankle length booties.

I lifted my heel off his foot and immediately stooped and snatched the knife. Next thing I knew, he had grabbed me by my hair and dragged me upright. Now it was my turn to scream but I pushed the blade into his belly hard enough to hurt without doing any major damage.

"Let me go, Fatso, or I'll gut you." I could feel the reluctance as he released me and we stood facing each other, eyes locked in the dim light, panting as if we'd both run long races. I slowly eased out of the alley, snagged my bags and sax from where they had fallen on the footpath and backed away until I had gone far enough to be confident that even if he made a sprint I would be able to reach my car before he caught me.

"Don't think this is the end of it," he shouted after me. "If you don't come up with the goods 'e'll come after you again."

"Tell him to send an army," I shouted back, sounding a lot braver than I felt. "He'll need it."

But I was sure he was right. I was in trouble. I had to do something.

* * *

My first step was to increase the security at the flat. As we owned both flats on the top floor, the freeholder committee allowed us to have a security door fitted at the bottom of the staircase leading up and an alteration to the lift that meant nobody could access our floor without applying a thumb-print to a special pad or by the lift being called from above. The work cost over twenty thousand pounds but made me feel a little safer.

I took to carrying my bamboo knife whenever I went out.

Any resolve I may have had to keep the money was fast evaporating. I was beginning to feel that, even if I couldn't trace it, maybe offering a sizable sum might be the best way out. Perhaps I should sell my assets and try to negotiate some sort of deal with him. But how much could I raise? And how much of a shortfall would Shepherd accept because there was no way I could get anywhere *near* the sum he was demanding?

It hung over my every waking hour. It haunted my

sleep. It insinuated itself into the rhythm of my music.
Thirty two point six million pounds.

* * *

With the repeated searches of my flat my belongings were in turmoil so it took me ages to find Shepherd's card but eventually I discovered it in the desk tray along with paperclips, spare staples and postage stamps. I dialled and got an instant response.

"Hello, Regina." *Does he do that to wind me up?* "You have something for me?"

"No. I searched everywhere and I've found nothing at all." It was pointless telling him about the H4SD. Without the dongle it was useless anyway and if I handed it over he could mess around with it, wipe the data and we'd be in an even worse situation. He swore ... at least, I think it was a swearword. It was said with the force and passion that usually accompanied expletives but I didn't understand it. It sounded like 'Bliad.' *Foreign? That might tie in with the H4SD being foreign made.*

"I do not want to hear this, Regina. Bruce owes me. Big time ..."

"But he's dead!"

"I DO NOT GIVE A SHIT!" he screamed down the line. "I NEED THAT FUCKING MONEY!" He sounded nearly hysterical, on the edge of a screaming fit, like a toddler going into a full temper tantrum. What could drive a man of his apparent suaveness into such a state? And then suddenly I got it ... *He's scared. It's not his money. He's a middle man or something. He owes it to somebody else. Was there an advantage in this?*

"Truly, Mr Shepherd," I said in as consolatory a tone as I could manage. "Can we do some sort of deal?"

"Deal? What do you mean, deal?"

"I've got money. And there's my parents' estate. If I liquidate all my assets—"

"How much?"

"I'm not sure. Half of my patents' money should go to my brother and it's held in trust. It depends what I can get out of him—"

"Cut the crap. How much?"

"Probably ten million. Maybe more—"

"Not enough. Nowhere near." He was shouting – almost screaming.

"How much?" I introduced a note of pleading into my tone now ... I thought it was quite realistic. "Meet me halfway here. What's your red line? There must be a figure you will accept. I'll see what I can do."

He took a deep breath, reasserting an ersatz calm that was as realistic as a soap opera plot. "Look, I know *exactly* how much money you have and ten is probably *more* than you can get in the short term so why are you haggling?"

"How do you know—?"

"Never mind. Thirty two point six million."

I tried a different strategy. "If you know what's in my bank then you'll also know I can't give you what I haven't got. Why not take what I *have* got?" There was a long pause and I hoped he was considering but got the impression he was struggling to bring his emotions under control.

Eventually he spoke, his voice almost mechanical. "It's out there somewhere. That much money can't just vanish." *Really? You've never been shopping with me and Maxie.* "Find it. Believe me, Regina, if you do not find it, I will make your life unspeakably awful."

There was a click.

It seemed he now had access to my bank balance. I needed to find out about this man so I sat at my desk, grabbed a sheet of A4 and started jotting down what I knew. I started with his business card that showed him as the managing director of a cleaning company. In the middle of the page I wrote his name and phone number. In the top right hand corner I wrote 'Cleaning Company.' What would a cleaning company have to do with thirty two point six million pounds? I wrote '$50m?' between them and connected them with lines.

Above his name I wrote 'foreign?' and beside it 'bliad' in brackets. I typed 'bliad' into Google and was offered a YouTube of a cat and then found the word was Russian for 'whore' ... but only if I'd heard it, and spelled it, correctly. But I wrote 'Russian?' in brackets beside 'foreign'.

I could add nothing more but, seeing his company office was in Crawley, jumped on Potex-1 and rode there for a quick reconnoitre. *Shepherd Cleaning Co* had a single suite among a dozen other companies in a nondescript block. I learned nothing except ... on a board outside headed 'Vacancies' ... that he was looking for a cleaning supervisor.

The next day I received a bullet through the post. There was no indication of whom it had come from but there was no guesswork about what it meant.

It was like being punched.

Chapter Twelve

"**N**o way!" Adam insisted in a fierce whisper, leaning across the table to glare at me. "There is no chance in hell I'm going to hack anybody's computer. I don't care how much trouble you're in. If I'm caught that's the end of my reputation and my career."

It had taken all my persuasion to even get him here. He wouldn't meet me in private so I'd selected a city centre restaurant. We shared a table in a green leather booth as far away from other diners as possible. Now he was on the edge of running out. A girl with plaits that made her look about twelve brought our drinks; one Estrella, one Pellegrino.

Leaning forward I lay a hand on his. "Please, Adam. You've no idea how much trouble I'm in." *Plan A: the sympathy vote*. I managed to screw a tear down my cheek and added a sob. "He's going to kill me." I kept my voice down, hoping he'd take the hint.

"No. No. No. Clear enough? NO!" He snatched his hand out from under mine and thrust his chin at me. The nearest couple stopped talking and sneaked looks, pretending not to.

Plan B.

I fitted on a sad face, showing all the regret I could fake. "In that case, Adam, you leave me no option but to have a chat with Becky …"

His eyes widened and his mouth moved several times before he managed to stammer, "What? You wouldn't." He tried to sound sure but got nowhere near. Then he slipped back in his chair, hands deep in pockets as if another thought had struck him. *As relaxed as a cat on firework night.* "She'll never believe you." He added a smile to confirm his confidence.

"No?" I slipped my phone from my bag and raised the screen into his line of sight. "It's very good, even if I do say so myself." Moans emanated from the speaker. His eyes widened and he added his own baseline groan in real time.

"You *videoed* us?" His voice was croaky as if the words were struggling to find a way out.

I shrugged. "Always useful to keep evidence of an affair."

"*Affair*? We're not having an *affair*. It was just a—" His voice was harsh. *You want to keep your voice down now, don't you?*

"You *dare* say 'fling'…" I let the thought hang but poised my forefinger over the keypad like an eagle waiting to swoop.

"But—"

"If it's not an affair how would you describe it?" He said nothing. "We first had sex about six months ago and the last time …?"

"A couple of days ago …"

I rolled my eyes to the ceiling with the glorious memories. "That sounds like an affair to me." I turned down the volume. "And, as sure as God made little apples, when I show Becky this and explain how you seduced me; how you promised to leave her—"

"Leave her? I never said that, you bitch—" Despite himself his voice rose in pitch and volume.

The girl approached carrying menus but Adam dismissed her with an angry jerk of his hand. She looked at me but I just gave her a miniscule nod and she backed away.

"No. Not 'a bitch'. Desperate. There's a nutter threatening to kill me." I pulled the bullet from my pocket and slammed it on the table where it sat between us. The thing might have been an ornament; pristine, polished silver and bronze, just nineteen millimetres tall but lurking as tall as Nelson's Column. "I got that in the post." I shoved my face into my hands and made my shoulders shake as if racked with 'uncontrollable' sobs. "What do you think it means? Because I've not a single doubt."

He shrugged. "So go to the police."

I was losing him.

"And say what? I've already told Leyland about Shepherd's demands but he dismissed me out of hand. Now what? Tell him about this?" I tapped the bullet. "I've no proof who sent it. "What do you think will happen?"

"I, I—"

"Nothing! Oh, they might ask Shepherd a few more questions and then, when my body turns up in a ditch, they'll ask him a few more. Then he'll go on his own sweet way." I rose as if about to walk out. "And you'll be happy because your grubby little secret will have died too." I grabbed my bag and turned. "Cause for celebrations all round."

I saw him soften and he leaned in, a hand reaching up to me.

"Come on, Josie. Don't be like that." He stood and came up behind me to steer me back to my seat as I 'cried' gently into my hands. There was no other sound in the place.

"I do care for you, Adam," I said. I had him now, I just needed to keep him. In the end he submitted so I gave him everything I knew about Shepherd.

He refused when I asked him back to the flat but I could see the debate going on in his head.

You're gagging for me, aren't you, Love?

* * *

Runner

I came back from my run. I'd intended to do my usual ten miles to the ruined West Pier and back but only managed half way before I turned back, feeling as if my trainers were made of lead. A chilly wet mist didn't help and tears hovered at the back of my eyes. I had never been this way in my life.

When Ray grabbed me outside Overton or when he tried again in a dark alleyway in Croydon it had been almost like an adventure. While intellectually aware he intended to hurt me, even scar me, I nevertheless felt no fear. Confidence in my own abilities ... and the natural male reticence to hurt a woman ... made me sure I would walk away unscathed. I was so intrigued by the experience that there was no room in my head for concerns.

I was well aware that a normal person would be scared; that I *should* be scared shitless but psychos find it difficult to do what psychologists call 'future pacing'; foreseeing outcomes.

But now my brain was mushy and I could conceive of no way out, no plan, no escape.

Bereft of ideas I carried a coffee to my desk and stared, unseeing, at the sheet of paper on which I'd scribbled my brain dump the previous evening. Rain pattered against the window in front of me. As I placed the coffee it knocked my pen, which fell to the floor. When I stooped to retrieve it my shoulder snagged against the handle of the flat tray in which I'd found Shepherd's card.

And I heard a distinct 'click'.

When I examined the handle it appeared to be deviated upwards by about twenty degrees. I wondered if it was broken but a slight downward pressure returned it to its correct orientation and I again heard a click. Intrigued, I pushed it up again and started investigating to find out what the action had caused. I discovered that the tray, normally captive to prevent it being accidentally pulled right out, now came free of its slot. I slid it out, dumped the contents on the desk and examined it. On the back edge was a small flap that slid easily to one side and a device, like a tiny USB flash pen, dropped into my hand.

There was only one thing it could be.

I grabbed the humidor and, banana-fingered in my haste, took several attempts to open it. Eventually, I got the flash pen plugged into the slot in the H4SD which I connected to my laptop. On the screen appeared a box with a blinking cursor and a line in Cyrillic script – the number '3' being the only symbol I understood. There were two buttons below the box: on one was written 'извлечение' and on the other 'хорошо'. So Adam was right about the H4SD being foreign and the script looked Russian. And Shepherd?

I hit a key at random and the letter 'h' appeared at the cursor. I continued to enter characters and counted 256 before the field was full and suddenly the mysterious file the police found on my computer made sense so I fired up *Word*, opened the file and copy-pasted it into the box. With a lead weight in my belly I moved the pointer over the first button, clicked and … the box disappeared!

I think I squealed.

After all Adam's warnings about the disastrous consequences if the data was incorrectly accessed.

I waited but nothing happened.

After all I had been through and now I'd ruined everything with a single key stroke. I forced my brain to concentrate.

In File Manager there was no sign of the drive. Then I worked out what I must have done: the button must have been the 'eject' button. Not knowing what else to do, I pulled the USB plug out then pushed it back in. When the box with the Cyrillic writing appeared it felt as if I had been holding my breath for an hour.

This time I clicked the other button.

My heart hammered as *Excel* booted up and a spreadsheet appeared. Names, dates, figures – each prefixed with a currency symbol – scrolled up the screen. Some fields looked like international banking sort codes and account numbers, others contained bank names in blue text, underlined to indicate a hyperlink. With pounding heart and a tremor in my hand, I clicked one at random. My browser started and the website of a bank appeared. I clicked 'Log in' and used the information from the spreadsheet to access an account that held thirty-eight thousand pounds.

Another contained less than two thousand. Still another, more than two hundred thousand. The accounts were designated in pounds, dollars, Euros or Swiss francs. Then one came up with fifty followed by six zeros – in U.S. dollars. Eighteen bank accounts held, between them, over forty million pounds.

I'd hit the jackpot.

Now what? I paced. Thinking.

The easy option would be to hand over the information to Shepherd when presumably … hopefully … the intimidation would cease. But would it? Or, having got hold of the money, would he then want to remove any witnesses? In his position, I knew what I'd do.

I copied the file onto another flash drive then, tinkered with the original before saving it. I put the H4SD, with the dongle still in place, back in the Chinese box.

My mobile blared its tune and displayed Adam's name. With any luck there was some news for me.

"Sorry, Josie. I've hit a snag …" *Oh sweet baby Jesus!*

"I thought you were able to hack into anything." I wanted to swear at him.

"That's the problem. His firewall … military grade. Never seen anything like it outside of GCHQ. No doubt I can crack it … but the job might take weeks." *Every single time!* He told me what we would need to do. And my heart sank further. With Shepherd breathing down my neck I didn't have weeks or even days.

I had to act. Now!

Chapter Thirteen

My mother's Volvo, adapted to carry Poo-brain in a wheelchair, was loaded with little brother, the Bablucs and all their luggage. I'd made arrangements, as secretly as possible, to get him into respite care in Cumbria where his two carers were to dump him before driving back to Luton and flying home to Romania – on full pay – for a month. *Lucky them.*

That was them all out of the way.

Diana wasn't expecting me and as I walked in I got her usual greeting. Today I returned it enthusiastically but then pulled away, turned my back on her and started crying. She came up behind me and wrapped her arms around me, cheek on my shoulder.

"Whatever's the matter, my love?" Through my sobs I told her about the 'evil man' called Neil Shepherd who wanted to take the money my parents left my little brother and I with threats to hurt us if I didn't hand it over.

As the story unrolled her arms tightened around me, as if she could make the world right by physical force.

"Have ... have you told anybody? What about the police?" she asked, close to my ear.

"Them? They're totally useless. They don't believe me!"

"There must be *something* we can do." *We?*

I ladled in a note of reticence and uncertainty. "I do have a friend who could help me gather evidence against him ... if we could get into the man's computer. But we can't," I said with finality; head down, shoulders slumped. "I'm really stuck and I'm so, so scared." I turned to face her and held her close. "I don't know what to do, my precious love." She really went for these over-the-top endearments.

Once she 'calmed me down', we went down to Steve's café where, over coffee, I allowed her to extract information about Shepherd, his impregnable firewall and how the only way to crack it would be if I could get a special program on his computer.

"The trouble is, I don't know anything about Breaking and Entering and he knows my face, so I can't just waltz into his office ..." I dropped my face into my hands for another bout of body shaking sobs. *I'm going to get a reputation in every eatery in this town.*

She burst out, "I've got it!"

"What? There's nothing we can do, my sweet."

She was suddenly enthusiastic, almost bouncing in her seat. "Yes there is! I can do it!"

I took her small hands between mine. "Don't be silly, my love. You don't know any more about breaking into an office than I do." I gave her hands a gentle squeeze and put on a brave look but she persisted.

"I'll get into his office somehow and put this program thingy on his computer." She stopped, a puzzled look on her pretty face. "Of course, you'd have to show me what to do."

We dashed back to her workshop upstairs and within an hour we'd written and printed her CV, along with a letter applying for the job as cleaning supervisor.

The next morning she drove over to drop it in. Shepherd must have been desperate as he interviewed her on the spot and told her she could start next day. She called me with the good news so that afternoon I delivered the flash pen and walked her through the process: simply a matter of plugging it in.

What with one thing and another ... *use your imagination* ... I didn't get home until well after midnight.

My flat was trashed. The humidor lay shattered on the floor and the H4SD was gone.

* * *

"Hello," Shepherd mumbled. It was two in the morning and the police had only just left. There was no need for the call but I wanted to see if I could learn anything … and ensure that I wasn't the only one losing sleep.

"Are you responsible for the carnage in my flat?"

"Regina?" I swore at him but he just chuckled. "If you had only done as I asked and carried out the search yourself then there would have been no need for my men to do it."

"So now do you believe me? You found nothing, right?" *Worth a bluff. Maybe he'd give something away.*

"On the contrary, our search revealed exactly what I wanted." I grinned. He still needed the password. "Yes," he continued. "I now have everything I need." That threw me. If Shepherd had got his hands on the password it was undoubtedly the same way the newspaper had got the photograph … from the police. Somebody on Leyland's squad was on the take.

But this raised another, far more serious concern … what about me? If he thought he had what he needed then I had suddenly become surplus to requirements. I had taken one precaution to protect myself because he'd got the H4SD but it was useless to him. Eventually Shepherd would realise the bank account details in the spreadsheet on the H4SD were false. Because I'd changed them all.

Up yours, Shepherd.

If he spotted the changes he was going to be mightily pissed off with me, if he didn't he might try to eliminate me as a witness. Either way, it was time for me to move.

I slammed the phone down. *About time I got a turn at doing that.* I packed, loaded Potex-2 – not much room for luggage but I didn't need a great deal. I would have liked to have left straightaway but with Diana starting the job a few hours later I decided to hang around to ensure she was all right.

* * *

I awoke with sick feelings of dread. I didn't know why and it was a new and unsettling experience for me.

I called to give Diane morale boosting love and best wishes. She said she was standing outside the door of her new workplace.

"Good luck, my love," I whispered.

She giggled. "I feel all sort of James Bondie."

"Don't do anything silly. As soon as you've plugged the thing in, don't hang around. Say you're going to the loo or something ... and get out immediately! All right?" She giggled again and made a kissy noise.

She only had to stick the flash pen into any USB port on any computer on Shepherd's network and walk away without being caught. What could possibly go wrong?

* * *

Adam took about seven or eight rings to answer.

"My mole will be in Shepherd's office in a few minutes," I said. "I can't know when she'll get access to his computer but you'll need to be ready."

"Don't tell me my job." He sounded aggrieved. "You have no idea how far I'm sticking my bloody neck out for you on this."

"I appreciate it, Adam. I really do."

"Yeah, right."

"Truly. And if it's any consolation, I never had any intention of squealing to Becky and never will."

I went for my daily ten-miler, then luxuriated in a bath fragrant with salts and pampered with lotions and makeup. But that didn't kill enough time so I went out and mooched around the olde worlde village; terraces of cute, shoebox sized cottages, worth over a million each. Time seemed to have stopped. I wandered, looking in shop windows at things I would never want, ending up by the duck pond but it was bone-achingly chilly and a vindictive wind blew straight off the channel so I bought a newspaper and I ducked into a café where I drank coffee until the caffeine gave me palpations and made my hands tremble. Eventually, when I could hold on no longer, I went home and called Adam.

"Oh, it's you." *Pleased to hear your dulcet tones, too.*

"Anything for me?" I asked.

"Yeah. Some good, some bad. I didn't get long … only about ten minutes … before his security was restored. The software on the USB drive built a tunnel through his firewall so I got into his network with no hassle … as far as his emails."

"And …"

"They're all encrypted."

"Damn!" Is the whole world out to wind me up?

"Indeed. But there is something I *did* get. I did something called 'Traffic Analysis': working out whom he was in contact with."

"Is that good?"

"That depends on what you want to know. Most of his communications have been with just a couple of IP addresses. One is in a place called Seversk." I asked him to spell it.

"Where's that? And what's there?"

"All I know is that it's a city in Russia." Russia. More

confirmation of Shepherd's nationality?

"Where's the other?"

"Syria."

"Any particular place in Syria?"

"Raqqa." I didn't need him to spell that one.

"Isn't that the …?"

"Yup. The so-called capital city of the so-called 'Caliphate' occupied by the so-called Islamic State."

As soon as I hung up, I Googled 'Seversk'. Professor Wikipedia revealed that it was a 'closed city' where the former USSR produced much of its highly enriched Uranium and Plutonium used in the manufacture of nuclear weapons.

My father and the Russian Mafia and atom bombs and terrorists and thirty two point six million pounds!

Dear God.

Chapter Fourteen

I drove uncharacteristically sedately ... and obeyed all road traffic laws ... getting to Dover where I abandoned Potex-2 on a double yellow where she would soon attract the attention of the local constabulary. I bought a ticket for Calais and boarded the ferry where, amongst assorted out-of-season holidaymakers, booze cruisers and lorry drivers, I had a light lunch. The sea was smooth and the journey uneventful.

In the first half-decent hotel I could find I had a long, luxurious bath, changed my clothes and caught a train to Paris. Outside the station I caught a taxi, the driver of which vehemently refused to turn a wheel until I pronounced *Le Bourget* to his liking ... although the offer of an extra €50 drastically improved his comprehension.

The plane, a twin-engine Piper Seminole, was waiting on the grass apron so I filed plans under the name of Vicky Siemann; the wife of the man who was giving me helicopter lessons and co-owner of the flying school. I'd told her husband, Phil, that I wanted a long solo flight to keep my hours up so Vicky and Phil had delivered it the previous day, flying two planes out and one back.

In the airport office, nobody bothered much about me ... everything about flying light aircraft is relaxed: people turn up, file plans, take off. Other planes land, people get out, leave.

I looked enough like Vicky to pass. Isn't it funny how when a married man has an affair he will often choose a woman who looks like a younger and much, *much* prettier version of his wife? *All except Graeme, who went for a really ugly bitch.* If anybody ever came sniffing around later I would be just one more insignificant foreign pilot who had pitched up, signed in and flown away.

The crows-flight distance from Le Bourget to Shoreham is about 400 kilometres so should have taken less than two hours but I battled headwinds all the way so it took nearly three. When I landed ... a familiar aircraft heading into its home base ... I never even spoke to anybody except the control tower and Phil who welcomed me home but I slipped away before he could claim any 'payments in kind' and caught a taxi to Worthing and from there a train to London where I booked into my second hotel of the day.

When they found Potex-2 in Dover I hoped they would assume I had left the country. The ticket office, CCTV and passport control would all confirm this. It would take hours of painstaking research to detect my return and my plan relied on them, stressed by budget and manpower shortages, not even bothering to look. My cover was gossamer thin but might just buy me the time I needed.

* * *

I hardly slept. First thing next morning I called Diana again and, as with the dozen or so times previously, it went straight to voicemail. I rang Graeme. I didn't want to but I needed help and I could think of nobody else. Especially as some of the help I needed was with Leyland. After our initial greeting he went for me.

"Where the hell are you? Leyland's having kittens. You're still on bail and he's heard you've skipped to France."

"Really? What little dickybird told him that?"

"Stop buggering me about! Where are you?"

"Sorry, Graeme, I can't tell you. There is a man after me and if I tell you where I am, you'll tell Leyland and the information will get back to him."

"Don't be ridiculous. How will that—?"

"There's a leak on his team."

"Leak? What do you mean 'leak'?"

"Well, for a start, somebody who went into Overton House after the murders stole a photograph of me and handed it over to the press. It had to have been the police because they were the only ones with access."

He chuckled. "Oh, come on, Josie. That sort of thing was going on when Peel was still on the orange. It's hardly 'a leak'."

"Well, this man I was talking about ... a client of my father's ... has got hold of details of all my bank accounts, including how much is in each. Even *I* didn't know that until Leyland pulled my statements. So how did that happen?"

"I don't know—"

"There's more. My father had put an encrypted file on my computer. Leyland's team found it and cracked the password. He told me the contents of the file were 'evidence' and wouldn't even give me a copy of it."

"So?"

"This fellow has now obtained a copy."

"How do you know Bruce didn't give it to him?"

"I didn't even know it was on my computer. It was hidden. It was password locked. It was encrypted. So it's obvious my father wanted it kept secret. I happen to know it would have been no good to anybody else without some other stuff –"

"What other 'stuff'?" Like I'm going to tell you about the H4SD. Adam hates me enough as it is.

"That's not relevant. The point is: How likely is it my father would hand out a copy of it when he'd taken such pains to keep it a secret?"

"Conversely, why would this other person – this client – now want a copy if it was only relevant in connection with this 'other stuff' you won't tell me about?"

"Because the situation's changed—"

"Josie!" He sighed: loud and theatrical. "If you won't be open with me, how in hell do you expect me to help you?"

"Well …"

"Just tell me where you are. I'll come and see you and we can talk. And I *promise* I won't squeal to Leyland." So I gave him the address of the hotel and my room number. He seemed surprised to find out I was in London but said he'd see me 'in a couple of hours'.

I hope I'm not going to regret this.

I opened the spreadsheet and logged on to the bank account in the Seychelles with fifty million dollars. It made sense to go for the one with the most money first. I had a bank account in the Bahamas – another gift from Granny along with the Hong Kong bank account and the flat, none of which the British authorities knew about. I transferred the money and closed the account in the Seychelles.

One by one I emptied all of my father's 'black' accounts and sent the entire contents to the Caribbean. *I know: Eggs, Baskets. What option did I have?*

Suddenly, and for no apparent reason, a strange tingling ran up my spine and my heart raced. I had no idea why. When we were still married, Graeme had sometimes complained about fugitives who'd slipped away just hours or even minutes before the police arrived. The villain may have been safely ensconced in a hidey hole for weeks but it was as if some sixth sense had warned him about the impending apprehension. And now I felt it. Without a second thought I slammed my laptop closed, stuffed it into my bag with all my other chattels and scooted down the stairs, out the door and across the road to the coffee shop opposite, from where I could view the hotel from behind a complimentary newspaper.

What the hell? Maybe I was overreacting but what

harm would it do?

The young Central European girl, micro-skirt and hair hefted high like a Hanoverian duchess, had barely brought my coffee and a bacon sandwich when a long, black car pulled up and three men leapt out while the driver waited on the yellow lines, engine running. All three were knocked out from the same mould: broad shoulders, shaved heads, no foreheads, but the man from the front passenger seat confirmed my fears. Ray! He sprinted with a limp.

I was incandescent! All my faffing about, all the ferries, taxis, flights and grotty hotels had been for nothing. I had hoped to gain a few days 'off the radar' but as it was I had managed little more than one night before my ex-husband had screwed me.

Again!

And I'd lost the use of my car because it was almost certain they would have somebody keeping watch on it.

I called Graeme and when he answered just hissed, "You treacherous bastard," before hanging up. I yanked the SIM out off my phone and slipped it in my pocket. I also kept the storage card with my music on it. Eventually, Ray and another man emerged and climbed into the car. They pulled away with a squeal of tyres but I assumed the third man was hanging around inside, ready to catch me if I returned.

Good luck on that one, Tiger.

Replete from my junk food repast, I left and lobbed the phone into a waste bin in case Graeme could track it. In a phone shop I bought a replacement with a prepaid SIM and loaded on a hundred pounds of credit.

I had to hide ... but that's something I've been doing all my life. There are two ways of hiding ... I call them 'mouse' and 'starling'. A mouse will find a small, dark place, crawl into it and hunker down: still and quiet – hoping the cat will not locate him. The starling will join with ten thousand fellows and behave just like them: wheeling and turning to confuse and confound predators. It would take a very clever hawk to locate an individual but the downside is that any one of his ten thousand compatriots could be a hawk and he had to be very alert to spot which one. I, on the other hand, had spent my entire life 'hiding in plain sight'; joining in, acting the part, faking being normal. Now I'd take it to the next level.

On a whim, I ducked into a barbershop where, to the amusement of the Asian clientele, I had my long hair cut into a short, androgynous style. Freshly shorn, I took a brisk walk to Euston, paid cash and caught a train to Birmingham New Street station, a bus at random and got off where the area looked seedy. I didn't even know where I was. I could have checked into another small hotel but wanted to stay away from anywhere that kept records. In the window of a small tobacconist I saw what I was looking for: a postcard advertising a room to let. I went in and got directions.

The ramshackle house was stuck in the middle of a terrace with peeling paint and miniscule, untended front gardens. I knocked on a door that looked on the point of exhaustion. After several knocks, a tiny, stick thin woman – indeterminately ancient – creaked it open, releasing a waft of furniture polish and boiled cabbage. She peered without really seeing me and even I, with no ophthalmic training, could see the mistiness of her cataracts. *Even better.* She was further hindered by the looming dusk, the miserable street lighting and the bare, sub-forty watt bulb in the hallway.

"Who is it?" asked a man's voice, overloud in a thick Scottish accent from somewhere in the interior.

"It's a little girl," the old woman called over her shoulder in a shrivelled voice that matched her shrivelled body. She asked my name so I made one up: Rosemary Smith.

"You have a room to let?"

She nodded. "Second floor, at the back, share the bathroom on the first. No pets, no cooking, no noise, do your own cleaning, eighty quid a week." It all came out in a rush, word prefect from practice. "Do you want to see it?"

"Yes please." She didn't show me up, just thrust a key in my hand and directed me. I wondered if she were capable of the journey. So I took the room, paid two week's rent and used the grubby, overused bathroom to modify my appearance still further with a mid-brunette hair dye I'd bought in *Boots* in Euston.

In my room I used my new smartphone to access the internet and create a Bitcoin wallet. I had never dealt with a so-called 'cryptocurrency' but it seemed to offer exactly what I needed. Within minutes I was the proud owner of several million pounds worth.

I was, with the addition of my own money, worth well over forty million pounds.

Despite Graeme's treachery, things were looking up.

Chapter Fifteen

My overseas account was a sort of belated thirteenth birthday present: part of Granny's legacy – like my three million quid, a flat, also in Hong Kong, the luxurious hair and the straight, white teeth. Okay, the 'straight' was augmented a teeny bit by my father's money and a good orthodontist in my teens.

We'd left my birthplace when I was nine and moved to England but when I was thirteen we went on a three month holiday to the Far East. For old times' sake, we took in the colony, still two years away from reverting to Chinese rule.

My father had gone off for the day to 'do a bit of business' – I know not what but now have to reassess everything I thought I knew about him. Left to our own devices, Granny took me on a tour, leaving my mother by the pool, baking in Asian-springtime sunshine. I vividly recall the bright floral swimsuit and, tall and gawky as I was, yearned for the day I had a curvy figure like hers. *Never did, never will.*

A taxi took us to Mongkok … a right dive but apparently even worse when she had lived there … and dropped us at a grey, monolithic tower block, looking like a scummy Christmas tree adorned with festoons of television dishes and washing bedecked balconies. Two Chinese heavies sat on the steps in the doorway and regarded us with dead eyes until Granny murmured something I didn't catch and showed them the inside of her left arm. They moved aside but said nothing.

Inside, we trudged up flight after flight of plain concrete steps, our footsteps echoing back from above and below. The smells, both strange and familiar, of packed humanity assailed us. By the tenth floor, fit as I was, my legs were beginning to feel heavy and my muscles burned but Granny just plodded on. At the fourteenth floor we walked to the end door – again under the surveillance of more marble-faced lookouts. The door opened as we approached and we were greeted in Mandarin by a young Chinese girl about my age. She bowed and led us through a stark hallway into a small room in which, unexpectedly, was another flight of stairs; dark, shining wood. As we emerged onto the floor above I nearly reeled backwards. Expecting to find another tiny apartment, I was staggered at the size; the walls of several flats had been removed leaving a single, huge hall.

Heavy, black teak tables jostled with long, cherry red, wooden sideboards. Rich tapestries, depicting mythical beasts in vivid colours decorated with pearls and semiprecious stones, hung on every wall. Light-limiting drapes covered the windows so most of the illumination came from cabinets displaying oriental art: mainly gold and ivory that shone and glinted under skilfully set spotlights. Boxes and panels were inlaid with mother-of-pearl and precious stones. Buddhas in various poses in an assortment of precious materials crowded shelves; glittered and shone. Heavy, exotic perfume hung in the air with an almost physical presence. In the centre sat an old man on what I could only be described as a throne.

Again I was surprised. With all this luxury and grandeur I was expecting him to behave like some haughty potentate, instead he laughed, rising with arms wide and greeted Granny with warm words in Mandarin. Short, bald and very thin, he grinned at her with a mouth more gaps than teeth.

"Hello, little sister. You have come to see me at last. Too many years have gone." Then he peered at me, waving me forward. "Who is this?"

"My granddaughter. Wei Yu." This was the name she always called me and meant something like 'unique bright light'. I considered it was just a pet name. She turned. "Say 'hello' to Deng. He is my honorary brother. You should call him 'Grandfather'." She urged me forward with a hand in my back so I gave greetings in my best Mandarin.

More gums. "She speaks our language. You have taught her well."

Now it was Granny's turn to beam. "Both Mandarin and Cantonese. She sounds like a native." I wanted to point out that I *was* a native but kept my silence.

The girl brought tea and we sat and sipped, the two adults talking like the old friends they were: catching up, remembering people and incidents … sometimes wistful, sometimes laughing, sometimes close to tears. I imagined that, in Hong Kong, they would speak Cantonese but soon realised they shared roots that went back a lot further; to pre-communist, mainland China.

Tea finished, we left but instead of heading straight back to the hotel, Granny took me to a dingy shop at street level and ordered me to, "Be brave, Wei Yu. Grit your teeth and bare your arm." For the next half hour I did as bid while the denizen of the parlour attacked the inside of my left upper arm with an electric needle that burred and buzzed and bored excruciating pain into my nerve endings.

Thinking back, it's strange. I asked her why and she simply said it was 'necessary'. I suppose, at thirteen, struggling with my condition and working hard to fit in, I was more malleable than I would have been just a few years earlier … or a few years later. Afterwards she told me that if ever I had real problems then all I had to do was come here and Deng would do 'whatever is necessary.' I smiled to myself. *That guy isn't going to be around long enough to help anybody.*

Later I examined the 50p sized mark but, upside down or reversed in the mirror, it was difficult to decipher. It was two Chinese characters one printed over the other: black on red. The top one was 云, Yún which means 'clouds', but the red symbol beneath was unclear and illegible. Only once Granny told me that it was 月, Yuè or moon, did I recognise it.

After my torture was over she took me to where she'd had her business in Wanchai. She was totally open about it. She told me it was 'a club' and had employed up to twenty girls.

"It was where I met your grandfather. He was a member. As soon as I saw him in his wonderful uniform I fell in love with him." Shades of *The World of Suzi Wong*. My grandfather, whom I barely remembered, had been a major in the British army.

I suppose, in a place like that, there were no secrets between them. They each knew what the other was there for.

Finally we took another taxi to Mid-Level where we went to the top floor of a tall block to a large, well appointed flat. Large flats in Hong Kong are rare and expensive.

"What's this place?" I asked.

She gave me a wide grin. "This is where your grandfather and I lived." She danced around, almost as if returning had stripped off the intervening years. "Now it is yours."

"Mine?"

"One day, maybe soon, I will go to meet my beloved husband and my honourable parents. All I can do is pass on the things life has bestowed on me. This flat is one of them. I don't know if it will ever be of any use to you or if you will just sell it and use the money – that must be your choice – but here it is." As she slipped a key into my hand I saw tears in her eyes.

We took the eight hundred metre long public escalator down to Central where her bank was situated. She introduced me to the manager and showed me the safety deposit box where she kept the deeds and various other documents then stood over me as I opened an account. When I asked her why I needed one she simply said, "You never know."

In subsequent years my business earned almost half its money overseas. With my fluency in Mandarin and Cantonese I was one of very few western business consultants in the world who could take their skills to the burgeoning new market of China. I saw no reason why the British taxman should take a slice of it. So, years later, the local bank account seemed like a very good idea. *Thank you, Granny*.

The only other outstanding memory from that day was the loud and ferocious argument between my mother and Granny … something I'd never seen before. As soon as she saw the tape that covered my new tattoo, mother seemed to see some significance in it that I had not. She launched into Granny as if the old lady had done me severe harm. My mother, who rarely spoke Cantonese even though it was practically her first language, now used it to scream and hurl abuse … something else she never did. Despite understanding every word, I never understood Granny's crime other than, according to my mother, that she had introduced me to *those people*.

In 1997, having been born there and owning property there, I was entitled to a residence permit for what became the Hong Kong Special Administrative Region.

The only other outcome of the whole trip was that nine months later, on my fourteenth birthday, Harrison arrived and I, now an inconvenience, was packed off to boarding school by loving parents.

Chapter Sixteen

I didn't get a lot of sleep in the tiny room equipped with minute bed, chair, a wobbly table and a table lamp which flickered. The mattress could have been made from Brighton Beach: hard and lumpy. I hadn't eaten and, despite the rules, the girl in the next room cooked bacon that she shared, laughing and joking, with her boyfriend. Then they had an energetic, noisy and prolonged sex session in a bed no more than a hollow stud wall away from mine. I felt as if I were in a vicarious ménage à trois. *They should be so lucky.*

I worried about Diane. I knew I was not to blame for anything that had befallen her. I kept telling myself that she had volunteered and gone into it with her eyes open. But from somewhere a little voice kept niggling – wouldn't leave me alone – telling me I had tricked her, used her, manipulated her. Still, I'm a psychopath – it's what I do. Why should it concern me? She was just furniture in the roomscape of my life and now she was gone. So what? She was just somebody I knew – a pretty girl, true, but with more breasts than brain cells.

So why did I keep remembering the way she was? Why did I keep crying? I told myself it was because I'd been betrayed – for the second time – by Graeme.

Needing somebody to talk to, I called Maxie from a box about three miles away from my digs – I walked to it – and hid my number.

"Josie, are you all right? I've been trying to call you but your phone's out of service. I've had the police here – some guy called Leyland – asking if I knew where you were. What's going on? Are you in trouble?"

I explained as much as I could … not a lot.

"Can I come and meet you somewhere?"

"Best not. If the police found out about it they could follow you. I can't take that chance."

"I hope you know what you're doing, Josie. This Leyland guy was talking about arrest warrants and even prison. Have you done something, love? Because if you have, you know I'll do whatever I can—"

"No, Maxie. I give you my word that there's nothing for you to worry about." *Except jumping bail and shipping a few million quid of illegal money around the globe.* "I'll stay in touch. Promise."

"OK. Why don't you give me a number so I can contact you if there's anything important? I won't tell anybody – I promise."

I apologised but refused.

When I called Leyland I was put through immediately.

"Where the hell are you?" He was as aggressive as usual … maybe more so.

"Sorry, Frank. I told you there was a nasty character after me and you ignored—"

"Hold on. That's not true. We followed it up and found nothing against him. We have laws forbidding us from harassing someone on nothing more than accusations." He was trying to sound sarcastic but I just heard 'patronising'.

"Be that as it may, he's now after me in a big way. A friend of mine, Diana Browning has gone missing and I believe he may be involved in it … maybe even killed her. If you won't do anything to protect me, I have to look after myself."

"I have reason to believe you've left the country—"

"Why do you think that?"

"Your car was found in Dover and we know you boarded the ferry. Are you in France?" *So Graeme ratted me out to Shepherd but not to Leyland. Strange.*

"Frank, you'll have to trust me on this. I'm staying out of the way because I'm in danger. I can't tell you where I am because somebody in your team is talking to Shepherd—"

"That's ridiculous." I could hear his anger: speaking faster, increased volume. "There's no way that sort of information would ever get out from my—"

"Rubbish!" I cut in. "I gave my ex-husband, your ACC, the name and address of my hotel and less than two hours later Shepherd's henchmen turned up. Explain that!" *Hear that splash, Graeme? That was you ... being dropped in it.*

"The ACC? Utter nonsense. Now you listen to me, young lady, you're still on bail and that means you're breaking the law. Get your arse back here or I'll have a warrant issued for your arrest. Then you'll be safe enough because you'll be in prison!"

"If you can find me, Frank, you go for it." I hung up. It was pointless discussing it.

Running low on funds, I contacted my bank in Hong Kong and had them send twenty thousand for collection at a bank in London. I was building an electronic signpost to my location but I had to take the chance.

Local bus and a cheap day return train journey, paid in cash, got me to London and three hours later I collected the money using my Hong Kong ID. *The wonders of modern banking.* Conversely, I was now wandering around the country with the sort of money people had killed for.

Back in Birmingham I went shopping to one of those shops that sells a complete outfit, made by two-year-olds in some third world country, for a tenner. The most useful item was a hoodie so I could keep my face obscured. *You can't be too careful.* Then I demolished a couple of hours running around a park – pushing myself as hard as I could. I've no idea how far I ran but by the time I finished I was almost incapable of walking and the day was over. Then a long bath, a restaurant meal and back to vicarious sex.

I wasted four days, calling Leyland occasionally to reassure him I was still alive. I got the impression he would be happy if I wasn't.

* * *

Diana's number was still unanswered ... except now her voicemail was full and accepting no more messages. I had to return home. There was no point in having all this money and skulking away in squalor and apparent poverty.

It would be difficult but, with forty million, I was in a better position to force Shepherd to negotiate. In extremis I could have him bumped off for a fraction of that. *That's a joke, right!*

I called him.

"It is you! Where the hell have you been, you stupid whore?" *You know I said I was joking about getting him bumped off ...?* He was irate. I could almost hear the foam hitting his mouthpiece.

"Tsk, tsk Neil. Calm down, there's a good boy. I've called to negotiate—"

"The bank accounts! You screwed up the account numbers on the storage device. You have no idea what you've done."

"What makes you think it was me—?"

"Do you think I am a total moron?" *Er, yes.* "The files are all time-stamped. I know to the second when the changes were made ... and they happened while you were telling me you had not found the device. You have no idea of the shit-storm you have brought down on our heads."

There's my confirmation that it's not your money. If I

could find out who the money belongs to, I may be in with a chance of achieving some sort of settlement and cut out this obnoxious thug.

"So tell me, what sort of shit-storm—"

"Oh no. You are going to have to sort this one on your own. You sowed the wind ... now the whirlwind is coming and I am not hanging around to feel the draft."

"Where's Diana?"

"I wondered if she was anything to do with you." The line went dead. *That hadn't changed ... he's still hanging up on me.*

There was nothing for it. I called Diana's husband, Garrett. It took a long time for him to answer and when he did he was barely coherent. He had just returned from the mortuary where he'd identified her body. A length of wire had been wound around her neck and pulled so tight it had almost severed her head.

I said lots of meaningless words before hanging up. My hand was shaking.

I called Leyland then Graeme and told them both I'd turn myself in tomorrow then arranged to meet Nancy Petterbridge, my solicitor, at the police station at one the following afternoon.

With my old SIM card in the new phone I was immediately bombarded with messages and voicemails. Stefan: checking I was all right ... and would I be playing Saturday? Maxie – before I'd called her – worrying. Others: clients, friends, Malone. Several from Leyland ... abusive but not quite enough to constitute harassment. Graeme claiming to be puzzled by the 'treacherous bastard' rant.

I purchased a first class to Brighton, using my credit card. It would ring alarms and have the police waiting at Euston so I got off at Watford Junction. I caught a taxi and, to the delight of the driver, ordered him to take me to Euston

Station 'as fast as possible' ... with a bonus if he beat the train. I strolled in with my face obscured by the hood. Just curious. I was not disappointed at how many uniforms waited at the gate. I directed a second taxi to the Park Lane Hotel where I paid cash ... I didn't need the cops knocking my door down in the middle of the night ... thrashed the gym, ate well in the restaurant, then had my first good night's sleep in over a week.

* * *

The train arrived in Brighton a few minutes before one but I wasn't going to be late for my appointment because Leyland, with six minders, waited for me as I walked through the barrier. I gave him a cheery wave and beaming smile as I strolled through.

"Well Frank, what a delightful surprise. Now I won't even need to pay for a taxi. I must admit I never expected such a party. Were you worried you wouldn't be able to handle me on your own?" I gave him another smile and winked at a young constable who coloured up. Leyland told me I was under arrest and snapped handcuffs on my wrists – a tad overzealously, I thought – before, with hand on my head, shoving me into the back of the car. *Hey Frank, you're helping me complete Hare's list. Now I can check off number 19, 'Revocation of conditional release'.*

I'd outsmarted him again because I had a text to Nancy prepared on my phone and pressed 'send' before they had time to confiscate it. It let her know I was in Brighton, under arrest and on my way to our rendezvous. She arrived while they were still processing me. From the look on his face, Frank would have liked to 'process' me in a blender.

In the same dingy interview room he allowed me a few minutes with Nancy then, accompanied by his poodle, Mullin, started on about where I'd been but Nancy cut in.

"Before we get to that, I demand you tell me if the CPS has decided to charge my client with the murders of her family?"

Leyland looked sheepish and took a long time to answer, shuffling the paperwork in front of him. "No. They've decided that—"

"So let's see if I got this clear: you are about to start harassing my client with a charge of failing to surrender to bail? But, if she was not to be charged with anything, then the bail should have been lifted ... true?" He shrugged. "So whilst Ms Trelawney is grieving over the loss of her family, you appear to be intent on making her grief worse." Leyland stiffened and his face set hard. He leaned across the table at her, fingers interlinked as if practising throttling somebody. *Nancy or me?*

"When she jumped bail she was still a suspect. How could I know the CPS was not going to charge—?"

"And why did she jump bail? She told you somebody was threatening her life but you—"

"We investigated her allegation and found nothing—"

"Except her friend has been murdered and she believes this man ... *Shepherd* ... is the culprit."

"We need more than the personal beliefs of your client to lock people up. Now let's get back to the 'failing to surrender' charge."

Nancy is an ex-public school girl with a cut-glass accent but she's a formidable woman: physically big and she'd cut her solicitor's teeth in the East End of London, keeping the local villains out of prison. She knows how to fight dirty. She leaned back in her chair, gave him a super-white smile and said, "Excuse me, Inspector, – and I'm sure you'll correct if I'm wrong – but aren't you rather, er, talking bollocks?" Leyland almost sputtered, just managed to hold it back, stood and headed for the door.

"Fuck off! The pair of you!" Mullin looked about to burst.

"Thank you, Inspector. I take it *all* charges have been dropped?" His only answer was the slam the door.

I was on the street in less than ten minutes. *One problem solved, bigger one still to go.*

Chapter Seventeen

The nondescript office block had a small entrance area occupied by a large and rather knocked about reception desk, two battered sofas and a low table with a scrappy, well-thumbed collection of out-of-date magazines. The reek of cheap air freshener completed the ambience.

I scanned the board by the lift, found Shepherd's company occupied the fourth floor and was debating whether to take the lift or the stairs, which would mean running the gauntlet of the hatchet-faced receptionist, when the person herself resolved the problem.

"May I help you?" she asked in a voice like a siren that contained not a hint of helpfulness. Maybe it was my biker gear. Or maybe she was just a miserable cow.

I smiled ... one of my 'little girl lost' affairs that generally worked. "I just need to nip up and see if—"

"Sign in." She picked up a clear plastic ballpoint pen, tapped it on a ledger and pointed the blunt end at me like an accusing finger. When I took it she demanded, "Company?" The telephone receiver hovered halfway to an ear that sported something long and dangly – probably from a Christmas cracker – finger poised over the keypad as if eager to start World War Three.

"Shepherd Cleaning." I pointed the pen over my shoulder at the board.

She sighed and replaced the instrument. "Nobody in." She picked up the trash magazine my unwarranted incursion had apparently disturbed and made a huffy, paper rustling show of relocating her place.

I've just wasted a perfectly good smile on you, Bitch.

I was considering whether I should try a charm offensive or ignore her and go for the stairs but suspected the first would be another waste and that she'd have a hotline to some sort of security to forestall the second. I'd had enough hassle for one day.

"Any idea when he might be back?"

"No." She didn't even look up.

Do charm schools do refunds?

Beaten, I headed for the revolving door as a man came in ... Ray. Instinctively, I felt for the knife in my cuff as he approached me: stiff-legged and bristling.

"Wha' you want?" He stood square on to me, feet wide apart, hands worked as if anticipating what they were going to do to my throat. *You've done that twice, Ray. I won't let you do it a third time.*

"Is Shepherd around?"

He looked, if anything, even more aggressive: chin thrusting, shoulders rising. "Buggered off. 'e said you'd fucked him over so 'e 'ad no choice."

"Language!" barked Miss Congeniality.

"So 'e fucked *me* over in turn." He glared at her, daring her to object but she just 'harrumphed' and got on with challenging her intellect.

"What did he do to you?"

"Didn't cough up me last month's pay, that's what." Then he smiled, like a shark eyeing lunch. "But 'e did say if I saw you again I was free to 'urt you ... lots."

"Then he cleared off and left you to carry the can. Brave man. Want to talk?"

"Why would I do that?"

"I might be able to help with your cash flow."

"Why would *you* do that?"

I shrugged. "You never know." I looked at my watch: 5:25. Out the corner of my eye I saw Cerberus packing her bags and shrugging on her coat and suddenly realised I was hungry. "Come on. I'll buy you dinner," then, when he hesitated, "Or at least a pint." He crossed his hands under his belly and heaved before letting it drop back, his belt like the underwire on a 66 double-F.

Near the edge of the trading estate we found a small pub rapidly filling with a mixture of office and factory workers. We fought to the bar, him leading – his bulk a massive advantage – and I ordered: fizzy water and a lager. "Pinta Wifebeater." *That would be about right.*

As he 'nipped out for a fag', I carried the drinks to a table already loaded with empty bottles and glasses.

He took his time returning. *A show of independence?*

Eventually he shouldered back through the crush, sat opposite me and downed half his beer in a swallow. "Well …?" He thumped the glass down and wiped his mouth on his cuff.

"Where's Shepherd?"

Lift. Swallow. Thump. Wipe. "Wha's it worth?"

I pulled a roll of notes out of the slit pocket in my leathers. "Five hundred?" I put it beside his drink.

"A monkey? 'e owes me a month …"

I placed a second roll alongside the first and could hear the cogs grinding. He was wondering if he could get more. Eventually, he nodded. "Go on then." He finished his drink and held up his empty glass so, while he went out for another smoke, I picked up the money but left my crash helmet to reserve our place. At the bar I ordered more lager, a half pound burger for him – "With everything," – and a prawn salad for me.

I put the money back on the table as he swallowed half his second drink, demonstrating his machismo.

"Okay, 'ere's what I know. Shepherd … by the way, that's not 'is real name … is some sorta dealer. 'e, y'know, buys and sells stuff but the sortsa stuff 'e buys and sells are not the sorta things you can pick up at your local Aldi."

"So is the cleaning company a front?"

"No. It's straight. 'e's got about thirty cleaners and if 'e don't come back I reckon I'll, y'know, 'ave a go at it meself."

"Ever run a business?"

"Not really. Shepherd didn't even do that much running of it. He had this little Chinky kid called 'u what did it all but 'e's gone, too." *Chinky? Careful pal.* I made him spell the name, Hu.

"What? Gone with Shepherd?"

"No, 'e just, y'know, didn't turn up one day, coupla months back. Just, like, pissed off. Never even called in for 'is dosh."

"Who sent you to my hotel in London?" He tried a look of wide-eyed innocence but it just made him look more guilty. I picked up the money and started to put it in my pocket until he clamped a ham-sized fist over mine.

"All right. Shepherd sent me and three others – some geezers 'e gets to do 'is 'eavy stuff."

"How did he know where I was?"

"Dunno, but 'e's got this, like, contact in the pigs. 'e gets these phone calls, y'know?" *Bingo!*

"Police? Any idea who?"

"Nah." Lift. Swallow. Thump. Wipe.

"What rank? Inspector? Superintendent?"

He chuckled, a deep rumbling. "Nah. Nothing so grand. I think 'e's, like, a detective and all but 'e's, y'know, just a grunt: a constable maybe."

Likely? Maybe not Graeme, then. Or maybe he gets somebody else to do his dirty work. Or maybe Heartthrob here doesn't know all he thinks he knows.

"You sure?"

"Sure, I'm sure."

"Tell me about the deal my father was involved in."

"All I know is this: Shepherd's some sorta middle man so 'e', y'know, gets somebody to buy something from somebody else—"

"What's this 'something' and who are the 'somebodies'?"

He shrugged and peered over the rim of his rapidly depleting lager. When it was empty he slammed it on the table, sighed, wiped his mouth and added a belch for embellishment. *Fancy a shag, Dreamboat?*

"I don't know nothing about that. All I know is there's four-a them … whatever they are. 'e called them 'tanks'. Said it made him laugh 'cos when they developed tanks … y'know, the things with tracks and guns … in the First World War they called them 'tanks' so as the Gerries wouldn't know what they was, like, talking about. Anyway, there's, y'know, four of 'em. Shepherd 'adta, y'know, get the money from these geezers, take 'is cut and pass on the rest to this other lot of geezers. That's where your old man comes in 'cos the idea was that 'e, y'know, does like that game on the pier where you hits the rat or something with an 'ammer."

"Whack-a-mole?"

"Yeah. He makes like whack-a-mole with the dosh. He chucks it in one 'ole and it pops up somewhere else, all cleaned up, like."

This all made sense to me except I couldn't see how my father would get involved in anything like that.

"You sure it was my father?"

"Absoluty-menty. Shepherd and 'im 'ad been doing it for donkeys' years. Mostly it was just, y'know, drugs 'n girls 'n that. Shepherd does the business and your old man sorts the wonga. This time, Shepherd reckons 'e's 'it the big time cos 'e's flogging these tank things to these guys for bleeding *millions*!"

Could these 'tanks' actually be nuclear weapons? Jesus!

"But it all went wrong?"

"For sure. Your old man gets the dosh but, y'know, snuffs it – no offence – afore he gets to pass it on. So now the guys who give 'im the lolly are, like, pissed off big time. Shepherd reckons 'e can, y'know, screw the dosh out of you but you truly fucked 'im over so now they're out to get 'im."

Maybe I've accidentally done the world a favour. If no money had got back to the Russians the bombs were presumably still safely tucked away in their bunkers.

"So he's skipped? Where to?"

He dragged the corners of his mouth down and shrugged. "Not sure but 'e mentioned that 'e 'ad a place in Mouldy-somewhere or another …"

"Malta?

He shook his head. "Na. Been there when I was in the Navy."

"Mauritius? Mauritania? Moldova?"

"Yeah, that last one sounds like it could be it."

"Will they come looking for him, do you reckon?"

"I would think so … least ways that's what 'e's scared of. And the guys what was supposed to be supplying these 'tanks'. They're after 'im too."

We stopped talking for a few seconds while our food was distributed and he immediately grabbed his burger and stuffed it into his mouth, ripping off a substantial proportion. I couldn't help noticing how black-edged his fingernails were. He chewed twice and swallowed. I pushed at my limp salad with my fork, speared a prawn.

"Why so? I thought you said they were *supposed* to supply four of these so-called tanks. Okay, they lost the sale but there must be others who would buy whatever it is they're selling." *Let's hope not.*

"Yeah." He spoke, grinned and ate simultaneously. "Sorta. They was supposed to be supplying four but they only supplied one ... justa, y'know, prove they could." He sprayed crumbs, some into my salad but I'd already lost my appetite. I stared into my untouched food while he went outside.

Was he telling me Shepherd had supplied ISIS with an atom bomb?

Chapter Eighteen

I needed to get any information that might be in Shepherd's office and abode. I kept hinting as much to Ray but he just drank more and more ... at my expense, of course. When he did finally invite me back to the office it was obvious what his intentions were so I ducked out and said I would meet him there the following morning.

Then there was my next problem. My mother's car, the Volvo, was in the long stay car park at Luton and Potex-2 was still in Dover. So despite having two cars I had access to neither. I called a company in Brighton and arranged to hire a medium sized Vauxhall for the day.

When the buzzer went I assumed it was the driver delivering my rental but I saw, on the tiny screen, Graeme, dressed in civvies.

"What do you want?" I tried to get plenty of aggression into my tone. It wasn't hard.

"Just to talk. Are you going to let me in?" I pressed the button and he moved out of vision. When the light beside the lift illuminated I pressed another button to bring him up. He stood behind the opening doors looking – what? Contrite? Puzzled? I don't know. I stood aside to allow him into the lobby but didn't invite him further.

He looked perplexed. "My God, what have you done with your beautiful hair? You look like a boy." He reached a hand out to touch it but I slapped it away.

"I cut it. What's it got to do with you?"

"Josie ..."

"Don't you 'Josie' me, you bastard." I was building up a head of steam and it would feel good to tear into him.

"Jocelyn ..." he tried the full version as if it was my own name I was objecting to rather than his use of my oxygen. "I got your phone call but I didn't understand it. What's all this about 'treacherous bastard'? What have I done?"

"Done? Don't you remember our last conversation? I said that if I told you where I was then you would tell Leyland and there was a leak on Leyland's team so this villain, Shepherd, would get to hear about it." Now I was sure, that *was* puzzlement on his face. "You remember that, don't you?"

"Yes, of course I do—"

"And you swore – *swore* – you would tell nobody—"

"And I didn't—"

"So how come a bunch of Shepherd's goons turned up and rushed straight to my room?" I didn't *know* that last bit but it was a reasonable guess.

"Josie ..." He reached out appealing hands. "I swear by everything I hold dear that I did not tell Leyland! I promise I didn't tell anyone!"

"Then how did Shepherd find out? Did you tell anyone at all?"

"No. Nobody. I swear. I was a bit delayed so it was nearly three hours before I got to the hotel. You'd gone but the receptionist told me somebody else had been looking for you." He seemed sincere. True, in his position he needed to be a consummate politician – for which read 'professional liar' – but, coupled with what Ray had told me the previous evening, I was half – no, a quarter – inclined to believe him. Then he hesitated. "I did enter the address into my electronic diary so I suppose ..." He took half a step forward and I was in his arms and he was kissing me. It would have been so easy. And you have no idea of the temptation: to cuckquean the woman who had cuckqueaned me!

But I stopped him and lowered him gently back to terra firma. *About a billion Brownie points there, Josie.* The truth is, I just didn't fancy it. That morning I had woken with stomach cramps, tender breasts and a deep loathing of all things masculine. *Here we go again.* Then the hire car arrived and the moment was over anyway but I was left with the warm and delicious feeling I could reel him in again if the mood took me. *Save that for when it might be useful.*

He made to leave but at the lift door turned.

"Villains demanding money and accusations of murder? Are you going to tell me what this is all about?"

"Maybe later. I think it's all right now." *And the last thing I need is you sniffing around my newfound riches.*

I sent him on his way and drove to Crawley, arriving half an hour after my appointed time with Ray. The epitome of charm behind the desk attested she had not seen him that morning, refused to allow me to go to the office to see if he was already there but did, with huffs and sighs, call his number ... with the clear implication she was going well beyond the call of duty. There was no answer and I sat on one of the uncomfortable sofas for nearly half an hour before he finally showed up and led me to the lift. He was unshaven and looked like he'd been to Hell and back – stopping to vomit on every step of the long, long staircase. His clothes, unchanged from yesterday, reeked of cheap perfume, beer and cigarette smoke.

"Rough night?"

"I met some mates and we 'ad some more drinks and then we pulled these birds and I got me end away so I didn't get 'ome till about five."

"Really? You got a girl?"

He looked offended. "I can get all the girls I want.*"
Really, Sexbomb? How much of my thousand pounds did she cost?*

In the office I found what I was hoping for but feared wouldn't be there: Shepherd's computers. There were three machines strung together in a network with a backup server. I circulated the office switching on each in turn and, while waiting, began a search. Within a minute I found the H4SD in the top draw of a desk in the inner office. My laptop told me that the contents remained unchanged. He'd probably abandoned it as useless to him. Maybe he'd left me a virus but my virus checker pronounced it clean so I wiped the data and slipped it in my pocket before Ray caught a glimpse of it and got curious. There was nothing else of interest but the industrial grade shredder was full of chaff.

"Let's see if there's anything on his machines." I looked at each screen in turn and saw the message, 'No bootable device.'

"What's the problem?" He leaned over my shoulder, sharing second hand beer and cigarette fumes. *Be still my beating heart.*

"Shepherd has wiped all the drives."

"Is that bad?"

"Yes. Everything on the computer is gone."

"Shit!" He banged the table and released an outrush of breath that nearly blinded me. "Does that mean we've lost all the client lists?"

"Looks like it."

"Well 'ow can I run the company if I don't know none of the clients? Nor the cleaners neither."

I wasn't fazed. Wiping a hard drive is damn near impossible. And I knew just the man who could recover one. In some ways Shepherd had done me a favour. If he'd left all the drives untouched then, first it would mean there was nothing on them worth seeing and, second, it was unlikely Ray would let me take them.

"Don't worry, I've got a friend who might be able to

recover everything for you." He helped me load them into the boot of the Vauxhall and I was soon heading for Hove.

Now all I had to do was turn on the charm for dear Adam. Time for some 'little finger wrapping'.

I caught him at home. Becky welcomed me with an air-kiss and coffee. *Is that a grey hair, Becky-baby?* Adam tried to act friendly for her benefit – and aggressive for mine. He failed at both and just came across as weird. Becky gave him a couple of sideways looks as if she might be sussing our – *his* – guilty secret. When I asked if he would recover the data she answered in the affirmative on his behalf and he just looked sour. I handed over the H4SD and told him to do with it as he wished.

Next morning I caught the train to Dover, a dreary, delay-riddled journey via London and a rain-sodden Kent countryside. The local police station informed me Potex had been towed away to the pound ... although I thought 'pound' was hardly the right word when I found out how much it was going to cost to gain her release.

With my credit card hammered I handed over the key to a young lad and stood outside the prefab office as he strolled the thirty yards to where it stood, its usual pristine white dulled by a film of dust and rain splatter, parked between a beaten up BMW and a smart Range Rover. I idly watched two pigeons fornicating as he vanished from view to snuggle into the driver's seat.

Then the world changed colour.

An intense, vivid sheet of flame blasted outwards and my Audi took off – for a fraction of a second I could see it completely above the roof of the Chelsea Tractor. I never heard a thing but felt a thump through my entire body ... pretty much as I imagine it would feel being hit by a truck. The percussion wave reached into my ears and met in the middle of my head. As I was lifted off my feet my vision gave out. Then gravity regained control and I found the ground. I remember the flying. I remember the falling. I remember the body-breaking impact. After that, I remember nothing at all.

Somebody was leaning over me, mouth moving but making no sound.

It took me over an hour before any vestige of hearing returned.

It would be weeks before I could move freely and without pain.

Chapter Nineteen

I lay all night in the hospital bed. Despite industrial quantities of pain killers, every part of my body screamed at me. Each slight movement caused me agony and tried to make me cry out. In the bed to my left, an old woman moaned and groaned while on my right, augmenting my tinnitus, was the sibilant rhythm from the earphones of a young girl who slept sound and snoring ... oblivious to the noise. At regular intervals staff walked past with squeaking shoes and rattling trolleys. Lights went on and off at random. But what *really* kept me awake were the thoughts swirling in my brain.

The constant niggle in my head was, 'This can't be right.'

The only person I could think of who would be out to get me was Shepherd. But surely he would still want the money and I was now his *only* route to it. So why would he put a bomb under my car? Killing me would blow – literally – any chance he had of getting it.

In which case who in hell had tried to blow me up? I had two other options. First was whoever it was Shepherd had sold the 'tanks' on behalf of. They seemed more of a possibility because they *may* have ended up 'giving away' a nuke – or whatever it was. At over thirty two million for four they were effectively eight million to the bad. Maybe they were prepared to just cut their losses and cash in on the three they still had. And that would likely make me a lose end to tie up. *A decided 'probable'*.

Second was whoever Shepherd had sold the 'tanks' to. But they were thirty odd million quid out of pocket so wouldn't they also be keen to get it back? Wouldn't all the reasons that ruled out Shepherd also apply to them? On the other hand, I'd heard ISIS was the richest terrorist organisation that had ever existed with literally *billions*. Maybe thirty two point six million pounds was a small enough amount to write off. *A definite 'maybe'.*

But did it even matter? If somebody was out to get me, did I actually care who pulled the trigger? My concern was to dodge the bullet.

Graeme turned up.

"Christ, Josie, you look a mess."

"Thanks. You really know how to boost a girl's self-esteem."

He pulled up a chair and sat, uninvited, by my bed and lay a hand against the side of my head as if I were made of brittle crystal. My throat swelled and my eyes burned at the touch but I couldn't – wouldn't – allow him to see me cry. "How're you feeling?" His voice was so soft.

"Rough. My ears are still ringing, I'm stiff all over and I haven't slept a wink. What are you doing here?"

"We had a report of the incident and somebody noticed the name … it's a bit distinctive. I called the hospital and they said you'd been kept in for observation but might be released this morning. Have you seen the doctor?"

"Not since I was admitted."

"They said you'd need some clothes as most of yours were destroyed by the explosion or had to be cut off you. Lennie sent some of hers." He held up a carrier bag. Leonora – Mrs Bergomay-Trelawney the second – was lending me her clothes. For a second I was tempted to tell him I would sooner go home by train, bare-arsed in the backless gown supplied by the NHS. *Bugger the pair of them.*

Eventually the doctor came and declared me 'fit to go home.' *I don't go much on your definition of 'fit'.* I needed to pee so I took the clothes, made my excuses, slipped out of bed and headed to the bathroom. Graeme wolf whistled at my bare bum – *if you've got, flaunt it* – before I managed to cover it with the threadbare towelling dressing gown, also the property of the state. In the bathroom mirror I saw my face for the first time: a Technicolor hamburger. Then I realised, I had no makeup. *Bugger it all!*

I'd also lost my pants but there was no way I was going to wear Nora's castoffs so I'd have to go 'commando'. Her clothes were tatty and hung off me. I would bet my millions she had taken great care in their selection and my occupation of them was the last waypoint before the recycling bin.

Outside, a chauffeur held the door of something long, black and stately while Graeme handed me in then slipped in beside me. I didn't realise he'd come in his official car but had no objection to travelling in style.

"We need to get you somewhere they can't get at you – a safe house." We cruised the motorway at well over the speed limit.

"No. I'll go to my flat. I'll be all right there. It has entry cameras and a high security door so nobody can get in unless I let them ... as you well know."

"Josie, be reasonable. We can't protect you there. Somebody put a bomb under your car. Next time it may be a rocket propelled grenade through your window!"

"Whoa! An RPG? Where did that come from? I was assuming I was dealing with some run-of-the-mill villain but you're talking about a completely different league. What do you know that you're not telling me?"

"Not a lot. But the explosives and detonators used on your car were military stuff ... not the sort of thing your 'run-of-the-mill villain' would have easy access to. I really think you should consider my offer of a safe house."

I was feeling battered, bruised and scared: an emotion

totally foreign to me until the last week or so. And my period had started so, all-in-all, I felt like shit. Now this. I fell against him, put my head on his shoulder and sobbed. He slipped a comforting arm around my shoulders and rested his face on the top of my head. He may even have kissed it. Afterwards I felt better – not least because of his physical reaction to the contact. *Reel him in.*

He was determined to find out why somebody was so keen on 'getting' me so I gave him a careful, and heavily redacted, account implying Shepherd was a crook who believed he had a call on my father's money. I made a big show of my belief that my father was completely innocent of any wrongdoing. While I was happy to have the weight of HM Constabulary on my side against Shepherd I really didn't want Graeme digging about into the family's finances. I was sure I had cleared everything away but could never know what he would dig up. Despite Graeme's imprecations I was determined to stay in the flat.

"Has anything got into the press about the explosion?" I asked.

"We've managed to quash details of the story – restricting it to simple details of the explosion and that 'a person had been fatally injured but police were withholding details until the family had been informed.' It will all come out sooner or later but it's the best I can do."

It meant I had a breathing space if the perpetrator believed he had succeeded in his mission.

As he left I said, "Please thank Nora for the loan of her clothes."

"Don't call her that. She doesn't like 'Nora'." *That's funny, I don't like Nora either.*

Chapter Twenty

I was interviewed by Leyland as if a bomb going off under my car was somehow *my* fault and, when I couldn't help him, he snapped, "You seem very relaxed by the fact that a young man has died."

That did it.

"I told you over and over Shepherd was out to get me but you just ignored me. You did bugger all and my friend was murdered. Now we find police security so slack that somebody can just stroll into a supposedly secure compound and plant a bomb under my car!" I got up and walked out, calling over my shoulder, "If being the victim of a murder attempt is a crime then arrest me!"

"It's not. But whatever else you're involved in might be." Nevertheless he made no move to stop me.

Poo-brain came home with the Bablucs who presented me with a bill for fuel and hotel bills in Luton and Cumbria. They hadn't stinted themselves. Still, I felt glad to have him home where I could keep an eye on him.

I handed Malone the problem of explaining to the insurance company why I expected them to buy me a new car. *Maybe something even more exotic. Potex-2a?*

Now they had brought the Volvo back, I had the use of a car so, despite the pain, I restarted my classes and kickboxing. That weekend I did a gig with Stefan: a wedding reception, with my face plastered under an inch of slap so as not to frighten the punters. I stayed at the rear and played my sax or sang backing.

Graeme dropped by regularly: "To see if you are okay," and one evening, because I knew which buttons to press, I levelled the score with wife number 2. *I bet he wasn't on your list of your cast-offs to pass on to me, was he Nora?*

Adam called and told me he had managed to recover everything from Shepherd's computers – "As far as I can tell."

"What have you found?"

"Nothing important from the two machines from the outer office ..." I groaned "... but some *really* interesting stuff on the main machine." If it's possible for a voice to 'beam' over the phone his did. In spades.

"So tell me ..."

"Better if we got together." *Uh-oh. Where's this going?*

"Your place or mine?"

"Whichever suits you." Sorry, pal, you're sounding just too casual.

"Becky there?"

"Not until after six."

"See you at seven."

"Okie-dokie." Did he sound disappointed?

* * *

"Right. First the guy's name ... it's not 'Neil Shepherd' but you probably guessed that already." Adam was grinning. "It's Nistor Serebrian or, at least, that's the name his Russian contacts called him by. But that could be false as well."

"Nistor Serebrian? What nationality is that? Any ideas?"

"I've Googled it and think it might be Moldovan," *Result!*

"Anything else?" He was too cocky for there not to be.

"Yes. I've also got his UK address and ... I've cracked his codes!" He was positively *crowing*. "He's using Public Key Encryption ... PKE. Now I don't know if you understand what that is but it works like this." Without waiting for an answer, he snatched a notepad and scribbled a rough circle with an 'S' in it. *I don't give a toss what PKE is but if a man – while doing me a favour – wants to brag about how big his willie is I'm not stupid enough to remind him I've already seen it. Okay, I was quite impressed but I won't tell you that either.* "Now say sender, S, wants to send a secret message to receiver, R." He drew a line to a second circle labelled 'R'. "His problem is: how does he do this so R can decrypt it but nobody else can. Supposing he wants to send the number '7'. R could tell him, "Multiply it by 4" so S sends '28' and when R receives it then he divides by 4 and gets 7 … job done. But the trouble is that R has to keep his key a secret between just him and S because, if it becomes common knowledge, then anybody can decrypt it. So he has to get the key to S without anybody else knowing. See?" I nodded. Becky brought coffee: all baking smells and laser beam smile. *At least two grey hairs.*

"So …?"

"So everybody always thought all maths were reversible: multiply A by B gives C and dividing C by B returns A. But in the nineteenth century a mathematician called Jevons realised that some maths are not and in the seventies a couple of nerds at GCHQ invented a new way of doing it. Now if you do something to A using B it gives C but reversing the process on C using B will give you a choice of E, F, G or a thousand others and if you want to get back to A you need to do a whole other load of maths with a completely different key. So R can publish his 'Public Key' and anybody can use it to encrypt messages to him but, because he's the only one with the 'Private Key', he's the only one who can decrypt them."

"So you've got his public key …"

"Yes … but I've also got his private key!"

Runner

"So you can decrypt messages sent to him?"

"That's how I found out the name his Russian contacts called him. He was incredibly stupid because he kept them as a file in Word. It had a password but I cracked that in seconds. Schoolboy error." I thought of the 256 character password to the H4SD I had kept in exactly that way on my laptop and hoped my face didn't give me away.

"Did you read all his emails?"

"Nah. I scanned a couple but there are *hundreds* of them and most are in Russian so I'll leave that to you."

"Anything else?"

"Not really. Just the public keys of all his contacts. Although I can't think what use they would be ... unless you want to contact the Russian Mafia or ISIS." He grinned.

We loaded all the computers back into the Volvo and he groped me in the process. I slapped his hand away but giggled. Becky invited me to stay for dinner but I made my excuses. Tomorrow I would take them back to Ray but keep the one with the emails. He was so intellectually challenged he probably wouldn't be able to count high enough to notice he was one short.

Tonight I had another task.

* * *

It was a block of flats – not unlike my own – stuck halfway along a quiet cul-de-sac near Crawley. Shepherd dwelt in a second floor, two bedroom apartment overlooking the well tended gardens: razor-cut lawns and sculpted bushes. The label on the buzzer panel by the door announced simply: **Shepherd** but a minute of pressing gained no response.

At a nearby shop I purchased a felt tipped pen and a fawn, padded envelope. As I left, I snagged a copy of the free local newspaper. I scribbled Shepherd's name and address in block letters on the envelope, stuffed it with the newspaper and presented myself at the front door of the block. Conscious I would be viewed on the camera I kept my visor pulled down as far as I could without looking suspicious – the constant drizzle helped. Starting with the flats on the same floor as his I pressed buzzers, working my way through the numbers on the floors above and below until I got an answer from somebody on the fourth. I explained I had a delivery and showed the envelope to the glass eye. A buzz confirmed my ruse had worked so I strolled in with the air of a bored despatch rider. To ensure the corridor was as empty as my poll of the doorbells had suggested, I knocked at the other three doors and, satisfied, broke in to Shepherd's flat by the simply expedient of slamming my steel reinforced motorcycle boot into the door beside the lock. At the second blow the wood split and the third gained me entry.

The flat was minimalist and tastefully decorated but smelled stale and unventilated. I carried a high backed chair from beside the dining table and jammed it against the front door. It was too puny to prevent anybody entering but would give the illusion the door was secure and give me a few seconds notice.

A systematic search of the place: every drawer and cupboard, revealed nothing so I bailed out ... jamming the door closed with a wedge of newspaper. *Another brick wall.*

I hadn't bothered with gloves so I'd probably left enough prints to guarantee a conviction for breaking and entering but if Shepherd or Serebrian or whatever his name was, had skipped the country ahead of a gang of murderous thugs then the last thing on his mind would be pressing charges against me for trashing his door. Anyway, I could insist that because Leyland hadn't believed me about how dangerous Shepherd was then I had the moral right to investigate the man myself.

Runner

Outside it was now dark but at least the rain had stopped and a fresh wind was drying the road.

The Yamaha is a highly desirable machine so whenever I leave it parked in a public place I secure it: not just with the built-in lock but with a long, heavy duty chain wrapped through the back wheel and the frame ... all held together with a hardened steel lock as big as my fist. Any would-be thief would need an oxyacetylene cutter. The problem with this arrangement is that I always end up crouching beside my bike, usually in the dark, fiddling with the combination. No sooner had I hunkered down to undo it, than the automatic security light above the front door went off, plunging me into darkness.

I was just digging out my mobile phone to use the torch when a car pulled up. Hunkered down as I was, the car's occupants didn't see me. They parked directly opposite the flats on the forecourt of a row of lockup garages, blocking three of the doors. Two men got out and headed towards the block. Nothing suspicious about that but there was something about them: their body language, their demeanour, the way they moved ... I don't know, but I kept down, watching them over the enormous back tyre. My concerns were justified when I noticed one of them held a pistol. With his arm straight, the weapon was pressed down by his thigh and, in the dark, almost invisible but as they approached the front door and the security lamp awoke, it highlighted them ... glinting off the gun.

I continued fiddling with the lock, working by the reflected light. At least my condition means I didn't panic. There's something about the sight of a gun that turns normal brains to mush. Eventually the lock disengaged and I had to grab it as the chain rattled free, loud in the night time silence, but at that very moment they gained access ... I'm not sure how, maybe they used the same trick I had ... and filed inside.

A few seconds later the lights in Shepherd's flat filled the windows: flooding the lawns ... and me. A rabbit in the headlamps.

Trying not to rush – which could mean cocking it up – I whipped the chain around my wrist, slipped the ignition key into its slot, turned it and pressed the button. Potex barked into life and, as I leapt aboard like a cowboy in a western, a figure at the window turned and saw me. Behind the double glazing and over the noise of the one thousand cubic centimetre, four cylinder, Genesis engine I couldn't hear what he shouted but his gestures and body posture were as good as sign language.

I stamped the lever into first gear and left a black stripe of rubber away from them. Stupidly, I'd parked facing towards the dead end of the road so as I reached the end I slithered to a stop and did a u-turn with one foot on the ground. There was a flash from above and the window disintegrated, exploding outwards in a cascade of fragmented glass. A lump of the asphalt leapt into the air in front of me and I yanked the throttle.

Ahead of me I saw the driver's door of the saloon opening and a figure emerging – preceded by another gun, while a fourth man leapt from the door behind him. They both started running around the vehicle into the road ahead of me. Adrenaline surged in my veins.

If I took Potex to a high enough cliff and threw her off she would take almost three seconds to reach sixty miles an hour. On the straight it takes less than this ... and I took every last drop of acceleration she would give me. The engine screamed like an animal in pain and the back tyre added a descant. Within yards the front wheel lifted as the forward acceleration overcame gravity. The world turned into a blur and it seemed no more than a fraction of a second before I was where they ought to be but, crouched over the tank, my view of them was obscured.

I must have really put the wind up them: a howling banshee, hurtling towards them at speeds that would be illegal on a motorway, with a high intensity halogen light and the front wheel at head height. One of them, near the centre of the road, aimed at me but I caught him a glancing blow with the faring and sent him spinning across the road just as I saw the muzzle flash of his pistol. The other, on my left, was also aiming but as I passed I lashed out with the chain wrapped around my wrist. Several pounds of tempered steel, swung in an arc from a vehicle travelling at speed is a lethal weapon. I didn't know what damage I did but I saw him collapse and a glance in my rear view mirror as I reached the end of the road, showed both men were still down.

At the corner I burst onto the main road. Thankfully there was no other traffic so I managed the manoeuvre without incident and I ignored every traffic rule until I was locked behind my own front door.

I called Graeme – Leyland would be a waste of time – and told him what had happened. He confirmed there had been reports of shots fired at the location and said he would come over, which he did accompanied by a uniformed sergeant who transcribed my statement. It was only as I was recalling the events I suddenly realised there was something else I should mention.

"They were East Asian."

"What?" they both said together.

"The men. All four of them were Chinese or something." The sergeant scribbled. Graeme looked pensive, chin on hand like a Rodin sculpture.

Russian Mafia, Arab terrorists and now Chinese. Where is this going to end?

The sergeant looked at my chain where I'd left it on the hall table.

"This what you hit him with?" He slipped a plastic ballpoint pen through one of the links and transferred it to a clear plastic evidence bag then Graeme dismissed him.

"What were you doing there?" he demanded, hands on hips, as soon as the door closed behind the departing uniform. I had no option but to confess to the break in. What would have been the point in doing otherwise?

That night he held me close in my king sized bed and for the first time in my life I felt the need to cling to somebody: needing the contact, needing the comfort. I was sorry when he left at two in the morning. In his job he could always come up with an excuse to his wife for being out so late. *He always had for me.*

Chapter Twenty-One

Ray was in when I turned up unannounced. I persuaded the harridan on the front desk to call him and he came down to help me transfer the computers to his office. All the time we were doing this he regaled me with his plans for continuing the cleaning company – renamed 'Ray of Sunshine' – and taking over Shepherd's clients and staff.

The previous evening's incident had given me an idea.

"You mentioned a young fellow called Hu the other day. What do you know about him?" I tried to sound casual as I assembled the cat's cradle of wires of his computer network. It's not my nature to be so helpful but he was the only lead I had. Okay, assuming this Hu was involved in the previous evening's fracas was bit like assuming all Britons know the queen but it was the only connection I had to anything Chinese.

"Practically nothing. Young lad, didn't look no older than about eighteen, skinny, tallish for a Gook." *Gook?* Robert Hare's, item 10, says that psychopaths have *'Poor behavioural control.'*

Do you want to find out just what that means?

"How tall compared to me?" He looked me up and down and I didn't like the thoughts I saw going on behind his eyes.

"Yeah. 'bout the same as you. Except 'e 'ad jet black 'air and slitty eyes." *Auditioning for the role of the Duke of Edinburgh, Ray?* Then I realised he could be describing Poo-brain, who had inherited far more of Granny's genes than I had or ... *The dead boy!*

"Do you know where he lived, friends, family,

anything?"

"Nah."

I snatched my mobile and eventually got through to Graeme. I allowed him to recap a few of the more memorable moments of the night before ... *Alone in the office, Graeme?* ... then interrupted him.

"Graeme, could you do me a favour ..."

"If I can."

"The lad who died at Overton on the night my family was killed. Have you managed to ID him yet?"

"No. Total blank so far. He may have been an illegal."

"Were there any PM photos?"

"Of course. Why?"

"Any chance you could send me a copy? Nothing gruesome, just the face."

"Well, it would be a bit irregular. Why do you need it?"

"I think I may be able to get you an ID."

"If you know somebody who has any information about him you should get them to come in—"

"That wouldn't be easy and if I'm wrong it would be a lot of work for no purpose. If you could just let me have a 'head and shoulders' ..."

He sighed. "Okay. Give me half an hour." Less than twenty minutes later my phone pinged and a text from my ex appeared. I opened the attachment and called Ray from the inner office where he had been drinking coffee and chain smoking.

"Unlikely, I know, but is that Hu?" He leaned over my shoulder – much closer than he had any need to – and studied the picture, at the same time sharing his own unique perfume. *Eau de Ray*.

"Yeah, that's the little slant." *Slant? How do you fancy another knee in the balls?* "Is 'e all right? 'e looks pig-sick."

"He's dead."

"What? In that picture? What sorta sicko takes pictures of dead people after they're dead?"

"Maybe people who realise you can't take pictures of dead people *until* after they're dead." I pushed him away from me with my shoulder. One thing about being around Ray, I could drop 'the act'. I didn't have to pretend to be 'normal people'. *Not smart enough to even notice, are you?*

"What 'appened to 'im?"

I wanted to see if he knew anything about it so I watched him carefully as I said, "He was taking part in a raid on a big house north of Brighton but one of the residents took a knife to him." He didn't react in any way other than I would expect from an innocent person.

"Bugger me. 'oo woulda thought the little git woulda been mixed up in anything like that." He tutted and shook his head before, still in my personal space, lighting a cigarette. I left him to it. *I give your new company about a month.*

Now I had another new lead to follow but would that, like every other lead so far, also vanish into a black hole?

* * *

As I drove away from Ray's office I called Graeme and tell him we had a hit on the identity of the dead boy. I gave him Ray's details and he said he'd have a squad car pick him up.

"I'll tell you something else: this Ray was Shepherd's driver and henchman. I bet if you start turning over the rocks in his background you'll find all sorts of slimy creatures lurking beneath."

"Friend of yours, is he?"

"I don't owe him anything, if that's what you're asking." *Call my Granny 'a Gook' and you deserve all you get.*

Graeme called me that afternoon. A body had turned up with half his head smashed in. It had been dumped in the footings of new office block being constructed near Gatwick Airport.

"They were due to pour the concrete at seven this morning. It appears whoever dumped him hoped he'd be buried but the hole was flooded by the rain last night. The builders were going to pump it out so some poor bugger went down with the hose and got a nice surprise to kick off his working day." I suddenly felt the full impact ... I had killed him. I'd realised, as I hit him, I was doing him a whole lot of no good ... but killing? Yet wasn't this something we psychos were supposed to be good at? Actually I felt nothing except a sense of satisfaction. He'd been aiming a gun at me and I had given him no more than he deserved. Nevertheless, I turned on 'the act'.

"Oh God! Are you sure it was the man from last night?" I tried to sound upset and concerned, my voice rose in volume and pitch. I think it worked.

"No, but it's early days. We're doing tests to see if it's his blood on your chain."

"What sort of trouble will I be in if it was me who killed him?" I gave him my little-girl-lost routine in case he was recording.

"If there were four of them, all firing guns at you, you must have been utterly terrified. I reckon a belt over the head with whatever you had in your hand will be classified as 'reasonable force'. We have recovered several bullets and cartridge cases from at least three different guns. We also have the broken window. The distribution of the shards indicate it was broken from inside the flat and forensics will be able to tell if it was smashed by a bullet. So, Josie, all in all I reckon you're in the clear."

"That's a relief." I put quite a tremor in my voice. *Nice*

touch that.

"Obviously, I won't be able to get involved personally but I'll have a quiet word in the right ear. That should do it."

"Do you know anything else about them? Who they are? Where they're from? Anything at all?"

"Sorry Josie. Nothing."

"So now what? I just carry on with my life and pretend last night never happened? Do I boost security and become a hermit in Fortress Josie?" I gave it the lot: tears, sobs, shaky voice. I didn't add: "Or do I run away again ... find a deep hole, climb in and pull the lid closed after me?" But that's what I felt like doing ... big time.

Have you ever been scared? I don't mean the-creak-in-the-darkness or walking-down-a-dark-alley-at-night type of scared ... I mean a sure, certain, unequivocal 'somebody is going to get you' terror. It muffles the mind and turns thinking into a Chinese puzzle. It makes problems insoluble. It feels like a weight is tied to every limb, every joint ... dragging you down. Life becomes impossible. I found myself crying for no discernible reasons at odd times and without warning. Worse, as far as I was concerned, is that this wasn't 'me'. My biggest problem at school, for instance, was that I wouldn't – just couldn't – cry, no matter what my classmates did to me. My psychopathy had always kept that sort of thing away from me.

In short, if somebody wanted to kill me I was beginning to feel it would be preferable if they just got on with it.

* * *

Something puzzled me. Graeme said the police had recovered bullets from three different guns. How could that be?

The next morning I rode back to the scene of the crime. The weather was fine and clear but cold and, for a change, dry. Apart from the boarded up window and sand on the road – probably to cover a pool of blood and brains – there were no signs of the previous night's drama. I parked Potex in the same spot I had the night before but almost superstitiously facing the opposite way. Then I realised I had no chain to lock her and put it on my mental shopping list.

I examined the scene.

I searched the road and found – right where I remembered it should be – a place where there was a chunk of asphalt missing. Several metres further on there was a chalk circle scribed on the road, maybe where a bullet had ended up.

The road sloped downhill to the bank of a river protected by concrete posts threaded with horizontal tubular steel. Two fences were parallel and overlapped by a metre giving pedestrian zigzag access to a set of steps, which dropped over a metre and a half to a stand of silver birches and a few other trees I didn't recognise: nature study having never been my forte. In one of the birches, only a few centimetres above the level of the road, was a hole in the trunk that looked as if it had been drilled with some sort of borer … maybe the police using specialist equipment to get a bullet out. With the back of my head against the hole I looked along the road and estimated the bullet must have travelled practically at ground level.

Back up the road I found a gouge in the asphalt exactly on the line between the pile of sand and the tree. Okay, I hadn't seen the man I'd killed fire at me but when I hit him he may have pulled the trigger and fired a bullet downward so it ricocheted off the road into the tree. Alternatively, it could have been fired by the other man. The birches were thin and well spaced so a direct hit was a huge coincidence but, in extremis, I could live with that.

Back at the river bank I found a second bored hole, this time even lower in a tree trunk no thicker than my thigh.

Really slim, okay? Another amazing coincidence as the hole was dead centre and had been bored right through the trunk.

Again with my back to the tree I could not work out any trajectory from where the man stood to where the bullet had struck. I followed the thick, black line of rubber left by my tyre to the point where I reasoned I had hit the shooter and the pile of sand confirmed it.

I walked around, retracing my escape route, endeavouring to recall all the events and their sequence. Then I remembered that, as he had gone over, the man I'd clipped with my bike had fired *up in the air*. I had to be sure. Back at the shop where I had purchased the padded envelope I bought an aerosol can of red paint which I used to paint the whole area of the tree around the bored hole. Standing at the point from which the gunman had fired I could not even see it. Only when I rolled Potex to about where he'd gone down, hoiked her onto the main stand and stood on the saddle could I see the red splodge. That was not a bullet fired by either of the men in the road. Could it have been from the window of the flat? But when I stood on the other side of the tree and peered through the hole the view was in the direction of the road. Unless bullets go round corners this one was not from the flat. The only way I could see the bullet getting there was if somebody had walked up to the tree and fired a gun at it from close range. *Curiouser and curiouser*.

Chapter Twenty-Two

Graeme was 'just passing' – he said – so he thought he would 'just drop in'. *Yeah, right.* But he did have some useful information for me. I made coffee and as we sat, side by side on my sofa overlooking a calm sea, he gave me what he had.

"Firstly, the labs have confirmed the blood on the chain was definitely from the dead man. But there's more." He sipped, almost as if stretching the tension on purpose. Sometimes I could hit him. *Actually, that's my default position.* He continued. "On an impulse I asked them to compare his DNA with that of the lad who was killed at Overton and they came back with a familial match."

"What? Brothers?"

"No, not that close; cousins perhaps. So it seems the murders of your family and the attempt on your life may well be connected."

"But who would want me dead? And why?" The words were out before I could censor them. It was not a hare I wanted him chasing.

"It might help if you told me the full story of you and this Shepherd and everything." *Damn.*

"I already have."

"No, the *full* story ... especially all the bits you've left out. You forget, I've spent my entire working life listening to people trying to convince me they were innocent of crimes I *knew* beyond any doubt they had committed. I can *smell* 'em, Josie."

So, with all my options exhausted, I did ... still heavily edited; I didn't mention the Russian mafia, ISIS or atom bombs but implied I suspected it was some sort of drugs deal that had gone wrong.

"That's why Shepherd is after me ... he wants the money."

"How much we talking?" he asked.

"Over a million." *I wasn't going to give him even a hint of the true amount.* His jaw dropped and his eyebrows took off towards heaven ... as if it had never occurred to him that so much money had ever been accrued in one place in the history of mankind. *Could that be genuine?*

"Where is it now? What did you do with it?"

I told him I had moved it from several places to a single account 'somewhere.' "Obviously, I'll hand it over to the authorities."

"So if you're prepared to hand it over, why go to all the trouble of spiriting it away in the first place?"

"I was worried if I surrendered it to Shepherd he may well kill me to tie up loose ends. I hoped I might be able to use it as a bargaining chip to get him off my back."

"That's a bit paranoid—"

"Really? You think so?" I shot to my feet and stood over him, hands on hips. "My friend, Diana, is dead – strangled – and he was probably the last person to see her alive and have every reason to believe he was responsible."

He shrugged. "Maybe you have a point." He took my wrist and eased me down beside him. "But about the money ..."

"Now he's gone that's no longer an issue so, if it's illegal, I'd just as soon get rid of it."

He seemed less than concerned. "If we don't know the provenance of the money or who has a claim on it, it may cause more problems than it solves."

"Except if the Chinese gangsters knew I had got rid of it, maybe they'd stop chasing me."

"And how would you tell them? Place an ad in the local paper?" I thought about it and came up blank. "Which bank is the money now in?"

I refused to tell him anything.

"I can see if Bruce had a million pounds of illegal money it could attract the attention of vultures," he said. "It's a crime with practically no risk for them. It appears that their original plan was to steal it from him. If they had managed it, he was hardly going to run to the police, was he? And if he didn't know who they were he wasn't even going to be able to set Shepherd on them."

"Except it all went wrong …"

He frowned and steepled his fingers. "As these things so often do. 'Mission Impossible' only works in films. It looks as if they planned to break in and coerce the information out of Bruce then get away with the money, free and clear but it all went south. A likely scenario is that Granny stabbed the boy and in the confusion Jeanne and Harry broke free and were shot. So instead of getting the information from your father by threatening violence against your family they had to try to torture it out of him but that resulted in his heart attack. Now they've not got the money but they have got murder charges hanging over them."

"In which case, wouldn't their best bet be to just keep their heads down?"

"Possibly. But, once they'd gone this far, they may consider that a better option is to see it through to the bitter end."

I contemplated this for a while. "I wonder how they knew about the money in the first place."

"This is just a guess but if this Hu was working for Shepherd in his legitimate business he may have somehow got wind of the deal Shepherd was cooking up with Bruce. He told his cousin and, with a couple of mates, they decided to rob them."

"How would they have got hold of the copy of my security card?"

"Did Bruce ever have client's call at Overton? Shepherd, for example?"

"Well yes. Occasionally. But only the most important ones. I suppose, with so much money involved, Shepherd is likely to have been one of them."

"There you are then." He pursed his lips and shook his head. "Bruce could have given it to him or Shepherd could have just picked it up when the opportunity arose."

"And Hu could have taken it from Shepherd ...?"

"Exactly. Of course, this is all conjecture but it hangs together."

"Wait up, Graeme." I put down my cup and swivelled to face him. "You're not off the hook yet. Can you explain how Shepherd's men turned up at my hotel a couple of hours after I told you the address?"

"Ah! I had the techies look at that. I put the address into my electronic diary. My diary is, of course, open to anybody with the appropriate access rights so they can book appointments and so on. It appears it was being regularly accessed by one of Leyland's team, somebody who did *not* have authority ... a DS called Mullin. Needless to say, he's now on 'gardening leave' for the foreseeable future."

Mullin! That also fitted in with what Ray had told me about Shepherd's mole in the police. That reminded me of something else. "What about Ray? Did you get anything out of him?"

"No. I had Leyland hold his feet to the fire but we've drawn a blank. I believe he genuinely knows nothing. The man's got a record as long as a roll of lavatory paper but all stupid, petty stuff: ABH, minor theft, receiving. He's too thick to do anything more ambitious." *I can believe that.* "If we had really stretched ourselves we could possibly have nailed him for something but he'd probably have ended up with no more than a fine. It wasn't worth our while so we let him go."

I cooked a simple meal of chicken breasts in a homemade Thai green curry sauce served on rice with stir fried mixed vegetables in an oyster sauce, though that was from a jar. He actually said he missed my cooking. Later, he demonstrated that it wasn't the only thing he missed.

Getting a lot from me you're not getting at home, aren't you Lover?

* * *

I ran. Hard. Thrashing my body, passing every other runner on the route. From Rottingdean along the coast past Hove Lagoon and back ... over sixteen miles. While I ran, I thought. Options and counter-options. Advantages and disadvantages. Pros and cons.

By the time I walked through my front door, breathless and dripping sweat, my decision was made. I had to leave. Somebody was out to kill me and I had no idea who or even, really, why. It's all right in books and films for an ordinary person to take on hordes of well armed, homicidal lunatics and even triumph but real life is not like that. And I didn't even have any idea who was after me so what chance did I have of fighting back?

I didn't want to die. Graeme had made it clear he was on my side and I was sure I could inveigle Adam into joining my little army and with their resources I would be better equipped than the average woman in the street. I also had Maxie, Stefan and a few others ... for what they were worth in this sort of situation. But I couldn't help feeling this game of lethal Blind Man's Bluff could only end in tears. *Probably mine.*

I needed a plan of campaign. Where to go? Hong Kong seemed the obvious place, at least as a first stop. I owned a flat there, I spoke Cantonese which, although not essential, would be helpful, I could stay there legally and I might find help in the form of Deng ... in the unlikely event he was still around.

The next problem would be to slip away unnoticed and that, again, would not be straightforward if somebody was keeping tabs on me ... and my skin crawled as if I had a watcher in every shadow, a stalker constantly behind me. How could anybody have known I was going to Shepherd's flat? Yet they did and arrived, armed and mob-handed, within an hour of my breaking in. Similarly with Shepherd's men turning up at my hotel. Were Shepherd and this Chinese lot working together? Or competing to get me? *I understand the attraction, boys, but let's not overdo it.*

On the other hand, if I managed to drop out of sight and get away I'd lose a lot: my flat, bike, car, a lot of my clothes but, hell, I had plenty in the bank to cover those.

And there was little brother to be taken care of.

So far there had been no indication of any attempt upon him even though he was a sitting duck. Anybody could have done anything when the Bablucs took him out for his daily constitutional and he was really obvious in his wheelchair so it wasn't as if he could be disguised with a false beard and dark glasses. Maybe whatever was going on was personal ... just against me. Still, if somebody wanted to get at me he would be a useful lever. That is, assuming they didn't know about my psychopathy which would mean, presumably, I wouldn't give a stuff about him anyway.

I needed help so I started with Graeme. He had access to the right resources and I had a certain amount of leverage on him.

"I've decided to go away," I told him as we sat in bed, side by side, backs propped against the padded headboard. He sipped a glass of white. I also had a glass but had barely moistened my lips with it.

"Why?" He looked at me abruptly, eyebrows raised.

"Surely it can't be that much of a shock that I would want to get away from a place where people are trying to kill me."

He pursed his lips and nodded. "Where to?" *Like I would tell you where I'm really going.*

"I thought maybe South America or maybe Australia. Somewhere I have no contacts and I'm not known. Somewhere these people will not think to look for me."

"There's no need for anything that drastic. I've already said we can organise a safe house—"

"For how long?" I turned on him, glaring. It always made him back down. "It's probably all right to keep a witness out of harm's way until some gangster gets sent down but you have no idea how long you'd have to keep me bottled up. In fact, even if the danger was gone you'd have no way of knowing it had. So would you keep me locked away for the rest of my life? I'd have to give everything: my friends, my hobbies, my business."

"You lose all that if you cleared off to Australia …"

"But at least I'd be free to make new friends or to start a new business … to start a whole new life."

He shrugged and his face softened. "Any idea when? I'll miss you." He pulled me close. *Really? What will you miss the most?*

"It's not simple," I mumbled into his chest. "I can't simply buy a ticket to Caracas or Melbourne and jump on a plane. These people seem to have far too much information on my movements. They turn up unexpectedly, apparently with full knowledge that I'll be there. Then there's baby brother. Even if I do manage to evade them there's nothing to stop them doing something to him to 'persuade' me to come back so I need to ensure he's safe."

"How will you do that?"

So I told him. He was so keen to get me into a safe house. Well I wasn't going. But Harrison could. I would send the Bablucs back home for another month's holiday and then Graeme would supervise Poo-brain's move to a new home complete with a fresh set of helpers. That way the Bablucs would have no knowledge of his new location and wouldn't be able to betray him even under extreme pressure. It was likely he wouldn't even notice the change in his circumstances so there was no concern about keeping him in Witness Protection for an extended period. As soon as he was settled I would do my vanishing act again until I could work out how to slip out of the country and away. After a month or so Graeme, if he thought it was all clear, could bring Harrison back to the flat and the Bablucs would take over again.

We discussed other aspects: where I would hide, how I could get false papers, how I would manage financially although, as far as he knew, I had a million pounds squirreled away.

"I'm still worried about one thing," he looked concerned. "You won't be able to put everybody you know in a safe house. What would stop these men snatching any of them and forcing you to come home." *Baby, you don't know how little effect that would have on me.*

"That would only work if they could contact me and tell me what they had done. When I say I'm going to vanish I mean 'vanish' … totally, completely, off-the-face-of-the-earth type vanish. All means of applying pressure would likewise vanish right along with me." He looked absolutely stricken. *Yes!*

Chapter Twenty-Three

"Hello, Ray," I gushed. He sat at the desk in the inner office of his business empire, pretending to labour at his keyboard, unaware I could see the on-screen card game reflected in the glass of a picture on the wall behind him.

"What ya want?" He jerked to his feet and I was sure that, but for the intervening desk, he would have launched himself at me.

"I think I can put a bit of business your way."

"You grassed me up to the filth." His voice was a snarl and his hands became bowling ball sized weapons of mass destruction.

"Of course I didn't. They were investigating a murder Shepherd was in the frame for. You were his right hand man so of course they snatched you. If you stand next to a target you might get hit by shrapnel."

"Tell me why I shouldn't wring your scrawny little neck." He stepped around the desk and towered over me. *You wearing the cricket box? I'm still wearing the kneecap.*

"Because I've got money you can earn … and I'm guessing your little business empire has not put you on the path to millionairedom yet." He looked sullen and his body language told me he was still deciding whether to strangle me.

"Go on then. What ya want?"

"I need a passport …"

"So go to the Passport Office, they do a nice little number for about seventy sovs."

I squared up to him. "Don't jerk me about, Ray. You know what I mean. Your boss, Shepherd, is out to get me so I need to get away for a while and to do that I need a hooky passport. Can you get me one?"

Now it was his turn to do the squaring up ... and he won at a walk. Instinctively, I felt for my knife. "I don't care what you say, I think you 'ad something to do with the pigs pulling me in so give me a bleeding good reason why I should 'elp you." He breathed stale ale and fresh cigarette fumes in my face.

"I can give two actually." I tried to appear absolutely calm under his looming bulk. I'm not sure I pulled it off but counted on him being too thick to see. "Firstly, if you put me on to somebody who can fix me up with a passport then you can be sure I won't be giving you away to any police because you'd have something to use against me and I'd be out the country anyway."

That seemed to sway him and I saw the menace in his frame ease slightly. "What's second?"

"I'll give you a grand over whatever the supplier charges me." That did it. He pulled out a mobile, minute in his gorilla-sized fist, and found a number. When the call was answered he spoke to somebody called 'Cal'. After he hung up he told me to go to Brighton Station and get four passport photos from the booth then get the train to Victoria where I was to wait in the cafe next to the exit to the underground station. I had to take a thousand pounds and had two and a half hours get there.

My 'date' kept me waiting for forty minutes and when he arrived – a black man in immaculately tailored pinstripe suit and a tie that may have belonged to some minor public school – he didn't even sit but just said, "Who sent you?"

"Ray." I took the envelope with the money and photographs from my bag and held them out. "It's all there."

"I know." He took them and walked off.

"Wait!" I called after him. "When will I get it?"

"Ask Ray," he said without looking round. Ray hadn't got my number ... he was the last person I'd give it to ... and I didn't have his so I would have to trek back to his office. I kept a low profile for two days before I dropped by but he wasn't there and the following day he had no news but on the third trip he pulled a well worn passport out of his desk drawer, thumbed through it, smirked at the picture and held it out to me but wouldn't let go until I crossed his palm with banknotes.

Phase one complete.

The next day the Bablucs took Poo-brain for his morning walk. The weather played its part: overcast, chilly and windy. They parked next to an ambulance in a car park in Saltdean, levered him into his wheelchair and wrapped him against the elements in a bright tartan blanket. Halfway through the tunnel to the beach they encountered a young man doing a similar favour for an elderly relative in an identical chair – except that the invalid was swathed in dull brown. The exchange was swift: blankets and hats swapped, wheelchairs spun through one hundred and eighty degrees and they emerged, as any watcher would have expected, pushing the easily recognisable form of my brother. The real Harrison was now being loaded into the ambulance clearly signed as belonging to a local care home for the elderly. An hour later the Bablucs returned and the fit, young plain clothed copper leapt from the chair and caught a bus back to the local nick. Soon after, the Bablucs took a taxi to the station for the start of their journey home and, at about the time they arrived at Luton airport, Poo-brain was being settled into his new room somewhere in Oxford. I hated letting him out of my sight but could see no option.

I kept an appointment with Malone where I signed lots of forms. As Harrison's next of kin I had become his guardian by default. In my absence somebody else needed to do the job and I passed the responsibility on to Malone and his partnership. I also signed over my flat to my brother's trust fund. Malone already administered the fund so it made sense that they deal with all other aspects of his care.

Phase two complete.

I called ahead so Becky was expecting me but Adam wasn't. That way he had no excuse to avoid me. He bristled when I walked in and I waited for Becky to set out on her safari to the kitchen before I told him what I wanted.

"I need you to book me a flight, please."

"Why don't you do it yourself?"

"Because with these maniacs after me I've decided I need to get away. The problem is that I don't know who I can trust so here's the plan." I got him settled in front of his computer. "I want you to go online and use your credit card to book me a Business Class ticket with British Airways to Dubai in this name …" I put a slip of paper in front of him with the name Arabella Wilson written on it, he just raised an eyebrow but said nothing. "Next week, returning two weeks later," I added.

"Business Class?" I heard a sneer in the words. *Jealous?* I ignored him so he continued. "I can see why you're using a false name but why wait a week before you leave and why return so soon after?"

"Several reasons. For all I know they may be watching the airports. If I go into hiding for a while then maybe – just maybe – they'll assume they've missed me and give up watching. I need a return ticket because many countries won't let you enter unless you've already booked your passage out. Dubai because I can enter on a British passport without getting a visa in advance."

"Then there's your next problem … where will you get a passport? You could end up in real bother if they catch you in a place like Dubai with a forgery."

"Don't worry. I've got it covered." I wrote him a cheque to cover the cost.

At the front gate, with Becky watching from the door, he gave me a chaste kiss goodbye and I whispered in his ear that at least his dirty little secret was getting on the aeroplane with me.

I dropped my luggage at Maxie's. She had promised to take it to Victoria and leave it in a left luggage place near the coach station.

My final stop was to call in on Stefan. I knew the band wasn't playing so I persuaded him to smuggle me into the back of his van and drive me to Leeds. That night. Without warning. I was fairly sure we weren't followed and the only items I took were my small overnight case with a change of clothes, cheap makeup, my handbag and a money belt with plenty of cash. Anything else I needed on my sojourn I would buy as I went along.

From Leeds I went by National Express coaches by a circuitous route to Birmingham and arrived at my digs the day before my rent was due to expire. The old dear told me off because I hadn't informed her I would be away or where I was going, for how long or when I'd be back. I was exhausted, stiff and utterly, utterly fed up so I snapped at her.

"You're not my bloody mother." I got right in her face. "I've paid my bloody rent so I'm entitled to come and go as I wish." I thrust a bundle of notes at her. "Here's my next month's rent." That smoothed her ruffled feathers.

Then, despite the horrific bed, I slept for fourteen hours straight.

* * *

With nothing to do but kill time for a week, I ran … lots … used local gyms and swimming baths, frequented local coffee bars and restaurants ... but not the same one too often and not once used a credit card. I insisted on sitting near the rear of restaurants facing the door with my back to the wall and if anywhere couldn't accommodate me on those terms I left and found somewhere that could. I made sure I was back in my hovel early each evening. I never went anywhere without my knife: either up my sleeve, in a pocket or in my handbag. I'm not normally a nervous person but the 'not knowing' was driving me insane.

Whenever I was on the street I found myself constantly looking over my shoulder. The weather aided my paranoia by being cold and wet so everybody was muffled, with covered heads and half hidden faces. Everyone looked as if they were trying to hide from me: skulking in the shadows or shop doorways. Sometimes it felt I was being followed only for the stalker to disappear when I rounded the next corner. At other times I'd be on an empty road but convinced eyes were watching from some window or alleyway.

I fought the feelings, did hand to hand combat with the almost overwhelming urge to run and run and run until nobody could catch me, run until I could run no more, run until my heart burst in my chest.

Eventually I stayed in my room until, two days before I was due to leave, I was driven out by hunger. Needing to do something – anything – I broke. Ignoring my own rule I caught the train to Solihull where I chose a phone booth at random and called Graeme. I dialled '141' to hide my number. I was bounced from one extension to another – further fuelling my paranoia – but when I finally got through to him, he assured me Harrison was fine and had settled in to his new environment well. He had a team of trained nurses and therapists attending him and was in a safe location, with twenty-four hour security, well away from anywhere the villains might think of looking for him. This settled my concerns on that score but then, all the way back to my bedsit I castigated myself for my weakness in making the call convinced that, despite all my precautions, the police and villains would have the means to trace me because of it.

By the day of my departure I just wanted to be away and was at the bus stop by eight ... more than an hour before the scheduled departure time, standing, huddled in my hoodie under a cheap overcoat against a penetrating drizzle aggravated by an insistent wind. Once more I used long distances coaches, zigzagging across the country; paying cash. I'd left my home a week before with over twelve thousand pounds in cash and still had most of it left, hidden in the belt around my waist. The single advantage of my downmarket, undercover lifestyle was that it was cheap.

The final leg of the journey finished just before five in the evening when I was deposited at Victoria: still cold and with the added attraction of diesel fumes and shoving crowds. I kept a sharp eye out for any suspicious activity or anybody hanging about without purpose ... but at a coach station that was practically everybody, so I took a chance and made a beeline for the left luggage office and was relieved to find my luggage awaiting me. Maxie had kept her promise.

Nearby, unable to shake my habit of sitting at the back of the café I grabbed a coffee and a salad and sat over it, recovering from the journey, collecting my thoughts and sorting through my chattels to ensure I had everything I would need for my new life. All appeared to be in perfect order except I noticed a small rip in the shiny, orange lining of my saxophone case and wondered how I could have done that. Still, it gets a bit of a pounding during gigs and if that was the only problem I had to face then everything was fine.

Next stop Heathrow. Rather than struggle on the coach with two suitcases, a shoulder bag, handbag and, of course, my saxophone, I took a black cab. The traffic was busy through central London but slackened off as we reached the A4 and we travelled west at near the speed limit. Nice and easy towards the M4, which would lead right to the door of Terminal 5. Tired buildings, terraces of houses and nondescript shops, slid past windows obscured by a persistent drizzle. The anxiety of the past few days slowly seeped away as if it were dripping onto the road as it passed beneath our wheels.

I took out my round, white calfskin case, flipped up the lid into a laptop dressing table ... with my *real* cosmetics ... and started my routine; so familiar, so reassuring.

In the past few days I'd had to put up with the gungy, stained bath shared by, it seemed, half the lowlife of Birmingham. What I wanted was water so hot I turned lobster-bright, bubbles tickling my chin, perfume that hung in the air and clung to my skin. I wanted candles and music and lotions and potions. But they would have to wait until the other end of the journey. If I couldn't have a decadent bath, I did have my Dior *Hydralife* cleanser. Then Chanel *Les Beiges*: like ambrosia for the skin after the tat I'd been using. Layer on layer, slowly, luxuriously applied. The drab, dowdy frump in the mirror, slowly dissolved and *I* reappeared: confident, elegant. The real me. *Whatever that is.*

There is a spa at Terminal 5. I wouldn't have time for any real treatment but my nails needed urgent attention so I would have them done there.

I relaxed. I probably even smiled. Sudden sun glinted off a bright glass of a new office block.

There were still four hours before my flight so I felt confident ... until we started to slow and move to the left. We were on the slip road up to M4 and the last leg of my journey to freedom.

I leaned forward and spoke through the aperture in the toughened plastic screen. "Why are we pulling over?" The nervousness that had dissipated as I got closer to escape started to flood back like worms burrowing into my brain.

"Police." He jerked a thick thumb backwards over his right shoulder and I saw the silver car, reflective blue and yellow squares on its flanks, lights flashing but without sirens, easing past us. Relieved, I slumped back in my seat, expecting it to hurtle past but instead, as the taxi eased over to the edge of the road, it pulled in front of us and the uniformed officer in the passenger seat leaned out of the window and pointed at the hard shoulder.

With both cars stopped he climbed out and walked back, pulled my door open and gave me his best 'meet the public' smile. "Ms Trelawney?" he asked, ignoring the driver.

I hesitated. "Yes?" Even I could hear the concern in my voice.

"I have an urgent message from ACC Bergomay-Trewlawney …"

Suddenly all the irrational fears of the past week hurtled back with full force … except they were no longer irrational. "What is it? Is something wrong?"

"I'm afraid I can't say, Ma'am. The ACC has passed a message through to the Met asking us to intercept you with an urgent message—"

"But how did he know where I was?" Then another thought struck me. "My brother …?"

"Please come with me." Without waiting for my response, he leaned over, hefted my two suitcases and marched off, dumping them in the boot of the police car. Still I didn't move. When he returned he smiled at me though the open door. "Don't worry about your flight. We'll take care of all that and, if possible, still get you there in good time." Filled with trepidation but seeing no alternative, I slid out and followed him towards the police car, suspicions high and

Runner

wondering if I should have just told the taxi driver to keep going and take me to the airport. Even if I had, with blue flashing lights in his rear view mirror, he'd probably have ignored me.

"Oi! What about me fare?" the cabbie, leaning out of his window, yelled at our backs and the constable dropped my other two bags beside their companions and walked back to him. For a few seconds they engaged in quiet discussion, heads almost touching. I wasn't sure, but the policeman may have passed over a banknote.

He caught up with me in time to open the rear passenger door and hold it for me. As I sat, about to swivel my legs round and slide in, I looked down at his shoes ... black trainers! A policeman in trainers? I half rose, intending to sprint back to the taxi but it pulled out into the stream of traffic and sped off. At that moment the driver reached through the gap between the front seats and grabbed my right wrist, yanking me off balance so the back of my head cracked into the doorframe. Panicking, I struggled but to no avail. The standing man lunged at me. I lashed out with my foot but he grabbed my left arm while the driver continued to heave my other arm through the gap, levering my elbow backwards against the edge of his seat. There was a sharp sting in the back of my hand and it felt as if I was filling up with warm water. As it reached my head it brought a swirling fog and blackness.

* * *

Everything after that was a misty haze.

I sort of remember being driven, slumped across the rear seat: it could have been minutes or days but I had the feeling it was a short journey. On another occasion I was dragged by my legs out the door of the car with somebody catching my head before it pounded onto the road. In later images I was bumped around in the filthy back of a panel van that smelled of vegetables and earth. I had impressions of a long journey, occasionally interrupted with stops that brought more injections. Sometimes we were on smooth, high speed roads at others short, stop-start legs with many turns and lots of jerky acceleration that caused me to slither backwards on the cold metal floor until I brought up hard against the rear doors followed by harsh braking when I reversed my track and slammed into the bulkhead separating the cargo bay from the cab.

My memories feel like a single, contiguous stream but the images overlapped, like I was in the car and the van simultaneously and it is likely I slipped in and out of consciousness. On a final stop I was dragged to the back of the van and given one last injection that threw me off the cliff of consciousness.

I awoke somewhere cold, ill lit and oppressive that felt underground like a cellar or dungeon. The walls were bare brick, the ceiling was peeling plaster with a single, large diameter pipe – like a domestic sewer pipe – running across the centre. In one place a joint dripped, adding to a loathsome puddle on the bare concrete floor: a liquid definition of my situation. There was the sickening reek of effluent. I didn't even know which country I was in.

I was prostrate on one of a pair of iron-framed beds on a bare, stained mattress. My right wrist was handcuffed to an iron ring bolted to the wall. The skin where the bracelet rubbed was already raw and seeping red. My head throbbed so hard I could barely focus. I was bruised, battered and I had a split lip.

I had wet myself.

Chapter Twenty-Four

I guess I lay there all night but all my jewellery, including my wristwatch, was gone and, with the constant illumination of a dim, unshaded bulb, there was no way of assessing the passage of time. I considered slipping off my disgusting, and now freezing, trousers but I felt vulnerable enough as it was.

I dozed and woke, dozed and woke. With my body still suffering from the effects of the explosion, coupled with my inability to move and the conditions, I was feeling stiffer and sicker by the minute.

Five metres beyond the foot of the bed was a door – steel with peeling, green paintwork – and what appeared to be a peephole. At regular intervals, maybe about once an hour, it would suddenly emit a bright light as a flap was slid aside then it would go dark, presumably when an eye peered in at me. Each time I made an obscene gesture at the watcher. I heard voices beyond the door but couldn't make out any words.

Occasionally I would hear a lavatory flush and water would rush and rattle through the pipe. The joint dripped. The smell got worse, augmented by the stench of stale, body temperature urine from my clothes. It got colder. My wrist chafed.

I turned my back on the watchers and cried.

* * *

I was wrenched into full consciousness as the door burst open and crashed against the wall. A seemingly endless stream of men came barrelling in, reminiscent of televised police raids on a drug dens. Each appeared to be shouting at the top of his lungs: a wordless, meaningless cacophony of noise intending to confuse, intimidate and subdue me.

It almost worked.

Five east Asian men: blue jeans, trainers and white tee-shirts, lined the side and foot of the bed and, at a signal from the man alongside me, short with broad shoulders and a face like the full moon, went silent. He leaned over me: face millimetres from mine, and screamed in Mandarin.

"Where is the money, whore?" He swung a hand at my cheek and the blow snapped my head around and made my ear whistle. I tasted blood and it felt as if one of my teeth had loosened. He screamed at me again, the same thing, over and over, each time accompanied by another brutal slap.

"I don't understand you," I screamed, in English, at the top of my lungs.

That gave him pause.

He looked at one of the others – a tall, slim and slightly effeminate lad – and, still in Mandarin, snapped, "Zheu, you said she spoke Putonghua."

The youth looked at his feet and wouldn't meet the aggressor's eyes. Maybe the thug didn't reserve his violence for women. "I don't know." He also spoke in Mandarin, his voice hesitant and querulous. "The Grey Man said she did."

The Grey Man?

"What did he actually say? Tell me his actual words."

"Er … he said, 'She speaks Chinese'." He said the last phrase in English in an almost music hall parody Chinese accent then, switching back to Mandarin, added, "He said she was born in China. Maybe she's bluffing."

"I speak Cantonese," I volunteered in Cantonese then I had to repeat it in English when they didn't understand me. *So you don't speak it.*

"Where were you born?" the boss demanded in English.
"Hong Kong."

He snapped a curse at Zheu then turned his attention back to me, this time speaking slowly in English. "Where is money?" I braced myself for the slap but it didn't come. Maybe he was only violent in Mandarin.

"What money?" That worked. The blow made me dizzy and it was some time before I could focus again.

"You take money from Russia man. You put money somewhere. I need know where is money. You tell me." Slap. "Tell me." Slap. "I need you tell where is money." Slap.

The strange thing was that, after a few blows, the pain from subsequent slaps seemed less severe. Was it too much to hope that he was running out of steam?

Maybe it was my adrenalin.

Maybe it was my natural resentment. I'm a 'doer' not a 'doee'. 'Do as you would be done by' has never been in my lexicon. Mine was 'do instead of being done by.'

I tried a new tack. "I don't know what you are talking about." My voice was raspy from thirst and the words were distorted by my now swollen face and lips.

"You tell!" he screamed along with the expected slap. On and on. Still I insisted I knew nothing and the more he hit me the more determined I became. I had no idea how far he was prepared to go. Probably it was this lot who had taken the pot shots at me outside Shepherd's flat. If he became convinced I was not going to talk he might do the same to me. Conversely, I was certain that if I *did* tell him, he'd have no reason to keep me alive and every reason to get rid of me. And nobody knew where I was. Anybody who would be interested: Maxie, Stefan, Adam, Graeme, thought I had caught an aeroplane and never expected to hear from me again. If my tormentor carried on the way he was going, that may soon become a reality.

I must have passed out because when I came round four of the men were clustered outside the open door. They spoke in Mandarin making no effort to conceal what they were saying. *That had been a worthwhile bluff.*

"She's never going to talk," said a harsh, grating voice I hadn't heard before.

"We need to find that money." The boss.

"Let's just bump her off." The unknown voice.

"No, Qi, we cannot do that." That was Zheu.

I was sorting them out. I had a face, name and voice for Zheu and a face and voice for the boss. Now there was a name and voice for this newest speaker.

"Why not?" The boss again. I was sure I would live or die on his say-so and it didn't sound good.

"Look Cho, the Grey Man said we can do whatever we like to her but we *must not* kill her." *Thank you, Zheu. The only good news on a terrible day.* "Anyway, what about the money he promised. Are you just going to give it up?"

So 'Cho' … the boss.

"What do you suggest, then?" This was another new voice. "Seems you can slap her until her head or your hand falls off."

"Got a better idea, Tung?" *That's four. Now only the absent man to go.* Tung didn't answer and after a while they slammed the door and, despite the fact that I was still chained to the wall, turned a key in the lock.

Echoing footsteps ascended hard – maybe concrete – stairs. I needed to pee and, despite having involuntarily done it once, was not going to piss in my pants again so I angled off the bed and did it on the floor where it trickled in a miniature stream to meld with the effluent lake.

I was starving but, far worse, I was absolutely gasping for a drink. I needed a plan. My first priority was to persuade

165

them to let me live. Only after that could I consider trying to improve my conditions. Later – maybe a long way down the track – escape. At least the thought process amused me. Hare's item 13:' *Lack of realistic long-term goals*'. What would Professor Hare expect a normal person to do, I wondered, just give up?

Sod him. Illegitimi non carborundum. I knew those hours spent conjugating Latin verbs would come in useful.

For thirty-two years I had survived in society by acting a part. Now I was going to have to call on all that practice to survive.

It was several hours before I next heard footsteps so I twisted around until my head hung backwards over the edge of the bed and kept my eyes shut. Somebody lifted my head by the hair and I just groaned. He slapped my face with the sort of slap used to encourage people to rouse rather than the brutal assaults of earlier. I allowed myself another weak groan.

"What's wrong with her?" This was Tung. I eased my eyelids so I could peer through the curtain of my lashes. He was medium height, slim with a 'pretty' face and full lips. Under other circumstances I could have quite fancied him. Today I wouldn't whip him with my pissed-in pants to put out flames.

"She may be dehydrated. Get her a drink." I heard retreating footsteps which soon returned and within a few seconds Tung was supporting my head while dripping water over my parched lips. *Bless you, Tung. Maybe I* would *piss on you then.*

Eventually, after I had swallowed nearly a glassful, I 'recovered' and with much groaning and a little coughing, 'regained consciousness'.

He lowered me back onto the mattress. "Better?"

"Yes. A little." I gave him my 'Little girl lost, please

help me, big, strong man.' I saw him going for it. I put a gentle hand on his wrist and his eyes jerked towards it. "Any chance of something to eat?" Pleading voice, flutter of eyelids, little brave smile.

"I see." He stood.

"Wait," his companion said. "Cho said make her as uncomfortable as possible."

"There is a difference between 'uncomfortable' and 'dead'." He left but returned shortly and dropped a crumpled box containing a half eaten pizza on the bed beside me then they left me to eat it. It was greasy, stone cold and tasted like heaven. I forced myself to eat slowly, chewing each mouthful to make it last, resisting the urge to wolf it down. I didn't know when – or if – the next meal would arrive.

When they returned, Tung carried another glass of water. I drank half, saving some for later then asked if could use the loo. They refused but I impugned their manhood ... "Scared you won't be able to restrain me" ... so they unshackled me and escorted me up one floor. It looked like an ordinary suburban house.

I heard them outside the door as I used the filthy, stained lavatory. I scrubbed my teeth with a wet finger and had a strip wash with some wetted paper. There was no lock but the choice was getting vulnerably naked or staying filthy. Pulling my trousers back on filled me with revulsion. I contemplated escape through the tiny window but as I eased it ajar the door crashed open and Cho stormed in.

"Out!" he screamed at me ... his default volume. He grabbed my arm and dragged me. My legs slipped out from under me so I slithered along the wooden floor and then bumped painfully, bone-jarringly down the concrete steps, the rough surface stripping the skin off my toes. I didn't fully appreciate his strength until he hefted me off the floor and flung me on the bed as if I were a toy. He turned and screamed abuse at the two men who had followed him down. They looked by the floor and took the torrent without comment. He finished off with, "Watch her!" and stormed out, slamming the floor behind him, deafening us all.

They chained me back to the wall. *Bugger! I hoped you'd forget about that.* Then left.

Hours passed; maybe a night.

Cho returned, two henchmen I'd not seen before trailing in his wake. Between them, they supported a young, blonde girl: skinny with gaunt features. I could see her skeleton through her skin like a medical student's diagram all overlaid with the red, blue and mauve evidence of a severe and sustained beating. She was naked except for a thick belt around her waist fitted with chains that bound her wrists down to her sides. Several turns of wide, brown tape enveloped her head as a gag.

Cho turned and took her from the other two, sweeping her up in his arms like a groom carrying his new bride across the threshold and held her up to me.

"This Natalia. She my girl but she decide no work for me. Girl must learn do what I say." He turned and threw her onto the other bed and one of the new arrivals added a further chain to her wrist and snapped it onto a ring similar to the one that held me.

Cho looked at me over his shoulder. "You watch. You learn." He ripped the tape off her mouth, eliciting a scream, and stalked out with his minions in his wake.

The girl, no more than about fourteen or fifteen, lay bound, naked and unable to move. I spoke to her, voice soft, to see if she had any useful information but, apart from confirming her name, she just added a few words in a tongue I didn't recognise. I guess she had no English but her tearful eyes on mine spoke all the words she needed.

Psychopaths are not great at reading expressions but I

didn't need an instruction manual to know that she was totally, completely, utterly terrified.

Chapter Twenty-Five

Their next visit seemed to have taken days to arrive. I would have gladly stretched the time to infinity. I had no idea what was coming but could only imagine it how would compare to things so far.

The door clanged open and the original five men trooped in, their faces hard and set. Their expressions said they knew things were going to get worse. Much worse.

"You watch," Cho said to me. His voice was icy.

Chinese is a tonal language and many native speakers, when they learn a non-tonal language such as English, never learn to use tones as we do, to emphasise, indicate questions and so on. This means their voices tend to be flat, with no inflections. It can be far more chilling than any ranting and abuse.

He loomed over the girl as she shrank away from him, legs scrabbling, whimpering, eyes wide. He gave her his trademark slap. "You know why you here?"

She nodded: a short, jerky, barely discernible movement of the head. I'm sure she didn't understand but his tone clearly demanded an affirmative. "You work for me. You do what I tell. You earn money." He leaned close, mouth just millimetres from her ear and screamed. "WHY YOU NOT DO IT?" She whimpered again and cowered away, her back pressed hard against the bare brick wall.

He stood back and, with jerks of his head, signalled two of his men forward and switched to Mandarin. "She has soiled herself. Clean her up."

They unchained her and, taking an arm each, hauled her to her feet although her legs seemed inadequate to the task of supporting her so they had to hold her upright. Her head lolled forwards and her face was hidden behind a curtain of hair. One of the others opened the locks on the belt that held her arms down at her side but left the chains dangling from her wrists. A third man slung a short length of chain over the waste pipe then between them they attached her handcuffs one to either end so she hung, toes off the floor, swaying gently, head hanging forward with her chin on her chest.

The fourth man had attached a hose to the tap and turned it on full pressure then, as she writhed and swung, they blasted her with a jet of water. What they did to her with that hose, that powerful jet, wasn't just a hosing down to clean her but an exercise in torture. She screamed and writhed, at one point trying to avoid the agony by levering herself upwards by the strength of her arms like a gymnast performing chin ups. Blood trickled down her arms where the bracelets lacerated her wrists but was instantly diluted and swept away by the jet.

I looked away but Cho strode over and grabbed me by the hair. "You watch. You see what happen to girl when no obey. She think she run away and I no find her. She fool." He yanked my head towards him. "You fool." Then he twisted my face back towards the scene. "Watch."

Eventually, after what seemed like hours, they stopped and left her hanging, swinging gently. She made no sound or movement so I couldn't make out if she was exhausted, unconscious or even dead.

From her point of view, death may have been preferable.

On Cho's instruction, the man called Zheu left while Qi and Tung gingerly lifted the fouled and streaked mattress off the bed, handling it as if it might explode, and hosed it down before propping it against the wall. Zheu returned with a fresh, but badly stained mattress and dropped it on the bed.

Tung unsnapped one of the locks and the girl collapsed

to the floor. Her head made a thud on the slick concrete and the chain rattled over the pipe and landed on her. Zheu and Qi dragged her by the arms, face down, head hanging, back to the bed, and flung her on it, face up. I heard her grunt at the impact. There was a smear of blood on her upper lip and a flow ran across her forehead and down her temple, saturating her hair.

Then they started on her.

They hurt her. They hurt her in ways evil men have always hurt women. They hurt her in ways that permanently damage and destroy. They hurt her in ways I could never have conjured up when planning the fate of my worst enemy. And *I'm* the psychopath! They hurt her for hour after hour. If they wanted to send a message to me they were succeeding. As each took his turn at some new and imaginative horror, the others cheered and jeered: raucous, spurring, encouraging like some sickening medieval sport. This must be what it was like in the Roman arenas.

When God makes psychopaths he leaves something out: empathy. We're unable to identify with others: to 'feel' their distress. But we still have all the other faculties so although I could not sympathise with the girl's distress, I was fully cognisant this was a demonstration, aimed at me ... that sooner or later everything they did to her was going to be inflicted on me. My stomach churned and bile rose in my throat. I wanted to vomit but held it down rather than let them see the effect on me. I had no idea how to react. I didn't know her, had never even exchanged a word with her and I was already sure – the moment they had brought her in – that they intended to murder her. If they killed her, what was it to me? There was absolutely nothing I could do about it anyway. Item 8: '*Callous /lack of empathy.*'

But I could not remain impassive as it would not aid my assertion that I didn't know anything about the money. The only way I hoped to convince them that I was unable to tell them what they wanted to know was if they thought I was terrified beyond reason but still adamant I knew nothing anyway.

So I went to 'Plan B'.

Reasoning that a 'normal' person would be distressed and plead for leniency for their victim I went for it big time. I cried, I screamed, I lunged against the chain that held me and clung onto Cho's sleeve until he flung me off.

"You want stop, you tell me where money." *So you get the money and I end up buried in some foundations.* "You tell or she suffer more. See what happen her. When we finish we do to you. Until you tell. If you tell I let both free." *Yeah right.* I reckoned I would remain alive as long as he wanted something from me ... and not one nanosecond longer.

From time to time they would stop. Sometimes they would even go away, leaving the girl, little more than a piece of blood smeared meat. She lay, unmoving, the only sign she was still alive was the rise and fall of her chest and the occasional long, drawn out moan.

Every time I thought that it was over, that they were satiated, that they'd had their fill of the sadism, the hate, the torture, the pain.

Each time they returned and started again.

Bit by bit my resolve weakened. There was a tiny voice whispering in my ear that he may be telling me the truth ... that he would let us go. I came so close to relenting but logic always won out and I beat the thought down, telling myself the consequences of revealing what they wanted to know.

Once more they finished and she lay, beaten and semiconscious.

I wondered if it was another 'phantom break' but, as their absence grew longer, I began to hope that I'd beaten them: that I had thwarted them in their attempts to make me tell.

They returned. I held my breath. Would it recommence? Would they try something new? Would they start on me?

Cho carried a roll of brown, shiny parcel tape: identical to what had been used to gag her when she arrived. Two of his men grabbed her arms and one held her head off the bed by her hair. Cho held my gaze with his own, his face a mask, his eyes dark, unblinking as he slowly and deliberately wrapped turn after turn around the girls face. He started at her chin. The next turn covered the first by half the width of the tape. Then again. And again. The final turn strained across her nose, flattening it, covering her nostrils so she was completely unable to breathe.

I saw her chest pumping as her air-deprived lungs toiled for respite and her body thrashed and jerked, her legs kicked. To avoid his gaze I dropped my head and her eyes met mine – a plea for assistance I was incapable of providing. It seemed destined to never end but eventually her thrashing stopped and she subsided, lying unmoving, inert.

If I could have got loose for a second I would have used every single trick I had learned in kickboxing on the odious Cho. He would find that women are not the only ones who can be taught lessons.

Suddenly, unexpectedly, viciously Cho ripped that last turn of tape off her nose and crossed to stand over me. Her chest heaved. I heard her sucking air into her starved lungs: a whistling, rushing near scream as if her airways were inadequate to the demand.

"You like?" He grinned and, for the first time, I noticed one of his upper incisors was gold. *Give me the inkling of a chance and you'll be digging that out of your next shit, Buster.* "You next." Slap.

Cho returned to the bed and straddled her. I thought he

was going to rape her again but what happened was worse. He knelt on the bed, one knee either side of her chest and, while one of his henchmen again held her head, he gripped her nose between finger and thumb.

Once more she began to thrash, flinging her head from side to side as much as her captor would allow, her legs hammered as if she were running a race and she scrabbled at the material of Cho's trousers with desperate fingernails. Slowly, over a period that was probably no more than a minute but seemed to last an eternity, her desperate fight ended as the life ebbed from her and, after one or two last feeble kicks, she lay still. This time I knew it was final.

He held her nose for a while longer to ensure his handiwork was complete but it was unnecessary and, eventually satisfied, he stood and crossed to me.

"You no want, you tell me where money." He turned and stalked out.

Between them his gang unshackled the corpse and again strung her from the pipe. They pulled the tape from her and, using the hose as before, they washed her inside and out – presumable to remove any forensics. This time there were no screams, no thrashing, no attempts to avoid or resist the pain of the jet. Her corpse just swung, propelled by the pressure.

Then they left her. I don't know if it was deliberate but she was facing me, eyes wide. Every time I glanced up she stared at me, a silent supplication or reproach. A silent warning.

I tried to turn her away but even stretching as far as my shackles would allow, I couldn't quite reach.

By the time they decided to move her she was stiff with *rigor mortis*. Zheu released the lock and her body fell, the feet hitting the floor then she toppled towards me. Her head hit the edge of my bed and she flipped sideways to lay on the floor giving me a final unspoken goodbye before they hauled her, heels dragging along the floor grinding a bloody trail on the rough material, out the door and up the stairs. I heard her thud on each step.

How long before I made that same ignominious journey?

Shortly after I tell him location of the money.

When I tell him what he wants, I will die. If I don't tell him then I'll live longer but probably in agony.

What a choice.

Chapter Twenty-Six

Another interminable and untimeable wait.
I was sure I would have at least a small breathing space if Cho's intention was to gang-rape me. Even rapists need recovery time.

Apart from being given some food and water and being escorted to the loo – where I had again taken the opportunity to grab a wash – they left me to stew. I dozed but each time I was awakened, crying, by vivid dreams of the horrors of the day, by the torture, by Natalia's pleading face which all too often morphed into the features of Diana.

I told myself I wasn't worried by the prospect of them raping me. I recalled the tipsy encounter with Davy Reilly and decided that I had not been at all traumatised by that experience. At the time I had shrugged it off as 'just one of those things that happens to girls' and, in fact, had probably thought less about it than Davy had – because he would be reminded of the incident every time he looked in his shaving mirror.

Natalia. I would remember her name. If I ever got away from this hell I determined I'd try to find her family. I didn't know why I felt this … it certainly wasn't in my nature. Maybe it was a distraction, thinking about the possibility, however unlikely, of escape.

What *was* in my nature was to use the girl's death as a learning experience. It had given me a few pointers that might help me survive a tiny bit longer. For instance, I now knew if I soiled myself I would get the hosepipe treatment but at least they were letting me use the lavatory. Also, I'd learned that if I struggled too much I would get the parcel tape wrapped over my mouth ... and I had seen how easily – and horrendously – that ended.

But when I heard the footsteps on the stairs all my resolutions flew out the – nonexistent – window. I once read in some Victorian adventure story that the protagonist had been 'unmanned' and thought it seemed a rather wimpish reaction. Now I knew exactly what it meant. My insides felt as if they were turning to liquid. Never, in my entire thirty-two years on this earth had I so much wanted the comfort of my mother. It felt as if death was walking with Cho and his confederates.

The door burst open and they piled in, screaming and bellowing – a typical intimidation tactic used by any raiding party but it failed in its intent because I'd anticipated it. *Don't try to shock a psychopath like that ... we're mentally incapable of the terror induced by that sort of intimidation.*

As I cowered, faking the reaction they desired, Cho loomed over me and pulled a knife that he opened with the click of a button. "Last chance," he growled but I just whimpered.

I thought he was about to cut me but he set about slicing my clothes away – none too carefully so I received several gashes. At one point he slid the blade upwards between the cups of my bra and, as the elastic parted to reveal my naked breasts, he turned to his colleagues with a smirk and said, "No wonder they call her Wú rǔfáng."

THEY?

Only one person ever used that name: Poo-brain! How would these people know it? What was his involvement with them? Whatever it was, it must have been from before the raid at Overton because he had been incapable of involvement in anything more complex than breathing and defecating since then.

Then another thought occurred to me ... the nickname

was in Mandarin and I had told them I didn't speak the language. Luckily, they seemed too stupid to spot it.

When he'd stripped me, Zheu unlocked the shackle and they dragged me to the far corner while Qi connected the hose and immediately began blasting me. It hurt. I can't imagine the agony Natalia must have endured when they ... did what they did to her with that hose.

But, as awful and humiliating as it was, I was determined to keep as free as possible so I cooperated. I scrubbed myself – even my genitals ... much to their enjoyment: hooting and whistling at my impromptu vaudeville act. When they were satisfied I allowed myself to be led back to the bed. I'd already been dragged across that concrete floor and lost skin in the process. I briefly contemplated making a break for the door but it was the entire length of the room away and the intervening space was packed with men: hyped up and ready for action. I made myself so biddable they didn't even bother to reattach my chain to the ring on the wall.

One man grabbed each of my limbs and Cho knelt between my spread legs and exposed himself to me. I felt no fear, no more than resentment at what was about to happen. I was still not going to make it any easier than necessary so I twisted, side to side, corkscrewing my body until one of them thumped me on the side of the head and momentarily stunned me.

Then everything changed. As he forced himself into me I felt the difference. I wasn't ready for him. It hurt. No – more than hurt. It felt as if he was ripping me apart. But there was more. As well as penetrating my body he was penetrating my mind, my soul, my psyche.

Involuntarily, I cried out and saw his smirk. It wasn't the sex he was enjoying, it was the pain he was causing, the control, the power.

He hammered into me, harder and harder, deliberately

hurting. I thought I was mentally tough, that I'd be able to face anything they could do to me. I assumed, after Davy Reilly, I'd be able to cope with rape but realised I hadn't mutilated Davy for raping me but for his bad manners. What he had done was unforgivable but, if he had asked nicely, taken it slowly, tried a little cajolery and foreplay, I would probably have cooperated and let him have his way. Cho was different. This was *real* assault ... not the physical assault but an attack on the intrinsic *me*.

Unlike Davy, he was keeping his face away from me, arching his body with arms straight either side of me.

He started grunting and pounding faster and it seemed almost as if my body, of its own volition, took over. My captors, distracted, had relaxed their hold on my wrists.

I snapped my arms down, elbows into his wrists, jerking his arms down so he fell forward onto me. His forehead smacked into mine and I saw stars but, as our faces met, I struck and I snapped my jaw shut. I felt my teeth rattle against his as they closed on flesh.

He screamed and tried to pull away and I realised I'd snagged half his bottom lip and some of his left cheek so I bit harder and his pulling achieved nothing but to inflict further pain. There was blood. First I tasted it: salty, metallic. Then I felt it: a warm, sticky wetness that trickled across my upper lip, down my cheek, along my neck towards my naked chest, into my mouth. I shook my head from side to side like a terrier with a rat – t*he 'rat' bit was spot on* – caused him to scream more. I may even have growled.

Other voices joined in: high pitched, loud, panicked. Fists pounded into me from different directions. Cho tried to punch me in the head but couldn't get enough leverage to hurt. The trickle of blood became a flow. Some went in my ear and my right eye. Trying to gain his release, Cho overbalanced and, with the greatest scream yet – so close to my ear it deafened me – he rolled sideways off the bed.

He'd escaped but I still held flesh between my teeth.

Blows rained down on me from all sides but I was free. They were panicking: a roomful of headless chickens. Now was my chance. My *only* chance. Ignoring the beating, I sprang to my feet. Qi came at me so I punched him as hard as could, squarely in the face and cartilage crunched. A grunt. More blood. More chaos. The place was becoming a charnel house. The blow hurt my hand and wrist but gave me deep feeling of satisfaction. Somebody punched me in the side of the head but I felt nothing and kept charging towards the door. I lashed out where I could; with fists, feet, forehead, elbows and knees, at any target that presented itself and was rewarded with squeals of pain and still more blood.

Zheu rose in front of me, seeming to appear from the ground, so I drove a full force kick into his midriff and he folded in half so I lunged for the door. As my fingers touched the handle and freedom was within my sights a hand snared my ankle and, unable to get my arms up fast enough, I slammed headfirst into the doorframe.

I could only have been unconscious for a few seconds and regained my senses as the chain on my arm was being clipped onto the ring on the wall.

Cho stood in the centre of the abysmal room, hands clamped to his face with blood pouring between his fingers and running down his arms. His tee-shirt, previously white, now glistened a slick, shiny red, bright even in the dim light. Qi likewise sported a bloody face and a red-stained shirt. All the men had contusions and abrasions. None was free of blood.

Between them, they escorted the two worst injured away.

At the door Zheu turned, hand against the edge. "Now you die." His voice was strangely calm and soul-shakingly malevolent.

There was no doubt in my mind of the veracity of the statement.

As soon as they had gone I found if I stretched out a leg I could reach my shredded trousers so I eased them towards me. I spat the piece of Cho's flesh into my hand, like a small slice of uncooked steak, and slipped it into the pocket. When they inevitably killed me, they would doubtless give me the same deep clean they had imposed on the pathetic Natalia. Then they would dispose of me in a shallow grave or some other clichéd resting place. Maybe they would also chuck in my clothes. In the unlikely event my remains ever came to light before all flesh had rotted away, the police forensics scientists may discover that small piece with Cho's DNA in it and my saliva on it. It wouldn't be proof that he committed the murder but it would certainly make him answer a lot of uncomfortable questions. *With a lisp.*

I arranged my clothes around me as best I could. I have no more concerns about being naked in front of people than I have in front of any other furniture ... but it gives *them* a sense of power and these were advantages I did not wish to bestow upon them.

That was it. I'd gambled and lost. I'd made my bid for freedom and it had gone wrong. Despite Zheu's threat it was all fine. One of the joys about being a psychopath is things like that don't bother me. It came down to item 6 on the PCL-R: *'Lack of remorse'*. That also means 'Lack of regret.'

But that one piece of resistance, that failed bid for freedom, had demonstrated that they were not invulnerable. They now knew this cat had fangs and claws. Cho would remember me for the rest of his life because the best plastic surgeon on earth would struggle to weld up the mess. Although if I had my way he wouldn't have long to regret it because if I got a micro-chance, regardless of any personal risk, he was going to die.

Most importantly, any fear fled. I still assumed I would die.

But I would die unbowed.

Resigned to my fate – whatever it brought – I lay out on the bed and waited.

Chapter Twenty-Seven

I lay undisturbed. Cho and Qi had, presumably, gone for medical attention but it was many hours – maybe a day – before the three uninjured men returned. Having no idea of their intentions I was sure they had come to finish me off so, with nothing to lose, I went for them as soon as they came within my reach – kicking, punching and clawing. With my right arm still held by the chain I was considerably hampered and, as I lashed out, one of them grabbed my left wrist and lay back, stretching me out so the handcuff ground agonisingly into my right wrist. I still had feet and used them liberally.

Tung produced a rubber tube, wrapped it around my right arm then took a hypodermic needle and slid it into the raised a vein. One his mates said, "Make sure you don't overdose her or Cho will kill you."

He eased the plunger down.

I was caressed by heaven. It was like nothing I had ever felt: warmth, floating, heavenly bliss. Cares vanished. Fears fled. I had no cognisance of the cold, hunger or pain. The stiffness of my joints dissolved.

I think they each took turns with me but I have only vague recollection of what they did, who did what or how many times. When I regained my senses, an indefinite period later, I was naked and alone. I doubled up with stomach cramps and uncontrollable shivering. I vomited on the floor. My head pounded and my vision swam. Despite the intense cold I was sweating as if I had run a marathon. I felt like hell.

Zheu brought me food; thin, lukewarm soup of unknown provenance, stale bread and a small slice of cold pizza. He refilled my beaker with water from the tap. The last thing I wanted to do was eat, but I realised I needed to grab whatever nourishment I could so I forced it down ... constantly on the point of bringing it straight back up. Then I got a trip to the loo and my usual strip wash. *Very little stripping required.* The prospect of one of them bursting in no longer phased me ... I had no dignity left.

Later Tung, the good looking one, gave me another shot of what I assumed was heroin and forced himself upon me.

Endless time passed, always the same. Food, drugs, forced sex. I had totally lost all sense of time. I would have said I had been incarcerated for about eight to ten days based on the number of times I had been fed and taken to the loo but they could have been messing with my head by deliberately varying my feeding intervals.

One of the characteristics of my condition is a low boredom threshold. Hare has it as item 3 *'Need for stimulation/proneness to boredom'*. I was scared I might be losing my sanity. I was freezing cold, ravenously hungry and thirsty all the time and the place smelt like a sewer. I had nothing to contemplate but being tortured to death. I never considered myself to be a coward and the prospect of death was nothing I had ever really worried about. The coming sadism, however, preyed on my mind.

I was now reliant on the regular injections of heroin. If for any reason my fix was delayed I started withdrawing. I hated it. I would have refused the drug if I'd had the moral fibre ... actually tried a couple of times ... but as the effects started grinding in on me I relented each time and meekly offered my arm.

Apart from Tung, who murmured sweet Mandarin words of love as he raped me, the others ignored me except when they fed me, escorted me upstairs or administered the injections.

I picked up snippets from their exchanges; all bad. Cho

was disfigured and the only reason I wasn't dead yet was because he wanted to kill me himself. Zheu argued passionately that 'The Grey Man' would be enraged if I were killed but the other two – now occasionally joined by Qi, the centre of his face hidden behind plaster – dismissed him with a sneer. Cho would do what Cho would do and 'The Grey Man' would have to accept it. I no longer cared. I had slipped into a half-life alternating between a drug induced haze and deep, self-loathing depression.

Death may even be welcome.

* * *

Cho arrived.

The last time he'd arrived with cacophony, action and violence. Now his demeanour was subdued. His face was a mess: the left half of his bottom lip was missing and so was a chunk from his cheek so even with his mouth closed several teeth were still visible. I could make out the shape of my lower teeth in the damage. The excised flesh had not come out cleanly but ripped away so a jagged zigzag of stitches ran from the centre of his lower lip almost to the point of his chin and a second marked a line from where the corner of his mouth had been towards the angle of his jaw. The edges of the cuts had been sutured with dark stitches and the whole was dotted with dark clots of what may have been congealed blood. Blue, yellow and mauve bruising smeared all over the side of his face as far as his eye.

He didn't speak to me ... didn't even look at me.

His men immediately set to work threading the chain over the pipe. They had not given me my regular fix and I was starting to withdraw so when they unshackled me and hefted me to my feet I was in no condition to resist. Just as with Natalia, they suspended me by my arms but being taller I was able to keep the balls of my feet on the floor.

He stood in front of me, feet wide apart, hands on hips and regarded me as he might examine a museum exhibit. Finally he spoke. His English was already poor so with the additional handicap most of what he said was barely intelligible.

"In China we have martial art, kung fu. You know?" He didn't wait for my response. "I am very good at kung fu. When I punch is very hard. Now you find out."

"The money—"

"Fuck money. Look face!" He sprayed saliva as he spoke. "Now you find how hard I punch. I smash you inside. You die. Very slow. Very painful."

Two of his men stood behind me and held me exactly as Owen, my personal trainer, used to hold the heavy punch bag to stop it swinging when I practised kicks and punches. This time I wouldn't be kicking or punching. I would be the bag.

He squared up, settled into a strong, low stance and smashed a fist into my belly just above my navel: like being hit by a battering ram.

When you are punched, say, on the arm, the blow crushes cells and splits the capillaries near the surface. Fluids leak out and collect under the skin as a bruise. The punch also shocks nerve endings, causing pain.

A punch to the stomach has all those effects but there's more. Behind the stomach wall are the intestines and these are loaded with pain receptors so a blow that deflects the muscles far enough will trigger these ... more pain. The stomach is also a sealed unit so compression will squeeze the internal organs such as the bladder. This will also cause more pain and may even cause the victim to wet herself.

Sitting on top of the stomach is the diaphragm and a severe shock to that will paralyse the nerves and make it impossible to deflect the diaphragm downwards so breathing will be severely restricted leaving the victim 'winded'.

But I had a few things going for me. Firstly, I suspect there are more exercises for the abdominal muscles than for all the other muscle groups put together ... and I know every one of them. In the gym I would do literally hundreds of them from simple 'sit ups' to complicated arrangements involving machines and mechanisms ... some looking as if they had escaped from a medieval dungeon. My abs were the nearest a woman's muscles can become to granite.

Also, if I raised my feet fractionally off the floor I added further tension to those muscles.

Finally, kickboxing teaches that when you are about to receive a punch you must exhale hard to minimise the compression shock.

So when he drove his fist into me it must have felt like punching the wall. He had the good grace to look shocked but it did not deter him. He nodded and the men rotated me by a few centimetres so his second punch landed a hand's width to the right of the first. They rotated me in the other direction and the third punch landed the same distance to the left of the first.

Clockwise and anticlockwise. Centimetre by excruciating centimetre he printed a row of destruction around my body and I could see how a constant and continuous beating such as this would slowly pulp the internal organs and cause the victim to die in slow, abject agony.

Despite tightening my muscles and getting my breathing right he was winning. I felt my grip on consciousness loosening. As soon as I passed out I would relax and immediately lose any protection my well-honed muscles offered. Then he would *really* start to damage me ... damage me more, that is, than he was already doing. I shook my head, fighting not to go under.

My peripheral vision was going but through a mist I

caught a clouded glimpse of his face: puce with rage or effort. Stitches had split in his face and fresh blood trickled down his cheek and neck, staining the neckline of his tee-shirt. The tinnitus, caused by the explosion, now came rushing back as a metallic whine but muffled, as if heard from under a blanket.

He caught me another hard blow as my breath was wrong. I gasped, fighting for breath, aware that I had to control it before they set me up for the next strike, terrified that I wouldn't. The ringing in my ears increased. My vision was almost gone. I hadn't got much longer.

The next blow caught me and shocked me to the core. The air exploded from my lungs as a scream. There was blood in the spray that splattered over Zheu's white tee-shirt. I was approaching the end. Many more of these and I would be unlikely to survive even if he stopped. In fact, maybe the best outcome would if he didn't stop ... at least it would end now. Just a few more like that and my churned up, battered and bursting internal organs would fail.

One or two more. That would do it.

"Fuck you!" I managed. Maybe if I incited him enough he'd finish the job. "Fuck your mother. Fuck your sister." I spat blood in his face.

When a westerner is surprised she will use an exclamation such as, 'Ah!, 'Jesus!' or 'Fuck!' Chinese tend to make a noise that sounds like a sort of eeaaiii.

As they lined me up to take a punch into the short ribs on the right side, one of my handlers – I think it was Tung – made exactly that noise and then, almost under his breath, whispered, "The clouds obscure the moon."

Cho, lining up his punch ... I'd lost count ... paused and looked at his man. "What?" he demanded through his ravaged lips, dribbling bloody spittle, brow furrowed.

There was a tremor in Tung's voice, almost a note of reverence, as he said, "The Hidden Moon." He stepped away from me as if I had bubonic plague. Released, I swung, rotating back to face Cho. Eyes wide, he scurried around me to stand beside Tung whom I could just pointing at the tiny red and black mark on the inside of my left arm, his other hand clamped across his mouth. With my arms above my head the symbol was inverted so Cho twisted his head, first to one side then the other as if viewing it from different angles would make it mean something different. But the look of horror on his face told me it didn't.

"What this?" he bellowed at me. Spit splattered my face and I felt it slither down my cheek.

I raised my head to meet his eye, a not insignificant achievement, and did my best to shrug – not easy when hanging by your arms. My body felt on fire and I was close to vomiting but I refused to show any distress. "Exactly what it looks like." I was on shaky ground, not really sure what it meant but, if it would help, I was going to run this hare as far as it would go. What had I got to lose?

"Has the Hidden Moon started recruiting westerners?" asked Qi in English so I wasn't sure if this was addressed to Cho or to me.

"I'm not gwai lo," I snapped at him. "I am Chinese."

Cho stabbed a finger at the tattoo. "Who put there?" I sensed anxiety. And I do love it when my enemies are off balance.

"My ..." I stopped. I had been about to say 'Grandmother' but suddenly had another thought. "My Uncle." Another pause. *Go for it, Girl*. "Deng."

I saw the colour drain from his face and I thought he was going to chuck up. He seemed to go weak and slumped to a seated position on the edge of the bed.

"Deng." He mouthed the word, almost as a worshipper might mouth the sacred name of his god ... or devil.

"Yes, Deng," I said. "And he is going to be very upset

about what you've done to me and my Grandmother."

"Grandmother …?"

"Yes. Grandmother." They exchanged looks so I added, "The woman who killed Hu." I could see the panic morphing into terror. I was feeling better by the second.

"How you know about Hu?" His voice was quavering.

"Hidden Moon knows many things. I know it was Hu's cousin I killed when he was trying to kill me – shooting at me outside Shepherd's flat—"

Cho cut across me. "He not try kill you. His gun have blanks."

"It wasn't a blank fired through the window of Shepherd's flat that hit the road in front of me."

"That me." He actually sounded apologetic. "I have real bullets because not know if Russia man there. I fire one bullet. I aim miss." *So if they were using blanks, who put the bullet holes in the tree?*

"I know something else you don't." I waited to let this sink in. I wanted to ramp up my small advantage and twist the knife. "My Grandmother – who you killed – was Deng's sister. Deng is *very* angry."

"It was not us!" Cho seemed to be almost weeping. "Only Hu. Not us. None of us." He was starting to jibber.

The others all started speaking at once, Mandarin tones ricocheted around the room, overlapping, cancelling and reinforcing each other. Cho remained silent, slumped on the edge of the bed, elbows on knees, staring at his feet.

Eventually Zheu outshouted the others. "We should just kill her and dump the body." Again they began shouting.

Cho finally spoke, his voice rising above the row of his subordinates. "No. If Hidden Moon knows about us and about Hu and she's one of them then we must keep her alive. The Grey Man knows she is Wú rǔfáng – maybe he is also of the Hidden Moon."

"So? If we get rid of her we can just deny all knowledge," Zheu said.

Cho suddenly leapt from the bed, lunged and grabbed him by the lapels, shaking him like a cleaner with a duster. "Idiot," he screamed. "Deny? Do you know what Hidden Moon does?" Cho's face was within millimetres of Zheu's. As he shouted, a spray of bloody saliva splattered Zhue's face but he made no move to wipe it off. "How long do you think you would last if Deng's men started questioning you?" He shook him again. "When some fifteen-year-old boy stole one of their cars they asked his father where the boy was hiding. When he wouldn't tell, they dragged the man's intestines out through his anus." He shoved Zheu away from him so he stumbled, falling with one hand in the filthy puddle. When he rose, he absentmindedly wiped it down the front of his shirt.

"What shall we do then?"

Cho paced for a minute then, seemingly resolute again, turned on Tung. "You have a relative who owns a brothel, yes?"

Tung nodded. "Yes. My brother, Ching. The place is run by him and his wife."

"Right. We'll send her there. They can keep her safe and out the way while we try to work something out with Deng ... if we can contact him."

They let me down, lowering me gently to the floor, catching me when my legs failed me, then led me back to the bed. Later Tung fed and watered me and allowed me to use the bathroom. I could barely walk and had to be supported every step. I even had a shower, leaning against the wall as the stream, no more than a tepid trickle, ran over my battered body. To me it was the most blessed, wonderful experience. There was blood in my urine.

Back on my bed, they gave me my next fix and I sank into ecstatic near-oblivion once more.

But I had thrown them into disarray and as I slipped under I'm sure I must have had a smile on my lips.

Chapter Twenty-Eight

They provided me with some old, ill-fitting clothes: ratty, threadbare jeans, flip-flops, ripped, stained tee-shirt and told me to get dressed – the first time in days. It was a slow, painful process. I could hardly bend, my shoulders felt as if they had been wrenched from their sockets and every movement brought me waves of nausea. I kept coughing up blood and, when I went to the loo I was still peeing pink. I had no way of knowing how serious any internal damage was ... but I was alive.

Hooded with a malodorous sack over my head and strapped up in the handcuff belt they had used to harness Natalia, Tung led me upstairs ... the stairs I had assumed I would ascend as a corpse ... along a passage and out into the open air where he hoisted me into the back of a van. From the smell and noise it might have been the one that had brought me here ... but I was drugged both times, so could be wrong. He loaded some other stuff in behind me, cardboard and wooden boxes, then we set off. I think it was Tung driving. He was totally crap. Once more I was thrown around: backwards and forwards or from side to side as the vehicle bounced and swerved, amplifying my agony and nausea. The boxes assaulted me; hard and heavy. I managed to work the sack off my head but it did no good ... there was nothing to see except the dim inside of the van and the boxes.

I had managed to retain my own clothes: the shredded shirt that had my blood on it, the jeans also with my DNA and a lump of Cho's flesh in the pocket. I stuffed them behind some wooden slats that ran along the metal sides. *You never know.*

The tops of the crates were nailed but a sharp end protruded from. I stabbed by thumb on the rusty point ... tetanus was the least of my concerns ... and dripped blood in every little crack and crevice I could find. In the microscopically small chance that anybody ever did a forensic examination of the vehicle they would find it awash with my genetic material.

The first part of the journey was full of halts, jolts and right angled turns, then a fast road and finally lots of slow, grinding stop-start progress with choking fumes seeping into my metal prison. I had no option but to accept it and my druggy state made it less awful. At one point we paused ... possibly in a traffic jam ... and I heard voices. I couldn't make out the words, or even the language, but I started hammering on the side of my metal prison and screaming. When we started moving again the driver took a violent left turn, flinging me across the space, followed by a screeching halt that hurtled me forward and made me scream in agony. Tung and a man I had never seen before climbed into the back, pulling the door close behind them, and spent a few minutes trying to persuade me to make less noise: mainly using their feet and fists. Finally, they refitted the sack over my head and gave me another injection.

The next thing I recall is jerking to a halt. The doors were yanked open with a bang and rough hands dragged me out, head first, face up, so my feet fell painfully to the ground and the hood was yanked off. We were in a small yard in the centre of a rectangle of three-storey buildings. It may have been the loading bay of a factory. The only way in ... where the van must have entered ... was though a square arch, the height of two floors ... presumably to allow the ingress of large lorries. There were only a couple of doors on the ground floor but rusty, metal framed windows, thick with grime, looked down on us from all sides of the other two floors.

Runner

Tung steered me inside and up several flights of rundown, bare concrete stairs, all painted white ... many years previously. I needed help but his supporting arm around my waist brought almost more pain than I could bear.

We arrived at a small, shoddy room under the roof, which smelled as if it had not been acquainted with fresh air in a long time and had a layer of dust on every surface. The walls were painted cream, but it took a lot of imagination to see it.

He unshackled me and left, locking the door behind him. At least I wasn't chained up. It was hot and stuffy but the window, rusty metal frame glazed with wired glass, opened so I flung it wide and found it looked out over the courtyard. I wondered whether it might be a means of escape but it gave onto to a sheer drop I would probably not survive. *A final way out, at least.*

Investigation of the rest of the room yielded nothing of use. It was about four metres by three with a grotty double bed opposite the door, placed centrally below the window. The mattress was covered in the sort of stains I did not want to contemplate. There was a bedside cabinet, dressing table, and a tiny wardrobe. A small, three-legged wooden 'milkmaid' stool completed the inventory. In the corner was a filthy washbasin but when I tried the cold tap it rattled and banged for a minute before emitting a gurgle of metallic smelling water the colour of diarrhoea engendering images of a rusty iron tank full of decomposing leaves and dead rats. I hoped this was not going to be my only source of liquid sustenance. The hot tap issued a similar idle trickle with no indication of any warmth. I left the water running full bore, hoping against hope to flush it clean. It also gave me a tiny sense of satisfaction, running up their water bill. *Petty? Guilty as charged.*

I lay on the mattress that felt as if was made of concrete

and waited. There was nothing else to do.

Tung returned with another Chinese man.

"This my brother. He own this place. Everyone call him 'Benny'.

I looked him over and could instantly see the reason. He was short, fat and moon-faced. In his tiny, bottle-bottom glasses I could easily imagine him being chased by a 'bevy of scantily-clad beauties' to the tune of *Yakety Sax*. The comedian Benny Hill died when I was 9 but I still remember him … and cringe.

"Hello," I said in Cantonese but, when he looked blank, I repeated it in English. He grimaced, crossed to the washbasin and turned off the taps then left, pulling the door closed behind him.

Tung grabbed me by the upper arms and tried to kiss me on the mouth but I turned my head so he scored on my right cheek. "It be all right. You safe here." He followed Benny out and locked the door behind him. *Define 'safe,' Arsehole.*

The place was disgusting with dust and grime everywhere. I found a raggedy sheet in the wardrobe, ripped it up for rags and moistened it with the filthy water then passed an hour cleaning the place as best I could: mainly just converting the dust to mud and smearing it around. But I did it anyway. Maybe I'd inherited some of my father's OCD. Better than boredom, anyway.

I started going into withdrawal: fidgeting, itching, nausea, so I hammered on the door and yelled. After what seemed like ages Tung entered.

"What you want?"

"I need a fix." He snorted and I felt like a low life. "It's all your fault. *You* forcibly injected me. *You* got me addicted," I snarled at him and he had the good grace to look away before he left.

Runner

He was gone so long I was beginning to think he had forgotten me and I was becoming desperate but eventually, he returned.

"Here." He held out a small polythene bag of white powder, a length of thin rubber hose, a needle, a spoon, matches and a nightlight candle.

I took them but, as he was about to leave, stopped him. "This is no good." He looked puzzled but said nothing. "I don't know how." When he still looked blank I got up in his face. "You and your pals used to hold me down and inject me. Now I need the shit but I've never prepared it. I need help to do it."

"I – I sorry," he stammered. Now it was my turn to remain silent. I just glared until he looked away. "I fetch someone." This time he left the door unlocked.

I chucked the drugs paraphernalia on the dressing table and, as bad as I felt, cracked open the door and peeped through the gap. The whole place seemed empty so I stepped out. 'My' room was about halfway along a corridor sealed by doors at either end. Metal framed windows lined the opposite wall and I assumed they looked out over something they would not want anybody to see because newspaper had been pasted over the glass, attenuating the light to a sepia glow. I scraped a small hole with my fingernail and caught a limited glimpse of a manky suburban street; tired, terraced houses and cars well past their use-by date. I twisted my head to left and right, hoping to spot something informative. *Useless*.

There were six other rooms: three either side of mine, but all the doors were shut and I didn't try any of them. Outside the door at one end of the corridor sat a man; moon face, almond eyes, reading a Chinese language newspaper but he just peered over it as I approached until I got within a couple of metres, when he waved me away.

"Hello," I tried in English but his expression remained

unchanged and he just made another 'shooing' gesture. When I stepped closer he reached inside his jacket in a gesture familiar to every aficionado of cop films. *No need to get snotty*. I retraced my steps but as I approached the other end of the corridor I heard voices beyond and scuttled back to my room. A few seconds later the door opened and Tung entered followed by a tiny, pretty girl in a red cheongsam with gold embroidery, looking like an extra from a 1950s film about a Chinese brothel. *The 'Chinese brothel' bit seemed spot on.*

"This Lilly." He waved at her. "She speak Cantonese, Mandarin. No English." He grabbed the drugs, thrust them at her and snapped, "Show her," in Mandarin then left.

"Hello," she said in Cantonese. Her eyes were wide and her voice shook.

"I am Josie. Will you help me?" I held out my arm.

She looked even more scared. "Tung told me I must not give you drugs. I have to show you how to do it. That is all." They were completing my degradation. It was one thing when they were forcibly injecting me but, now they'd got me hooked, they were going to make me do it to myself. I felt sick.

She lit the candle and stood it on the dressing table then tipped the white powder into the spoon. When she added a few drops of water from the tap I cringed. Did I really want that gruesome liquid in my veins? *Oh God, yes! Desperately!* She held the bowl of the spoon over the flame until the mixture bubbled, stirring it with the tip of the hypodermic before sucking the golden brown solution into the barrel.

As I sat on the edge of the bed, she showed me how to use the brown rubber tube as a tourniquet to lift a vein and watched as I gingerly eased the point into it – my natural trypanophobia overcome by my dire need. I felt shame, embarrassed by my shame, ashamed of my embarrassment. As heaven filled my body and swamped my brain I slid backwards on the bed. She patted my hand and whispered, "Sleep, poor baby."

* * *

I'd found that immediately after a fix I would drift into a state somewhere between wakefulness and sleep ... drifting in a sea of warm ecstasy for a couple of hours. After that I'd revive and be able to function semi-normally until I started to come down, when the need for the drug would grow and grow until it became a raging monster, ravaging my entire being, making thinking nearly impossible.

When I roused, it was dusk. I lay, full consciousness seeping back, when there was a gentle tap on the door and Lilly entered with small, hesitant steps, head lowered, eyes to the floor.

"Would you like tea?" She placed a tray with two cups and a large, white pot on my bedside cabinet and poured. I patted the bed beside me and she sat, cradling one of the cups. I took the other and sipped the pale, green-brown Chinese tea. It tasted wonderful.

"Thank you." She just smiled. She looked very young. "Do you know where we are?" I asked. "Which town?"

"No. We are in England. That is all I know." Haltingly, with many hesitations and prompting on my part, she told me her story ... not at all strange to anyone who follows current affairs. She grew up in a tiny village in Central China, which she had never left. Her family was poor and life was grindingly hard. When she was fifteen she – actually her father on her behalf – had been offered a well paid, exciting job in the west. Her father had been given a 'large' sum of money, actually just a few pounds.

She was unclear of details after that: a flight to a city, possibly somewhere in Eastern Europe from her description, where she was met by a man who accompanied her by bus, coach and train to somewhere she was put in the back of a lorry, then a van to a place similar to where we were now. "Benny said it is England and all the customers speak English."

Customers? Of course.

"How many women are there here?"

"About twenty. They come and go. This is my third place – Benny owns them all. I have been here six months. Maybe they will move me again soon. We all live in the other rooms along this corridor." Six other rooms, so three or four to a room. *Fantastic*.

"They make you have sex with these 'customers'?"

"Yes. Sometimes ten, twelve or more every day." She dropped her face in her hands and sobs shook her. I put my arm around her shoulders and held her until they abated.

As we shared the tea I pumped her for more information. What went on behind the door guarded by the man at the end of the corridor? She wasn't sure but thought they were making drugs. I asked how they got away with running a brothel and a drugs' factory. Surely the police must know. She shrugged, not sure, but offered that there was a genuine factory on the ground floor ... a sweat shop making Chinese herbal remedies. That might be a half decent cover. At the front they had a 'Gentleman's club': membership only. *They probably bribed a few local police officers, too, I would guess.*

I also discovered something else of immense interest: the girls weren't locked up.

"So why don't you all run away?" I burst out. I couldn't believe they wouldn't make a break for it at the first opportunity.

"We are in a trap. They got us all hooked on drugs and keep us supplied. We are scared of running away because we would lose our drugs – we know that England is a very honest society and the police are very strict so it is impossible to obtain drugs and we have no money to buy them, anyway. None of us speak English and the police will arrest us. We will be locked away for years in a labour camp if they find out we are prostitutes and drug addicts. After that, we will be deported and the men who brought us here will harm our families ... because they know where they live." She started crying again. I wasn't surprised. I tried to explain that half the things she had been told about Britain and the British police were not true but soon realised she had been so thoroughly brainwashed that I may never get her to see the truth. I had none of the girls' reservations and would be gone at the first opportunity but whereas they were free to escape and didn't want to, I did want to ... but wasn't free. I would need to cultivate Lilly and as many of the other girls as possible. *But cultivating people is what I do.*

She showed me where the bathroom was: the end room to the right of mine, and I showered but still only had the clothes I stood up in. I thought of asking her for a loan but nothing of hers would fit me so I slunk back to my room and did the only thing I could: sleep.

For the next few fixes Lilly brought the drugs and watched me as I brewed up the mixture but on about the fourth day it was Tung who brought the blessed sachet. When he held it out to me he said, "How about sex?"

I leapt up, outraged, hands on hips. "No. Absolutely not," I screamed in his face.

I expected him to react, get angry, lash out, but instead he just smiled, shrugged and slipped the packet back into his pocket. "See you later." He shrugged, smiled and sauntered out, radiating confidence, patently sure of his ultimate triumph. After an hour he returned and we reran the scene but this time I was less emphatic and he was even more assured.

On his third visit I caved in.

As he 'had' – no, let's not beat about the bush: raped – me, he murmured more phrases of eternal love and devotion. *What a deeply wonderful and caring person.* Any shame I felt previously now morphed into a deep self-loathing. I knew the drugs had been forced upon me but I believed I should be able to resist – both them and Tung.

After he left I looked at myself in the misty, black-spotted mirror: the dull, matted hair, the face that had started to sag and develop lines. The rest of my body was also becoming raddled; muscle tone going, my belly – previously like a washboard – getting flabby. If I was like this after only this short period of time, what would I be like after months? ... or years?

I'm ashamed to say, I dropped my head into my hands and cried as I have not cried since I was a child. There's no more loathsome emotion than self-pity ... and I went for it big time.

A small, soft hand drifted across my shoulder and I squealed and jumped.

"Oh, Lilly! You nearly made my heart stop!" I gasped as she wrapped her arms around me. She kissed me on the cheek, lips like butterfly's wing. I don't know why I did it – maybe the need for comfort but suddenly I was kissing her and she was kissing me back. After Tung's attentions and my episode of depression she was just what I needed.

Chapter Twenty-Nine

Lilly brought me some cleaning materials and, as a tiny act of defiance, I set about my room: cleaning and scrubbing, polishing and shining. They could keep me in squalor but I refused to be degraded.

Away from Cho's cellar – and attentions – the terror that had gripped me turned into a mind-numbing boredom, alleviated by the regular drugs ... and Lilly.

And there were the less welcome visits from Tung. I decided that if he was going to 'use' me then I was going to return the compliment ... and I could do a better job on him than he could on me.

More defiance: when alone I restarted my training. There was nowhere to run but there were star jumps, plenty of static work: press-ups, sit-ups, squats and lots and lots of yoga.

And finally: when Lilly brought me my next fix I poured the powder into the spoon but then scraped out a tiny amount with the nail of my little finger and flicked it back into the Ziploc bag. Usually, Lilly took all the works away with her – instructions from Benny, she said. I asked her if I could keep the bag and she just shrugged.

Then we brewed up and injected as usual.

It was probably psychological but I swear I started to come down sooner than usual. I fought it and held out until my next scheduled fix. With the next fix I did the same, adding the miniscule amount of heroin to that in the bag I'd kept.

"What are you doing?" she asked, a tiny vertical crease between her eyes.

"Building our escape kit." *Building* my *escape kit*. She still looked puzzled so I explained. "By saving some of the drug each time we can accrue enough to see us through when we escape." I said I was also trying to wean myself off. She swore she would do the same but never actually managed more than the most minor reduction in her intake. I can't say I blamed her ... I wasn't being screwed by a battalion of baboons on a daily basis.

Just Tung.

The next time Tung brought the drug it was obvious from the look on his face what he was after but this time I played up to him, inviting him to my bed before he had the chance to ask. *Demand.* I acted enthusiastic to his attentions. As he forced himself upon me I poured forth a barrage of filth and vituperation ... but all in Cantonese that he did not understand and all in the sweetest tones. Afterwards, I told him what a wonderful lover he was. *Like you do*.

Afterwards, he sat, back propped against a pillow and smoked a cigarette: dropping ash on the floor while I snuggled into his rancid armpit making satisfied, smoochy noises.

"Darling," I whispered up to him, "Would you do me a favour?"

"Mm?"

"I would really like some make up. You know, not a lot. Just a bit of lipstick, something like that. Any chance?"

"Why?"

"You'd like me to look nice for you, wouldn't you?" He shrugged, dropped the still burning dog end on the bare wooden floor, rose, dressed and left without speaking.

There was more to my request than the need for beauty products. Psychologists say the best way to get people to like you is to get them to do you a favour. This might feel counterintuitive because you would think it would be more effective doing *them* a favour but this can actually make you seem eager to please or needy ... not an attractive trait. The theory, if I remember it from my degree, is that their subconscious tells them they wouldn't do you a favour unless they liked you so if they have done you a favour then they *must* like you. The – normal – human brain is weird. *My brain? You'll always be just furniture to me.*

The next day he arrived with a present ... my makeup kit! Of course. When they snatched me, they'd also taken my bags so they must have them stashed somewhere. He opened the catches and upended it on the bed, prodding around in the contents, presumably looking for anything I shouldn't have.

"What's this?" I almost couldn't breathe, I felt the pulse hammering in my temple. My knife! To him it must look like a piece of bamboo. If I wanted to keep it – and I *so* did, of course I did – I had to think fast.

"Let me show you." I took it from him and put the knife on the dressing table then, with my fist against my temple, rolled the back of my upper arm backwards and forwards across it. "It stops me getting flabby arms." *Oh come on! I think that was pretty good on the spur of the moment.*

He pulled me close and shoved his tongue down my throat. All while I was holding the knife. *You just don't know how close you are to losing your balls, Scumbag.*

Soon!

Things were *definitely* on the up.

* * *

The delight. Lilly and I spent the whole of the next morning showering, washing our hair in decent shampoo, slapping on body lotions, manicuring and pedicuring to our heart's content. Then we made free with my makeup until, by the time I was finished with the girl, she would have died for me.

Jags Arthurson

But I didn't want that.

Exploring the place had become an obsession but was proving harder than I had imagined. Tung and Benny made sure I was kept secure. The door to my room was no longer locked – I think they became fed up with letting me out to use the loo – but I found anywhere beyond the doors either end of the corridor was out of bounds to me.

There was another corridor at right angles to 'ours', opposite the bathroom door. It had a scummy kitchen and, adjoining it, a room they used as a recreation-cum-dining room. I figured the kitchen was over the entrance arch. My mind went into overdrive. A hole through the floor perhaps? If I could get the tools. Even if I succeeded in digging it undetected, it would still be a long drop.

There was a coffee machine and, whether I was allowed or not, I helped myself to a mug of the bitter, black liquid. The first I'd had since Victoria Station a lifetime ago.

In the angle of the two corridors was the 'forbidden door' that opened onto a staircase to the floor below. In the corridors beneath ours, Lilly told me, was another set of rooms, much more luxurious than ours: each with a king-sized bed and bathroom … like a decent hotel. These were where the punters took … in every sense of the word … the girls.

I met the other women: all mandarin speaking Chinese, and detected resentment: three had been moved from the room I now occupied … further increasing the congestion in the other rooms. And because I, supposedly, did not speak their language, they left me alone. At least there was no actual physical aggression.

Whereas they were pretty free within the confines of the building, every time I opened the door to follow them to the floors below, a thug would stop me and order me back. He sat in a chair at the bottom of the stairs facing away, so I reckoned his real job was to stop the punters coming up rather than me getting down. Whatever, he was very efficient at it.

In the no-go area beneath our recreation room was, apparently, a luxurious bar they called 'The Gentlemen's Club'.

"That is where the men come and choose the girl – or girls – they want," Lilly told me.

This was getting good. "How do the men enter?"

"There is an arch under the building. At the courtyard end it is blocked by a gate and just before the gate, under the arch, is a door with a doorbell. Madame sits behind a desk in the foyer. She sees the men on a television screen and presses a button that releases the door."

"Can you open the door from the inside other than with the button?" I could barely breathe.

"No. She must press the button behind the desk and anybody leaving has a few seconds to go out the door, otherwise it locks again." Seconds? If I ever got the opportunity to press that button I would be moving at the sort of speed that would make Olympic sprinters look like tortoises on Mogadon.

The bathroom was 'cleaned' by a roster of the girls – they were not very good at it. I was starting to feel a little better: still bruised and stiff but I needed to do something so, partly to ingratiate myself with the other inhabitants but mainly because I loathed using the place, I set about cleaning it. All the necessary materials were in a cupboard under the kitchen sink. It took a couple of hours but eventually it was sparkling so I switched my attentions to the kitchen but, by then, I had run out. By a stroke of luck I saw Benny so I accosted him.

"I need cleaning materials." I shook an empty tub of scouring powder at him. He looked puzzled as if he'd never seen the like before.

"Why?" *Men!*

"So that I can clean the kitchen."

"Why you do that?" *Like I said ... Men!*

"Because it is disgustingly filthy." *Because I will go insane if I just sit in my room all day.* "Just get me the stuff and I will clean everything."

He said nothing to me but snapped at Lilly in Mandarin, "Fetch Madame." Lilly left but returned after a few minutes accompanied by what looked like a skeleton in a gold cheongsam. She wore long, dead-straight hair, possibly a wig. Her face was submerged under makeup that looked layered on with a trowel ... presumably to hide the numerous, deep wrinkles in her leathern skin. She had the longest fingernails I've ever seen.

"She wants polish and ... stuff. For cleaning." She too looked puzzled but jerked her head, indicating I should follow her and she led me through ... *the door!* With a pounding heart I stepped into forbidden territory. As we emerged the man on duty at the bottom of the stairs stood, stiff legged, nervous, eyes never leaving me but the Golden Skeleton just nodded so he relaxed back into his chair and resumed his newspaper. She jerked her head again and I followed her into a foyer – noting everything I could on the way.

Everything was as described by Lilly but now I was able to estimate distances and, more importantly, assess how long it would take me to cover them. The space was over five metres square, with luxuriously deep, scarlet carpets; heavy, maroon flock wallpaper and gold, or gold leaf, fittings throughout. Sofas and chairs, reproduction antiques, also in gold and red, lined the walls. An exotic, overblown chandelier hung from the high ceiling to almost head height. A reception desk, with telephone, occupied half of one wall.

The whole setup was a tribute to tackiness.

The front door! What were my chances of making a sprint for it now? Probably close to zero. I'd have to overcome the Madame, locate the button, press it and sprint. *Better not to go off half cocked.* I had made one abortive escape attempt and ended up worse off. Mess this up and only a lunatic would let me have a third. My next attempt *must* succeed.

Through a door behind the desk, she led me along a short corridor to a small room. Half a dozen men looked up from a noisy, rattling game of Mah-jong as she directed me to a set of shelves loaded with boxes and packets.

"Take what you need."

I was loading myself with polish, scouring powder and cloths when I looked up at the top shelf. My suitcases. Could I grab anything? Or even have a look to see what was there?

Before I had the opportunity, she snapped, "Have you got everything?" She slapped me around the back of the head: more demeaning than painful. *I'll remember that, Sweetheart.*

Back in the kitchen I set to. During the process I found a cheap disposable lighter in a drawer and slipped it, along with a spoon, into my pocket. One more minor triumph. I was elated.

This had been a great day.

* * *

That evening I did more training but had removed eight scrapings of heroin from my last fix so I was starting to withdraw. I played my saxophone for a while … another 'gift' from Tung … but even that soon lost its charm.

I thought of my small stash but had no needle and momentarily wondered, despite the risk of infection, if one of the girls would let me use hers. I had to fight it. When it became almost unbearable I thought of one last, desperate tactic. I centred the nightlight on the stool, lit it and sat cross legged on the bed. My yoga teacher had taught me meditation but I'd rarely used it: pseudoscientific mumbo jumbo. Now I'd try anything.

I stared into the tiny, flickering flame, cleared my mind and immediately hit my usual problem. As soon as I thought my mind was clear I realised I was thinking about having a clear mind. But at least I wasn't thinking about my next fix. The flame danced at me. I felt as if I was falling into it. It filled my brain. It sucked me in. It grew and seemed to be exploding, forming a mushroom cloud, a blast wave roiling towards me. As I was hurled backwards to oblivion I came to.

From the declining twilight I judged an hour or so had gone by and I was still sitting on the bed. My legs were completely numb. As I moved, daggers of pain lanced through the muscles. But over it all a huge question mark haunted my brain.

A nuclear bomb.

THE nuclear bomb.

I knew – or, at least, I thought I knew – that Shepherd was supposed to have sold four bombs to some terrorist group but had only supplied one. But here was my concern ... if the terrorists had even just one atom bomb WHY HAD THEY NOT LET IT OFF? Was that credible? Why would they hold off?

Okay, I had been incommunicado for quite a while: over six weeks based on my menstrual cycle, but even so I was pretty sure that if somebody had set off an atom bomb anywhere in the world I'd have heard *something* about it. They still didn't know I spoke Mandarin so Benny, Tung and all the others talked freely in front of me. Surely somebody would have mentioned it?

But nothing.

What conclusions could I draw?

While I was thus conjecturing, Lilly arrived with my next packet of magic powder and the next couple of hours slid

Runner

into the unrecorded past.

Chapter Thirty

The threads were coming together. One day I went to clean the bathroom but found it occupied by Jasmine, an exotically beautiful girl from southwest China. There was no lock on the door – Benny wouldn't allow it – so I walked in on her as she showered. Beside the basin was her hypodermic. She had her back to me so I grabbed it and scuttled away. There was no way I would use it because that's a great way of contracting HIV and other nasties but immediately after my next fix I handed Jasmine's needle to Lilly and kept my 'own'. I didn't let Lilly see me do it. Some things should be 'need to know.' *And you don't.*

I now had almost a complete kit: the lighter and spoon that I'd swiped from the kitchen, a candle and now the needle. All I needed was the tourniquet. I had, approximately, a whole measure of heroin and had started a second bag. I was removing up to ten small scrapings from each ration so would soon accrue enough. I was determined to escape but going into withdrawal while on the run was not an option so I had to have enough to see me to a place of safety. Assuming there was such a place.

My only worry was that I had to keep it in the drawer of the bedside table. It would only take one snooper to uncover it. I was constantly on the lookout for an alternative hiding place but could find nothing. It was essential it was close to hand because I would never know when an opportunity to escape might present itself. If it did, I wouldn't hesitate to go for it … but not without my supply.

With my escape kit ready they would make one slip – just one – and I would be gone.

Runner

* * *

I was still 'playing' Tung ... like Yehudi Menuhin at The Carnegie. When he next came to see me I asked him about getting hold of some of my clothes 'to look nice for him.' I only expected him to choose something ... any money you like it would be 'short and skimpy' ... but he actually brought up my suitcases. Once more he went through the routine of searching them for something I shouldn't have but he was too late ... I'd already got it all!

The only things missing from my belongings were my purse, valuables, mobile and, of course, my ten-thousand pounds.

We played 'dressing up' like schoolgirls. Well, I did the 'dressing up' ... lots of squealing and twirling ... he just lay back and letched. He got so wound up by my antics that eventually he could hold back no longer and lunged for me. I thought he was going to rip the dress to shreds ... just as I'd got my hands on it. Not that I would have been overly fussed because what I really wanted was jeans and trainers ... I wasn't planning to go on the run in silk and killer heels.

When he left he sorted out a couple of dresses, shoved the rest back in the cases and took them with him. *Damn!*

I played my saxophone whenever I wasn't training or cleaning. As I was putting the instrument away I noticed again the tiny tear in the lining and had sudden inspiration: the perfect place to hide my drugs and syringe. It wasn't obvious, none of them had any reason to look in it, and it was easy to grab for a fast exit.

Gently, I increased the size of the rip and was just about to start easing the barrel of the syringe into the hole when I felt a small lump. I edged it out: a small, flattened, black device about the size of my little fingernail and, like a precision machine, the bits slipped into place in my brain.

I had wondered how they knew where I was and how they could snatch me from a taxi on the M4 Motorway. And here it was. All the subterfuge of travelling to Birmingham and hiding out for a week in a slum had been a total waste. True, they had no tracker on me there, but all they had to do was wait until I picked up my bags at Victoria after which they could take me any time they wanted.

And they bloody had!

Now I had to work out who'd put it there.

Over the next week I inveigled Tung into returning more and more of my clothes until, finally exasperated, he dumped the two cases on my bed and snapped, "Just keep all. I piss off keep lug up-down."

Amongst the clothes were belts, any one of which would serve as a tourniquet, so my escape kit was complete.

* * *

Benny was screaming at somebody in Mandarin. I was in the kitchen and they were in the adjoining rest room. The door between the two rooms was ajar but it would have made no difference if it were closed because he was so loud I would have heard it in the courtyard.

"She is a leech. I will not keep her anymore. She has to earn her keep!" I peeped through the crack of the half open door and saw he was on his feet, towering over Tung ... although perhaps from his five feet two inch height 'towering' was, perhaps, a bit of an exaggeration.

His brother sat in an armchair, legs stretched out in front of him, hands thrust deep into trouser pockets, chin on chest. He scowled up at Benny. "Are you stupid? She has the mark. If anything happens to her then *The Hidden Moon* will turn Cho inside out ... literally. Can you imagine what he would do to us to prevent that?"

"Cho this. Cho that. Listen ... He said I must keep her safe, feed her and supply drugs to keep her quiet. And Cho said he would reimburse me for the cost. I've fulfilled my part of the bargain. Hundreds of pounds every week I pour down her ever-open maw or stick into her scrawny little arm. So where is your precious Cho with the money?" *You talking about me? Just give me the opportunity to wrap this 'scrawny little arm' around your scrawny little throat, Bud.*

"He will pay, believe me."

"So where is he? Do you even know?"

"Yes. He went to Beijing. He wanted his face rebuilt and he doesn't trust British surgeons. As soon as he's recovered he will go to Hong Kong where he'll contact Deng and negotiate the return of the girl in exchange for our safety."

Benny stalked across the room, away from where I lurked, towards the door to the corridor then pulled up sharply as if a thought had just occurred to him. "*OUR* safety? *US?*" He was, if possible, even louder, his voice box seemingly on the edge of bursting. "*US?*" He crossed back to his brother, waving clenched fists at him. "Are you including me in this '*US*'?"

Tung just shrugged and smiled again. "Well, she's here, under your care. If anything happens to her I would think Deng might include you in 'us' whatever I say, don't you?"

Benny leaned in so his face was millimetres from the seated man. "FUCK YOU!" He strode into the corridor, slamming the door behind him. After a few seconds he returned, re-crossed the room and bellowed into his brother's face, "I know you are soft on her but listen carefully ... in three days I either get some money or she starts earning her keep and I don't care if Cho, Deng or Mao Zedong himself says anything to the contrary." Then he stormed out again, the slamming of the door drawing an exclamation point on the scene.

Oh shit.

I had no alternative but to accelerate my escape plans because there was no way I was working as a prostitute. There was going to be trouble.

Suddenly, it felt as if they had increased their watch on me. Whereas, previously, I had seemed free to wander throughout what I considered to be 'the open area', Benny or Tung now constantly ordered me back to my room. When I was cleaning or cooking one or other of them would tell me it was not required. Even when I just sat around drinking coffee, Cho told me to drink it elsewhere. *Love to. Brighton, for example?*

Two days passed and I heard nothing further – good or bad – on Benny's ultimatum. I was awakened in the early hours by Lilly as she eased into bed beside me. We made love for an hour then slipped into satiated sleep.

When I awoke, a dismal morning pattered rain onto the windowpane above my head and a miserly daylight eased in begrudgingly through the window. This was the third day since the ultimatum. Today, ready or not, I was going to have to make my break.

Lilly woke about the same time, nuzzling the side of my neck, and we started where we'd left off the night before. As we kissed she suddenly went stiff. I opened my eyes and saw she was transfixed on something behind me. Fearing the worst, I swivelled my head until I could track her gaze. Tung's face was glaring down into mine.

"You enjoy?" he asked with a smile. But this smile moved nowhere on his face beyond his mouth and showed absolutely no humour or amusement.

Chapter Thirty-One

He dragged me out of bed by my hair. I wished that, instead of having it cut shorter, I'd had the lot shaved off. I managed to clamp onto his wrist but could get no leverage and first my heels then my hip thumped onto the wooden floorboards. He hauled me up so I half crouched, only partially clothed, before him. My immediate reaction was to lash out, not doubting my ability to kick him into oblivion. But at that point I would need to follow through. Grab what I needed, somehow get past the guards, down to reception, press the release and get out the door. Even if I succeeded at all that, I had no idea where I was or where I was going.

But when *would* be the right time?

I had to play for time. And the words were ready, neatly lined up like the carriages of a train waiting to leave the station. "It was nothing to do with me. It was all her. She gave me my fix and then, when I was knocked out, climbed into bed with me. Punish her ... not me." So easy. Hare's Psychopath Checklist, Item 16: *'Failure to accept responsibility for own actions'*.

But they wouldn't come. The accusation died on my lips.

My mind was in overdrive. For all his professed love for me, albeit only ever expressed in a language he thought I didn't understand while he raped me, I had no illusions. If he ever lost his fear of Cho or Deng, if he got fed up with me, if I somehow offended him ... I was a 'goner'. And now I had offended him big time.

"You pervert," he growled at me, face so close to mine

I could smell his breakfast. "You have sex with woman. Not natural."

"It's not how it seems." I tried to sound contrite but sexy at the same time. *If you think it's easy, try it.* Then, ignoring the pain in my scalp, I pulled him close and kissed him deeply. "We've been planning a surprise for you," I said when we came up for air. He released my hair so that was some relief. I turned to Lilly as she cowered in the bed and ripped the sheet off her. "Help me out here," I said in Cantonese. She looked terrified, eyes wide and staring, but rose and joined me. Under my guidance she started kissing him and nibbling his ear. Eventually he relaxed and we really set to work on him.

For over two hours we made him feel like a potentate, a powerhouse, a sex god. Without doubt it was the best couple of hours of his life. It wasn't so great for Lilly and me. He strutted out feeling like a real man. Isn't it every man's fantasy to satisfy two women at once? Or so I've heard. Although the 'satisfaction' bit was a very one-way street as far as the distaff side of the transaction was concerned. But I had managed to pull our arses out of the bear trap. *Maybe.*

It was more time chopped out of my diminishing reserve. I had the rest of the day before Benny's ultimatum ran out. My options were closing down. I had to act but when I left my room I found one of the heavies who usually guarded the stair had been reassigned outside my door. Had they guessed I'd overheard their conversation? That I spoke Mandarin? Or were they just being overcautious? God knows, but it was certainly limiting my freedom to act. Even when I went to the loo my 'new best friend' accompanied me and stood outside the door until I emerged. *Enjoy that, Pal?*

I tried the window in the bathroom but, slim as I am, there was no way I could fit through the tiny gap. Back in my room, I tied sheets together and fixed one end to the leg of my bed but when I dropped my makeshift rope out the window I estimated it was about ten metres short of the ground. I was even prepared to attempt a drop from that height but as soon as I put some trial weight on the antique material it parted like tissue paper.

So there were two options left. If Benny did not carry out his threat today, I would make my break that evening. The man outside the door would be no problem. I had the stool and my knife. If I opened my door he would assume I was going to the loo and I could hit or stab him. It might be even better if I could somehow lure him into my room where any fuss was more likely to go unnoticed. Then I would have to tackle the man on the stairs. With customers on the premises he may be less likely to fire his gun so a mad rush, led by the stool and accompanied by my knife, may just succeed.

If that worked, the next steps were the reception area, the Golden Skeleton and the door. That had to be played by ear. If it didn't work then a bullet would at least be a quick end to my worries.

The alternative was if I was sold to a customer. Another 'make it up as you go along' situation.

We spent the rest of the day chilling out and shooting up. Lilly was called to the *Gentlemen's Club* about seven and I waited an hour before deciding to make my break.

My door was locked.

Another plan gone.

Another day gone.

And the next morning Lilly was gone.

My warden let me use the bathroom and I accosted Benny as I passed him in the corridor, demanding to know where she was.

"She gone."

"Where?" I threw myself at him but the thug grabbed

me, arms around me like a steel band, before I could hurt the little rat. Benny sneered as if I were some lower form of life. Let's be honest, I was.

Benny got right in my face. "Now I one girl short. Tomorrow you make up money you owe me. You go with customer."

I struggled but his bodyguard maintained his bear hug so I shouted, "You let me lose with one of your scumbag punters and I'll rip his face off. See what that does to your business."

Benny smiled, "You see," then walked away.

* * *

They left me locked in for the rest of the night and all the next day: no food, no drugs. They were softening me up. If I was withdrawing, I would be more amenable. Eventually I had to dig into my stash. I took the smallest charge I could ... just enough to stop me getting the shakes and the cramps. But it left me just one full dose and a bit.

It was very early in the morning when the light came on as Benny burst into my room followed by two other men: one tall and slim, the other shorter and massively wide, like a gorilla with the hair shaved off. *Laurel and Hardy – but not so funny*. For the second day in a row, I was dragged brutally from the escape of pleasant dreams and the big man held me by the back of my neck on my knees in the centre of the room.

"You have too much my drug," Benny said in a calm voice intended, I assumed, to intimidate. "You think me charity?" He paused. I really think he expected a reply.

"Hey, Buster, if you don't want to pay for my keep ... let me go. Easy."

He grinned, a sort of lopsided grimace. "No way. Cho say keep safe. I keep safe. But you pay for drug."

Against the downward pressure of the huge hand on my neck, I forced myself to my feet. "Tough shit. I won't. And you'll never make me." Benny just nodded at the big man. "Them? Punters? You think I'm just going to lay back and take it?" I managed quite a decent sneer of my own.

"No, I think you make trouble for client so men show how we train girl." He backed towards the door and started to pull it shut.

"Wait," I yelled and he looked round, eyebrows raised. "Tung will not be happy about this. He will be very angry when he gets back."

He chuckled. "You right, Tung not happy. Tung not happy with you. Say do this." He gave a tiny mock-bow, said, "Enjoy" and left. I heard the key turn in the lock.

I regarded my opponents. Chinese, like all the others, I had the impression I'd seen them around … maybe as door guards. 'Laurel' didn't seem as if he would give me much trouble.

"You make easy or you make hard?" he said so I drove a roundhouse kick at the side of his head and he blocked it with simple ease. Then 'Hardy' slapped me across the face. I say 'slapped' but that implies a stinging cheek and a red mark. This one spun me round, pirouetting onto the bed from where I bounced onto the floor. I lay still for a second, my ear ringing and head whirling, and he kicked me in the kidneys. As I started to recover, he stood astride me, grabbed my hair and slammed my head onto the floor several times … I don't know how many because I was too busy hurting to keep an accurate count. All my previous pains and injuries reawakened in an instant.

They tell you that if you're ever attacked by a grizzly bear to play dead. This guy wasn't a grizzly bear but it felt he might be closely related, so I let myself go limp and he stopped working me over. They lifted me onto the bed: Hardy by the shoulders, Laurel on my ankles, dumping face up. While the big man held my hands down hard against the mattress, Laurel stood at the foot and dropped his trousers. In order to undress, Laurel had released my right ankle and as he started to climb over me I realised the big man's weight on my wrists gave me a tiny advantage. I pushed up on the restraining hands and I guess he thought I was trying to escape … he grinned and pushed down harder allowing me to use the leverage to get my free leg up, knee almost to my chin and let the tall man have it right in the face. My heel connected solidly and there was a crunch. *Now* that's *how to really get satisfaction from a man.* He made a muffled noise and jerked upwards before toppling backwards and falling onto the floor with a crash. I half expected him to get up but he just lay on his side, curled up like a foetus with his hands cupping his face as if to hold his nose on. There was a lot of blood from between his fingers.

The big man released my hands to attend his colleague and I used the opportunity to leap off the bed and returned the compliments of the kidney kick then started pounding on the door. When Benny finally opened it I just waved an arm at his soldier.

"I think you'd better get your monkey out before I *really* hurt him." Benny turned to call another henchman and I slipped past him and hurtled towards the door and freedom. As my hand grasped the handle, the door came at me like a train but I swivelled and avoided it. I wasn't so lucky with the man who'd opened it. As I tried to duck around him, he smashed a fist into my head and sent me reeling backwards. Then muscleman came up behind me put an arm lock around my neck and dragged me back into the room. On the way, we passed Benny and another man, supporting the injured skinny man away. *Not such an easy touch, was I?* But my latest escape bid had failed and it tasted like acid in my mouth.

Surely, they wouldn't be stupid enough to give me a third chance.

Benny was gone, along with his cockiness and threats. I was left alone with a man who had come to do me harm, to break my spirit like a cowboy breaks a wild bronco. Tung arrived and stood outside the door, glaring at me with a look of pure hate until my attacker slammed it shut. *Shy, are you?*

As soon as he released me I went for him big time. Feet, fists, fingernails. Attacking a tank with a feather duster. I didn't hold out a lot of hope but my options had closed down. Now it was 'all or nothing'.

Each time I attacked, he retaliated: a backhanded slap, a punch to the stomach, a kick to the side of the knee, each was like being hit by a truck. At one point I had the backs of my knees against the foot of the bed and he pushed me over backwards. I had no illusions about how these people worked: kidnap, imprisonment and rape into submission so I assumed he would dive on me as I lay spread eagled. Instead he grabbed my ankles and twisted me until I was face down then he held one of my ankles while he opened his zip. His weight landed on my back and I felt as if I were trapped under a falling tree but I started wriggling up the bed, grabbing anything I could get my hand on. I reached for the rails of the bed head, hoping I might be able to pull myself free but his hands around my waist started dragging me back towards him. My flailing hand fell on the handle of the bedside cabinet and the whole drawer came out, scattering its meagre contents. I swung it around with as much force as possible but it skidded off his shoulder and went clattering across the room.

With a hand on the back of my head he pushed my face into the mattress so I could hardly breathe as he worked at ripping off my pants.

"I'm going to split you open," he said in my ear in a voice like a boulder rolling down a hill as he lowered his full weight on me.

I felt something at the very tip of my fingers. My saxophone case. The lid was open. My spike! I stretched, I wriggled, I fought. It was in my hand. I thrust myself forward, partially freeing myself from his grip and, without thinking, twisted around and swung it in an arc. I had no idea where it would strike but four centimetres of steel needle into any part of the body would give him pause.

It hit something.

There was a moment of utter stillness and silence as if the world had stopped.

Then he screamed. He jumped backwards but kept screaming. Seizing the opportunity I rolled sideways off the bed, landed, twisted and sprung up – whirling around to face him.

He stood in the middle of the room, arms wide and still screaming, my needle hanging from the centre of his right eye. He continually reached for it but as soon as his hand touched the plastic cylinder he jerked it away again as if contacting high voltage electricity.

Still he screamed and screamed: a deafening, ear damaging siren of a noise that went on and on. I had to stop it so I snatched up the three-legged stool and slammed it into the side of his head. The shrieking ceased instantly and he crashed to the floor with a thunder that shook the room.

Now I was in *real* trouble. There was no way they were going to let me get away with this. Gang rape was now the very *least* of my worries. The die was cast. All my options had gone. I was on borrowed time and had to get out.

Now!

Escape or die.

I was standing in the centre of the room, throwing on my clothes, when the door burst open, slamming hard against the wall, and a man whom I had only ever seen occupying the chair by the door barrelled in, closely followed by Tung. They took in the sight, the unconscious man, a trickle of blood running from his temple and needle still dangling from his eye. The man reached inside his coat as I'd seen him do every time I approached his guard post but this time he completed the action. The gun seemed huge. With his left hand he gripped the top and slid the mechanism back, it made an ominous, mechanical swishing and finished with a click. Then he raised it until I was looking straight down the infinite black tunnel of the barrel and the irrelevant fancy rushed through my mind that I might actually see the bullet before it smashed my brain out the back of my head. Under my left hand, on the dressing table, I felt a hard wooden cylinder.

"You die now." His voice was a grating whisper. They were the first words I'd ever heard him say. They'd probably be the last words I'd ever hear.

I held my knife in front of me so I could take the other end in my right. I saw the tightening of his jaw, the physical effects of determination working its way from his brain to his trigger finger so I slipped the blades apart raised one to his chest and pressed ... expecting instant oblivion as the spasm of death reached his hand. Instead I saw a look of amazement rush across his features: eyebrows rising, mouth opening in a silent 'O'. It was so simple. Even the physical act had been easy ... no rattling of blade on ribs, no massive resistance of flesh to the passage of steel, no protest from my brain at the morality of it.

Tung stood, open mouthed, as his colleague slumped to the floor. Was he with me or against me? My bridges were ablaze and I was in danger of oblivion in the conflagration. I had to get out ... now! It would be easier with Tung on my side so I stepped over to him and gave him my best little-girl-lost-needing-a-big-strong-man-to-help-me-out. I wrapped my arms around him and gave a small sob.

"Tung, thank god it's you. Please help me. I'm so scared. Help me. Please." I capped it off with another pathetic sob. *I thought it was quite a good performance.* He reached up, gripped my wrists and untangled my arms, pushing me backwards ... but not, I noticed, too roughly.

"What you do?" His voice sounded distant, as if he had not got full control of it. "You kill man. You kill ..."

"Please, Tung. He was going to kill me ... shoot me through the eye. You love me, I know you do." I flung my arms back around him, whispering in his ear, persuading, soothing, cajoling. "We can run away. I have the money ... millions of pounds. We can go away, just you and me. I can contact Deng and call off *The Hidden Moon*. We will be safe and we could have a good life—"

"Not sure." *Got you!* I waited, aware a wrong word or move might break the moment. "We could, maybe. I could tell Benny." He thought some more. "Maybe I tell Benny these two get in fight ..." *Wait up, what's Benny got to do with this?*

"Tell Benny? Why tell Benny anything? Let's just grab our stuff and go."

Against the wall the big man had started to regain consciousness. At the moment he was groaning, probably still groggy but any second he was going to recover ... and remember. Then he'd start screaming again and that would attract more attention. I *really* didn't want that.

"No. I tell Benny these two have fight. *He* ..." he indicated the dead man, "... stab *him* with needle so *he* stab *him* with knife. "You tell me where money is and I square with Cho and Benny. Then all OK." *Yeah, right. In your dreams.* The man on the floor started screaming again. *Shit!*

"But why? Let's go ..." I grabbed his arm and started pulling him towards the door.

"We need keep him quiet." He was right about that, at

least.

"No problem."

I was getting heartily hacked off with Tung and even more so with the screaming man so I could have reacted to either of them. On balance I decided the screamer was the highest priority. As he sat up and finally worked up the courage to grasp the syringe and yank it from his eye I stepped behind him and grabbed his hair – *it works both ways, guys*. With my knee forced into the back of his neck I ran the blade across his exposed throat.

Maybe I wasn't slicing hard enough at the start but by the time the knife was directly under his chin a jet of blood sprayed in front of him. As I completed the cut, the blood was cascading in an arc of about seventy degrees. Fascinating the way, with each beat of his heart, it sprayed outwards, down his chest, across his legs, over the bed, some even splattered the walls. Each beat seemed to reduce in power and force. As the life squirted from him, his legs jerked and his feet beat a tattoo on the floor. I held him until the spasms stopped.

When I glanced across at Tung he just stood, open mouthed, eyes bulging, face a sort of green.

"What?" I snapped. I was still hacked off with him.

"You … you … you kill!"

"You said we need to keep him quiet. He's quiet."

"No. I mean persuade him not talk … not *kill*." He voice had become almost a wail. *Man up, you wuz.*

"Why would I care what he said?" *Is this conversation real?* All I wanted to do was hit the road.

"Then Benny let you stay and you be my girl. Dirty whore, Lilly, gone so you stay here just for me."

WHAT? Was he totally insane? Completely off his box? He really expected me to stay here and be raped for his pleasure. *Okay, fellow, last chance.*

"Come on. Let's get out of here." I stepped towards

the door but he grabbed my arm.

"No go. Stay here." I turned to face him and he had a gun in his hand. For the second time in minutes I was staring down the barrel of a gun. *Fuck this. Kill me or die.* I brought the knife, still in my hand, up to his chest so the point pressed into his flesh.

He squeezed the trigger.

I jerked.

Nothing happened.

I was still alive. Then I realised what he'd done.

"Hey stupid, you know that slidey thing on the top? You have to pull it back before your toy will work." A look of terror crossed his face: wide, unfocused eyes, quivering lips. His hand flew up and scrabbled with the mechanism but I just smirked. "Too late." I put my weight against the knife and felt it slide into him, seeing, once again, the look of surprise as *The Grim Reaper* tapped him on the shoulder.

Those burning bridges were now ashes.

Chapter Thirty-Two

There was no time for planning or pondering. I had no idea how many men Benny had on the premises: the size of the army he could send against me. I had to act ... NOW!

I stuck my head out and scanned the corridor, relieved to see all was clear, so I returned and searched the three bodies. What I hoped for most was a phone but was disappointed. The big man was so drenched in blood that I just patted his pockets but felt nothing. The other man, the guard, wore a black, knee length leather coat ... unfortunately, miles too big for me. In the inside pocket I found a wallet with a few pounds and a credit card. There was also a lump in one side and it turned out to be a set of car keys. *Result.* If I could get out and locate it I was *really* in with a chance. All Tung yielded was a pair of wraparound aviator sunglasses. And, of course, there were the two guns.

Now I just had to get out ... and away.

By the time I was dressed: jeans, tee-shirt, trainers and hoodie, I had formulated a plan ... of sorts.

The corridor was still empty ... the usual doorkeeper was on the floor of my room and wouldn't be resuming his post this side of the resurrection. I stuffed the guns into my pockets and ducked out. A few doors along, a couple of the girls were in their room.

"Where are the others?" I asked in Mandarin. Their heads snapped up, eyes wide. One of them told me most were in the recreation room. "Grab any others you can find and meet me there as quickly as you can. It's really important." I sprinted to the room and was soon joined by an assortment of women – it was obvious some had been dragged from their beds. I called for attention.

"We didn't know you spoke our language," said one.

"No. I am here as an agent of the British Police. We are going to get you out … to rescue you from these men. Go back to your rooms, get dressed and get anything you want to take with you. Then come back here," adding, "As quickly as you can. It's really urgent." There was a crush in the doorway as they fled.

Back in the corridor I hurtled through the door and down the stairs. The man with the newspaper leapt to his feet, reaching inside his coat but I already had a gun pointing at his head so his hands changed direction and went straight up towards the ceiling.

"Turn around." He did so and I smashed the gun barrel into the back of head as hard as I could and he went down as if dead … he might have been. I didn't know how much damage I did him and, frankly, didn't care. I caught 'Madame' in the foyer and she was putty in my hands … most people are with a bloody great gun stuck in their face … as I know from personal experience. Men who rape and prostitute women are evil but there is a special place in Hell reserved for women who collude in the process. So I smacked her about a bit … mostly because she deserved it but personal satisfaction played a part in the process.

A head appeared around the corner from the corridor that led to the store room. We saw each other simultaneously and for the shortest instant we both just looked then, almost without thought, I whipped up the gun and fired. It was so easy. Pulling the trigger was not hard … just a gentle squeeze and there was a loud bang. The gun jumped in my hand with an unexpected force and a lump of plaster exploded near his head. He squealed like a girl and ducked back down the corridor. *Any other girl … not me.*

I jumped up from where I crouched over the skinny woman and chased him. "Stay there," I ordered her over my shoulder as I turned the corner, just in time to see the door slam. A moment later it opened again and a second head appeared, this one accompanied by a hand holding a gun, so I fired in the general direction and it vanished back to where it had come from.

Once more in the foyer I caught the woman bolting for the door into the brothel, so I grabbed her hair from behind and banged her about some more.

Behind the desk was a high backed office chair on wheels which I trundled through the door and along the corridor. This time I was greeted by two shots from around the doorframe so I pulled out the second gun and sent a barrage of bullets towards them from both guns at once. I had no idea about aiming or anything so I just pointed them in the general direction and pulled the triggers. The noise, in the small space, was ear-splitting and bullets went everywhere: chewing lumps from the door, the doorframe, the wall and the ceiling. I received the satisfaction of a howl of pain then chucked the chair on its side and lay it between the door and the wall opposite. The door would now only open about twenty centimetres. This time, when I went back to the foyer, I found Madame had not moved from where I'd left her.

"Which town are we in?" When she hesitated I hit her in the mouth with the gun and then pushed it into the side of her head – hard. "I *will* shoot you. There are plenty of others I can ask."

"Leedth," she mumbled through split lips and broken teeth. *God, Leeds. I'd been here a few times before. I always hated it.* I made her give me our address, which I scribbled on a page ripped from the desk diary.

"Where is the nearest police station?"

"Wha'?"

"Police! Where are they?" She gave me directions and it seemed, from her description, to be remarkably close. *Wouldn't you know it, a brothel on the doorstep of the local cop shop?* There was one more thing I needed to know. "Where's Lilly? Where did they take her?"

Her eyes darted about and I couldn't work out if she was confused, dizzy or looking for a way out. *No chance.* Eventually she said, "I don't know. Maybe ask my husband."

"Husband? Who's he?"

"Ching. English people call him 'Benny'."

"Of course." I would have liked to have tied her up but had nothing to hand so I kept whacking her on the head with one of the pistols until she stopped moving or making a noise.

Just as I was about to return to where I was to meet my fellow inmates, a buzzer sounded and, on a small, monochrome screen behind the desk, I saw an image of Benny, patiently waiting outside, idly looking up at the camera, scratching his balls and picking his nose. *Who said men were useless at multitasking?* Just the man I wanted to see.

I pushed the button and dashed around the desk to lurk just inside the entry as the door eased open. When he walked in, I hit him behind the ear with the gun before he had a chance to react. *I'm getting good at this.* He dropped to his knees then, with my foot between his shoulder blades, pitched forward. I crouched beside him as he lay, face down on the floor.

"Where's Lilly?"

"I didn't know you speak Mandarin."

"There's a lot of things you don't know about me." I pushed the gun against the side of his head as hard as I could. "Last chance. Where's Lilly?"

"I don't know. Tung took her to Manchester. That's all I know. You must to ask him."

"Fuck!" I stood and kept kicking him in the ribs until he flipped over on his back. "You sent two men to rape me, you bastard. You send men to rape women when they won't do what you want." He had no answer so pushed the barrel into his groin.

"No!" He was begging. I wondered how many young girls had pleaded with him ... and how many of those pleas he had acceded to. *We know the answer to that one, don't we?* I pulled the trigger and he started screaming. I grabbed the diary with its pen attached by a chain and scooted.

In the dining room I found the women waiting for me and rattled off the directions to the police station and handed one of them the page with the address. I'd added a quick scrawl that explained the bearer was one of a group of women who had been trafficked and used as sex slaves and that none of them spoke English, only Mandarin. To really get the police's interest, I noted that there were three dead bodies in a room on the top floor. I told her to hand the note and the diary to the officer behind the desk and they would all be helped. *I wonder what secrets the diary of a whorehouse will reveal.*

They took a bit of persuading ... and quite a lot of shoving ... but eventually I got them moving.

In the foyer, I released the door and they filed out, each carrying a miserably tiny parcel of belongings. Several of them couldn't resist giving Benny or Madame a kick as they passed. Can't say I blamed them.

In the side corridor an arm protruded through the gap and was easing the chair out of the way so I threw my weight against the door and got a very satisfying bellow. Then I reset the chair and hurried back upstairs.

Now all I wanted to do was get out. Over the previous few days, ever since Tung had returned my cases, I had been packing, unpacking and repacking to select what I really wanted to take. It wasn't just about my possessions ... I would have liked to leave no evidence of my presence but knew that, what with DNA and the stuff I couldn't take, it would be a forlorn hope. My problem was that I had no idea where I was going. With no money or any other resources, whatever I took would have to last me until I found some sort of sanctuary. And that would have to include a period of 'cold turkey'. *God knows how long that will be. Or where.*

As I was about to leave I had one final thought. On a whim ... item 13: '*Impulsivity*' ... I dropped my bags, took out one of my bamboo knives and scribed the Chinese symbol for 'moon' in the plaster of an unbloodied wall. I dipped a corner of a sheet into the congealing blood, so liberally splattered over the bed and other parts of the room, and quickly daubed the character for 'clouds' over the first. The whole work of art was about a metre high and without grace or polish but, even to my unpractised eye, clear enough for any who could read it.

I had no idea if Cho had managed to contact Deng in Hong Kong. If he had, I'd have loved to have been a fly on the wall for that conversation: with Cho begging for mercy and Deng having no idea what the hell he was talking about. If he hadn't and I could make Cho think *Hidden Moon* had a hand in this massacre, it may deter him or the mysterious *Grey Man* from giving chase.

Back in the foyer, I pressed the button and hurtled towards the front door and freedom. There was a small movement in the corner of my eye and a shot rang out from somewhere to my left but I ignored it and catapulted through the door as if my feet were on fire. I heard the door click shut behind me as a body thudded against it ... a few more seconds gained if he had to go back and press the release again. I sprinted through the archway and reached the road just as a second shot rang out.

Damn! That was quick.

I dropped my case, grabbed the guns, spun and fired back at the door, causing my hands to jump around as if each was holding a wild animal. Bullets went in all directions, ricocheting off the walls and shattering windows. After just a few seconds both guns clicked and would fire no more but that should dissuade all but the bravest – or most foolhardy.

In the road: red brick terraces of houses probably slung up in Victoria's reign, I was confronted by rows of cars but repeatedly pressing the fob brought no answering flash of indicators. Left or right? I had sent the other women to the left so, based on that alone, went to the right. After about twenty metres there was another road on my right: most likely the road I had been able to see from the corridor opposite my room. This time a press on the key fob caused lights to flash on a big, red, four-wheel-drive Kia about halfway along. The tailgate slowly and majestically started to rise. I hadn't noticed which button I'd pressed and apparently I'd hit the one to release it.

The sound of shouts in the road I had just fled added wings to my feet. With a continuous terrace of houses both sides fronting directly onto the footpath ... without even front gardens ... there was nowhere to go: no alleys to slink down, no walls to duck behind and I knew I had no chance of climbing into the vehicle, starting the engine and driving away before they came around the corner: guns in hand and shooting up the place. I sprinted to the car, chucked my bag into the open boot and dived in after it. A second stab on the button and the descending door plunged me into a comforting darkness.

I was free. It was a decidedly precarious freedom but, in my book, it still counted. Anybody opening that tailgate was going to find a wildcat with teeth bared and claws unsheathed. There was no power on earth that getting me back in that place alive.

* * *

I lay in the dark and, for the first time in my life, contemplated the similarity between 'womb' and 'tomb' ... both the words and the concepts. Outside I heard muffled shouts in Chinese and the clatter of running feet. After what seemed an hour, but was probably just a few minutes, this was replaced by the screech of sirens. One of my tactics had worked. My note about dead bodies may have intrigued the police but I suspect a fusillade of shots, turning a residential street into a warzone, was probably the major factor. Soon I heard more voices – this time in English – and the distinctive timbre, staccato speech and electronic bleeps of radio chatter.

Through a crack along the edge of the board that covered the luggage compartment I watched the light draining out of the day and only when it was fully dark did I operate the button that again opened the back and scrambled out, trying to look in all directions simultaneously. Just along the road a police car sat diagonally across the junction, blocking traffic in all directions, its roof light washing blue swathes across the surrounding buildings. A light drizzle was falling, whipped about by a chilly breeze.

Because of the small dose I had taken for my last fix I was feeling the first stirrings of withdrawal: a sort of restless nervousness and an itching along the skin of my arms and legs. There was no way I could shoot up here so I had to get away ... the sooner the better.

As I shut the tailgate and strolled around to the driver's door a constable, buttocks hooked over the wing of the plodmobile, looked up and I gave him a noncommittal wave. He nodded but did no more. I climbed in, started the engine and drove away. As soon as I was around the corner and out of sight of the officer, I set the satnav and hightailed it for the M1 and home.

With hood pulled up and, to lessen the chances of recognition by any cameras, wearing the sunglasses despite the dark, I forced myself to drive slowly ... over the speed limit by one or two miles an hour because driving too slowly is as suspicious to any traffic patrol as driving too fast

Twenty-five minutes later I arrived at Woolley Edge Services where I parked at the back of the car park and gave myself a fix. There was no way I could do the whole journey without chemical assistance. But that was my last full fix; I only had the half bag left. *Stupid! They must have had loads of the stuff on the premises. I should have found it before I left. Too late now.*

Stretched out on the back seat, I dozed until I was fit to drive then nipped back into the coffee shop where, with the dead man's credit card, I bought hand wipes, coffee, a pie and enough chocolate to satisfy even Aunt Tazzy. Thank God for contactless credit cards. Then I hit the road. The gauge showed the tank was almost full so it should get me all the way.

There was the usual boring slog of a British motorway journey, broken only by the regular news reports of the slowly unravelling drama of shootings, mass murder, a drugs factory, people smuggling and prostitution in a back street in Leeds. Somebody would have some questions to answer about that. I contemplated using the cruise control but wondered if I would be likely to doze off, so decided not.

It suddenly occurred to me that the onboard computer was displaying the date. It allowed me to calculate how long I had been incarcerated. 76 days.

Nearly four hours later I drove into Gatwick airport, tucked the Kia in a slot way back in the long stay car park and wiped the interior with the hand wipes to remove my fingerprints. The longer it stayed there before coming to the attention of the authorities the better.

Still wearing the sunglasses, I queued amongst sun tanned, case-laden travellers for a ticket to Brighton ... another charge to a credit card for which the bank was never going to be reimbursed ... and from Brighton station caught the bus, using some of the money in the wallet.

Thanks to the upgraded security of my flat ingress was actually no problem ... the thumbprint recognition entry system buzzed and let me in. Inside, I took the tiny amount of heroin that remained and ordered up a massive takeaway: solid food the like of which I had not seen in nearly two months. Replete, I put the residue in the refrigerator and set the security system on 'lockdown mode', which disconnected the electronic locks so they would not operate without me entering a password. Then I went to bed and fell into the agonising arms of heroin withdrawal.

If I ever did a single thing in my life of which I am supremely proud it was in battering down the monkey that sat on my back all those hours and of fighting the almost irresistible urge to dash out and buy some relief.

It was five days of horror and hell before I emerged from my flat. Let's not reconstruct the episode except to say I bagged my bed sheets and chucked them down the rubbish chute. The mattress would go to the tip as soon as I could organise it.

When I'd escaped from Benny's 'establishment' I was hacked off. After five days of vomiting, hallucinations, diarrhoea, cramps and screaming agony I was absolutely spitting blood and feathers. I had been turned into a junkie against my will. I'd been imprisoned, raped, tortured and degraded.

Now somebody was going to pay. I mean really, really, *really* pay.

Chapter Thirty-Three

I started gradually: gentle runs, yoga, the gym. Every hour, on the hour, my body screamed for the drug I denied it. I rode to Eastbourne and donated the clothing to various charity shops and clothing recycling schemes.

My body needed restitution so I gave it a glorious treat: from my split ends to my toenails and every pore between. My shins, underarms and bikini line proved Darwin's assertions of human relationship with monkeys so some of the treatment involved hot wax and pain. I created a fictitious road accident to assuage the curiosity of the beautician.

Justin, my hairdresser, moaned and complained.

"It's like straw, Love." He trotted around me like terrier at a lamppost, occasionally stopping to rub a strand of my crowning glory between finger and thumb. "Who on earth did this? It looks as if it was cut with a knife and fork ... by a baboon ... in the dark. Honestly, I've seen haystacks in better conditions. It will take months ... just months ... to get any life back in it, Sweetie." He called a colleague and they discussed options as if they were planning a moon landing.

The fourth day after my re-emergence I took Potex – no longer Potex-1 – and went to Shepherd's, now Ray's, office in Crawley. At the reception desk the usual viper was missing and a younger woman occupied her throne.

"Is Ray Poulter in?" I grabbed the pen and started scribbling lies into the book.

"Yes." She reached for the phone. "Who shall I say?"

"Ms Trelawney. I'm his business partner. Don't bother

calling him, I'll just go up." Without waiting for a response that might be a refusal, I headed for the stairs.

"I didn't know he had a part—" was all I heard as the door closed behind me.

"Morning, Ray," I said as I walked in without knocking. His head jerked up from behind the screen and a look of confusion and doubt raced across his face. "Dirty pictures?" I nodded at the monitor.

"No! I...I..." His mouth suddenly became a straight line and his jaw protruded. "What do you want? I thought you'd buggered off somewhere."

"Nice to see you too, Ray. How's business?"

"Not bad ..." He hesitated. "Look! Whadya want? I'm kinda busy 'ere so if you don't want anything just bugger off again."

"I need some information ..." I sat opposite him.

He half rose, knuckles on desk and leaned over, stubble clad chin still jutting, broken nose whistling. "Yeah right. Last time I supplied you wiv information I ended up 'elping some fat pig wiv 'is 'in-quiries' so you can just piss right off." I unzipped a pocket and pulled out a wad of notes. His eyes flicked at the roll and back to mine. "Still no." He seemed adamant and I couldn't work out if he was serious or it was just a ploy to up the ante so I reached down the back of my waistband. This time his eyes widened and he tried to step back as I pulled out the pistol. As the back of his knees caught the edge of his chair he thudded down. I grabbed the mechanism and slid it back. It made a satisfyingly ominous sound.

"Which will it be, Ray? The left ..." I wiggled the money. "... or the right?" I twitched the gun. "I don't care which." I hoped there was no way to tell there were no bullets in it. The pallid complexion and slack jaw told me he couldn't. His gaze was glued to the weapon. *I know just where you are at this moment, Ray. Been there, done it, got the pissed in the pants.*

"Wha'?" His voice shook and the words seemed to struggle to pass his throat.

"It's simple, Ray. Did Shepherd have any sort of storage? A shed? Warehouse? Lockup?"

"N...n...no." He shook his head – a little too vigorously.

I rose and stood the cylinder of notes on the desk then pointed the muzzle at the middle of his forehead. "Don't lie to me." He still shook his head but the fear hung about him like a bad smell. *Okay, that too.* Then it dawned on me why he was so reticent so I lowered the gun. "Look, Ray, I'm not interested in any contraband you may have there. I give you my word I won't touch it and won't tell anybody." His eyes still never left the gun, so I slipped it back in my waistband and saw his features relax; like watching a candle left too close to heat. I waited. "It's just that I believe Shepherd had some stuff stored there and I need it."

"No, nowhere. Jus' this." He waved an expressive hand around the office.

"This is a cleaning company?" I waited. He nodded. "So where are all your mops and buckets? What about polish or scouring powder? Scrubbing brushes? Dusters? Chamois leathers? Carpet shampoo? Sink plungers? Toilet duck?" Another wait.

His face went 'shifty' again: eyes darting left and right as if his brain was ponderously searching for a mental plan in the physical world. *Never going to happen, Ray.*

Eventually, he nodded. "Lockup garage. Right opposite 'is flat." Of course! I'd noticed them the night I broke in and got shot at by the charming Cho and his cheeky chums. *Why hadn't I thought of that?* "But there's nuffink there. I been through it all." He shook his head. "Nuffink," he said again with a puzzled look, almost as if doubting his own statement.

"You got a car?" He nodded so I stood. "Let's go." I picked up the wad and thrust it at him. "Here." His eyebrows shot up but he grabbed it and stuffed it in his pocket in case I changed my mind.

"How'dya get 'ere? Ain't you got no car? We can go in that."

"No just my bike. You lead in your car. I'll follow." Like I'm going to have you sitting on the pillion with your groin against my buns and those hands on my chest!

He snatched a glance at his watch. "I ain't got a lotta time."

"Let's not hang about then."

The garage was only a few minutes away, one of a block of ten: identical, pristine white, up-and-over doors, identified with black numerals. Number two had a laminated 'For Sale' sign taped to it with wide, brown tape. Ray undid the central lock on the door numbered '9' then released two padlocks, each as big as my fist, hooked through hasp and staple catches bolted to the ground. *Excessive for a few cleaning products.*

Inside he flicked a switch and harsh strip lights blinked on. The sides were lined with shelves, apart from a set of wooden lockers towards the back against the right hand wall. Every shelf was filled with the sort of stuff I would expect. Down the centre, stacked on wooden pallets, were cardboard boxes which a brief examination confirmed held rolls of paper towels, polish and so on.

"Have you been through these?" I nudged the bottom box with my toe but he shrugged.

"Nah. Not really. No point."

"Mind if I take a look?"

"Knock yerself out." Instead, I strode to the back and

Runner

tried the first of the wooden cupboards. It was locked. As I examined them I was impressed ... and puzzled. There were three of them and they were constructed from beautifully finished hardwood, lacquered to a high gloss. The wood was between two and three centimetres thick and the doors were wider than the average room door. I tried the others.

"Keys?" I held my hand out.

"Well ..."

"Don't mess me about. I guess this is where you stash the stuff you wouldn't want Mister Leyland to know about but I give you my word, I'm not interested in it."

"Still an' all ..."

"Look," I snapped, "I know they're here now. If I wanted to drop you in it, all I'd have to do is tell Leyland. Do you think he'd ask nicely for the keys? Or would he get some beefy plod with a crowbar and a no manners to open them?" He sighed and shook his head before reluctantly offering me a key ring.

"The three little ones."

I opened the first door. Inside were some more cardboard boxes that contained several dozen iPhones. I picked one out and held it up. "Supplements the income from the cleaning?"

He found something very interesting on the toe of one of his shoes, scraping an arc into the dust on the floor. I sighed and stuck the phone back and pulled out the carton. Underneath was another – this one with satellite navigation units.

"They're all like that." He tried to stop me pulling it out. "I know everything what's in there."

"And the rest?" He shrugged so I went to the next locker where I found clothes, a briefcase and a laptop computer.

Ray looked at his watch. "Hey Babe, I gotta split.

You'll 'ave to come back later." *'Babe'? You forgotten the evocative caress of kneecap on gonads?*

"No. Leave the keys. I'll drop them in to you when I leave."

"No friggin' chance." He held his hand out but I pulled out the gun.

"Leave the keys."

"Fuck you, bitch." He stalked off and a few seconds later I heard his car drive away. I continued searching the cupboards. The laptop battery was flat but I put it aside for later examination. The clothes yielded nothing and the briefcase was locked. None of the keys fitted.

The final cupboard contained a couple of workman's toolboxes with a cardboard box of toilet rolls stacked on top. With a screwdriver I forced the locks of the briefcase. Just papers. All in Russian. I dragged the contents out of all the lockers and sorted through everything. Nothing.

I searched the rest of the garage. Nothing.

I opened every box. Nothing.

After two hours I locked up and went to a nearby greasy spoon for a coffee, then returned to repeat the search. As I stepped over the threshold I noticed the two 'hasp and staple' catches had twin brothers on the inside. Who needs to lock themselves *inside* a garage?

Inspired by this discovery, I examined the cupboards again, thinking it strange such workmanship had been lavished on them when a set of metal locker would have sufficed. They appeared to have been handcrafted for the purpose – exactly fitting the space. And why were they so *wide*? The only thing I found of interest was in the middle locker where the tiniest groove ran top to bottom on the left hand side about one centimetre in from the back. Closer inspection, using the 'Flashlight' app in my phone, revealed what appeared to be a minute gap along the bottom, up the

Runner

right side and across the top. But all pushing, pulling and even an attempt to pry it with the screwdriver were to no avail.

Frustrated I resolved to call it a day but, on a sudden, totally uncharacteristic, impulse I decided to put some of the stuff away. That was when I found I couldn't shut the door of the third locker: the cardboard box of toilet paper stood proud, preventing its closure. *Funny, it fitted before.* Then I realised. No, it had fitted in the next locker – the intriguing middle one. I pulled it out, shoved it in its original place *et viola*, the door closed. I scrabbled in the toolbox and found an engineer's tape measure and it confirmed my suspicions: the middle locker was nearly three centimetres deeper than the others. I rapped the sides, the tops, the bottoms.

Nothing.

I wanted to scream. I kicked the end door and it banged closed but the only result was the satisfaction of the action so I did it again. I started putting the clothes back and realised I hadn't looked at the shelf. It seemed firmly fixed, except, when I gave it a yank it jerked forward by a centimetre ... no further. Convinced I had done something important I sidestepped to its next door neighbour.

Nothing.

I screamed. I kicked boxes. I threw everything I could put my hands on. Eventually, exhausted by the outburst, I slumped to sit on one of the pallets. I was absolutely convinced beyond all reason there was something to be discovered here. I could hear Granny's words: "Patience and perseverance leads to great knowledge." *How about impatience and a bloody great hammer, Granny?*

Tantrum worn out, I returned to my study and found it almost immediately. I slipped a finger into the gap between the back edge of the shelf and the wooden wall behind it and slid it along. About ten centimetres along I felt a small raised lump.

I pressed it.

There was a click.

In the next locker there was now a small gap down the left edge of the back panel – and what I had originally thought was a groove was actually a fillet of wood affixed to the edge: a sort of 'top to bottom' handle. The whole back slid smoothly, left to right exposing a void filled to the brim with an inky darkness.

Using my phone torch I stepped through. On my left I found a light switch and flicked it. Four overhead tubes buzzed, flashed once or twice and flooded the room with searing white light.

I was in the garage next door; identical in size and construction to the one I had just left, but here the similarities ended. Racks of shelves lined all walls. Two more sets ran down the middle, filled with boxes. I looked. *You have to, don't you?*

Guns. Lot's of them. AK47s I thought but I'm no expert – packed in straw. Conundrum solved; that's why somebody would want to lock themselves inside a garage.

Without hesitation I rushed back into Ray's garage, shut the front door and secured it with the padlocks on the inner catches. Now I could go back through the cupboard to search the secret storage without danger of disturbance.

I found metal boxes of ammunition, hand grenades, stuff that looked like blocks of putty that may have been plastic explosive – expertise lacking there, too – and much, much more. On one shelf was something on a tripod that looked like a metal box with a drain pipe sticking out the front and double handle on the back. Four metal boxes beside it contained what was probably the ammunition: shells longer than my hand and as thick as my wrist. Antiaircraft? Antitank? Who knew? Long tubes that any schoolboy would identify as bazookas or launchers for antiaircraft missiles ... and the shells that went in them. I found boxes of handguns of different shapes and sizes, along with bullets; maybe ammo for my gun but I had no idea which ones. One crate contained knives with what looked like knuckledusters for handles.

While I had been examining my find, something else niggled at the back of my brain, then I suddenly realised what it was: there were shelves on all four walls and I saw the front wall, where the door should be, had been bricked up with large concrete blocks meaning the door from Ray's was the only way in ... or out.

But most important was what sat in the middle of the floor at the end of one of the racks. A simple wooden crate, about two metres long by a third of that in width and height. On the lid were stencilled Cyrillic letters. It seemed to *lurk* like some beast of prey.

And I felt like the prey.

The screwdriver made short work of the lid.

Inside were three wooden supports, each a square of wood about two centimetres thick, mounted laterally. Each had a hole through the centre and was divided, just like the pillory through which a medieval criminal's head was pushed before being closed and padlocked shut. Only these three did not hold necks. They held, between them, a long, matte black cylinder. It was cold and smooth under my touch with no detectable seams or joins.

This was it. I had no doubts. I'd found what I was looking for.

I slumped back against the shelf, legs straight out in front of me, brain in neutral. I may have sworn. I probably did. But what words would be adequate to discovering you are sitting within inches of total annihilation?

It was the weirdest experience. It is often said that psychopaths cannot feel emotions. This is absolutely not true.

Jags Arthurson

I am capable of feeling every single one of the emotions that a *normal* person can feel it's just … difficult. Firstly, emotions do not impose themselves on me the way I believe they do on 'empaths'; suddenly popping up unbidden. I have to stop and examine myself. What am I feeling now? What caused it? What does it mean? Secondly, once I do feel an emotion I'm not necessarily sure which emotion it is or, indeed, if it's the correct emotion for the current circumstance. Imagine a person who was born deaf but suddenly gets her hearing. She will hear sounds, hear they are different from each other, but have no idea what each is. Is that music? Is that speech? If so, what does it mean?

I remember, when I was a child on a trip to the zoo, I stood a few centimetres from a venomous snake. It was secured in a glass vivarium with no way to reach me. But my throat contracted, my palms were clammy, my heart hammered in my chest. But I wasn't sure if I was scared of the potential death, so close. Or impressed by the power, the killing potential, of so tiny a creature.

Now I sat, centimetres from something far more lethal than a small, slim, white, green and red serpent. And I was terrified. I felt the emotion and was sure beyond doubt what it was. I had no idea how much damage this thing could do but felt as if, at any second, I would be vaporised.

After a while, I've no idea how long, I regained control and realised I was shaking as if I had a fever. I walked around my find, taking snaps from all angles with my phone, ensuring I captured every detail of the writing on the device itself and on the packing case.

Back in Ray's garage I reclosed the secret door and restored the whole place to some semblance of order. My next stop was a hardware shop that advertised: 'Key's Cut While You Wait.' I waited. They cut. *There's no way I'm losing access to that baby*.

Back at Ray's office I walked in on him as he was handing out assignments to a group of foreign men and women: none of whom seemed eager to meet my gaze. If I had whipped out my camera phone at that moment Ray would have found his workforce stampeding for the hills.

When we were alone I handed back his keys. "Thanks. And sorry for the trouble. You'll find it's more or less as you left it."

"So you never found nothing, right?"

"No." I sighed and shook my head. "Although that reminds me. I wonder if you can do me a favour." I pulled the gun out of my waistband and, as he jerked backwards, placed it on his desk. "Can you get any bullets for this thing?"

"Bullets?" *Am I speaking a foreign language?*

"Yes. Bullets. You know, the long, thin things that go bang and shoot people. It's empty and I don't know where to get any more."

"Empty?" *Yup, you're definitely struggling with the language.*

His face grew red, starting from the neck and rising up though his cheeks. I thought he was on the point of exploding – spraying me and the office with guts and blood ... no brains. Instead he started to laugh.

"You been threatening me wiv a empty fucking gun?" he gasped between guffaws. I nodded. "I ought to come round there and ring your scrawny, fucking, little neck." He laughed some more. Then wiped his eyes on the back of his cuff. "I'll say this for ya ... ya got more bollocks than most men I know 'cos they wouldn't even 'ave the bottle to threaten me wiv a *loaded* gun." He stood, picked the gun up and turned it over in his hand. "See what I can do." I turned to leave but he stopped me. "Whereya going?"

"Home."

"Not wivout this fucking fing, you ain't. I ain't 'aving it 'anging round 'ere. 'ere!" He lobbed it at me and I caught it before it hit me in the chest. "Take it wiv you." I stuck it down my back and left.

Once more in my flat, I slid to the floor as soon as the door clicked behind me. I was shaking. And I had some serious thinking to do.

Chapter Thirty-Four

I thought and I planned and I scrapped the plans and created new plans. My ideas ranged from, at one extreme, handing everything over to the authorities to, at the other, actually setting it off.

Eventually I had a plan that might – just – work so I felt free to spend the rest of the day in the gym then a long sauna and another luxurious massage and facial.

The next day Ray called.

"I got them fings what you wanted," he told me so I drove out and picked them up. He showed me how to load the magazine, cock the gun and fire it … without a round in the chamber. I didn't tell him I'd done quite a bit of the latter – for real – at a brothel in Leeds.

As I was about to stick it down the back of my jeans he said, "You don't wanna do that without making it safe. Them ones don't 'ave no safety catch so you 'ave to make sure it ain't got one up the spout otherwise, you go over a bump it's likely to go off and shoot yer pretty arse off." *Two Brownie points: one for caring and the other for the observation. Keep this up, Ray, and I might even start to like you. Okay, bit OTT there. How about 'not loathe'?*

He showed me how to eject the round in the breach and reload it in the magazine but added, "You wanna go easy wiv that. You got no idea 'ow to use it proper and if yer not careful you'll end up doing yerself a mischief." I thanked him and left. For all my inexperience with firearms I was glad to have it.

I put my plan into operation. It felt a bit precarious and if any one of its elements failed, the whole thing would collapse and I'd have got nowhere. In fact there was every likelihood I'd actually be even worse off. But I had to do *something*. There was not a 'do nothing' option.

The estate agent turned up exactly at the appointed time outside the garage that was for sale and whooshed open the door as if revealing the climax of a magic trick. Inside, it was identical to the others: bare, grey concrete blocks, except – to my delight – it had an inspection pit: about a metre and a half deep, a metre wide and three long with, at the front end, a set of steps leading down into the oil stained depths. The young Scottish man: baby pink face, livid red spots and vivid red hair, said the asking price was twenty four thousand pounds but confided that the vendor would probably take less. I offered the full asking price for a quick sale and a call on his mobile confirmed it was mine as soon as the legal work was done.

* * *

I was sitting astride Potex at the top of the ramp that led down to the car park beneath my block of flats, waiting for the portcullis to grind its slow way up, when I noticed a nondescript black saloon parked in the side street opposite. I couldn't be sure, but I could have sworn it had been there when I left and there were two men sitting in the shadows behind its tinted windows. I tried to recall if I had seen it anywhere on my sojourn to Crawley. Apart from Ray and hairdresser, I had contacted nobody: not Graeme, not the kickboxing club, not Adam, not even Maxie. But somehow, I felt sure, they had tracked me down. I wondered how. I wondered *who*. Had Shepherd reappeared? Or was it the Chinese back on the scene?

At least I had spotted them so I could take extra care if I needed to go anywhere or do anything I didn't want them to know about. Meanwhile I tried to act as if I hadn't seen them.

In my parking space, safe behind the garage's security gate, I examined Potex and found the tracker within minutes. *So that's how you found me.* First my saxophone case, now Potex. Jesus, I must have been carrying more tracking technology than a NASA launch.

I didn't touch it in case they had some means of telling if it had been disturbed. I was heading for the lift to my apartment when a thought struck me that sent me scurrying back again. I started a second search, this time using spanners and screwdrivers and, after nearly half an hour, found the second. One for me to find and one to track me with. *Tricky buggers.*

Safe behind my front door I picked a Brighton-based solicitor at random and hired her over the phone to handle the purchase of the garage – in my mother's name: Jeanne Trelawney. The most superficial check would reveal the subterfuge – dead women tend not to buy too much real estate – but if my plan worked I would not need to maintain the cover for long. By the time anybody investigated I would have vanished into the wide, blue yonder.

Over the next few days I got a great deal of enjoyment taking long rides, zipping in and out of motorway traffic and watching the black limo, in my rear view mirror, struggling to stay on my tail.

On the fourth day I broke cover ... if the enemy knew where I was then how could it hurt if my friends did? I arrived at Adam's front door unannounced. Becky welcomed me into an atmosphere of baking cake, waved at the spare room Adam used as an office and headed for the kitchen. *Getting a tad wider on the hip, I see, Becky.*

"Coffee?" she called over her shoulder.

Adam was hunched over a computer.

"Josie?" his voice half an octave above normal. He

craned his neck to look past me. He wore his conscience like a dunce's cap.

"It's okay, she's in the kitchen," I said in a stage whisper, further fuelling his paranoia.

"What do you want?" he asked, his voice hoarse with guilt. To his credit he seemed less aggressive than when we'd last parted. Becky appeared bearing a tray loaded with all the accoutrements of coffee and served it.

"Gosh, Josie, you've lost weight," she stood back and looked me up and down then offered a plate holding a dozen cup cakes, all elaborately decorated with multicoloured bits and pieces. *They would soon put the weight back on. It was certainly working for her.* I smiled and declined so she placed the offering on the table and left with a, "See you later."

"All right, what is it?" He swivelled his high backed office chair to face me, peeling the paper off a yellow bun.

"I need to send an email ..."

"So sign up for Gmail." He took a bite, leaving a cream moustache. *Yummy.*

"No. I need to send an email the way Shepherd did to those guys in Russia and Syria. You know, The Dark Web."

"It's called 'The *Deep* Web'. The populist media call it 'The Dark Web' because it sounds more sinister and they want you to think it's only used by criminals to sell guns and drugs." *And atom bombs?*

"Whatever." I shrugged. "I just need to send emails that can't be traced back to me."

"Sure. No probs." He wiped his mouth with a paper napkin, swung back to his machine and called up a browser. "Here you go. You need this special version of *Firefox* to access something called *The Onion Router* or *ToR*." He fired it up, logged on and started flitting from one screen to another. Most showed drugs and guns. *No atom bombs.* I reached into my rucksack and pulled out the laptop I'd appropriated from

Ray's garage.

"While we're at it, can you see if there's anything of interest on there, please?"

He plugged the machine in, booted it, plugged in a cable sticking from a socket on his desk and, for the next half an hour, faffed about with flash pens and CDs before declaring there was no new stuff. It seemed to be a copy of the files he'd recovered from the other machine. At my request, he loaded the special browser on it then set up all the required accounts. Eventually, two cups of coffee each and three buns ... all eaten by him ... later he snapped the lid shut, unplugged it and handed it over like a king handing down an honour.

"Connect to WiFi and you're ready to rock and roll."

With all the usual hugs and air kisses and encouragements to stay for dinner, all from Becky, of course, I escaped and headed home ... followed by the same black car.

Next day I went to the solicitor's office to sign forms for the garage. I met the young woman whose name I immediately forgot and presented a cheque, signed by *J Trelawney*

She promised completion within a few days. "Conveyancing of something like a lockup garage is much simpler than residential property."

"When can I have possession?" I asked.

"Theoretically not until contracts are exchanged – maybe a couple of weeks – but I've spoken to the agent and, apparently, the owner has moved up north and has no further use for it so you can move in immediately if you like. Again, it's not like a house where there would be major upheaval moving out again if anything went wrong. It would be a case of simply moving your car out and handing back the key."

Well, not quite. But I'm not telling you that. She handed me two keys looped on a piece of wire.

I assumed somebody was watching me when I left the office but, in the crowds, I couldn't identify any overt watchers.

On the internet I found a general builder in Crawley and got a quote for filling in the inspection pit, accepted it and told him I'd send the key. I scribbled the address of the garage onto the back of my business card, stuck it with one of the keys and a cheque for half the cost into a padded envelope and strolled into Rottingdean to post it.

There was an unexpected bonus because I finally got a look at the man who followed me and was puzzled. I had expected Chinese features but this guy was Middle Eastern in appearance with a wild, dark beard. *Okay, now I am worried.*

On the way back I saw the black saloon snarled up in traffic in the narrow high street of the quaint *Olde Worlde* village. Maybe they needed to bring the car in case I took other transport. I was tempted to catch a bus to Eastbourne or somewhere, just to see the panic as they tried to extricate themselves from the jam but didn't bother because suddenly the fun was going out of it. Assuming I was being stalked by Cho's lot and, having crossed swords with them and won every round, I had no worries. This was a whole other issue. If these men were who I thought they were, then the game was moving onto a completely different playing field.

But at least my plan was coming together ... or so I thought.

* * *

It was dark on the landing. It shouldn't be: there were detectors on each landing that switched the lights on as soon as anybody entered. But the hallway outside the security door at the foot of the stairs to my floor was black. Undeterred, I pulled out my phone to use the trusty torch but a hard blow sent it spinning from my hand. Strong hands grabbed me, slammed me against the wall and I felt as if I'd been punched hard in the right hip ... followed by agony. When I touched the area it felt wet and sticky and I realised I'd been stabbed. Two men held me against the wall and one of them switched on a torch: the beam no more than a dull glow. The one directly in front of me placed his left forearm across my throat, leaning heavily on it. In his right hand he held the blade of a knife against my cheek with the point pricking my lower eyelid.

The man with the torch leaned in to me and a rough voice in a foreign accent growled in my ear. "You want more pain, we can give you more. Much more." I could smell garlic on his breath and the touch of coarse whiskers against my face.

"Why would I want that?" I could feel my gun grinding into the small of my back and I wondered if I stood a chance of reaching it while retaining my eye.

"Where is Shepherd?"

"God knows. He's cleared off. I heard maybe he's gone to Moldova."

"Why were you at his store?" *Ray's garage?*

"His store?" I don't know what you mean?" The man in front of me pushed harder and I was starting to feel dizzy. The other, beside me, punched me in the ribs ... a reminder of Cho's attentions. My eyes watered.

"I followed you. You and the fat man. You both went in. He leaved, you stayed." I eased the bamboo knife out of my sleeve. *Knife fights: a game for all to play.*

"The garage?" I croaked. "It's not Shepherd's. It belongs to Ray Poulter: the fat man. He keeps cleaning material in it."

"Not Shepherd?" He sounded unsure. They spoke a

few words each in Arabic. Finally my inquisitor snapped something that sounded like, "Aqtiluha." The light went out and my captor withdrew the blade from my cheek and in the dark I sensed him drawing it back – maybe to strike – so I twisted sideways and lunged forward with my own blade. He gasped, clasped his gut and dropped to his knees. His knife clattered to the floor.

I was free.

Sensing the position of his colleague, I lashed out with my foot on no more than instinct connecting with thin air, stabbed my thumb on the illuminated sensor and was only able to breathe again when I heard a click and the door unlatched. I dived through and slammed it shut a fraction of a second before a solid body thundered into it. *Give it your best shot, Pal.*

Now I had Arabs threatening me ... possibly attempting to kill me ... looking for Shepherd and, presumably, what was in the secret store. Sure as hell they weren't after the scouring powder.

In my bathroom, I undressed and treated the wound. It hurt like hell. When I swabbed it with antiseptic it hurt even more. At that instant I hated ... detested ... loathed ... anything with a Y chromosome. If I previously desired revenge now I was gagging for it.

Chapter Thirty-Five

I fired up Shepherd's laptop. There was no reason I used his instead of my own. Just superstition I suppose. Google translate told me the text I wanted was 'Вы хотите это?' – Do you want this? I composed an email and attached a picture of the device in the secret storeroom and encrypted it using the public key of Shepherd's contact in Raqqa. I logged onto ToR, clicked the *Send* button and the message hurtled off into the ether.

Early next morning I was just rousing from a deep sleep when I was brought fully awake by the ping of an incoming message on Shepherd's computer. Despite my bleariness I set about putting it through the reverse process using Shepherd's private key. The message, when translated was simple and to the point: *Where? When?*

I made the sender wait until I'd risen, bathed, tended my wound and dressed. I munched a slice of toast while composing a reply, also simple. "Wait. It is held by enemies. Soon." I sent them a list of instructions, all very simple: I didn't want to overstretch Google's Russian translation skills. I finished with: "Contact me when you are ready."

Outside my front door I found my mobile lying on the floor beside a congealed puddle of blood – too much to be mine. I fetched a bucket of soapy water and washed it away. There was no sign of the knife with which I'd been stabbed. Both light bulbs were broken so I reported it to the maintenance man who lived somewhere at the other end of the internet. The CCTV was supposed to be monitored 24/7 but he claimed not to have been on duty the previous evening so had no knowledge of any interlopers. He couldn't tell me who had been.

I went to the gym – nobody followed me – but my leg hurt and I couldn't concentrate so just slung a few weights around then showered, changed and headed home. Graeme was waiting for me, dressed in civvies and sitting behind the wheel of a small, tatty Ford. As I waited for the garage gate to open, he walked over.

"Hello Josie." He looked older: slower, somehow 'saggy'. His hair, a distinguished hint of grey at the temples when I married him, was now almost totally grey and seemed to have abandoned part of his forehead.

I flipped my visor up. "Hello. How did you know I was back?"

"It's my job. Can I come up?"

We drank coffee then went to bed and it made a nice change to do it from choice. My leg and other bodily damage hampered proceedings a little. *Not too much*.

As soon as he'd gone I checked the emails. Nothing except spam. *Even on the deep web!*

On my own machine I searched the web and located a picture of one million pounds ... a huge stack of notes ... saved it as .jpeg file then composed another encrypted message, this time to Shepherd's other contact. The message was the same, in the same language. It was only the picture that was different. The response was almost immediate: long, encrypted and once I'd deciphered and translated it – a job that took over two hours – it turned out to be a rant of accusations, threats and demands to know where I ... 'Serebrian' ... had been.

By that time I'd had a response from the Syrians. They needed a week.

I ignored the Russians' threats and simply sent them an identical message to the one I sent the Arabs. Within minutes I had the response. "Two days."

I didn't answer. It will be nice to have somebody waiting for me for a change.

The next day, Graeme called again but this time he was accompanied by a female detective constable called Alderton. Quite pretty really. Large bosom. Just his type. *Shagging her, are you?*

They settled down with cups of my best medium roast and he made it clear this was totally unofficial and 'off-the-record'.

"In view of our personal relationship, I probably shouldn't be doing this but I discussed this with Leyland and we felt it might be an easier way to start."

"Start what?"

"We've been communicating with a couple of other forces ... particularly Leeds. They've raided a, er, factory or something. It seems this place was involved with drugs and prostitution. The other day there were five murders ..." *Hmm, wonder who else didn't make it? I hope it was Benny and his wife.* He trailed off as if unsure how to continue so I prompted him.

"Really? Why are you telling me this? What's it got to do with me?"

"Oh, Josie." He looked genuinely downcast. "Don't pretend you don't know. We know you were there." He opened a folder and riffled through papers. "Your DNA – we had it on record after your parents' murders. Clothes, shoes, even your saxophone ... with your name and address on a card in the case." He sighed and his shoulders slumped. He *did* look old. "Do you want to tell me about it?" I pondered for a few seconds while they leaned forward, expectation on their faces. So I told them.

"On the way to Heathrow – when you all thought I was leaving the country – I was stopped by a couple of bogus policemen and kidnapped. I was drugged and taken somewhere ... a cellar ... I don't know where. I was tortured, repeatedly raped and injected with regular doses of heroin." I pulled up my sleeve to reveal the track marks. "A girl called Natalia, with whom I was incarcerated, was tortured and suffocated to death in front of me." As I filled in a lot more of the graphic details, the DC beside him on the sofa went white and kept swallowing excess saliva. *You chuck up on my Persian and they'll be a sixth murder.*

"Any idea why they abducted you?" Graeme asked.

"Same reason Shepherd was harassing me. They were after this mythical fortune my father was supposed to have." His eyes jerked down.

"Did they give any hint they might have been involved with your family's murders?" he said.

"Nothing. But they weren't interested in giving information – just getting it." He nodded. "Eventually they chucked me into the back of a van and drove me to, I later found out, Leeds."

His eyebrows went up. "Why did they do that?"

"God knows but I think there was something to do with some sort of war going on between them and another gang ... or Triad, I think it's called."

He looked at his companion as if it fitted with something they already knew. "Hidden Moon," she said, *sotto voce*, and he nodded.

"All the time, I was kept addicted to the heroin and regularly raped by a man whom I knew as Tung. I had no idea how long I'd been held there but one day there was a load of shouting and guns going off. Three men: one of them – this 'Tung' – came barrelling into the room in which I was kept but some other men wearing ski masks and dark glasses came after them and led me out. That's all I know."

"A group of women turned up at the local police station and said you had set them free. They had a note from you ..."

Runner

"Good. I knew about the other women. They'd been trafficked and forced to work as prostitutes. I asked the new men to release them. They refused but in the end allowed me to write the note and direct them to the police station."

"Right. Then what?"

"They took me to Gatwick in a big four-wheel-drive car …"

"Make? Model? Anything?"

"Sorry, no. It was red. I think." The woman leaned forward and spoke to me for the first time.

"We think you drove the vehicle."

"What makes you think that?" I got every inch of surprise I could into my voice: higher register, rising inflection.

"Cameras. On the motorway. In the service station—"

"I was locked in the boot! I never even got inside the cab—"

"Like I said, there's somebody who looks like you on cameras—"

"Looks like? How … 'looks like'?"

She referred to something in the folder then passed me a photograph.

I laughed. "You're joking! Hoodie, shades. Even *I* couldn't tell if that was me." I thrust it back at her but she missed and it spun to the floor at my feet. Our eyes locked but I made no move to pick it up. Eventually she lost and relented. She held out another picture. "Gatwick Airport. You, buying a ticket. That *is* you, isn't it?" *Shit. Same clothes.*

"Yes." I had to think fast. "But when they threw me out one of them gave me the coat and sunglasses. He said I had to wear them until I got home—"

"And you did?" She sounded aggressive and looked fierce. *Not so pretty now, Sweetie.*

"Somebody had me incarcerated, tortured, raped and drugged ... I pulled up my sleeve and thrust my needle tracked arm at her again ... before the others locked me in the boot of a car and bounced me around for two-hundred and fifty miles. When I found out they were letting me go I would have travelled naked with a daffodil up my arse if they'd told me to."

"Still got the coat?" Graeme interrupted.

"No. I binned everything." She scribbled notes. *Good luck on locating any of that.*

"Why?" she asked.

"Sorry, was I supposed to hang onto them for sentimental reasons?"

"Why didn't you report all this to us?"

"What? Like I reported Shepherd? That went well, didn't it?" We glared at each other.

"Anything else?" Graeme broke the deadlock.

"Yes. Two guys turned up here the night before last and demanded to know where Shepherd was. They looked like Arabs. If you check the CCTV in the foyer you might get something."

"What did you tell them?" Brünnhilde started in on me again.

"Nothing. And they asked me ever so nicely. Oh, and one of them stabbed me. Want to see?"

The cow actually did. I flashed a look at Graeme who could have confirmed my wound but he wouldn't meet my eye. They left with promises that I would 'need to give a full statement later.'

* * *

Runner

Ray obtained me another fake passport and Stefan bought me some aeroplane tickets. This time there would be no trackers in my luggage and I truly would vanish. Completely.

I needed to spend a few days visiting Poo-Brain so had to lose my tail. I pulled both trackers of the bike, slipped them in the back of my gloves and set out towards Rottingdean. The road pattern in the village is like a giant letter 'P' running north from the sea. In the centre of loop is the Village Green which acts as a giant roundabout but the stem of the letter, The High Street: narrow and congested, has two-way traffic. On the coast road I checked for the black saloon and slowed to let it get closer as it followed me into the village.

Just past the road on the right where the loop of the 'P' joins is a second road, Whipping Post Lane, a narrow, private road that serves a small terrace of cottages. I turned into this and accelerated past two parked cars to the other end. They tried to follow but soon realised there was insufficient room. As I turned right at the end I glanced back and saw it trying to reverse out.

Within seconds I was turning left, back onto the High Street heading south. To my right I saw the chaos as my followers were backing into the stream of vehicles but a supermarket delivery van was too close behind and was blocked, in turn, by the car behind. I sneaked through jammed up traffic and dropped one tracker into a pickup truck heading north and flicked the other into a lorry unloading outside the supermarket.

I took the coast road, up to Wilson Avenue and from there to the A23. I stuck to speed limits and on the outskirts of Birmingham, stopped at a cheapish business hotel for the night, paid in cash, and continued to Cumbria the next morning.

Harrison looked much the same. I talked to him …

talked *at* him. I needed to know what he remembered of *that night*. Did he have any recollections of the events? Did he remember who shot him? I got little more than largely incoherent mumblings.

They told me he was 'greatly improved' but I couldn't see it. I stayed over – they had a room for visitors – and drove back nonstop six days later.

Emails told me everything was in place.

Just one more piece to go.

Chapter Thirty-Six

Graeme claimed to have been 'just passing by' and 'thought he'd pop in.' I didn't believe a word. I would bet large sums he had somebody watching me; probably the woman who spent all day washing, sweeping and polishing the public areas of the building was keeping him up to date on my movements.

I invited him in. I made it sound like I was doing him a favour but actually it was great timing. We sat in the solarium, bright sea spread before us, open doors admitting cool sea breezes and the distant sound of traffic.

"Sorry about Terry – DC Alderton – yesterday. She's a bit … you know …" He tapered off. *Even better. Start at a disadvantage.* I sat, head in hands, shoulders slumped, silent. After a while, he placed his cup on the low coffee table and moved closer, sliding along the sofa. I felt his arm around my shoulders. "What's wrong?" *Do I detect genuine concern? That's a first.*

I sighed, long and shuddering. "I think I've made the biggest mistake of my life and I don't know what to do."

"What is it? Anything I can do to help?" *Now you're interested.*

"I'm not sure." I twisted around to look at him, face so close it was almost touching mine. *Burberry Aftershave.* "It's the money my father had …"

"The million pounds …?"

"No. Not *million* – singular. *Millions.* Plural." I let it sink in.

One eyebrow rose. He used to practise that look in the mirror. "Millions? What exactly are we talking about here?"

"Probably about forty million. Maybe more. I'm not sure."

"Jesus Christ Almighty!" he burst out, springing to his feet as if propelled by several thousand volts up his rectum. "Forty ..." he stepped around the coffee table and strode to the window where he stood, staring out to sea, with his hands behind his back, rigid shoulders speaking volumes. Occasionally he slapped the back of one hand into the palm of the other then rose on the balls of his feet before rocking back on to his heels.

"Graeme, you said— "

"Said what?" He rocked some more: toes, heels, slap hands. Toes, heels, slap hands.

"You said not to worry about it. When I thought it was a million. You said not to mention it to the authorities. What's changed?"

"If you can't see the difference between *one* million and *forty* million then you're more stupid than I took you for." *Careful. Men have died for less*.

"Of course I see that. And that's what's worrying me about it ..." I paused.

"What is?" His voice snapped like a whip as he spun to face me, suddenly the policeman again.

"Well, it's a bit difficult. It's not in money, you see, it's in gold."

"Gold?" He strode across and towered over me. For a second I thought he might actually hit me. I don't know why.

"Good grief. Do you know where it is? Have you seen it? How big a stack is it, for God's sake?"

"Not so big. I was quite surprised at how small, actually. A cubic metre of gold weighs over nineteen tonnes and is worth about ten million pounds. When I stuck a tape measure on it, I found it measured—"

"Christ!" He spun around and stalked back to the

window where he took a deep breath, as if to calm himself, and turned back to me. "You know where it is?"

"Yes. And I'll tell you." I paused deliberately and held his gaze. "But first I want some information from you."

He nodded. "What?"

"You obviously know more about this ... the Shepherd connection and so on ... than you've told me. So tell me now."

"What do you want to know?"

"Everything. Who is he? *What* is he? And ... most importantly ... what's the connection between him and my father?" I needed to find out what the police knew.

He sighed and slumped down on the sofa once more, picked up his coffee, sipped and screwed up his face. "Cold."

"I'll get another."

"No. Don't bother." He lay a hand flat across the cup but made no other move. I waited. Eventually he said, "Shepherd is not whom he claims to be. He's not even British. As far as we can tell he's Eastern European. And he's a dealer; drugs, arms, people."

"And my father?"

"Bruce? Not too sure but I suspect he was laundering Shepherd's money. I don't know all the details but I think Shepherd did a deal for something big – again, not sure what – with some nasty characters in the Middle East ... may well be connected with terrorism." *Definitely connected with terrorism.* He made a moue and shook his head. "Most things out that way are to do with terrorism, it seems to me. Anyway, Shepherd did the deal and Bruce got the money on his behalf but then put it somewhere that nobody else knew about." He sipped some of the coffee, seemingly forgetting it was cold, and pulled another face.

"Go on."

"That's it. That's all I know. We can only surmise

that, somehow or another, somebody else – these Chinese characters – got wind of it and decided to swipe the money off your father but it all went south. When Bruce died, we assumed all trace of the money had died with him." He put his cup down and swivelled to me. "So now it's your turn. What do *you* know?"

"The gold is all in ingots. My father kept it in a garage in Crawley – in my mother's name. I found details of the place in some of his papers and, when I went there, I found it was empty. There was one of those inspection pit things and it was hidden in there. It had wooden slats over it – so nobody fell in, I assumed – but when I lifted them up I found it was full of gold."

"And it's still there?"

"Of course. Even a single bar is too heavy for me to pick up. That's where it's all going wrong. What the hell can I do with load of gold that I can't even lift?" I dropped my head in my hands again, gave a sob and rubbed my eyes. *Reel him in.* "I didn't know what to do so I got this load of concrete delivered and chucked it on top of it."

"So what's the problem …?"

"You know I told you and DC Busty I was assaulted by a pair of Arabs the other night …?"

"Yes." He nodded vigorously.

"Well it wasn't just Shepherd they wanted. They also knew about the gold and that it was in a lockup garage. Just not exactly where …"

"And …?" I could see his eagerness shining out of his wide eyes.

"They also knew where Harrison is and said that, unless I gave them the details they would kill him."

"Did you give them what they wanted?" He was on his feet now, arms wide, eyebrows arched high, chin thrusting.

"What choice did I have? They stabbed me!"

Runner

His face was a mask of fury. "You stupid ..." He reached down and grabbed me by the upper arms, hauling me out the seat, thumbs grinding into my biceps. I acted scared but actually felt a warm glow of satisfaction. After a few seconds he became calm again but I was sure it was an act ... he almost buzzed with tension. "Okay. So I ask again, 'What's the problem?' You're scared of something. What is it?"

I shoved him away, hand in the centre of his chest and pushed so hard he staggered back, almost falling over the table.

"The reason they didn't kill me is that they wanted to make sure the gold was there. They made it clear if I was lying they'd come back and 'ask' again." I started crying, even managing, under cover of my cupped hands, to lick my palms and wipe it over my eyes. *Smeared mascara is always makes them go all gooey.*

"But you *didn't* lie to them, did you? They've gone now. There's nothing more to worry about." His teeth seemed glued together and I saw the strain in the muscles of his jaw. But then, who wouldn't be hacked off at seeing a few million pounds slip through their paws?

"Don't you see ...?" I tried my Are-you-a-total-moron? look. "You, yourself, just said they were terrorists. You also know what terrorists do ... they *kill* people. Usually in pretty gruesome ways."

"So ..."

"So once they've got the gold there's a good chance they'll want to eliminate any witnesses ... me!"

"Oh stop exaggerating. They're *terrorists*. They don't give a stuff if anybody knows they exist—"

"Unless they're a cell operating in secret in this country!" I fired back at him. "If you were organising an attack on, say, a public event, would you want to leave anybody around who knows who you are and who could identify you? Like I say, the only reason I'm still breathing is because they needed to check if the gold is really there. Once they have, I'm dead!"

"Okay, answer this ... why didn't they just take you with them? Something else terrorists are noted for is kidnapping. Why would they make an exception in your case?" *Shit! I didn't think of that one. Think fast!*

"I managed to get the knife off one of them and stabbed him. If you've looked at the CCTV you'll see that, as they're leaving, one of them doesn't look quite as spry as he did arriving. While he was doing his *Dying Swan* act, I nipped in through my front door ... my *high security* front door." *Phew, got out of the one.*

He didn't seem one hundred percent convinced but let it go.

"Where is this place? Crawley, you said?" I gave him the address of my new garage and he headed for the door. "I'll get things moving," he called over his shoulder as he headed out. I saw him pull out his mobile as the door closed on his back. *No hanky-panky this afternoon then, Superstud?*

I grabbed a bag I'd packed and headed to the garage. Twenty minutes later I pulled up in a quiet cul-de-sac about fifteen minutes walk from Shepherd's flat and garage. I slipped off my leather jacket and unrolled the skirt of the dress I wore beneath then took off my jeans and exchanged my boots for sandals, sticking the shed clothes into a couple of shopping bags. Now I was an ordinary woman you might pass on any suburban street. *If you're really, really lucky.*

I gained entry by tailgating a delivery man who held the door open in exchange for a beaming smile. Nothing had changed in the corridor outside the flat: the broken door was held closed with a padlock and crisscrossed with police tape. A repeat of my previous performance with a foot against the door ripped the hasp out of the woodwork.

With the laptop connected to my phone I set it up as a mobile hotspot to access the internet. I sent two emails: identical except for the recipients' addresses. Both simply enquired, "Are you ready?" Within minutes I had positive responses to both.

Then I set myself up in Shepherd's bedroom: nice, comfortable armchair behind the net curtains with a good view of all the garages.

If my ex was doing as he said, I would expect to soon hear the sound of sirens and be treated to the sight of numerous plods levering open the door to my newly acquired property. Or maybe he'd set up a discreet observation post to keep watch and see who turned up. *Should be interesting.*

I waited.

About ten the next morning, fortuitously rousing from a light doze, I spotted a lone man strolling, too nonchalant to be credible, past the garages and as soon as he'd spotted his target, turned and fled ... all signs of insouciance gone. It was difficult to tell at the distance but, if forced to decide, I would say he was Chinese. A few minutes later a large lorry turned into the end of the road and coasted to a halt directly opposite me. Men jumped out, a crowbar or the like was produced and the door forced. More men started unloading long handled sledge hammers and bars that could have been chisels or crowbars. I would have sworn I recognised a few of Cho's men.

Most vanished inside and the door clanged shut. A few hung around outside and distributed a line of traffic cones to make the work 'official'. I kept a special look out for Cho but, if he was there, I didn't spot him.

I grabbed the laptop and fired off an email. It simply gave the address of the garage. From opposite I could hear hammering and was somewhat surprised the neighbours were not complaining.

The work had been going on for less than half an hour when a car: long, sleek and black, oozed around the corner and slid gently towards the men idling behind the truck. A sudden burst of automatic gunfire from the rear passenger window sounded almost like ripping cloth. Some of the standing men were catapulted backwards by the flying bullets, others dived for cover, scrambling underneath the lorry while simultaneously trying to draw weapons.

I hit the 'send' button and hurled another email into the void.

With a scream of tyres the car accelerated away but, with a dead end in front of it, was forced to slither to a halt as the driver performed a three point turn. The garage door burst open and men erupted, guns blazing. A second vehicle – another truck – pulled into the road and stopped crosswise, disgorging more men and catching the defenders in a devastating crossfire.

I dialled triple nine, my number concealed, and reported heavy gunfire. I gave the location and made it clear there were machine guns being used until the operator got too inquisitive about my identity when I disconnected the call.

The gunfight lasted several more minutes and the Chinese had been just about overwhelmed when a third lorry turned into the road, smashed into the side of the one that blocked the way, driving it sideways for a dozen or so metres and spinning it through over ninety degrees. A new group piled from the back and added to the affray. The latest arrivals were swarthy with thick beards and a tendency to yell 'Allahu Akbah' at regular intervals, audible even from my remote location.

Bullets peppered the surrounding properties. One smashed the window beside me and showered the floor with glass. I wonder what moron coined the phrase 'Friendly Fire.'

Runner

How ironic would it be to have set up this cabaret only to be taken out by a stray?

People were dying, maybe a dozen or more. What did I feel? As usual, not a lot. Okay Professor Hare, chalk up a point for number 7; 'Shallow effect.' But these were all men involved in, between them, attempts on my life, kidnapping, torture and murder. Should I *really* be concerned?

With the losers vanquished – dead or wounded – the Arab victors now occupied the garage and hammering once more issued forth from the interior and all reigned – relatively – peaceful again. None of them seemed to be concerned about the casualties and the newcomers didn't even bother to close the door so I could see them attacking the concrete it had cost me so much to have installed just a few days before.

I was surprised by how long it took for the authorities to arrive but when they did, they did it in style. The clatter of rotor blades chattered above and the helicopter hung, as if by magic, fifty metres above. A man stuck his head out of the building and, almost casually, let lose a few rounds at the big machine, which listed heavily as it veered away. A few seconds later an armoured car burst into the scene of carnage and the gunfight resumed. The difference this time was that the latest attackers were obviously skilled professionals so the defenders were soon overcome ... although most chose to die, charging en masse, guns blazing rather than surrender. *Jihadis are a bit like that, I hear.*

Calm was eventually restored and they locked the area down, tapes were stretched across roads for streets around, roadblocks were set up: lorries or armoured cars manned by men in khaki battledress, toting weapons that would not normally be seen off the battlefield.

I'd anticipated this and brought enough food and bottled water to last a couple of days so I settled down for the wait. I'd brought my music and several books although the show on the street below kept me diverted as ambulances carried away injured or corpses – considerably more of the latter than the former, it seemed – and police vans conveyed the rest, in handcuffs, presumably to cells and interrogation.

The Triad members, who had arrived first, had been totally massacred by the Russians who, with their military efficiency, would have wiped out the Syrians too except for the latter's superior numbers and a faith-inspired, fearlessness that bordered on a death wish.

* * *

With troops occupying the street outside and the rest of the block evacuated, I dared not show a light so at dusk I had a snack and went to bed lying, dressed in my biker gear, on Shepherd's musty, dusty sheets. The army had set up powerful arc lights outside so I pulled the curtains to try to restrict the brightness ... with only partial success. With the sound of jack hammers, digging up my new concrete, I slid into a sort of half-doze.

When I awoke I thought the light was artificial but on cracking the curtains saw it was daylight and, despite the odds, I'd actually had a good night's sleep. I felt great. After a cold breakfast and a colder wash, I packed everything ready to leave as soon as I was able then settled back in the chair and waited for the squaddies to finish. Eventually they must have been satisfied the hole contained nothing. *Your sources must have got it wrong, guys.* So I watched as they dismantled barriers, packed everything into canvas topped military trucks and departed.

My cue to do likewise.

I sneaked along the hall, cracked the door open the smallest amount ... and it hit me in the face. As I staggered back, holding a bruised mouth, it came fully open and a man

filled the frame.
 Shepherd.
 And he was not alone. He brought a friend: a bloody great revolver.
 And it was looking straight at me!

Chapter Thirty-Seven

I raised my hands and backed away as he followed me in, flicking the door closed behind him with his heel while all the time the gun remained rock steady, aimed straight at my face. He reached into his pocket and pulled out a pair of handcuffs, swinging them on an outstretched finger, as if we were about to start a game. He grinned: wide, taunting.

"Hello, Regina, be a good girl slip and these on." *Fancy something a bit kinky, do you? I'm up for a bit of SM ... providing I'm the 'S' and you're the 'M'.* When I'd done as bid he lay the gun on a shelf beside him, grabbed my wrists and checked I'd fastened the bracelets securely. In doing so he found my knife secreted up my left cuff and, apparently intrigued by what looked a stick of bamboo, took it out and examined it, eventually sliding the blades apart and together again a few times. "Pretty little toy." He slipped it in his pocket.

He spun me around – a little too enthusiastically – and pushed me back towards the room I'd just vacated. I felt the hard muzzle between my shoulder blades. *A bit optimistic to hope he'd forget it to pick it up, I suppose.* He made me sit on the bed, unshackled me and rerouted the chain through the rail at the foot of the bed. *Not again! I'm getting heartily* PISSED OFF *with being chained to sodding beds!*

He put the gun on the dressing table and stood by the window, surveying the scene below, now devoid of all life, the only evidence of the former activity being the smashed-in garage door, hanging drunkenly from its frame, revealing the garage full of rubble and bullet holes in walls, doors and the road surface. A few cones held blue and white tape that

Runner

fluttered in the breeze and suggested no one should enter but offered no resistance should they ignore it.

"I suppose you organised this little sideshow?" he asked without turning around. He seemed remarkably calm ... especially compared to how he was the last time we spoke.

"I may have had some small part in it." I twisted my wrist in the faint hope there might be some leeway in the cuffs. There wasn't.

"I have to hand it to you, I never expected you to get out of the mess I left you in." He turned, smiling. "Let me see what I can deduce from all of this ..."

"Go for it, Sherlock."

He looked puzzled. "Sherlock?" Then he brightened. "Ah yes, the fictional detective. "

"I don't suppose you had much time for the English Classics, did you, Mister Serebrian?" His eyes narrowed, just a flick, but I'd caught him off guard.

"Touché." *French as well.* He refitted his smile. "You got into my emails?" I nodded and so did he. "Yes. It's the only way you could have summoned up the hordes." He waved a hand out the window. I just smiled. "I am guessing the Chinese had something to do with Hu ..."

"Who?"

"Hu was ..." He realised the trap too late but just pursed his lips and shook his head. "He was the little bastard who started this whole shit storm. I am guessing that when he was working for me he overheard something, or saw, something he should not have ... we will never know. It would not have been so bad if he had even succeeded in stealing the money. I would have tracked him down and got it back." He picked up the gun and sighted along the barrel at me. "I can be *very* persuasive." He replaced the weapon. "What did they think was there?" He jerked his head towards the window and the garages beyond. "The money?"

"Gold – to the value of. Fifty million dollars would have been an absolutely *huge* amount in cash. They would never have believed it."

"Clever. And the others ... the Russians?"

"Also gold. They were very efficient by the way. They could have beaten all-comers but were too heavily outnumbered. Mind you, they were all on a loser when the army turned up."

He shrugged and sighed. "I guess. Still it got them off my back. Well done." He went suddenly serious. "And the Arabs? What did they come for?"

I made him wait but eventually said, "You know what they wanted."

`"And that is ...?"

"I think you called it 'a tank' did you not?"

"Ah! So Ray talked. I assumed he would. Too stupid to keep his mouth shut." He pondered. "I never thought they would have put themselves on the line for money ... they have already got *billions*. But it is a pity really."

"Oh?"

"Yes, because they did not all die and I guess, once the security services start interrogating them, they will admit what they were here for. Then we will have MI5 and co looking for it."

"And the logical place to start would be other garages." That made him really start. I saw the eyebrows jerk up, even his mouth made a momentary 'O'.

"So you know about that, too?"

I just nodded. "Just like Lucy, Susan, Edmund and Peter ..."

"Who? What are you blithering about?" His fists clenched and he took a half step closer.

"Some children went through the back of a cupboard and found a whole secret world." He towered over me, body

Runner

stiff. "Just another English Classic." I said. "Forget it."

He nodded and pinched his bottom lip between finger and thumb. Suddenly he thrust a hand in his pocket and pulled out a mobile phone, hitting a number. After a few seconds the other party must have answered.

"Ray?" he asked then, after a few seconds, added, "Yes, I am back. Meet me outside the garage. Do not forget to bring the key." Finally, after a few more seconds of unheard protestations from Ray, he snapped, "I do not give a flying fuck. Just get over here." *I just knew the good mood wouldn't last.*

He resumed his lookout and eventually Ray must have arrived because Shepherd unhooked me from the bed but immediately re-secured the handcuffs. He hooked my long-handled bag over his shoulder so he could keep his hand with the gun out of sight and propelled me to the door, forcing me to precede him out of the building and across the road. Parked outside was a small, open-backed truck with a tarpaulin stretched across the load space. He'd come prepared.

Ray stood by the door, anxiety radiating from him as he shuffled his feet and the coins in his trouser pocket. *I hope they're coins.*

"Open up." Shepherd waved an impatient hand at the door while we were still some metres away then followed us in and switched on the lights before closing and padlocking the door behind us.

"What's going on then, Mister Shepherd?" Ray asked, eyeing my handcuffs.

"Shut up and do as you are told." Shepherd pulled the gun from the bag and shoved past us, keeping the gun trained on me. I couldn't work out whether he was threatening Ray with it as well. I wondered if Ray suspected the danger he was in.

Shepherd went straight to the third cupboard, "Open

this one. And this." He slapped the next door and Ray complied, allowing Shepherd to pull out the shelf and push the button.

"What's going on?" Ray asked me this time.

"Your mate, Shepherd here, has another garage next door and the only way in is through the back of that cupboard."

"Another garage? What's he want that for?" *Not the ripest plum on the tree, are you Ray?* "What's in there?"

When Shepherd didn't respond I supplied the information. "Guns. Lots and lots of guns ... and ammunition, of course. And grenades—"

"Shut up!" Shepherd turned on me, grinding the gun into my forehead.

"... and a bloody great big atom bomb!"

The impact of the barrel on the side of my head made me dizzy but I didn't go down.

"Shut up!" he screamed again. He tried to push the muzzle through my skin but from somewhere deep inside I managed to dredge up a smile. Ray gave a small cry and made a move at him. *Ah, Ray, you* do *care!* Shepherd swung the gun to face him and the big man stopped dead in his tracks.

"Don't worry, Ray, he can't kill us yet. Can you, Neil?"

"Oh, and why not?"

"Well, if I'm not mistaken, you now want to move that crate in there and that's going to take at least two people ..."

"Ray and I can do it ..."

"But how will you lift your end while keeping the gun trained on Ray?"

"I will not need to. Ray will help me voluntarily."

I smiled at them, as they stood, side by side. "Except as soon as you've moved the bomb you'll have to kill us both

anyway, won't you? Dim as he is, even Ray can see that."
For a moment I thought the blow had fractured my skull. One second I was 'The Big I Am', mouthing off to the man with the gun and next I was on my knees with blood streaming down my face, vision gone and a humming in my ears like standing next to a beehive. I thought I was going to chuck my breakfast over his feet.

Ray made another half-lunge but Shepherd had the gun on him too quickly.

I slumped back against a packing case, legs stretched out ahead of me, and untucked my tee-shirt to rip a rag out of the front, using it to staunch the flow. Shepherd dragged me to my feet by the collar of my jacket and herded us before him, through the tiny corridor into the stygian dark beyond. We waited while the lights buzzed, flashed with a sort of popping noise and finally deigned to favour us with illumination.

Ray just stood, staring around him like Aunt Tazzy in the Harrods sale. When he reached out to touch a Kalashnikov, Shepherd banged him across the knuckles with the pistol barrel.

"Leave it." Shepherd's voice was overloud to my ringing ears. Ray yelped and stuffed his knuckles in his mouth.

Shepherd stayed near the door but directed us to the crate.

Ray stepped up so close behind me, peering over my shoulder, I could feel his breathe on my ear. The lid was still off and the black monster inside seemed to crouch, ready to erupt and vaporise us all.

"Whassat?" His voice sounded distant, filled with awe.

"That's what an atom bomb looks like, Ray," I offered.

"Jesus Christ Awmighty!" His voice was barely more than a whisper, sounding almost religious. I took a tiny step, as if backing away from this epitome of destruction. I was now pressing hard against him.

"Ray, do you remember what you thought could happen to my pretty little arse?"

"Pretty little arse …?"

I took another small step so I was now grinding my back into him, buttocks against his groin. I felt him stiffen. *Not like that. Your mind is like a sewer.*

"Ray, come around this side," Shepherd demanded.

"Yes, Mister Shepherd." Ray was about to step around me but stepped on the edge of the lid, dropping to one knee. As he went down, I felt him lift the gun out of my waistband. Shepherd sighed and rolled his eyes up to a God he would never want to meet. Somewhere behind me, near the floor, I heard the distinctive noise of the mechanism being cocked so I gave a loud cough, then something hard came up between my legs. *I've already warned you about your mind.* When the shot rang out the pistol jumped hard, giving me a nasty kick in the crotch and Shepherd jerked backwards, folded in the middle and fell backwards half through the door. I looked down and it seemed as I had grown a six inch penis that oozed a gentle waft of smoke.

When I decided he'd kept it there long enough, I pushed it down with a fingertip.

"Good shot, Ray."

He bent forward and muttered, "I never shot no-one before."

"Well, there's a first time for everything." I kissed him on the top of the head but jumped backwards as he vomited in front of my feet. *That's gratitude.*

"Ray." I shook him as he stood hunched over, one hand on a shelf, the other on his knee. He looked up, face like a full moon on a frosty night.

"Wha…?"

"We need to clean up."

"Wha …?" *You're really not getting any smarter, are you?*

"There's a dead body over there. We've got to do something about it. We need to remove our fingerprints and any indication we've been here. Including that." I pointed at the pile of vomit.

"We could move 'im. Chuck 'im in the river up the end." He jerked his head back, pointing with his chin then looked like he wished he hadn't.

"That's no good, there are all these guns. And an H-bomb, for God's sake! Even if we shift the body I don't want to be associated with any of this other stuff."

He sighed and we set to.

It took us quite a while to clear up and remove any forensics. I recovered my bamboo knives from where they had fallen half under a shelving unit when I noticed …

A bolt like electricity shot through me.

"Where's Shepherd?"

"Wha …? *You're starting to sound like a cracked record.*

"Shepherd! He was here!" I pointed at the empty space where the body had been, indicated by a pool of congealing blood. Ray came up beside me.

"Bleedin' 'ell."

A shape loomed in the entrance.

"The report of my death is greatly exaggerated … Mark Twain. A little bit more literature for you." He held the gun. And he wasn't about to let me get to mine. He made me reach in my waistband, left handed, and toss the weapon at his feet.

He staggered, arm wrapped across his midriff and nearly fell. I almost made a lunge but hesitated for a fraction of a second too long by which time he'd recovered and welded the gun back into its allotted space … pointing at me.

"I will be leaving you now." He slid the door closed. I dived, full length, for my gun but by the time I got it sighted there was no more than a gap.

"I have left you a puzzle," he called out.

"Really?" I scrambled to my feet and charged.

"Yes. The bomb. I have triggered it to go off in half an hour." The door shut with a click. "Enjoy your last moments." His voice was muffled.

"Wait!" I flung myself at the door. "It's an H-bomb. It will get you too!"

He laughed. "Nyet. It is only a little one. The blast range is no more than about five miles. By the time it goes off I will be more than fifteen miles away. I should get quite a good view, though."

Ray stepped up behind me. "Fuckin' 'ell."

* * *

I fired at the wood but there was the whine of a ricochet like a cowboy film shootout and a lump flew off the brickwork on the end wall. When I examined where the bullet had hit the door there was no more than a scratch and a silver gleam.

I could find no indent around the edge of the door or any way to get a purchase on it. I tried charging it with my shoulder. Then slamming my foot into it. It didn't even tremble under the impact.

"What the fuck we gonna do now, then?"

"I don't know." I wanted to hit him. *No reason, it would just feel good*.

We returned to the monster in the box. It just sat, menacing. Nothing about it moved, ticked or flashed.

"'ere. 'e can't 'ave set the bleedin' thing goin' or there'd be flashing numbers on it." *That was the reason I was looking for.*

Runner

I really lost it.

"You stupid, fucking bone-headed moron. This isn't a fucking James Bond film. Why would an H-bomb have countdown timer? Who's going to be looking at fucking red numbers counting down as it drops from a fucking aeroplane at forty-thousand fucking feet?"

He looked like a whipped pup: dropped his head, hands deep in pockets. "Sorry." It was almost a whisper. I checked my watch. Four minutes gone. "Any ideas?" he asked, still subdued.

"Well, there're plenty explosives here. Maybe we can blow a hole in the door."

We started searching. I found some grenades but had no idea how to make one work. They had no levers or pins or anything, just a cylindrical hole down the centre where I assumed a fuse or detonator or something was supposed to go. They were probably in another box somewhere but even if we found them I was far from sure I'd be able to get one working … or do so without blowing myself up. I had an atom bomb to do that for me.

More than ten more minutes had gone. Something over fifteen to go – assuming Shepherd wasn't lying. If I got out now, Potex would get me about fifteen miles away. Still time.

I fired eight more bullets, with increasing desperation, at the slab that barred our way, trying to hit exactly the same spot each time. With each shot the silver dent appeared slightly deeper but even with nine hits … all from close range and within an area no bigger than demitasse … it held resolutely stubborn against shoulders and feet. Smoke hung, almost a solid wall, in the air, burning my lungs and stinging my eyes. My head pounded. Blood seeped down the side of my face and neck.

Seven more minutes wasted, eight to go. Eight miles. Tops. If I got out now. If I got out. If.

Too late.

Time for really desperate measures.

I returned and examined the bomb. On one side a panel had been removed and a black box hung through the gap, connected by a spaghetti of wires that vanished off into the interior. A metal lid was held on by four cross-head screws but these were loose and barely finger tight so I undid them. Inside was a printed circuit board with, here and there, Cyrillic characters. I held it in tentative fingers, feeling as if one jolt would set the device off. A tiny red light flicked on and off, about once a second.

"There's your flashing light. Happy now?" My voice still worked. I was surprised. I wished my brain would.

"Do you think we should cut one of the wires?" The voice, a few millimetres from my ear, unexpected, was like an alarm going off in my head. Despite myself I screamed, dropped the box and jumped backwards. My heart hammered and my chest felt taught.

"Jesus Christ, Ray. You moron."

"Why do ya keep calling me that?"

"Because you're a moron." I slammed the heel of hand into the centre of his chest and he took a half step backwards. As I retrieved the box my hand was shaking like an alcoholic after a day sober.

"'ow long we got?" His voice showed no sign of any tension. Maybe he was just too thick to be able to imagine dying in a thermonuclear holocaust.

"Five minutes." *Too late now. Even Potex would struggle to get me out of range.* "Nothing for it." I took a deep breath and pulled the gun, still warm, from my pocket.

"What yer gonna do?" Did I detect the slightest tremor in the vocal cords?

I pulled the box out as far as the wires would let me, then put the business end of the gun to the back of it.

"Bugger me. You ain't gonna shoot it, are you?"
"Got a better idea?"
Three minutes.
"No." He paused, thinking. I could almost hear gearwheels grinding. "Ain't you worried it'll go off?"
"Of course I am! But in a couple of minutes we won't have any options at all." I took a deep breath.
Two minutes.
Nothing for it. I pulled the trigger. The box jumped and shattered.
Ray screamed, a high pitched, feminine sound and dived behind a shelf.

* * *

It took more than an hour to break out. I took the tripod from the anti-tank gun. It had a spike on the bottom of each leg that I used to attack the brickwork above the door. We took it in turns to chip away at it until I could slip a hand into the small gap and release the catch. We were free but I wondered how long it would take my nerves to stop jangling. Maybe I was becoming an empath.

In the other garage I slumped onto a pile of boxes and found myself sobbing and hating myself for showing weakness. Ray crouched beside me and enveloped me in arms like tree trunks and I hated him even more. No. I *wanted* to hate him even more but couldn't.

Sometimes people are like pets and he was tuning into a big, floppy mongrel. A big, floppy, *smelly* mongrel.

After I'd pulled myself together, I shut the door and helped Ray move contraband from the garage to his car ... as much as would go. It would take a few more trips to remove all the incriminating evidence.

"Have you got somewhere safe to keep all this until the

fuss has died down?"

"Yeah, no sweat. But I don't understand why I needed to get everything out."

"Because there's a bloody H-bomb in there. And it was set to go off. Do you want to live near it?"

He mumbled something that I took to be a 'no' then he fumbled in his pockets for no discernible reason.

"For all we know, it would only need a good thump to set it off. We can't just leave it and hope nobody ever finds it." I pointed. "You get the rest of your stuff out, then keep a low profile. In a while – I don't know how long – I'll get onto the authorities and tell them about it. I expect they'll turn up here mob-handed with lots of shouting and waving and during that time you'll lose access to your garage. Just keep cool. Tell them the truth about being Shepherd's employee – they know that anyway – but say he cleared off so you took over the business … and the garage. Deny you ever knew anything about the secret doorway or what was beyond."

"Pity. I coulda made a decent few quid off them guns …"

"Really? You've seen how arms dealers end up." I gave him a peck on the cheek and a cheery wave as I walked towards the end of the road.

"Will I see you ag—?" he called after me and sounded almost pathetic.

"No. Goodbye, Ray."

He climbed into his old Toyota and waved as he passed me. At the T-junction I stood and watched as he drove out of sight. I doubled back and blagged my way back into Shepherd's block. I had left my crash helmet and other stuff when Shepherd had marched me out a lifetime ago.

At the flat, the door stood slightly ajar and I couldn't remember how we had left it.

I mentally tossed up whether to go in or just run. What

the hell. I nudged the door open enough to peep in. and found the owner full length on the hall floor. Blood pooled, in a large circle, underneath him.

I needed the bathroom so I stepped over him but as my foot touched the floor a hand clamped around the ankle and I pitched forward. The breath left me as I hit the floor and when I looked around I was looking back down the barrel of that same bloody gun.

Now I was really, utterly, completely pissed off.

Without a thought for the consequences, I lashed out with my free foot, getting a glancing blow on the gun – deflecting it upwards – and finishing with a full blooded impact into the centre of his forehead.

He must have been stunned because I managed to dive on the weapon before he had time to re-aim. I twisted it from his grip and briefly thought about shooting him but decided the noise may attract attention.

"Help me," he mumbled. The blood was forming a larger pool and, when I flipped him over, I saw the front of his shirt was completely red.

"Sure," I said and slipped my bamboo knife out of my sleeve. "Have this one on Diana." His eyes opened wide and he made a sound that may have been a plea but I wasn't interested. A single stroke across his throat did the job. That solved his problem. All I felt was a warm sense of satisfaction. On the wall, above his body, I repeated my art exhibition with the Chinese symbols carved and daubed in blood.

I washed my face and stole one of Shepherd's designer shirts ... he was beyond needing it. *Always thought I looked better in a man's shirt than any man.*

It was already early afternoon and I hadn't eaten anything except the energy bar for breakfast so I walked back to the bike and drove around until I found a café. I had a few hours to kill then all I had to do was put the final phase of *Operation Sod-em-all* into action.

Chapter Thirty-Eight

It was risky. I'd never done such a long distance, never over water, never so low and never once, not even a lesson, in the dark. Now I was about to attempt all of them together.

This time my escape attempt was going to work. Stefan had bought my tickets: out of Heathrow to Abu Dhabi and then onto Lagos. Maxie would once more take my bags to a left luggage office. All were dummies. I would not be using the tickets. I would not be collecting the luggage ... mainly stuff I didn't want anyway ... so even if anybody had managed to hide a tracker in them again they'd be out of luck.

I had no illusions. I hadn't damaged ISIS, but I'd sure as hell disrupted their operations in Britain. It was possible that every active member in the UK had been thrown into the operation to wrest control of the bomb and they were all now dead or under arrest. With any luck, all knowledge of what they had been up to was now dead or locked up with them – if only until MI5 inveigled it out of them.

The Russian mafia was harder. I had no reason to believe they were active in Britain so assumed the men who attacked the garage had been sent specially ... but what do I know? It was unlikely they knew anything outside the details of their operation. But it would mean there was now a break in their contact with me. If I vanished they would have no way of following me.

On my visit I had arranged to have Poo-brain moved. He would be taken to another private nursing home, this time in Suffolk, and in a few months time he would spirited away to Canada. By the time they realised they had lost track of me they should also have lost track of little brother, too.

The Chinese were the easiest of the lot. I knew they were only a small band. If any had survived they should be too weak and disorganised to present any threat.

I'd driven to Worthing along the A27 and dumped the bike, easing her gently into the car park of a shopping centre, the engine barely more than a burble as I manoeuvred up the concrete ramps. It always surprised me that such a powerful machine could be so subdued when driven sedately. I stuck her in between the back of an industrial waste bin and the wall of a loading bay. As I hefted my pack I couldn't resist giving her a pat on the saddle. I'd miss her and was briefly concerned at how she would end up. A police pound until she rusted? I rather hoped not. Or maybe some enterprising thief would nick her. That would be preferable as the fewer clues I left the better. I left the key in the ignition and my helmet.

I changed my clothes then flagged down a passing taxi: a small risk but one that was unlikely to come to light: some random, nondescript woman.

It was dusk when we arrived at the small aerodrome but a few people were still hanging about, clearing up, wiping a windscreen, pulling a cover over their pride and joy. A small Cessna, barely beating the waning daylight, banked in steeply over the distant flyover and swooped gently onto the grass, pitching and yawing a few times before veering off towards the hangars.

As I leaned in the window and paid the driver, I glanced over my shoulder at the tower: nobody there, no lights. No aircraft engines other than the latecomer, disturbed the air, none seemed to be waiting to take off. The whole place was bedding down for the night.

Phil Siemann's hangar was, as I had expected, locked but several months ago he'd given me a key so I could sneak into his office for when he could get away from his wife for a couple of hours. I settled on the sofa that Phil and I had so often used for – let's just say 'other purposes' – and waited. It was almost midnight when I emerged.

I stuck my head out the door and was gratified to find the place deserted but I was under no illusions. I wouldn't have long.

Inside again, I flicked on the lights. It was chancy because the light would escape around the edges of the door facing the airstrip and, worse, through the wired glass window facing the road ... although there was a hedge obscuring the view.

Phil's Bell 206B III Jet Ranger gleamed in the bright lights, sitting, red and white, on its skids in the middle of the large empty space. By the book, I should carry out all pre-flight on the pad but I really didn't want to take it out until the last minute. I walked around, examining all the externals, pulling and pushing the control surfaces and checking everything the way Phil had drilled me.

Satisfied, I turned out the lights, eased the big roller door up, squealing and protesting, thankful there was nobody to investigate the cacophony. *You really should give it a dab of grease sometime, Phil.* The chopper weighed nearly three quarters of a ton and had no wheels, just skids, but Phil also owned an electric cart to lift and haul it out. I connected it up and towed the chopper out into the gentle chill of the midsummer night. The moon was about five days old and the sky was cloudless so the night was a mosaic of bleached silver and razor edged shadows. The tiny tractor whined its way out to the large circle with a two metre high letter 'H' painted in the centre. As I was going to be the only pilot operating for the next five or six hours there was no logical reason to use the pad. Just superstition, I suppose. Every helicopter flight I'd ever undertaken had started and finished at that exact spot and I could see no reason why this one should start any differently. It wasn't going to end here.

Ready as I was ever going to be, I abandoned the little tractor, grabbed my bag from the hangar, took a deep breath and strode out into the gloaming as the moon slid down the sky.

"Hello, Josie." The voice caught me mid-stride and mid-heartbeat. I finished the first but the termination of the second was touch and go. *Not another sodding man with a gun! Any minute now there will be handcuffs and a bed.* I dropped my rucksack as I whirled to face the voice, ready to launch an attack, hand at the back of my waistband on the comforting hardness of the pistol grip, only recognising the speaker at the last instant.

"Graeme?" I peered into the gloom of the shadow of the hangar. I could barely make out his tall form. Then I noticed a man-sized bundle at his feet. "Who's that?"

"Your friend and mine; Cho."

"What are you doing here? How did you know where I was?" I approached them, half a step, still wary, hand still on the gun. Cho lay, unmoving.

"I was following him and he led me here. Then I saw you messing about in there ..." He jerked his head towards the hangar. "I guessed Cho intended you no good so I gave him a thump."

"Then how did *he* know I was here?"

"I'm not sure but I would guess he had a tracker on your bike. I was watching him as he was watching you park it up in Worthing—"

"But I found the trackers."

"Ah-ah! He got you. The trick is to put one tracker where it will be easily found and some people will find it and fall for it—"

"But I didn't. I kept looking and found a second."

"Exactly. So the canny spy will hide *three*. When you

find either of the well-hidden ones you will think there could not possibly be a third."

Okay, I'm the fool.

I took my hand from the gun and recovered my pack, slinging it over my shoulder. There wasn't much in it: a few changes of clothes, a bit of makeup, toiletries and so on; just enough to keep me going until my next bolthole. Everything of value, money and some bearer bonds ... enough to get me to wherever I ended up ... were in a sealed belt around my waist.

"Sorry Graeme, I'd love to stand and chat but, you know, mountains to climb, worlds to conquer."

"Where are you going?"

I made a zipping gesture across my mouth. "Sorry. No clues."

"Can I come too?" I couldn't see his face but he sounded wistful. "I've been realising, over the last few months, how much of a fool I'd been. I should never have left you. Can I ever say how sorry I am?"

I felt anger rising. "Just like that? You cheat on me with Nora. Then you cheat on Nora with me. Now you just turn up and expect to just pick up where we left off ..."

"Because you're going away." His shoulders dropped as if a heavy weight had perched on them and he took a half step forward. "When you went before I thought I'd never see you again and realised what a fool I'd been. Now I've got a second chance but if you leave this time I know it will be for good." He closed the gap between us, arms wide. "If I don't tell you how I feel now, I know I will have missed the chance forever." His eyes glinted with reflected moonlight.

"And you'd just throw everything over and run away with me ... with nothing but the clothes on your back?"

"If that's what it takes ..." He enveloped me in his arms.

For a second I was torn. Did I want to do this? It would probably be better – easier – to just go. Revenge would be so sweet. I made my decision. "Jump in." I opened the passenger door for him but he returned and grabbed the prostrate Cho and dragged him by the collar towards the machine.

"What are you doing with him?"

"We can't leave him. He'll be awake soon and then he'll start making waves. If we take him with us we can drop him off somewhere." I wondered how much of a *drop* he had in mind. A thousand metres sounded good. Frankly I didn't care. We bundled him into the back seats and Graeme lashed him in with the seatbelts while I completed the pre-flight checks. With everything green I started spinning her up.

"Buckle up," I told him. "And put the headset on or we won't be able to talk." *And I really want to talk.*

I eased up on the collective to create some lift and felt the weight come off the skids. When we were just a metre or so up I let her hang for a while, to reaccustom myself to the feel.

"Don't we have to file flight plans or something?" I heard his voice, tinny and electronically distant in the headphones.

"Supposed to …"

I gave her some more wellie and we went up like a lift. I heard him gasp. *Perhaps a bit too enthusiastic there.* At about a hundred metres I brought her back to a hover, swivelled due south, dipped the nose and set off. *Goodbye old life. Hello world.*

"Where are we going?" *Nowhere you're expecting, that's for sure.*

"Isle of Wight. First I need to go and get the money."

"Money …?"

"Yes. Forty million quid."

"God, Josie. In gold? How will you transport that?"

"Not gold, bearer bonds. Forty bonds, each worth a million. Fit in your pocket."

"So there was no gold ...?"

"No—"

"So why the cock and bull story?"

"I told you before. There was a leak in your department. I had to keep everything tight or the whole thing would have fallen apart." I stole a quick glance sideways and saw his eyes, seeming to gleam. The instruments didn't emit a great deal of light but with the external darkness they seemed to illuminate his face like spotlights. *Avarice?*

We crossed the coast and through the Plexiglas there was an almost perfect black except for starlight above and their reflections flicking from the waves below. The gauge told me I'd slipped down to a height of about fifty-five metres. I slowed and let her drop lower, still heading south.

"Then where?"

I ignored him. "Do you remember the last time I took you flying?" I tried to sound wistful, nostalgic. "Want a go? Just to see how it feels?" I'd taken him flying when we were still married and he'd loved to take a turn. He looked at the controls as if they might bite.

"How's it all work then?" He sounded unsure, suspicious.

"Simple. Three controls. The cyclic: that's the joystick between your knees. Whichever way you tilt it makes it bank that way ... and whatever way we bank, that's the way we go. You only need worry about making it go forwards." I demonstrated. "The collective is the lever like a handbrake on the floor between us. It makes us go up and down." I took her up to three hundred metres so hard we felt our intestines crushed down and he yelped. Then I dropped her to about five metres. A big enough wave would splash us. I wondered if he would notice just how low we were. "And finally, the pedals ... to keep you pointing the way you're flying ... because a helicopter's quite happy flying sideways or even backwards but the passengers tend to be more choosy." I got his hands and feet placed and had him shadow me: sensing how everything moved in unison. "How's it feel? Okay?"

"Not bad." He still sounded dubious.

"They say it's a bit like juggling while riding a unicycle. Do you want to take over? I'll keep my hands on, shadowing you."

"Go on then." I felt his grip firm through the dual controls.

"You have control," I said using the formal words of handover.

"I have control." The machine swayed a bit but he was really quite good for a first timer. I unlatched my seatbelt and reached round for the map in the door pocket, then gave the controls a gentle nudge to correct a small yaw he was introducing.

"You're doing well. Feel okay?"

"Yes. Not bad at all."

After a few minutes I took back control and brought her to little more than a hover. "I'm puzzled by a few things and wonder if you could help me out." I tried to sound casual.

"Puzzled? About what?"

"Oh, you know: things that people knew, for example ... and how."

"Like what?"

"Do you remember what Harrison used to call me? The nickname?"

"Yes." He hesitated. "Titless," he added with a snigger.

"No, in Mandarin."

He hesitated longer this time until I prompted him.

"Wú rǔfáng," he said at last.
"Yes. I thought it was you. Why did you do it, Grey?"
"Do what?"
Again I snatched a glimpse. This time he was looking straight at me, face a mask of professed innocence. *No chance.* "Why don't I work my way though it and you tell me where I go wrong, or fill in any blanks? Okay?"
"I don't know what you're talking about." He was trying to sound puzzled and missing by a country mile. I've had to spend my entire life studying people's emotions so I can act normal. I can spot an act before the actor realises he's acting.
I brought the chopper to a complete standstill and allowed it to slide even closer to the millpond smooth sea. "Who were you on to first? Shepherd for his arms dealings or my father for the money laundering?" I waited but he said nothing. "I'm guessing it was my father …"
"Bruce …?"
"He was the only father I had." I was feeling snippy. "What happened? An overheard telephone call? A glimpse at a paper? Something like that?" He was silent so I continued. "Following the trail brought you to Shepherd, right?"
"Keep going." His voice was strange, distant with a sort of *musing* note even the headphones couldn't disguise."
"Hu? Was he one of yours? Caught out as an illegal immigrant and 'persuaded' to work for you? A perfect spy to put into Shepherd's camp."
"What put you on to me?" *The truth at last.*
"They called you 'The Grey Man'. Grey. Short for Graeme. Of course, that was in Mandarin. You told them I spoke 'Chinese' but you didn't bother to tell them which one and I convinced them I could only speak Cantonese. Then there was my nickname: Wú rǔfáng."
"Come on, you're building a mountain on the

foundations of the tiniest of molehills. Pun intended."

What happened? You found out about the deal Shepherd was setting up and you got Hu to carry out the robbery—"

"No! I never knew about the money until later—"

"Bullshit. And I guess Hu decided to double cross you."

"It wasn't like that at all. I knew about Shepherd and Bruce's money laundering but I was going to blackmail them to cut me in. It was only afterwards ... after the murders ... that I got an inkling of the size of it ... when Shepherd started putting pressure on you to get the money."

"I just don't believe you, Graeme. Who else could it have been? You found out about the money, ordered Hu to get it and my family died because of your schemes."

"No. That was nothing to do with me. I admit I was using Hu as you said but the raid on Overton was down to him alone."

"And Mullins? Was he a mole?"

"No, that was a smokescreen. He's clean."

"How did you end up working with Cho's mob?"

"What made you think I was?"

"Well if you weren't, how did they know about the supposed gold concreted into the inspection pit in the garage?" I snatched a glance at him. "The only person on earth I told was you!"

He sighed, a fizzing through the headphones. "Okay. By the time Hu was killed I had enough on Cho to force him to work with me."

"So you ordered him to kidnap me. And he ended up torturing me ... nearly killing me."

"It was never supposed to be like that."

"But it's what happened." I let the words hang in the air like the machine we rode. I knew how well he got on with my parents. The murders had probably hurt him more than it had me. "Did you know just how much money there was?"

"No. Just that it was a huge sum."

"Why? Just for the money?"

For the first time he showed emotion. "*Why*? You have to ask me *why*? Being married to you was like living with a robot. You never showed any love or affection and, when I went and found it elsewhere, you acted like you didn't care—"

"I thought it was what you wanted … to have a fling on the side—"

"Bollocks! You didn't give a toss. It was always 'me, me, me.' Look at the divorce. You took me for everything you could. You even made me sell the house my parents left me and then pissed it away on stupid cars and motorcycles—"

"You bastard," I grabbed a quick glance away from the instruments. "It was *me* who was all alone when I lost the baby. Where were you? Out screwing your whore, that's where!"

"How was I to know …?"

"So you had a wounded ego and my family had to die as revenge—"

"I told you. I had nothing to do with the robbery or the murders of your parents. It was only Hu, working alone. Nothing was meant to happen that way—"

"But it did. And it was ALL YOUR FAULT!" Despite myself the helicopter bucked and I took a second to correct it.

"You'll never believe me … but we are where we are, so now we're going to play this out to the end. Just give me the money and we'll call it quits." He twisted in his seat and snapped, "Cho!"

I caught a movement in the corner of my eye, looked around and once more I had a gun pointed at me.

"Another gun loaded with blanks?" Again I snatched a

look at Graeme. "That's another thing, what was it all about with your chums firing blanks at me?"

"You were the only one who knew where the money was. I didn't dare risk them actually shooting you …"

"But you had your men drill holes through the trees as if to recover bullets …?"

"Of course. I knew you'd go and check … and I was right wasn't I? I went back and fired some bullets into the trees with a silenced gun."

I suppose nobody queries what a copper in uniform is up to.

"You realise that I could have been killed when you blew up the Audi?"

"That was nothing to do with me. I would *never* have risked killing you. I guess the Arabs did that." I heard him chuckle. "But I wasn't unhappy they did."

"Bastard," I said again.

"Take down." I barely heard Cho's voice over the noise. "This real bullet." He reached the weapon between the seats and prodded me. Then the full impact of the situation hit me and I laughed … *really* laughed, the machine swinging with my movement.

"Oh, come *on!*" I could hardly speak and had to wipe my eyes on the back of my sleeve. "You're *really* pointing a loaded gun at me? *Honestly*? What do you think will happen to us all if you pull that trigger?" I turned and snared Graeme's gaze, keeping the machine steady by instinct alone. "Call your boy off."

Eventually he reached down and tapped the barrel. "She's got a point. Put it down. She'll have to land sooner or later."

"You think so, Graeme? You never know. I've lost everything: my mother, my father, Granny. Even Harrison is the next best thing to a carrot. Now you want to take the money. With nothing left I might be suicidal."

He curled his upper lip. "Not you, Josie. Nobody comes close to loving you as much you do."

Cho lowered the weapon and we sat without speaking for a while. I wondered if they realised we were just hovering, poised in the air, not going anywhere.

"So this is just about the money? That's it?"

"Yes, just the money."

"What about the *side benefits*? I wonder what Nora would say about our sessions of afternoon nooky."

"She knew."

The helicopter slewed and kicked and I struggled to regain control. I heard Cho gasp but Graeme laughed.

"Leonora's attitude is, 'If I've been there once then what's the problem with a return visit?' Just to 'grease the wheels' as they say." *Been there? The cow.* Again conversation lapsed ... what was there to say after that?

I nudged the cyclic towards me by the merest fraction and the chopper started drifting backwards towards the beach.

"Where are we going?" he asked. "It doesn't feel as if we're moving."

"Deceptive when you can't see what's outside." *Deceptive when you can't see what's under your nose.*

"Take control for a second will you? I need to check our bearings." I shuffled the map in its clear plastic case on my lap.

"Well ..." I could hear the doubts.

"Only for a second while I look at the map. What sort of stunt do you think I could pull that wouldn't endanger me as much as you?"

He reached out, taking a couple of goes to set his hands comfortably on the levers.

"You have control."

"I have control." *That's what you think.*

"Right. Now for the next phase ..."

"What ..."

"Sorry, Graeme. Been nice knowing you." I reached down to the collective lever and yanked up as hard as it would go and rolled sideways into fresh air. The skid hit me across the left hip and I was flipped, end over end and plummeted, still rolling. I began to wonder if I had misjudged it and been higher than I had estimated ... altimeters are a bit inaccurate at very low levels ... but then I hit water as yielding as concrete and was plunging into icy coldness. A roaring filled my ears, bubbles rushed around me and my chest was crushed by the pressure. My lungs heaved, involuntarily trying to gasp air due to cold water shock but I slammed my hands over my mouth and clamped my nose between finger and thumb.

After an age the surface hit me again ... almost as hard as going in ... and saw the helicopter hurtling straight up, an indistinct black shape against the slightly lighter shade of the sky.

I sucked air, ice cold and wonderful but a wave caught me in the face and I breathed seawater causing me to cough and gasp.

High above, the chopper started to pitch, roll and yaw. I watched, fascinated as each deviation was corrected then overcorrected by the novice pilot panicking at the controls. One overcorrection too far and it suddenly lurched, stood on its side, landing gear pointing at the horizon, and plummeted towards the black water below. Another wave caught me but I managed to ignore it. In the final rays of the dying moon I saw the Jet Ranger edge on as, for the briefest of moments, the tips of the rotors touched the water and it seemed to be driving along like a demented, one-wheel paddle steamer. Then it flew apart in a sheet of spray that glowed with a faint biological iridescence, disintegrating into a myriad tiny pieces. The sound followed a second later: the screaming of tearing and tortured metal and plastic, like the dying howl of a beast: half a million pounds worth of machinery self-destructing in foam.

Chapter Thirty-Nine

The swim was long and tiring. Fit as I was, the weight I carried and my saturated clothes were dragging me low in the water. I dropped the gun and took off whatever clothes I could – a trade off between keeping warm, buoyancy and freedom of movement – but even stripped to the minimum I felt constricted and weighed down. Despite the season, the sea was bitterly cold and sucked the warmth out of my body. All I could do was keep the lights of the shore ahead of me and swim. The knife wound in my leg had reopened so the kick on every stroke lanced, excruciating, from knee to hip.

Somebody must have raised the alarm because I heard the roar of boat engines and, soon after, the chatter of rotors as another helicopter quartered the area with bright beams ... but they were much further out from where I laboured. I made no attempt to catch anybody's attention.

I was exhausted beyond measure but I just ground on, stroke by agonising stroke. The salt water burned my eyes, my throat and the back of my nose. Occasionally I swallowed another mouthful which made me vomit. Vomiting caused me to swallow more water.

The shore caught me unaware. My leaden foot touched pebbles on the down kick but it was three more strokes before I realised the water was shallow enough to stand. My body disagreed and I was forced to drag myself on hands and knees up the stones, each of which had a vendetta against me. I realised if I stayed where I was, hypothermia would make all my efforts redundant and the thought drove me to my feet. Barefoot, stumbling, I ground my way to the promenade.

Hove seafront. I had come up among green lawns and very pre-dawn joggers.

My teeth chattered and my body was so racked with uncontrollable tremors I could barely make my limbs obey me. In desperation I made for a shelter where I sat, dressed in nothing but pants and shirt: exhausted, soaked and shivering.

"You okay, Love?"

The voice came from the dark corner and I grabbed for the handle of the knife at my wrist. "Yes. I'm fine." I forced my voice to remain flat and expressionless despite my chattering teeth.

A shape detached itself from the gloom and slid along the bench towards me. Big and shaggy with long hair and scruffy beard, he was still wrapped in the sleeping bag that was obviously his shelter for the night. I could feel the heat radiating from him even at half a metre. I could have smelled him at ten times that.

"You're frozen." He made a move as if he was going to put an arm around me but I shrank away and raised a protective hand. It shook like a geriatric's.

"I need a coat," I told him.

"Only got the one on me back."

"I'll pay. How much?"

"It ain't for sale …"

His appearance said it was not for sale. His voice said it was not for sale. Five, ten pound notes said it was for sale. Another of the notes added a pair of knackered boots. Despite my relieving him of his only protection from the elements he seemed overjoyed by the cash. All through the transaction I kept my other hand near the handle of my knife in case he tried to renegotiate the price. Even thus dressed, I was still frozen and needed warmth.

"Anywhere serves hot food that'll serve me dressed like this?"

"Up there." He pivoted so he could point inland. "It's called 'Kahvalti.' S'alright."

I chose a place in a corner at the back and let the blousy Turkish woman see a ten pound note to assure her I had the means to pay. By the time I had wolfed down a Full English accompanied by two enormous mugs of weapons grade tea I was starting to feel more human. The shaking had stopped and my skin was beginning to return to its normal hue.

For the rest of the morning I upgraded my appearance: first in a charity shop and then in a cut price chain store before finishing in a more upmarket establishment. Going straight to the latter, dressed in the homeless man's garb would have raised eyebrows and I really didn't want to draw any attention to myself. At each upgrade I donated the discarded garments to a homeless person. It was not just altruism – I reasoned the clothes would vanish into that milieu whereas anything dropped in a skip could always come to light.

I stuck my thumb out and started travelling. This time I was vanishing once and for all.

Chapter Forty

There's little point in detailing the long, arduous and intensely boring trip. My thumb, augmented by a coach and local buses took me indirectly to my intended original target of the ferry terminal at Dover.

The lorries backed up along the ramps as men in yellow tabards directed them on board the boat. I stole into the back of a trailer. It was easy. Nobody was looking for, or probably even cared about, stowaways in that direction. *An illegal emigrant?*

The journey was stuffy, uncomfortable and smelly, so similar to my enforced trips in the back of Tung's van. But eventually it ended. When the lorry stopped in a café in Central France, I slipped out and approached the driver – unaware he had been my unwitting chauffeur.

"You English?" I asked, putting on an accent that could have originated anywhere from Northern Canada to Southern New Zealand.

"Sure," he said.

"Where are you heading? Anywhere nice?" I catalysed it with a nice smile.

"Naples. You after a lift?" He ogled me. *Weighing up your chances?*

So a few kind words and the hint of a promise I never kept got me a ride. From there I used ferries, first to Greece then Turkey and overland via Armenia, Baku and another ferry to Kazakhstan with a hop on a lousy local airline to

India. It was a wonder the plane managed to get in the air, let alone stay there. In contrast, I reached Jakarta by luxurious ferry and finally made it, weeks later, mentally and physically shattered, to Hong Kong on a filthy tramp steamer that, under normal circumstances, I wouldn't have trusted on a duck pond.

At the entrance to the tower block in Mongkok, even more dilapidated than in my distant teenage memory, I was stopped by a pair of heavies, so I showed them the tattoo and asked them – without a great deal of hope – if I could see Deng. One of them nodded me through and, for the second time in my life, I made the long ascent.

In the same huge room; fixtures and fittings unchanged in two decades, I reintroduced myself to the frail old man, now little more than a toothless, hairless skeleton.

We were served tea and cakes by the same girl; now a frumpy, middle aged, rotund woman.

Sitting on a low stool at Deng's feet I recounted the story and saw tears spring to his eyes when he heard of the fate of Granny. He muttered revenge on Cho's gang but I assured him there were few, if any, members left ... definitely none of the principals. He just smiled, nodded and tapped my knee with the dagger-like nail of a skeletal finger as if he expected no less from me.

Through him I got a message to British Intelligence about the bomb. If Deng was as smart as I suspected then he ought to have made some money out of the information. *Keep him on side*.

I took possession of my flat in Central – although I could never think of it as anything but 'Granny's Flat' – and settled into a new life. Deng helped me with a new identity and all the necessary paperwork to make it legal. I am now officially *Wei Yu*.

Over the following weeks and months I established a

life. I kept the flat but also bought a villa in the New Territories and moved in as soon as I was able. I have a staff of five, all young local girls.

No men.

Ever.

Deng promised to make enquiries about Lilly but, so far, has come up with nothing. That's a worry. I remember telling her things, during my drug fuelled 'outages', things I really shouldn't have. A secret is a secret while only one person knows it. Maybe she's met her end. Girls in her position tend not to have long lives. I'll have to keep my ear to the ground.

About twice a day I get an overwhelming longing for a shot of heroin, which I have so far managed to resist and each day it feels slightly less of a struggle. I still train hard. I have a trainer, one of the highest graded women martial arts instructors in Hong Kong. We kick and punch each other black and blue four times a week.

I run – lots – and whenever I set out on the local roads there is always a long, black car creeping along behind me and it only leaves me when I'm safely back home. Deng being overprotective.

I bought another Yamaha and replaced Potex-2 with a Lamborghini Veneno Roadster: Two hundred and twenty miles an hour. God knows where I'll ever get anywhere *near* close to that here.

Oh, and I finally bought my Jet Ranger.

* * *

Deng arranged for Poo-brain to join me but after I'd been here for about a month one of Deng's men came and collected me.

"Wei Yu. I have news of your brother, Harrison. It is not good, I'm afraid." Deng's voice showed concern but his face remained inscrutable. "As you requested, we were bringing him here via America and the Pacific. We located him in Canada, as you said, and he was being transported by ambulance across the border and through New York State."

He paused while the same woman poured tea from what could have been the same pot from twenty years previously.

"Go on," I said. I knew it was bad manners in this culture but couldn't restrain myself.

"According to witnesses, they were on Interstate I90 and were overtaking a camper van which pulled out and drove them head on into an oncoming sixteen wheeler. All on board were killed instantly. The camper had been stolen the previous day and was found, a few hours later, as a burned out wreck. I guess we'll never know if it was a genuine accident but we kept everything so secret that we have to assume that it was."

I could do nothing but nod. Without another word I stood, bowed and left. I managed to hold in my smile until I was alone on the street.

Epilogue

Part of the problem was I had only heard one end of the conversation. But the end I heard was enough to make me prick up my ears.

My father was saying, "No, we don't need to launder the whole fifty million dollars."

I was about to walk in and ask him for the loan of a printer cartridge but the words *fifty million dollars* pulled me up short so I hovered outside the partially open door. It was worth the wait.

"When Jubali transfers the money to me I'll take out fifteen percent; your ten and my five. After I've worked my magic they'll reappear as clean as the driven snow. That will leave forty-two point five million which I'll pass directly to your principles. We won't need to clean that up. In fact it won't matter if it's dripping in blood because by then it'll be their problem."

He was quiet, listening.

"No. There'll be hardly any delay. It's practically instant. The wonders of modern banking ... it's just the press of a key away. It'll be in my dark account for a couple of days, say three at the most ... just while I create the paper trail to *prove* it's legal." He snickered, quite like a horse. *I'll always remember his laugh.* There was another pause before he continued. "Yes. It will just pop up in your account, seemingly the post-tax proceeds of the sale of some investments you made in an oil company a while ago."

A couple of days. Three at the most. I had to act quickly.

Harrison had been my only error in the whole process.

I should never have got him involved but with such a constrained timescale I could think of nobody else on the spur of the moment. All he had to do was organise a couple of friends. You wouldn't have thought that was beyond the wit of man, would you? But it was obviously beyond the wit of my 'shit for brains' brother.

It was simplicity itself. He would meet is pals, bring them to the house and they could take the family hostage. I told him that mere threats to my mother and grandmother would be all that would be necessary for my father to reveal the bank account details ... he was never much of a man.

Another major piece in the jigsaw was Jordan.

I'd met him at a gig a couple of weeks earlier. Despite being engaged, he was having a fling with Maxie. Jordan said he was going to ditch his fiancée, some girl by the name of Priti but, as he was employed by her father, he had to hold off until he started a new job. It was through Jordan, via Maxie, we got the gig to play for Priti's father's company. I knew Maxie wasn't really struck on Jordan so would have no objection to my giving him a 'run around the block' that evening. He would fit in very neatly.

Jordan had a problem ... he liked a gamble. His weakness was the horses. It was just that he wasn't very good at it so he'd racked up a debt with some people he *really* didn't want to upset ... the sort who *always* get their money, one way or another.

He was starting his new job the week before the dance. The timing was perfect.

In exchange for payment of his gambling debts all he had to do was manufacture an argument with Priti at the dance so she would storm out ... apparently a regular occurrence ... and I could be seen to go off with him, to all appearances to spend the night. I needed an airtight alibi for the night because if Poo-brain messed it up he was not going to take me down with him. They could suspect me all they liked ... and Leyland did ... but they had to prove, beyond reasonable doubt, that I'd had a hand in it. Jordan and all the witnesses at the dance would be enough of a 'reasonable doubt' to keep me off any uncomfortable hooks.

Once Harrison and his pals had extracted the details of the accounts where the money was secreted, the accomplices were to leave my family, including Harrison, tied up and the bank information written on a slip of paper in the hall. I would dash home at about two in the morning, access the bank account and transfer the fifty million dollars to my overseas account. Then I would clear off back to Jordan's and return home the next morning to 'find' them all tied up and call the police.

Of course, my father would immediately log in to the banking system to try to prevent the theft but it would be too late.

That's how it should have worked.

But Harry – as I feared he would – cocked it up. No wonder I called him Poo-brain. He thought he knew better and that he and this lad, Hu, could do it alone. But even though Harrison was dressed in a ski mask, Granny recognised him and starting abusing and berating him.

Psychopathy is to do with the function of the brain. It is likely some components are hereditary and Poo-brain was just as psychopathic as I am. But whereas I have learned to control it he was never that bright. He lost his temper and shot her.

My mother took the opportunity to break away and made a dash for it. So he shot her too. When they tortured my father for the details he had the heart attack which killed him.

When I got home I found carnage and disorder. Hu and Poo-brain were screaming at each other, hurling accusations and blame. Hu had somehow got hold of the gun and was threatening Poo-brain, demanding money. I took one of Granny's bamboo knives and stabbed him. That solved one problem. He was the first person I'd ever killed. I had often wondered what it was like. Truth to tell, it was no big deal. I wiped the knife but obviously missed one print. *Stupid.*

That left only one loose end.

I grabbed the gun but Poo-brain must have guessed my intentions and made a bolt for the stairs. I'd never used a gun before so, despite aiming at the middle of his back, I hit him in the head. I was sure he was dead.

I dumped the gun in a river on the way back to Jordan's, returned to Overton later on the Sunday morning and called the police. You can only imagine my horror when I was charging upstairs and discovered Harrison was still alive. I couldn't kill him then because I know enough about forensics to realise they'd work out his true time of death ... and how he'd died. When the police rang the doorbell all I could do was grab the phone and call for an ambulance. I had to hope he wouldn't pull through or, if he did, wouldn't remember anything until I'd had time to deal with him ... permanently.

And that, I thought, was the end of it.

The mistake Leyland made was assuming a connection between the disparate groups when in actual fact the only connection was Hu; working for Graeme spying on Cho, Shepherd and, indirectly, my father. Graeme had encouraged Hu to take work as a general dogsbody in Shepherd's cleaning business. That's how Hu met Harrison. He had come to Overton when he drove Shepherd to visit my father and they realised they had the Mandarin language in common.

When he turned up dead at Overton it must have put Graeme in a tailspin because, although he knew who the dead boy was, he not could say anything. My identification,

Runner

through Ray, must have been a godsend for him.

Hu had not told Cho or Graeme about the raid on my family ... perhaps he thought he'd be able to keep all the proceeds. There is no reason Harrison would have mentioned how much money was involved but Hu would have realised it was a substantial sum to make it worth our while holding up our own family.

During his period of recovery I continually pumped Harrison to see what he remembered. He always said he recalled nothing but I couldn't take the chance his amnesia was permanent. When Deng offered to get him to Hong Kong I made careful note of dates, times and routes. It cost quite a bit but solved the problem. I considered asking Deng to get it done. The Triads have strict rules about harming family so he would be against me killing Poo-brain although if I told him – truthfully – that Poo-brain had killed Granny, he may have obliged. But that was a can of worms to which I didn't want to take an opener.

After the whole operation had gone bad I assumed the money was gone forever and just wrote it off to experience. And, apart from the obstruction that was Harrison, I was at least still in line for the house and all the family's savings. All I had to do was set us up in our new flats with a couple who spoke no more than a smattering of English and await my chance to take care of him.

It was only when Shepherd started digging that I realised that maybe the money hadn't slipped entirely out of my grasp.

Do I feel guilty? No, I'm worth every penny and Hare's item 2 is '*Grandiose sense of self-worth*'.

So what's your problem? You're 'disappointed' in me? You know you're beginning to sound just like the head teacher who chastised me for stabbing some little oik who had insisted on calling me 'Regina': "You've let your parents down, you've let the school down and worst of all you've let yourself down."

But right at the very start I told you I was a psychopath and that psychopaths are habitual liars. Now you're getting all upset when you find out that I had acted like … well … a psychopath.

Tough.

THE END

About the author

JAGS ARTHURSON IS AN author based in Brighton, Sussex, UK. He has lived, worked and travelled in over forty countries and had various careers including research chemist, a director in a Middle Eastern construction company, a business analyst, an IT infrastructure expert and a business consultant. For more than twenty-five years he has been the managing director of his own company. He is sort of retired and is now enjoying life even more and dedicating it to the three things he loves: his family, his charity work and his writing … but don't ask him to put them in order of priority.

You can contact Jags directly on **jags@number90.co.uk**.

If you enjoyed *Runner* by Jags Arthurson, he would be delighted if you would go to www.amazon.co.uk and leave an honest review.

Jags Arthurson

Other books from Jags Arthurson

Pagan Justice: A Karl Pagan Crime Thriller

Printed by Amazon Italia Logistica S.r.l.
Torrazza Piemonte (TO), Italy